"Religion is the sigh of the oppressed creature, the heart of a heartless world, the spirit of soulless stagnation. It is the opium of the people."

—Karl Marx, *Works, Vol. 1*

"Every religious idea, every idea of God, even flirting with the idea of God is unutterable vileness, vileness of the most dangerous kind, contagion of the most abominable kind. Millions of filthy deeds, acts of violence, and physical contagions are far less dangerous than the subtle, spiritual idea of a God decked out in the smartest ideological costumes."

—V.I. Lenin, *Works, Vol. 1*

"The most beautiful excitement which we can experience is mystical. This is the progenitor of all real art and science. The man to whom this excitement is foreign is no longer able to experience wonder, or to stand bewildered and in fearful admiration, just as if he were dead."

—Albert Einstein

VAMPIRE IN MOSCOW

Richard Henrick

Cover Art
JEFF EASLEY

TSR, Inc.
PRODUCTS OF YOUR IMAGINATION™

**To Morning Star—who taught me that
the vision in the flame was but a reflection
of one's own inner soul.**

VAMPIRE IN MOSCOW

This book is protected under the copyright laws of the United States of America. Any reproduction or other unauthorized use of the material or artwork contained herein is prohibited without the express written permission of TSR, Inc.

Distributed to the book trade in the United States by Random House, Inc. and in Canada by Random House of Canada, Ltd.

Distributed in the United Kingdom by TSR UK Ltd.

Distributed to the toy and hobby trade by regional distributors.

DRAGONLANCE is a registered trademark owned by TSR, Inc. FORGOTTEN REALMS is a trademark owned by TSR, Inc. TM designates other trademarks owned by TSR, Inc.

First Printing, August, 1988
Printed in the United States of America.
Library of Congress Catalog Card Number: 87-51449

9 8 7 6 5 4 3 2 1

ISBN: 0-88038-552-9
All characters in this book are fictitious. Any resemblance to actual persons, living or dead, is purely coincidental.

TSR, Inc.
P.O. Box 756
Lake Geneva, WI 53147
U.S.A.

TSR UK Ltd.
The Mill, Rathmore Road
Cambridge CB14AD
United Kingdom

1

On the Appian Way—54 A.D.

The dawn broke clear and warm as young Nicholas of Carpathia guided the ox-drawn cart down the smooth, lava-stone roadway. With reed whip in hand, the strapping eighteen-year-old walked beside the bull, prodding the beast's haunches whenever its attention strayed. The road stretched out ahead of them, level and clear, and Nicholas was able to keep his jabbings to a minimum.

He and his father had been traversing the Roman highway for a good two days now. At first Nicholas had been amazed to find that such a thoroughfare existed. He had never seen anything like it in the village where he was raised. Now he could not help but imagine what other wonders awaited him in the capital city. Not only would this be his first visit to Rome, but it also marked his first real journey away from the village of his birth.

The fascinating tales of the elders had done little to prepare him for the astonishing new world that awaited beyond the Carpathian foothills. Each bend of the path seemed to beckon him with the promise of untold adventure. This was especially true once he and his father completed the ferry trip over the Adriatic Sea and began their way across Italy on the Appian Highway. Here, an entirely new way of life was in evidence.

His father, who was a veteran of several such trips, took in the young traveler's gasps of wonder with a calm shake of his head. He was never one to outwardly display his emotions; not even the passing of an entire legion of armed soldiers could break the look of bored indifference that seemed perpetually painted on his face. This was not the case with Nicholas, whose wildly pounding heart almost burst from his chest as the legionnaires marched by.

Nicholas found it equally hard to believe that anyone could possibly sleep, knowing that the greatest city that ever was, was only a few hours away. Yet his father's snores were clearly audible from the cart's covered interior. Nicholas wondered if he should wake him now that they were approaching Rome's swarming outskirts.

The majority of vehicles sharing the roadway were covered carts much like their own. Whether pulled by oxen or horses, these wagons were solidly built for speed and endurance. Every so often, a chariot would flash by, usually driven by a toga-clad plebeian. Careful to steer well clear of such speedy means of transport, Nicholas kept to the right portion of the roadway whenever possible. Here he passed the slower-moving foot traffic.

Nicholas looked curiously at the crowded thoroughfare. He had never seen such a mixture of people and races. Fair-skinned Celts walked side by side with swarthy Arabs and black-skinned Nubians. The majority carried their wares beside them and were dressed in typical Roman fashion. The most popular garment was the tunic, a short-sleeved piece of clothing that hung to the knees. Over this, either a toga or cloak was draped. Men and women alike wore sandals. Proud of the similar outfit that his mother had crafted for him, Nicholas felt at one with this crowd. Like them, he was but another

Roman citizen, called to the capital city to pay homage to the new emperor.

The gift that he and his father were carrying to Nero was a lavish one. The people of Carpathia had spent weeks trapping and preparing dozens of exquisite fur pelts. As village elder, Nicholas's father was chosen to convey them to Rome. When Nicholas was asked if he wanted to accompany him, the lad breathlessly accepted the offer. What stories he'd be able to tell around the fire-circle!

Nicholas was forced to pull the ox to an abrupt halt when a small train of men broke before his cart. The lad was prepared to curse their carelessness, when he noticed their cargo, a magnificently ornamented sedan chair, carried by four people. A warm breeze gusted from the hills and parted the sedan's curtains, allowing Nicholas a brief glimpse of its sole occupant. The youngster's eyes opened with appreciative awe as he viewed the face of the most beautiful woman he had ever seen. Her hypnotizing dark stare, pure white skin, and bright red lips were practically etched into his consciousness when a gruff, familiar voice broke from his right.

"For Jupiter's sake, son, please watch where you're going! Why, that stop of yours almost broke my neck!" Sticking out his beard-stubbled head from the cart's interior, Grigori of Carpathia hastily surveyed the surrounding landscape. "By the gods, lad, I had no idea we were making such progress. The capital's southern gates are almost upon us. Why didn't you awaken me sooner?"

Ignoring his father's question, Nicholas watched as the sedan chair was conveyed across the roadway. Eventually it disappeared into an adjoining stand of trees. Its occupant's bewitching spell held him captive as his father jumped from the cart and stretched his cramped limbs.

"What's gotten into you, son? Are you just going to stand there all day? Why, beyond those hills the ruler of the Roman Empire himself awaits us."

Torn from his brief reverie, Nicholas pivoted and noted the warm smile on his father's lips. As a pair of gleaming chariots passed to their left, Nicholas returned the smile. His father winked.

"That's more like it, lad. All that you see this morning is nothing compared to Rome. That I can promise you. Now let's be on our way, while the day is still young."

Infected by his father's unusual display of enthusiasm, Nicholas inhaled a deep breath and raised the reed whip overhead. With a snap of his wrist, Nicholas persuaded the ox to move on. There was a slight jerk as the cart rolled forward and their journey continued.

It wasn't until dusk that they finally crossed through the Appian Gate and entered Rome itself. Confused by the mass of humanity that now surrounded them, Nicholas was content to seat himself in the cart and allow his father to lead the way. Gone was the broad pavement of the Appian Way. Replacing it was a dimly lit, narrow roadway that twisted past building after building, many of which were several stories high.

The stench of ripe garbage and the constant chatter of the inhabitants filled his senses. Without a single tree or plant in sight, Nicholas found it difficult to orient himself. Even the stars themselves seemed absent from the night sky. His father identified a wide, elongated clearing as a central marketplace known as the Roman Forum. Here Nicholas was able to just make out the crescent moon. Seeing this familiar orb gave him a renewed sense of confidence—he was not in an alien world after all.

Nicholas jumped from the cart and joined his father.

The inn that they were seeking adjoined the Forum. Having stayed there on a previous occasion, Grigori was able to guide them there without getting lost. Both travelers were anxious to properly rest after their long journey, and were somewhat dismayed at finding the inn's tavern packed with dozens of curious patrons. Unable to pick out the innkeeper in this crowd, they allowed their attentions to be drawn to the back of the room. Here, a table was placed on a slightly elevated platform. All eyes seemed focused on this portion of the tavern. Standing on his tiptoes, Nicholas was just able to see over the mass of heads.

The table held a handful of seated men, each one facing the crowd. Most seemed to be middle-aged, except for a handsome blond-haired youth who could not have been much older than Nicholas, and a single, white-haired elder. The buzz of nervous chatter that had filled the room abruptly faded when this elder suddenly stood. Without speaking a word, he silently appraised his audience.

Though Nicholas was well hidden in the rear of the room, the youngster could have sworn that this old-timer's vibrant green eyes actually met his own. Curiously affected by this brief glance, Nicholas found himself swaying dizzily. When he regained his balance, the mass of people surrounding him seemed to fade away, and he focused all of his attention on the wizened stranger. Close at his side, his father seemed likewise captivated.

When the old man finally spoke, his voice trembled with constrained power. "Greetings to each one of you, fellow citizens, on this festival of the new moon. I have been called into your midst this evening to personally bear witness to the miracle that has changed the world for all time. For with my own eyes I have witnessed an event that will alter the very course of history.

"I speak to you about the one Father, whom even Jupiter and Nero must bow down before in reverence. Creator of all things, the Father sent to us his beloved son. For nine glorious months, I had the honor to walk at this Master's side. The miracles that I witnessed were many. He who caused the lame to walk, the blind to see, and even allowed the dead to live again, rose from the grave himself. In this manner, the Ascended Master returned to the one Father, his mission completed."

"And what mission is this?" cried a gravelly voice from the crowd.

Taking a moment to silently scan his mesmerized audience, the elder eventually answered. "The Ascended Master was sent to issue humanity a final warning. For a creature exists whose purpose is to impede man's journey to the final paradise. This evil one is also known as the great deceiver, Satan. His ways are those of waste and sin, and they lead to eternal damnation."

No sooner were these words spoken than a disturbance rose from the tavern's doorway. Nicholas turned in time to see a column of armored centurions enter and begin pushing its way toward the impromptu stage. Sensing trouble, Nicholas looked on as the lead soldier pointed at the white-haired elder and shouted commandingly, "John of Ephesus, by order of the emperor I place you under arrest for the crime of treason!"

Nicholas watched as the blond-haired youth beside the prophet jumped to his feet. The boy's fists were clenched, and his eyes were narrowed in angry defiance. Yet it appeared that the elder only had to touch the lad on his shoulder to restrain him. By this time, the soldiers had made their way to the table. With hands on the hilts of their swords, they looked up as the old man humbly bowed, and without displaying a hint of resistance, climbed down to surrender. Then, with their prisoner in tow, the centurions pivoted toward the exit.

By the time the last soldier ducked out the doorway, excited chatter filled the room. This was followed by a mass exodus, as the onlookers spared no time in leaving the tavern. Minutes later, the room was practically empty. This allowed Nicholas and his father a chance to corner the innkeeper and to arrange accommodations.

Their room was a cramped affair located above the stables. It had barely enough room for two stuffed mattresses and a cracked, tile wash basin. Though Nicholas wanted to talk more about their strange encounter with the so-called prophet, his father was snoring away contentedly in a matter of seconds. Unable to fall asleep himself, the youngster decided that some fresh air would help clear his head.

Outside, it was dark, hot, and humid. The air was heavy, reeking of strange spices and garbage. Even at this late hour, the streets were crowded. Not daring to wander far from the inn, Nicholas sat down on the building's narrow porch. He had barely settled himself into this position when he was accosted by a tall, red-headed woman with dark eyes and huge, jutting breasts. Her mere glance spoke her intentions, and Nicholas felt an alien stiffness in his loins.

He had heard stories that such women—prostitutes—existed. Making their living by selling sexual favors, they were a phenomenon of almost every large city. If the rumors were correct, he merely had to offer her a coin in order to be invited into her den of pleasures. His mouth was dry, his heartbeat pounding, as he reached into his pocket and touched the silver denarius that his father had given him earlier. He was just about to pull it out when another individual emerged from the darkness. Nicholas was quick to identify this blond-haired stranger as the same young man whom he had seen sitting beside the prophet, inside the tavern. Without speaking a word, the stranger eyed the prostitute, then linked his gaze with that of Nicholas.

Mesmerized by the utter intensity of this blue-eyed stare, Nicholas felt his sexual longings suddenly dissipate. Shame flushed his cheeks as he regarded the gentle, all-knowing face of this virtual stranger. Little did he care when the woman of the street slunk back into the shadows. All that he was aware of now was this newcomer.

"Blessed be, citizen," greeted the stranger smoothly.

Nicholas was forced to clear his throat before he could respond. "I saw you in the tavern earlier, didn't I? Where did they take the old man?"

"Most likely, straight to the chamber of tortures," returned the blond-haired one. "Yet our Master knew the risks. I can only pray that his sufferings are brief."

"Are you a servant to this man?" quizzed Nicholas.

The stranger shook his head. "Each one of us owes our obedience to the blessed one Father."

"But what about Jupiter and the rest of the gods?" countered Nicholas. "Surely one can't ignore their existence."

The stranger shot back. "Such pagan beliefs are mere fairy tales. The Master we bow to is the true creator of all."

Impressed with the virulence of this reply, Nicholas continued to probe. "Did you also witness the miracles that the elder spoke of?"

"My name is Dmitri, and I am a Greek by birth," said the stranger, whose tone had lightened. "I have only been following John of Ephesus for thirty days now, but in that time I have come to know the true meaning of spiritual peace. I did not know the Ascended Master, for my time had yet to come."

"I am Nicholas, from Carpathia. I arrived in Rome, along with my father, only this afternoon. We are here to pay tribute to the new emperor."

Dmitri nodded. "You have indeed traveled far. Welcome to the city."

"Thank you," returned Nicholas, whose brow was still knit with thought. "Tell me, Dmitri. I, too, have spiritual longings that not even my parents know of. Is it possible for even the simple likes of me to share the same peace that you experienced? And if so, what initiations must I go through to gain this insight?"

"The one Father is found by those who don't put him to the test. All that is needed is a pure heart, an open mind, and a strong will. For those who thirst for enlightenment, the Ascended Master exists like a well in the desert. Remember this, and perhaps you, too, will be called by the light that needs no fire in order to burn.

"Now the hour is late, and I must return to my vigil outside the master's cell. Peace be to you, Nicholas of Carpathia. And if it is so willed, perhaps our paths will cross again."

Without waiting for a response, he bowed and then turned to disappear into the night, leaving Nicholas alone on the inn porch. Again, a strange sense of contentment possessed the eighteen-year-old. It was almost as if in that brief conversation, his thoughts had aligned themselves in some perfect order. With a clarity he had never before experienced, Nicholas pondered the vast mysteries that had kept him awake on many a sleepless night.

The Roman gods came along with the Roman conquest. They were accepted now by his people, and they served to satisfy spiritual needs and longings. Yet, alone in the ancient forest or climbing the majestic mountaintops, the lad had heard another calling, one that spoke with a primal simplicity. For what need was there for intricate temple rituals and rote prayers, when the real creator expressed himself in the simple splash of a brook and the cry of the gusting wind?

Could this essence be the one Father that the blond-haired Greek had spoken of? And if so, perhaps he, too, might share in the strange peace that obviously filled this stranger's being. Issuing a wide yawn, Nicholas decided that it was time to return to his mattress and let his dreams explore the answers to his questions.

Hours later, Nicholas and his father entered the court of the emperor. They had been summoned to the baths of Nero by a messenger. Here they were instructed to wait in a large, marble-walled anteroom. With their load of fur pelts before them, they nervously waited for the moment when their audience would begin.

Both looked up expectantly when a distinguished, toga-clad patrician entered. This gray-haired aristocrat solemnly nodded and introduced himself.

"Greetings, citizens. I am Marcus Flavio, the emperor's chief political adviser. I do hope that your journey here was a smooth one."

Grigori cleared his throat. "That it was, my friend. We arrived here without incident and are looking forward to this morning's audience." Suddenly remembering his traveling companion, Grigori added, "I hope that you don't mind, but I've brought along my son, Nicholas."

"Why, of course we don't mind," returned the patrician. "The emperor will be pleased to meet with both of you. Is this your first visit to Rome, lad?"

"Yes it is, sir," responded Nicholas shyly.

Sensing his bashfulness, Marcus Flavio spoke warmly. "Well, I'm certain that you've seen an eyeful already, my boy. Enjoy our city's hospitality, and know that you are always welcome here. That goes for your friends as well. For you see, the emperor is most pleased with the loyalty of all of the Carpathians. You are a brave, industrious people, and all of Rome can rest easy, knowing that our northern border is under your expert scrutiny. I do hope that the barbarian rabble is not giving you much trouble."

"It's nothing that we can't handle," answered Grigori firmly. "Our main concern is with a tribe known as the Rus. They are a wild, fair-skinned people who have recently pushed down from the north. Though we've yet to confront them in a major battle, we've fought back several border incursions. In each instance our troops prevailed, yet not without sustaining much injury."

"We have also had contact with this same tribe," replied Marcus Flavio. "The Rus are fierce warriors. They have actually been seen drinking the blood of their slain enemies. Such godless savages must be kept from the empire's borders, and we are depending upon the Carpathians to be our first line of defense."

"You can rely on us," returned Grigori.

Marcus Flavio was about to continue, when a toga-clad Nubian entered the anteroom and informed them that Nero was ready to see them. With the patrician leading the way, they shouldered their gifts and began walking down a wide, column-lined hallway that led directly to the structure's central room.

Nicholas audibly gasped as they entered, for he had never seen such a grandiose chamber before. Feeling humble and small, he followed his father down the red mosaic pathway that bisected the room.

In the foreground, Nicholas spotted several large blue pools of water. Each contained a gurgling fountain and was graced by dozens of magnificent life-sized marble statues. Set between these pools was a single throne. A bearded, corpulent man in a white toga with gold trim sat there, his attention riveted to the scroll he held in his lap. Nicholas breathed in sharply. Was this really Nero? The man was flanked by a pair of armored centurions, each well over six feet tall. Nicholas imagined that they were representatives of the infamous Praetorian guard, whose loyalty to the emperor could never be questioned.

Marcus Flavio was about to announce their presence when a loud, resonant gong sounded. Nicholas stopped his advance and turned around in time to see a messenger enter. The messenger was obviously on a mission of great importance, for he hurried past them without breaking his long, fluid stride. Seconds later, he was breathlessly kneeling before the man seated on the throne. He whispered a message, and even though Nicholas could not discern its nature, he clearly saw the manner in which it affected the emperor. Nero screamed with rage and threw his scroll to the floor in disgust. A moment later, the emperor caught sight of Nicholas and his father. A curt order was conveyed, and the two guards immediately advanced to escort the Carpathians back out into the hallway.

Stunned and perplexed, Nicholas followed quickly on his father's heels. Without an explanatory word, they were led through the anteroom, where they were instructed to deposit their pelts. No sooner had the furs hit the ground than the two were ordered outside.

The morning sun was rising hot in a crystal blue sky as they emerged on the exposed vestibule of the baths. The continued presence of the two guards beside the entrance made it obvious that they were no longer welcome inside. This left them no alternative but to return to the inn to await some sort of explanation.

As they were crossing the forum, an agitated circle of merchants caught their attention. Nicholas and his father attempted to penetrate the crowd, and they soon learned the reason for the emperor's rage and their hasty dismissal from the baths. Only minutes ago, they were told, word of an event of miraculous proportions had reached the streets.

It centered around last night's arrest of the white-haired elder known as John of Ephesus. This advocate of the traitorous cult of the one Father had been imprisoned and subsequently immersed in a vat of boiling oil. The so-called prophet not only failed to react to this immersion, but when he was pulled free of the scalding liquid, was found to have experienced not a single burn!

"Such a thing is impossible!" shouted Nicolas's father, who led him out of the crowd. "It's not the first time that such a groundless, wild rumor has spread through the streets of Rome."

"Why do you say that?" countered Nicholas. "Maybe it's true. Maybe it really is a miracle."

Grigori shook his head. "Oh, come now, son. You can't be serious. That mob is talking nothing but pure foolishness."

Though Nicholas instinctively felt otherwise, he held his tongue as they made their way across the square.

Waiting outside their inn was a large cart surrounded by spear-toting soldiers. Inside this vehicle was a solitary, white-haired figure. The prophet! Nicholas thought. John of Ephesus!

Several of the men who had been seated at the table beside this man were now being escorted toward the cart. At the back of this line of solemn figures, prodded by the soldiers, walked Dmitri. Without a second thought, Nicholas ran to intercept the blond-haired Greek.

"Come back here!" vainly cried his father.

Oblivious to this cautionary shout, Nicholas pushed his way through the throng of curious onlookers. Crawling beneath the legs of one of the soldiers, Nicholas was able to catch Dmitri's eye just as he was about to enter the cart.

"Is it true what they say?" queried the Carpathian breathlessly. "Did the prophet truly escape the boiling oil as it has been rumored?"

"Yes, my friend, such a miracle indeed occurred," returned Dmitri.

"Then, may I ask where you are being taken with such haste?"

The blond-haired Greek answered without hesitation. "Because the emperor remains deaf to the cries of the one Father, he has ordered us banished from Rome. We are currently on our way to exile on the Mediterranean island of Patmos."

"But how can Nero ignore what surely is a miracle?" asked Nicholas.

"Too often, the truth creates fear. Today this same truth leads to our banishment. The time will yet come when all men accept the word of the one Father. Until then, we can but go where fate sends us."

A captain broke from the ranks and squeezed in behind Nicholas. Lifting up his shield, he pushed forward and toppled Nicholas into Dmitri. When their feet intertwined, both fell instantly to the ground.

Not certain what was happening, Nicholas felt a pair of powerful hands grasp his shoulders. He found himself lifted up and carried forcefully toward the cart like a puppet. He squirmed, kicked, and shouted that this was all a mistake, yet his efforts were to no avail. Tossed into the covered cart on his back, he looked up in time to see its gate barred shut. The cart then jerked forward with a sickening jolt.

Nicholas sat up. Across the way he could see the horrified face of his father, who was frantically attempting to break through the crowd. Nicholas fought to control his panic. As he struggled to catch his breath, he became aware of the men beside him. They sat on the straw-covered floor of the cart, their eyes wide with calm acceptance.

Looking past the compassionate, blue-eyed stare of Dmitri, he focused on the elder responsible for this misunderstanding in the first place. The man known as John of Ephesus merely nodded to him and issued the barest of all-knowing smiles. The result was almost instantaneous. In a heartbeat, Nicholas lost his anxieties. As the cart continued southward through the crowded streets of Rome, the young Carpathian forgot his fears.

They arrived at the sea by nightfall. Under the cloak of a dense fog, they were transferred to the hold of a galley. Twice Nicholas attempted to speak to the officer in charge to explain his predicament, yet each time he was turned away. When he realized that the ship was actually setting sail, a new wave of panic possessed him. Once again he cried out to the guards, yet this time in response he received a painful blow to his head.

It proved to be Dmitri who pulled him away from the guards before they could dole out further punishment. Led back into the hold's dark recesses, Nicholas collapsed to the deck, emotionally and physically exhausted.

He awoke to find the light of dawn illuminating the compartment. His head throbbed, and it took him several seconds to reorient himself. Nicholas studied his new traveling companions. There were twelve in all. Most were approximately the same age as his father.

Dmitri initiated the introductions. Drawn from the far corners of the world, Nicholas met men from such diverse places as Gaul, Britain, Africa, Arabia, India, and China. As a group they seemed surprisingly content, accepting their banishment without a single utterance of complaint.

John of Ephesus remained somewhat detached from this troop. His need for privacy was never questioned. This was especially evident in the hold of the ship, where he took a corner of the compartment all for himself. Here he read constantly from a small, black, leatherbound book, whose pages were illuminated by a single flickering candle. Dmitri explained that this book included a detailed account of the miracles initiated by the Ascended Master. Though Nicholas was eager to hear more, he was once again overwhelmed by exhaustion and fell into a deep sleep.

This time when he awoke he found the hold masked in darkness. From the pitch of the deck beneath him, he knew that they were well out to sea. As his eyes gradually adjusted to the black of night, he spotted his companions. Each of them were on their knees, facing the forward bulkhead and the standing figure of John of Ephesus.

Nicholas was quick to join them. Kneeling at Dmitri's side, he listened to the words that were so eloquently flowing from the white-haired elder's mouth. He spoke of mysteries, miracles and sacrifice. He spoke of things that Nicholas had never imagined. In such a way the night passed into morning, and the young Carpathian learned more about the short but full life of the Ascended Master.

After brief stops in both Malta and Crete, the galley finally made port in Patmos. By this time, Nicholas realized that he must face the truth and give up any hope of being reunited with his father. That part of his life was over now. He had been called to something greater. It seemed that his very outlook on life had changed as they made their way onto land.

Their new home was volcanic in origin and stretched barely ten miles long and six miles wide. This included a thousand-foot peak, whose slopes were covered with thick groves of palm trees. It was in the midst of such a grove that they set up camp.

It was sometime during their second evening on Patmos that John of Ephesus disappeared. Nicholas feared that the elder might have become lost, and he offered to lead a search party to find him. Strangely enough, the others begged him to be patient. They argued that John was quite capable of taking care of himself and that he had disappeared just as abruptly on several occasions in the past. "Try to wait," they told Nicholas. "You'll see what we mean."

Nicholas was kept busy preparing the large cavern that they had chosen to live in. He helped the others construct grass mats to sleep on and proved an accomplished food gatherer. Figs, dates, and shellfish were abundant. Such selection proved more than adequate to keep their hunger under control.

Nicholas found himself looking forward to the nights, when the twelve disciples would assemble around the fire-circle and exchange tales of their homelands. Called from the far corners of the earth, each man went on to explain how he first received word of the Ascended Master. Drawn by this common bond, they had their shared faith to link them together as a family.

The sixth evening of John's absence arrived with a violent thunderstorm. Black storm clouds had been gathering on the western horizon all afternoon and did not vent themselves until the sun had dipped. To escape the torrents of rain and hail, the twelve disciples took shelter in their cave. Here they waited out the storm by immersing themselves in individual prayer.

The storm's fury, clearly audible inside the cavern, only added to the uneasiness that Nicholas had felt all day. For the first time in almost a week, he seemed to have lost his faith—in St. John, in the one Father, and most of all in himself. Called to the entrance of the cave by the wild gusting of the wind, the crack of lightning, and the distant boom of thunder, the young Carpathian looked out to the tempest, feeling alone and abandoned. It was all a horrible mistake. He did not belong in this desolate wilderness—he should be with his father, on the road back to their homeland.

The cult of the Ascended Master had painted an alluring vision of miracles and the promise of a glorious paradise to be. Yet what did it really mean to him? What could have possessed him? He had been brought up with the gods of the forest, stream, and sky. The idea of the Ascended Master ran contrary to every belief that had ever been handed down to him.

A deafening bolt of lightning cracked overhead, and Nicholas anxiously stirred. The elder known as John of Ephesus must be a master magician who was able to mesmerize his followers. By weaving such a powerful spell, even a fully grown man could be tricked into becoming one of his disciples. Now that this so-called prophet was gone, his spell was wearing off, and Nicholas believed he was the first of the men to come to his senses.

Nicholas felt his spirits lighten. He had been strong enough to resist the warlock, and as a result, he had set himself free. As the rains fell and the winds whipped the grove with a torrential ferocity, the eighteen-year-old mentally formulated a plan. After the storm was over, he would secretly leave the cavern and make his way down to the beach. There he would assemble a raft and then say good-bye to this cursed island. Proud of his newfound courage, Nicholas leaned back against the cave's smooth rock wall to await the moment when the cloudburst would end.

The hypnotic patter of the rain caused Nicholas to drift off into a deep slumber. He began dreaming almost instantly. In this vision he was transferred to the hills of his birth. Seated beneath a majestic oak tree, with a field of thick, green clover around him, Nicholas tended the village's communal sheep herd. With a pair of spirited dogs doing the majority of the work, the lad was able to sit back and properly enjoy the warm, summer afternoon.

Suddenly, in his dream, he was transported to an isolated, desolate crag, situated deep in the Carpathian mountains. An angry, cold gale raged. From the black heavens, lightning streaked the sky, while the thunder boomed incessantly. The icy rain fell in a deluge, as the storm-soaked Nicholas desperately searched for shelter. Straining to see through the fog, with his teeth chattering, he barely spied the opening of a tiny cave cut into an opposite wall. His body seemed weighted down as he fought his way into this cavern's entrance.

With the storm still raging outside, he realized with a start that he was not alone. On the rock floor was an intricately ornamented sedan chair. Nicholas's heart pounded in his chest as he approached the sedan chair and pulled back its curtain. The musky scent of rich perfume was enough to make him choke, and he took in the somewhat familiar face and figure of a tall, redheaded woman with dark eyes and jutting breasts. Her mere glance spoke her intentions.

Raw sexual desire inflamed Nicholas's total being. Satisfying this lust was everything!

The woman's brightly painted, ruby red lips beckoned, and Nicholas experienced an aching hunger the likes of which he had never known was possible. To satisfy this craving he leaned over to merge his quivering lips with hers. Inches away from fulfillment, her mouth suddenly opened in a wolflike sneer. With one look at the pair of razor-sharp incisors that protruded from her clenched jaw, Nicholas was overcome with terror. The scent of death almost suffocated him as he pulled back to see the spiraling red spheres of fire that had replaced her dark pupils. One terrifying look was all he needed to understand that what he faced here was not a woman at all. This was the Evil One!

Nicholas snapped from his nightmare with his heart pounding and his forehead soaked in sweat. A resonant boom of thunder echoed in the distance as he struggled to adjust to his surroundings.

His companions were nowhere to be seen. Quickly he

looked outside and saw that a new day had dawned. Rain was still falling lightly. He ducked through the cavern's entrance and was met by a swirling gust of wind. Within minutes, he was wet to the skin. Doing his best to follow the narrow trail that led from the cave, he climbed down to the clearing where the fire-ring had been situated. As lightning flashed, he spotted his companions.

Set in a semicircular grove of wildly swaying palms, the grotto faced a hundred-foot-high, elevated rock shelf that was set into the clearing's eastern edge. Completely oblivious to the storm, a line of kneeling figures faced this outcropping.

Curious as to what had drawn them outdoors, Nicholas turned and approached the line of kneeling penitents. Through the gusting squalls, he picked out the blond-haired figure of Dmitri. His friend was deep in prayer as Nicholas approached him.

The Greek's piety shamed Nicholas. How very strong his faith must be!

A resounding boom of thunder exploded overhead, and portions of his recently concluded nightmare rose disturbingly in his consciousness. Was he so spiritually weak that he could not resist temptation? For was not the act of running away from this holy place the ultimate act of cowardice? Tears rolled down his cheeks, and Nicholas knew that if he wanted to be at peace with himself, he had no other choice but to surrender his soul. Without another thought, he knelt down beside Dmitri.

The Carpathian emptied his heavy heart of doubts. He filled the cold void with meditations of the one Father. A sudden feeling of warmth possessed him, and he was absolutely certain that he had made the right decision.

The howl of the wind interrupted his deep pondering.

Opening his eyes, he looked up to the elevated rock ledge that lay immediately before them. For a moment, the rain seemed to slacken. Then a jagged finger of lightning broke from the heavens and struck the outcropping with a deafening blast, releasing two spiraling balls of intense red light. Zooming down to the clearing, the spheres left in their wake a hideous vision of Hell itself. Monstrous, slime-covered demons cavorted in the thick air, their bansheelike cries echoing with piercing abandon.

Several of these creatures appeared to be almost human in shape, yet they were composed solely of bone. Following this assemblage of skeletons was a shaggy, four-legged beast that resembled a horse—except for its misshapen, lolling human head. There was also a massive, dragonlike animal, on whose back a naked man and woman were frantically copulating. Their cries of passion were swallowed by an angry, deafening scream that emanated from the mouth of what looked like a tall, muscular mortal. Yet instead of skin, this creature was covered with black scales and had a long tail, with a head capped by two pointed horns. Beckoning toward Nicholas, this horned beast revealed a man's bearded face. It was only when he opened his mouth to cry out that Nicholas spotted a set of razor-sharp fangs and noted the tortured red glow in this creature's eyes.

Shivering in awareness, Nicholas realized that he was viewing the cohorts of the Evil One himself. The vile, putrid stench of death met his nostrils, and Nicholas was beyond fear. Pure terror possessed him as he turned to see the manner in which his companions were meeting this devilish onslaught.

Immediately beside Nicholas, his face glowing red by the light of Hades, Dmitri trembled with dread. His companions seemed equally affected, and Nicholas knew that the very limits of their faith were being tested. Feeling weak and defenseless, Nicholas could but pray for a quick, merciful death.

Just as the demons were almost upon them, a vicious whirlwind descended upon the plateau. The howl of this cyclone rose above the cries of the hordes of Hell. Forced to grab onto Dmitri's hand in order not to be sucked away, Nicholas wondered if this was how death would take them.

The winds tore at his body, the whirling gusts rising in a deafening crescendo. Yet as suddenly as they arrived, they evaporated. This brief reprieve allowed Nicholas to focus his line of sight back to the foot of the rock outcropping, where the pair of swirling red spheres still circled. The crimson balls of evil seemed to be merely teasing them, when all of a sudden his attention was drawn to the ledge that topped the wall. His heartbeat fluttered upon identifying the figure of the man known as John of Ephesus.

The white-haired elder stood facing them. With his arms outstretched and his white gown blowing in the wind, the prophet spoke out forcefully.

"Demons of Hell, I command you to begone!"

This powerful invective only seemed to irritate the swirling spheres, which began circling more violently. Seeing this, John of Ephesus again shouted:

"By the staff of the one Father, I demand that you return back through the gates of Hades!"

John of Ephesus lifted a slender wooden staff in his right hand and pointed it down toward the clearing. Instantly, a blinding finger of lightning shot from the heavens. This was accompanied by an ear-splitting boom of thunder that caused the very earth below to shudder.

Deafened by this blast, Nicholas found himself shaking uncontrollably. Only when the smoke finally cleared did his nerves settle—for the swirling red spheres and the demons that had accompanied them were miraculously gone! The young Carpathian sheepishly looked up and focused his attention on the white-haired elder, who continued standing on the ledge above them. A glowing golden nimbus surrounded the elder's head as he lowered his staff and began to speak.

"Blessed be, brothers of the faith. Open your hearts to the glorious one Father, from whom even the beasts of Hell flee back to their dens.

"For six days I have been called to the wilderness, to bear witness to the greatest of revelations. In this apocalyptic vision, the Ascended Master himself appeared to me. Called from his father's side, the Holy One warned of the evil intentions of the Beast, who also goes by the names Satan, Lucifer, and the Devil.

"As there is light, so there must be darkness. Thus to satisfy his insatiable hunger for human souls, this evil one spreads his gospel of greed and sin. Woe to those mortals who dare stand in his way, for even the mightiest men are powerless before him.

"To insure this earthly paradise, the one Father has been forced to call down his angels. Together with a great chain and the key to the bottomless pit, they have seized the Evil One and bound him for a thousand years. After this period of time has expired, it is written that Satan must be loosed once again, to test the strength of men's hearts.

"As fellow disciples, you have been chosen to await the beast's reawakening. You must fight the Evil One with the only two weapons you have: your own faith, and a spear that was cut from the cross on which the

Ascended Master died. The Master himself has handed down this spear to me. Now you must spread out to the far corners of the planet. Here you will perpetuate our mission by passing down our sacred responsibility to the generations that follow. For on that fated day when the Evil One awakens, we will be all that stands between the hordes of Hell and the community of man. Know this and never falter, or eternal damnation will be humanity's reward."

Nicholas shivered in complete understanding as he listened to the words of the prophet. Gone were the petty insecurities and weaknesses that had once held him back. In their place was an unquestioning, indomitable will. Like a man who had died and had been reborn in the spirit, his purpose was now perfectly clear.

It had been the divine will of the one Father that had brought him to Patmos. Here his life had at long last been given a real direction and purpose. He was an initiate of St. John the Pursuer now, dedicated solely to tracking down the Evil One, wherever he might be.

Turning to his left, he caught the stare of his fellow disciple, Dmitri. His friend's pupils flashed, and Nicholas knew that he, too, had accepted his calling. Nodding in awareness, the young Carpathian turned his attention back to the stone ledge. This time he was forced to shade his eyes when the dawn sun broke the horizon, engulfing their master in a golden, pulsating veil of radiance.

2

The Soviet Ukraine—The Present

The first day of spring in the Carpathians dawned wet and cold. To Colonel Sergei Koslov, commander of the Ministry of Defense construction unit attached to the Fifth Military District at L'vov, the arrival of the vernal equinox had been eagerly anticipated. The winter just past had been an unusually severe one. The accompanying snow, ice, and sub-freezing temperatures meant that the projects assigned to his unit were three months behind schedule.

If only his superiors would estimate reasonable time limits, taking into account such weather, he could do his job without undue pressure. Yet somehow the bureaucrats snuggled warmly inside the Kremlin expected miracles from him and his men. Work in isolated mountain valleys, such as this one, was hard enough without the elements to contend with. Because the nearest city of any size was more than a hundred kilometers distant, just achieving an adequate supply line was in itself a major project. Add to this the poor state of repair of their equipment, and the colonel found himself facing one delay after another.

His superiors were not interested in excuses. What they demanded were results. The installation of the twenty-four SS-18 ballistic missile silos was a major priority. Because of the latest round of strategic arms talks, just beginning in Zurich, a decision had been made to install as many new launch sites as possible in the immediate future. Since an ensuing treaty would most likely limit the amount of future warheads, the Soviet Union wanted to have their latest, most advanced weapon system well-entrenched, so that it could not be used as a bargaining chip.

The SS-18 was the world's most powerful ballistic missile. With a range of more than seventy-five hundred miles, each rocket carried ten warheads, which could strike almost any target in the Western Hemisphere with an amazing degree of accuracy. By deploying it here in the Carpathian mountains, the Soviets hoped to take advantage of the region's unique physical characteristics. The missile site would be well hidden from any reconnaissance satellites, for the area was shrouded by thick virgin forests and an almost constant cloud cover. The Motherland could rest easily, knowing that at least one of its defensive installations would remain intact in the event of an American attack.

Looking out the frosted window of the small log cabin that served as both his current living space and the unit's headquarters, Sergei Koslov understood the importance of his current assignment. Outside, the rain fell in a fine mist. A dense fog had arrived with the night, completely enshrouding the surrounding woods. The muddy, one-and-a-half acre clearing where the silo command center was currently being excavated was barely visible before him. His men looked like heavy-handed ghosts as they dug into the sodden ground. They were dressed in long, burdensome, soaking wet greatcoats. Sergei shivered in his warm cabin.

Because of an almost complete breakdown of their earth-moving equipment, the men had been forced to resort to picks and shovels. At first the rocky, half-frozen soil had been almost impossible to penetrate, and it was only in the last few weeks that any real progress had been made. Although the work was slow and tedious, gradually the excavation deepened. With the help of laborers conscripted from the nearby villages of Vorochta, Zabje, and Rachov, the work progressed—as it had to—under the awful weather conditions.

As Sergei watched the men pull up the mud-filled buckets and then empty the mucky contents into the awaiting carts, he found himself thinking back to a time more than forty years ago. He was an army conscript then, fresh off his family's communal farm on the outskirts of Kiev. After a minimum of basic training, his first duty had brought him far to the north, to the capital itself.

At that time the nation was under siege by the ever-advancing Nazi hordes. The army was furiously attempting to construct a defensive barrier around the outskirts of Moscow. Sergei was assigned to an excavation brigade much like the one now working under his command. He would never forget the frantic digging, or the way his bare hands had been scraped raw and bloody. Even a shovel was a luxury then.

Catching his own reflection in the cottage window, Sergei was abruptly brought back to the present. How different was the paunchy, bald-headed figure he saw before him from that tightly muscled, blond-haired youth of forty years ago! But even today he was working for the defense of his homeland.

The encroaching tide of capitalism was a deceptive evil. Like the Nazis, the Imperialists would not stop until the entire world was under their greedy spell. That was why installations like the one he and his men were working on now were so vital to the nation's security. Tens of millions of men had already given their lives in order to keep Mother Russia secure. Their deaths must never be in vain. This was the guiding principle that Sergei Koslov had sworn to uphold.

Sergei's thoughts were interrupted by the arrival of his aide. The scrawny, tight-lipped Siberian padded into the cabin almost soundlessly. He gently placed a silver serving tray on the surface of the room's only table.

"Your tea, Comrade Colonel."

The burly officer, who had been looking forward to some breakfast, found himself unable to respond, his attention diverted to an unusual disturbance which was taking place at the dig site. Here, the men had stopped pulling in their buckets and were now excitedly pointing toward the hole's interior. Sergei looked on as other workmen came running over to peer down into the muddy depths.

Not knowing what was distracting the colonel, the orderly cleared his voice. "Sir, one of Dr. Lopatin's students was by earlier to see you. He said it was most important that the doctor have a word with you, as soon as it possible."

Sergei did not respond.

"Sir?" the aide repeated, stepping closer.

"I hear you, comrade," Sergei snapped. His eyes were riveted on the dig site. "The good doctor is just going to have to wait her turn. All I need is a nosey archaeologist wasting my time. It looks like something unusual is going on at the site. Be so good as to run out there, and have Lieutenant Nosovka report to me at once."

"Very good, sir," snapped the orderly, who disappeared from the room as quietly as he had arrived.

Seconds later, Sergei watched as his khaki-uniformed aide scrambled out into the clearing. Oblivious to the falling rain, the hearty Siberian, who had not even taken the time to don his overcoat, pushed his way past the dozen or so gawking figures who still huddled around the hole's interior. A full minute passed as several of the men crouched over to help a co-worker climb out of the pit. Even though the man who emerged was covered with mud, Sergei had no doubt as to his identity, for he clearly dwarfed all those who stood around him.

Sergei's aide anxiously led the muddy soldier to the colonel's cottage. The soldier, Lieutenant Georgi Nosovka, seemed oblivious to the fact that he had tracked a trail of dripping mud into Sergei's spotlessly clean cabin. He snapped a smart salute and spoke out breathlessly.

"Colonel, we have just made a most startling find. Several minutes ago, our picks struck what appeared to be solid rock. Since our core samples showed no such strata in this immediate area, we proceeded to clear away the surrounding dirt to see what we had hit upon. We've yet to totally uncover the object in question, but at this point, it seems we've unearthed some sort of ancient relic. It appears to be a type of sarcophagus."

With this revelation, the colonel's expression noticeably soured. "That's all we need to delay us now, an archaeological find! Knowledge of this discovery must be kept from the university people at all costs. National security is at stake here!"

Sergei Koslov's head was pounding as he turned to look back out to the clearing. There, a thickening line of drenched figures stood, gaping into the large hole, which lay barely half a kilometer distant.

"What do the men think they're doing? Is this a holiday? Lieutenant, get them back to work this instant!"

"But the relic, Colonel?" pleaded the junior officer.

"To hell with that relic!" cried Sergei, his face beet red. "Remove it at once, and get back to your duty! Any more holdups and we'll all be sent off to Siberia. Do you hear me, comrade?"

Georgi Nosovka straightened his muscular frame and saluted. "I'll have the men get back to work at once, sir. I'm sorry for the delay. It won't happen again."

Sheepishly, he slipped out of the room. Turning again to the window, the colonel managed barely a smile as he watched the lieutenant angrily barking out orders to the men in the clearing. It took only seconds for the men to scatter and return to their duties.

Sergei knew that he was fortunate to have such an officer working under him. Now, if only his luck held, news of the discovery would not reach the ear of Dr. Yelena Lopatin.

Three kilometers southwest of Colonel Koslov's cabin, in an adjoining wilderness valley, a handful of student archaeologists stood beneath the canvas awning of their instructor's tent. To the accompaniment of the patter of lightly falling rain, they listened, completely fascinated, to their leader's discourse.

Dr. Yelena Lopatin was one of the Institute of Culture's brightest professors. One of the top experts in the field of ancient Russian civilization, she knew more about the origins of the Soviet people than almost anyone else on Earth, quite an accomplishment, considering that she was barely thirty-six years old.

The tall, redheaded professor stood before a portable table, carefully chipping away at the flakes of clay that still stuck to the morning's gruesome find. The petrified human skull was in almost perfect condition. Though the teeth had long since fallen from their sockets, the only apparent aberration of the cranium was the manner in which the top section had been cut off and the interior hollowed out and smoothed down.

"It must be Scythian in origin," explained Yelena. "In the fifth century B.C., the Greek historian Herodotus described just such a skull cup. Yet until today, one has never been exhumed intact."

"If this relic is indeed Scythian, that would make it almost two thousand years old," offered an alert student. "Shouldn't it have deteriorated by now?"

Yelena answered while chipping a thick piece of mud from the relic. "It must have been protected from the elements by a waterproof capsule of clay. We've exhumed dinosaur bones that were preserved for much greater lengths of time because of just such a phenomenon."

"Could this skull possibly date back before the Scythians?" quizzed another one of her students.

Yelena shook her head. "I seriously doubt it. As you know, the village site that we were excavating when we came across our little treasure here held several primitive iron spear points. Since the Celts introduced iron to the peoples living on the continent and then drove the Scythians out of the Balkans and into these hills in 300 B.C., I'd say that our relic dates from such a time."

One of the younger students, who was completely transfixed by the morning's activities, dared a question. "Miss Lopatin, what was this skull used for, anyway?"

A girlish gleam sparkled in Yelena's eyes as she answered. "That's a good question, Sasha. Herodotus seems to think that they were first designed by the Celts. These same warriors supposedly drank the blood of their enemies at their high feasts, using cups made from the skulls of their foes."

A chorus of squeamish groans rose from her audience as she brought the artifact to her lips and pretended to drink from it. This rare moment of levity was abruptly interrupted by the excited shouts of a man who approached them from the nearby mist-covered forest.

Completely soaked and out of breath, graduate student Konstantin Ustinov reached the cover of the tent flap. "They've found something, Doctor! The army engineers have stumbled onto a great find!"

"Easy, Konstantin," counseled Yelena softly. After carefully putting down the skull cup, she continued. "Now take a few seconds to catch your breath, and then tell us exactly what they've come across."

Accepting a towel from one of the other students, Ustinov wiped the rain from his bearded face and uncovered hair. As he bent over at the waist, his wheezing lungs gradually returned more normal rhythm. Straightening up, he caught his professor's crystal blue stare.

"I had just finished delivering your message to the colonel's aide and had taken a few minutes to watch their dig's progress, when they made the first contact. This was at a depth of about ten meters. After that, it didn't take them long to completely uncover the object, which appears to be some sort of stone sarcophagus. Strangely enough, it was buried lengthwise."

"On its end, you say?" repeated Yelena thoughtfully.

Accepting the student's nod, the archaeologist broke into a warm smile. "I bet it's the tomb of a Scythian war lord! Herodotus mentioned that this was the strange manner in which their chiefs were buried. Do you realize what such a find could mean? We must get over there at once, before the soldiers open the coffin's seal and ruin whatever lies waiting inside."

Reaching out for her poncho and bag of excavating tools, Yelena beamed like a young schoolgirl. "Come on, comrades. What an incredible morning this first day of spring is turning out to be!"

She immediately took off for the distant woods. Infected by her enthusiasm, they slipped into their own jackets and left the shelter of the canvas awning to surrender themselves to the raw, icy drizzle and the great mystery that lay beyond the tree line.

By the time Colonel Koslov neared the dig site, the volume of rain had noticeably increased to a steady shower. Even with the cover of his woolen greatcoat and fur hat, Sergei was thoroughly chilled as he peered down into the pit's dark interior. Here, the muddy walls had been sufficiently hollowed out to allow three men just enough space to surround the massive granite object.

The monolith, which appeared to have been cut from a single block of stone, was several centimeters taller than the figure of Lieutenant Nosovka, who stood beside it. Beside him, two enlisted men were busy attaching a thick, canvas sling around the relic's midsection. The strap was connected to a steel cable, which led upward to the hydraulic hoist mechanism. The long-armed, diesel-powered lift would be responsible for transferring the stone block to the surface.

The colonel watched these preparations and stirred impatiently. "Lieutenant Nosovka, get on with the removal! We've wasted enough time with this already."

Impervious to Koslov's commanding tone, the lieutenant continued his study of the stone slab's surface. "There's some sort of writing etched in the rock here, Colonel. It's unlike any language I've ever seen."

"Comrade!" Sergei bellowed angrily. "I ordered you to remove that block at once. Finish the attachment of the cable, and get that obstacle out of there. This delay is inexcusable!"

Koslov looked on as the junior officer backed away from his close examination of the granite block and bent over to give his coworkers a hand in fitting the sling. Satisfied that this delay would soon be overcome, Sergei turned to make his way back to the shelter of the cottage. It was then that he saw the line of strangers emerging from the woods to the southwest. He cursed to himself, for in a moment it was clear just who was approaching.

Koslov knew that it would be useless to try to keep them from the find for long. The archaeologists would pester him endlessly. Besides, there were members of the government who supported the discovery of such relics. These same individuals were responsible for funding the archaeologists. Better to let them have their look now, so that his men could get back to their work without outside interference. Sergei signaled his aide to inform the guard at the periphery to let the professor and her flock of students through. Then he slowly crossed the soggy field to intercept them.

"Good morning, Dr. Lopatin," he greeted the professor. "To what do we owe this honor?"

Pushing back the soaked ringlets of red hair from her forehead, Yelena met the officer's glance evenly. "Come now, Colonel. You really didn't think that you'd keep news of your find from us, did you?"

"What find is that?" returned Sergei carefully.

Yelena's response was tinged with impatience. "This is certainly no time for game-playing, Colonel. One of my own students saw for himself the relic that your men have stumbled upon. From his initial description, the piece appears to be of great importance."

"Your intelligence network impresses me, Doctor. In fact, I was just about to send one of my men over to inform you of our little discovery. You don't really think that I'd dare keep such a thing from you, knowing your interests as I do?"

Yelena studied the colonel's shrewd eyes. Although she knew that he was most likely not telling the truth, she decided to play along with him.

"No, Colonel, I'm certain that you understand how important our excavation in this valley is to both the institute and our country."

Sergei accepted this reply with a nod, and beckoned toward the dig site. "Then, if you'll be so good as to follow me, I'll show you the object that brings us together on this wet, gray morning."

The group did not have far to go before it was standing at the pit's edge, staring down into its murky depths. Each of the curious observers could clearly see the huge stone monolith as it was pulled to the surface.

To the whine of the straining diesel engine, the object inched its way upward. Supported by a tense steel cable and a canvas sling, the relic was guided by three mud-soaked workers who stood on the pit's soggy floor.

Certain now that her initial suspicions were correct, Yelena's heart pounded with excitement. Everything, from the depth at which the object was found to its dimensions and the manner in which it was buried, indicated that it was the sarcophagus of a Scythian war lord.

"Colonel, are you certain that your hoist is of sufficient strength to lift such a heavy object?"

Koslov responded with an incredulous look. "Dr. Lopatin, have you already forgotten that you are dealing with a Soviet military engineering unit? I think that we can handle a minor extraction such as this one without undue concern. Relax, comrade."

His last words were emphasized by a distant boom of muffled thunder and the increased patter of falling rain. Looking up into the darkening heavens, Sergei sensed that the brunt of the storm would hit them at any moment. It was time to be on his way back to the warm confines of his cabin. Only a fool or a conscript should be subject to such a needless soaking.

As he glanced down to monitor the progress of the relic, the first winds hit. Sweeping in from the northwest with an icy fury, the gusts struck with the intensity of a full-force gale. Struggling to keep his balance, Sergei fought to keep himself from being blown into the pit.

"Everyone, back away from the edge!" he commanded.

The strained grinding of the hoist's diesel engine rose above his cry as the wind grew even stronger. Sergei shielded his eyes from the stinging spray of rain. He could see that one person had yet to heed his warning. With her poncho blowing wildly, Dr. Lopatin still stood precariously near the edge of the pit, gesturing wildly at the hoist crew working the opposite bank.

"Lower the relic until this storm passes!"

Not knowing if the men working the hoist could even hear her, Yelena attempted to signal her request by gesturing more slowly. At this point a massive gust of wind struck the archaeologist full in the back, sending her teetering toward the muddy abyss. The colonel's iron grip on her shoulders kept Yelena from plunging downward to certain injury. Pulled back to safety, she was just turning to thank Koslov when a loud metallic snap, followed by a dull thud, sounded out behind them.

The first thing Yelena noticed was a section of slack, frayed iron cable hanging uselessly from the hoist's topmost arm. Just as she comprehended that her greatest fear had been realized, a pained, unearthly wail emanated from the hole's, followed by a panicked cry.

"Somebody help us! Lieutenant Nosovka has been crushed!"

Against the pit's opposite wall, the loose sarcophagus stood, firmly implanted on its end. Covered by several inches of water, the monolith's base was well entrenched in the muck. On each side of the stone object, a young soldier was busy, frantically trying to claw into the mud wall that it rested against. It was evident from their actions that their unfortunate coworker was trapped between the relic's far side and the wall.

It proved to be the colonel's deep voice that snapped the rest of his men into action. "Get some men down there with shovels! Replace the hoist cable, reattach the sling, and get that infernal relic off of him!"

As the men hurried to carry out these orders, a deafeningly loud crack of lightning split the dark clouds above, followed by waves of solid rain.

Why did the unfortunate victim have to be Lieutenant Nosovka, of all people? Sergei thought hopelessly. The young officer had served under Sergei for more than five years now. Beyond his great physical strength, the lieutenant was loyal and honest to the core. Although at times Sergei had been harsh with him, this was always meant for his own good. Drafted into the army as a mere boy, Nosovka grew not only in height, but also in mental prowess. A quick learner and a natural leader, the youngster had quickly risen through the ranks. He was the type of officer that the colonel could always rely on to make certain that his directives were carried out properly.

Nosovka had been an invaluable member of his staff, having assisted him with such varied projects as the submarine pens at Petropavlovsk, the missile command post at Semipalatinsk, and the barrack complexes in Kabul. He was not a man who could be easily replaced.

Cursing his misfortune, Sergei made his way over to the side of the frantically working hoist crew. Without wasting a second, they had replaced the broken cable and were busy attaching it to the canvas sling. Meanwhile, workers had positioned themselves inside the hole on each side of the monolith. With quick strokes of their shovels, they dug into the earthen wall.

The renewed whine of a diesel motor sounded. Even though the torrential sheets of rain still veiled the progress of the rescue, the colonel breathed a sigh of relief. The steel lift cable abruptly tightened.

"We've got him!" shouted a raw voice from below.

Fighting the gusting wind, a pair of medics lowered a field stretcher into the pit. With the help of two others, the men managed to pull the litter back to the surface.

A massive, inert, mud- and blood-soaked body lay strapped to the wooden frame. Koslov joined the kneeling medics as they hastily examined the crushed man. Far beyond first aid, Georgi Nosovka stared upward with unseeing eyes. The colonel closed his junior officer's eyes for the final time. While wiping the mud from the lieutenant's stiffening face, Sergei could not help but notice that one of Nosovka's arms had popped out of its nylon restraint and was dangling over the pit. From his torn wrist, a current of blood dripped down into the abyss.

The rising drone of the hoist's engines signaled that the sarcophagus responsible for Nosovka's death was nearing the surface once again. With eyes streaked both with tears and the effects of the icy shower, Koslov looked up as the huge block of smooth rock was lifted out of the hole and laid flat on the muddy ground. As he expected, the first one to its side was Yelena Lopatin. Stiffly, he rose to join her.

"I'm sorry about the loss of your man, Colonel," noted the archaeologist as she checked the find.

Sergei could see that the sarcophagus had suffered no external damage. He watched her bend over to examine its sealed lid. Carved in the stone here was the writing that Lieutenant Nosovka had noticed earlier. The young officer's blood had seeped into the indentations upon which the individual letters had been formed. Thinned by the rainfall, it spilled out onto the lid and then trickled down into the mud.

Yelena's voice distracted Sergei from his macabre observation. "It appears to be some sort of ancient form of Cyrillic. I'll need to get a copy of this writing back to the institute in order to make a translation."

"Take the whole infernal thing away with you, if you'd like," returned the colonel abruptly. "It's done enough damage already." Noticing Yelena's expectant beam, Sergei added, "I'll even supply you some space on our truck for the trip back to Moscow.

"Your help is much appreciated," returned the archaeologist. "If this sarcophagus indeed holds the remains of a Scythian war lord, it fills a void in our interpretation of the Motherland's past."

Koslov grunted. "Unfortunately, my priorities are focused on a different goal, comrade, for it is my responsibility to protect our country's future. I'm afraid that unless I get this project back on schedule, my own future service will be somewhat in doubt. Go in peace, Doctor."

Yelena could not help but sense the colonel's sincerity. At that moment, he looked tired, old, and extremely vulnerable. There could be no doubting the great pressures that lay on his shoulders. The discovery of the tomb and the death of his lieutenant were merely obstacles in the carrying out of a duty he was sworn to enforce.

Gathering together her group of students on the rain-soaked field, she told them of Colonel Koslov's offer to transfer the relic back to Moscow. Although a moan of disappointment fell from the lips of those who had anticipated opening their new treasure back at camp, she explained how invaluable the institute's laboratory would be in ensuring a proper examination. Because she wished to supervise the proceedings herself, Yelena would also return to the capital city. She promised to keep them well informed of the progress of the study.

The rain fell with renewed intensity as Dr. Lopatin led her group across the wet grounds and into the swaying tree line that led back to their camp. Behind them, the soldiers returned to their excavation under the watchful eye of their commanding officer. Tired, chilled, and thoroughly soaked, the troops surrendered themselves to their picks, shovels, and endless mud-filled buckets. Few of them even noticed it when the body of their recently fallen comrade was wrapped in a tarp and carried off to be slung in the back of a nearby lorry. After all, to dwell on the lieutenant's tragic passing would be but a waste of time, and time was one of the many commodities they could ill afford to waste.

3

Dusk arrived with a deceptive swiftness in the Carpathian foothills. The thick woods and deeply cut valleys seemed to completely swallow the sun only seconds after it had dipped beneath the western horizon. Oblivious to the chilled, ever-darkening twilight gloom that surrounded him this first day of spring, Alexander Sergeyevich hiked briskly down the narrow footpath. He knew every twist and turn of this trail by memory, and would need no light to continue his journey. Besides, he did not have much farther to travel.

Even though his day had been an exhausting one, he could not look forward to a proper rest until he had finished his business in Vorochta and returned to the construction site. If all went without a hitch, he would be back before the midnight bed check. Alexander removed a leathery strip of beef jerky from his jacket pocket and bit off a mouthful. The meat was tough and salty, but it did temporarily appease the hunger pangs that gripped his empty stomach. Alexander ground the meat between his teeth as he lengthened his stride and began to make his way up a steep incline.

Fortunately, the twenty-nine-year-old was in superb physical condition. A lumberjack by trade, Alexander had spent most of his years in these very woods. He was able to follow the ascending footpath with a minimum of effort.

As his climb took him upward, he passed through a thick patch of gnarled, leafless oaks. Soon the limbs of these ancient trees would be filled with the green buds of a new year's growth. This was an event that Alexander most anticipated, for it signaled the end of another cold, dark winter, and hinted at the warm, glorious summer that would soon follow.

A raven cried harshly, and Alexander turned to see if he could spot it behind him. Veiled by the ever-darkening shroud of twilight, he could pick out only a brown mass of twisted trunks and bare limbs. A chilly gust of wind shook the forest, and the woodsman pushed himself onward.

When Alexander reached the summit of the hill, he was afforded an excellent view of the lower section of the forest.

A thick, foggy mist still hovered above these trees. The dark canopy of branches appeared as a single mass as he looked out to view the western horizon. Painting the sky here were the colorful last remains of a most glorious sunset. Deep bands of rapidly dissipating reds and oranges merged with the oncoming black of night. Crowning this purple twilight was a sickle-sharp crescent moon. The evening star glowed with a sparkling iridescence all its own. Awed by this sight, Alexander took a moment to appreciate it fully.

The clarity of the sky indicated that the storm front, which had kept him chilled and soaked these last few days, had finally passed. This was most welcome news. The army construction unit that he was currently assigned to had been proceeding with its frantic efforts regardless of the rotten weather. Never before had he been forced to work under such inclement conditions. The colonel in charge of the operation must have been faced with an extremely critical deadline. Why else would he push his men so vehemently?

Not only did the rains make the work extremely uncomfortable, the foul weather also made things dangerous. An army lieutenant had been killed that very afternoon, crushed to death in the midst of a severe thunderstorm. Though Alexander had been deep in the woods, felling trees at the time of this accident, word of the incident had spread quickly. Only hours ago, Alexander had seen for himself the object responsible for the soldier's death.

Alexander had arrived at the clearing just as the massive stone monolith was being loaded into the rear of a truck. Kept from a detailed examination of the object by a stern-faced guard, Alexander was able to edge close enough to make a cursory inspection. A chill of awareness streaked up his spine when he identified the piece as being similar to a relic he had helped his great-uncle exhume only last fall.

Uncle Dmitri was actually his mother's uncle, yet for as long as he could remember, Alexander had been as close to the old-timer as he was to his own father. A warm, vibrant man, Dmitri never seemed to be without a smile, a hug, and an interesting tale to tell. His position as elder priest of Vorochta's solitary church surrounded him with an additional aura of mystery.

Some of the villagers looked down upon Dmitri and treated him disrespectfully. One gang of teen-age toughs in particular seemed to despise him. They called him crude names and spat on him in the street. When he was growing up, Alexander had been confused by this show of disrespect and spite. It was only as he entered his teen

years that the source of this ill feeling became apparent.
It dawned on him slowly that some villagers regarded
Dmitri as a symbol of the Old Russia.

Having halted his formal education at the eighth
grade, Alexander was not the type who sought to comprehend the intricacies of history or politics. All he had
ever wanted was to become a woodsman like his father,
and like his father's father before him. Far from being a
political activist, Alexander had never been interested in
joining the Party. He even managed to stay away from
the Pioneers, a young people's organization designed as
the first step toward Party membership. Whether they
were political or social in nature, groups were simply not
for him—

While he was enrolled in his final year of state school-
ing, a lesson was presented to his class detailing the Soviet Union's unique relationship with religious
institutions. Here he learned that organizations such as
the Church his uncle led were considered anachronisms.
Barely tolerated by the state, they preached superstition
and spiritual doubt, two concepts far removed from the
teachings of Lenin and Marx. Immensely popular before
the revolution, the Church had no place in modern Soviet life. It existed only to console the old and confused.

Alexander himself was not an overly religious fellow.
Dragged to church on Sundays on the arm of his mother,
he nevertheless found himself looking forward to the
soothing hymns, sweet scents, and the mystical pageant
of the mass. Of course, he could also look forward to
watching his great-uncle lead the faithful onward. Surely the prayers the devout shared and the sermons that
followed were not intended to harm the security of the
country. Rather, his great-uncle preached charity, for-
giveness, and peace through understanding, qualities

that each Soviet citizen would do well to strive for.

Confused by the state's position, Alexander had, after his sixteenth birthday, approached his great-uncle. Cautiously at first, Dmitri explained that if tolerant of the existence of the Church, the founders of the modern Soviet Union would reaffirm the importance of religion. The political concepts which the revolutionaries promulgated were radically new and without precedent, whereas the teachings of the Church were almost two thousand years old. Fearing any institution more powerful than their own, the Bolsheviks instinctively moved to stem the influence of the clergy.

To give the youngster a better perspective on their homeland's long history, Dmitri invited Alexander to join him on an archaeological dig. An amateur researcher, he was actively searching for relics of past civilizations. His years of field work had led him to a variety of artifacts. These included ancient coins, jewelry, farm implements, pottery remains, and even a bone or two. Alexander had immediately accepted his great uncle's invitation, and thus began their first field trip into the surrounding forest.

These trips, which had become a yearly occurrence, had culminated in an expedition to the rounded peak of Mount Goverla eleven years ago. During the summer of his eighteenth year, he had accompanied his great-uncle to the summit, which rose more than two thousand meters above sea level. That summit was only a few dozen kilometers north of the Rumanian border. To the south, the foothills of Transylvania beckoned. Beyond lay Bulgaria, Greece, and the Mediterranean Sea. Alexander and his great-uncle failed to uncover any ancient artifacts on Mount Goverla, though they did chance upon the remains of a buried Nazi observation bunker.

But the trip had opened Alexander's mind to the outside world. Since then, he never failed to accompany his great-uncle on the annual digs.

Last fall, though he was getting old, the grizzled, gray-haired priest insisted on pushing deeper into the forest. As usual, Alexander was at his side, handling the pick and shovel without question. His great-uncle appeared in the grip of some compelling wanderlust. When Alexander's shovel uncovered a stone sarcophagus, he could not help but sense his uncle's feverish excitement. Dmitri's face seemed to fall when Alexander pried the coffin open, exposing only the dried bones of the tomb's long-dead occupant. But what had he expected? Alexander mused. Did he think that the ancient one would be alive? Alexander had managed to hold back his questions, yet he could not forget the discourse that followed.

"Please, Alex, you must swear to me that if you ever chance upon a sarcophagus like this one again, you will inform me at once!" Dmitri had whispered urgently. "My days of wandering the woods are over, and I'm relying on you to be my eyes and ears out there."

"But what's so important about a musty old coffin?" Alexander asked. "Surely there are more interesting relics to pursue."

His great-uncle did not reply, but the intense look that projected from his eyes had been enough to stop Alexander in his tracks. And now, only a few hours ago, the shovels of the army construction team had uncovered something so like that first sarcophagus that Alexander knew he had no choice. He had to tell Dmitri. He never questioned what he must do. Slipping away from his work detail was not difficult, and the hike to and from Vorochta could be completed in plenty of time for him to return to camp and not miss the inevitable midnight bed check.

Alexander knew that the news would be heartily received by his uncle. During his last visit to town two weeks ago, Dmitri had certainly looked like he could use some cheering up. Ravaged by a chest cold that had dragged on for the entire winter, Dmitri looked feeble and exhausted. It appeared to be an effort for him simply to stand and serve mass.

Now, Alexander found himself anxious to reach his village. Taking one last look at the crescent moon, the evening star, and the last colors of twilight, he turned from the clearing. With a light step, he proceeded into the thick, pine forest.

The trail here was narrow, yet smooth and most familiar. Winding his way through the maze of thick tree trunks, Alexander drank in the night sounds. Over the endless creaking of the wind-blown branches roared the tumbling, icy-cold brook that eventually cut past the village. The mournful cry of an owl pierced the air and the young logger remembered a time, more than a decade ago, when this wood was all that he knew of the outside world. How mysterious and frightful the forest at night had seemed then! During childhood it seemed that ghouls and ghosts waited behind every tree to snatch the soul of any child who was unfortunate enough to be caught there after dark. In reality, he knew that such tales served parents well in keeping their children indoors at night where they belonged.

Smiling to himself, Alexander continued his brisk pace. It was only as he traveled farther into the pine forest that he discerned the unnaturally loud roar of the water. Minutes later, he found the source of this commotion.

Two and a half kilometers from the village, in the midst of the wood, the path crossed a mountain brook. Because the passage was a well-traveled one, a wooden footbridge had been built. As Alexander approached this spot, he soon found that the previously gentle stream had turned into a raging torrent. Fed by the melting snows and the steady rain of the last few days, the current had swelled over its banks. In the process, the waters had apparently undercut the bridge's foundation and washed it away. Just wide enough to make a running leap most difficult, the stream could easily sweep a full grown man away.

Alexander studied the swirling rapids and decided to look for a safer place to cross. Although he hated to leave the convenience of the path, he turned upstream and began picking his way through the underbrush.

The pitch black night and the thickness of the trees themselves made his going slow. Only when he stepped into a bush of razor-sharp brambles did he seriously consider returning to the path and risking a jump. Cursing loudly, he attempted to free himself from the spiky thorns. As he lifted up his legs, the brambles tore through his thin cotton trousers and ripped into his skin. The pain was intense, and he instinctively stopped his struggle. Still waist-high in the thorn bush, he took a second to catch his breath and decide his next course of action. Then an alien crackling sound caught his attention. Slowly, he turned his head.

From behind him, another branch snapped. Alexander froze. Something was out there watching him! His heart thumped wildly, and a thick line of perspiration formed on his forehead. A full minute of sheer terror possessed him before he regained control.

Come now, the woodsman chided himself silently. For

a man who makes his living in the forest, you scare as easily as a mere child. What would your great-uncle think if he saw you trembling so?

A forced smile broke on his face. He was merely hungry and tired after the long day of work. This unscheduled hike only inflamed his frayed nerves that much more.

After gulping three deep breaths, he managed to center his thoughts. First, he had to pick his way out of the brambles, then find a safe spot to cross the swollen stream. As he bent to unhook the stickers that had cut into his leg, the sound of rustling underbrush again caught his attention. Unable to ignore the noise this time, he yanked his legs upward, oblivious to the pain, and backed out of the thicket.

He decided to return to the path and take his chances at crossing the stream at the site of the washed-out footbridge. When a series of piercing, high-pitched howls broke from the nearby forest depths, Alexander took off running. This was no animal—at least not one he'd ever heard before.

Blinded by panic, he sprinted through the tree line. Sharp pine boughs scratched at his face and torso, but he pushed onward. Beyond the pounding of his own heart and the sounds of his limbs as they crashed through the brush, he could hear the ever-encroaching steps of a pursuer. Whether it was a bear, a pack of wolves, or a creature from an unfathomable world, he would never know for certain. Not daring to look back, he somehow reached the trail, and without halting, leaped across the swollen stream. Running with long, fluid strides, he quickly covered the two remaining kilometers to the outskirts of Vorochta.

Father Dmitri Stanislaus felt tired and worn. This evening's special mass was scheduled to begin in less than ten minutes, but he could not seem to pull himself from his bed. Focusing on the icon of the Ascended Master that was hung on the wall before him, he petitioned the one Father for strength. As if in answer to this prayer, he was seized by a violent fit of coughing. Centered deep in his lungs, the painful spasms expelled a thick wad of viscid mucus into the back of his throat. He spit into his handkerchief and could not help seeing that the phlegm was speckled with bright clots of blood. The volume of blood had been increasing noticeably these past few days. The end could not be that far away.

Resigned to his own fate, Dmitri sighed. He had lived a full, rewarding life. In his years, the Motherland had grown under the protection of a new social order. As a child, he had witnessed firsthand the bloody revolution that brought this new system into power. Even isolated villages such as Vorochta were touched by the hands of the ensuing violence. To give life some semblance of stability at this chaotic time, the Church of the Old Believers stood as a bulwark.

His first memories were of masses overflowing with the faithful. Then, as an altar boy, Dmitri was able to become a participant in this greatest of all mysteries. He lost himself in service to the one Father. To become a priest was his only goal.

In 1925 his dream came true. After years of unselfish study and sacrifice, he was admitted to the Orthodox order that was to become his life. For the next decade and a half, he served under a most reverend father. His duties brought him to congregations throughout the Ukraine. Although the revolution was still a fresh experience, these were blissful, innocent times. As it had for centuries past, the Church prospered. But a dark, malevolent cloud was rapidly developing on the western horizon, one that was destined to change the nation for all time.

The invasion of the Nazi army affected every Soviet household. Struggling for survival, the population rallied against a common evil. Fortunately, Dmitri was spared capture by the rapidly approaching Germans. Led deep into the surrounding forest by one of his coworkers, he found refuge in a secret monastery that was hidden in the foothills of Mount Goverla.

There, in the protective confines of the abbey of St. John the Pursuer, Dmitri passed the war years. Even though he had practically grown up in the region, he had never known that such a holy enclave existed. Staffed by only half a dozen monks, the monastery occupied a massive, castlelike structure whose cornerstone was originally laid in the eleventh century. Much to Dmitri's surprise and delight, he found that it housed a magnificent collection of ancient icons, jeweled chalices, and expertly crafted vestments. The abbey was also home to a superb library. Many of its manuscripts were centuries old, and provided Dmitri hours of fascinating study.

The monks were dedicated to scholarship and holy contemplation. They lived simple, reclusive lives. Their only contact with the outside world was through the young man who guided a supply-laden donkey through the abbey's arched portals each month.

As word arrived of the continued advance of the Nazis, Dmitri was called into the abbot's office. He would always remember this fated morning, for it was the first time that Father Nikon, the abbey's senior priest, revealed his flock's true purpose. Instructing Dmitri to seat himself in one of the two high-backed chairs that faced his desk, the white-haired abbot initiated an amazing discourse.

"You have lived with us for nine months now, Dmitri, and it's time you knew the true reason for this abbey's existence. Almost two thousand years ago, our holy order was founded on the island of Patmos. It was originally conceived by none other than the disciple, St. John of Ephesus, the author of the Divine Revelation.

"In his apocalyptical vision, St. John warned of the evil that was destined to walk this planet every one thousand years. Our sole purpose is to track down and contain this black tide, using a spear carved from the Ascended Master's own cross. This spear is our greatest and most powerful possession, and we keep it close to us beneath the abbey's central altar.

"Because of your pure heart and conscience, you have been chosen as an initiate. As such, you have been invited to join the ranks of a most select group of individuals. Our numbers are small, but we are spread across the planet, lying in wait for the Evil One's reawakening.

"Will you join us on this all-important holy crusade, Dmitri of Vorochta? For if the Beast escapes unchallenged, the hordes of Hell will be free to roam the earth—and we mortals will be doomed."

Dmitri's initial reaction had been one of total disbelief. Yet the seriousness of the abbot's gaze attested to the fact that this was not mere fable. Though Dmitri was full of questions, he found himself agreeing to join the order, and on that very same night, he was formally initiated.

In the days that followed, he learned many a wondrous thing, and soon all of his questions were answered. He was even allowed to view the only weapon that could contain the Prince of Evil. The spear was kept in a velvet-lined case, hidden beneath the limestone altar. Formed from a slender shaft of ashen wood, it had a formidable, finely honed blade. Yet could it actually accomplish the job for which it was designed? Dmitri wondered if he would ever learn the answer to this. Eventually, as the Nazis were driven from the Motherland, he returned to Vorochta to reassemble his grateful flock. Sworn to secrecy, his experiences in the monastery of St. John the Pursuer were soon replaced by more immediate concerns.

Dmitri returned to the abbey every year to renew his vows. For the last three seasons, however, he had been unable to do so because of illness. He wondered who would replace him in the secret order once his earthly time was over. His age was advancing, and sickness had kept him confined to his bed for much of the past winter.

A loud knock on the door of his study brought Father Dmitri Stanislaus abruptly back to the present. Once more a fiery pain seared his chest. With an effort, he lifted his head and cleared his throat.

"You may enter," he said.

With this, the door popped open, and in walked the disheveled figure of his great-nephew, Alexander Sergeyevich. The young lumberjack quickly forgot about his own concerns when he saw the pale figure of his great-uncle lying before him.

"Uncle Dmitri, are you all right?"

Alexander crossed over to the bed, feeling more concerned with each step. As Dmitri doubled over in another coughing spasm, Alexander pressed a cool hand against his forehead.

"Why you're burning up! Where's Doctor Korsakov?"

With the help of his great-nephew, Dmitri sat up. "Easy now, lad. It's only this cold that's had me in its grasp all winter. I'll be licking it once the spring sun shines again."

Alexander looked down and could not help but notice that Dmitri's handkerchief was stained with bright red blood clots. "I still think that Dr. Korsakov should be called in to have a look at you."

The old man responded strongly. "I'll take no more poking from that woman! Now please, be so kind as to help this old man with his vestments. I've almost forgotten about tonight's special mass."

Alexander could not believe what he was hearing. "Certainly you're in no shape. There are only a handful of people waiting in the sanctuary. At least postpone the service until tomorrow, after you've had a sound night's sleep."

Heedless of his nephew's words, Dmitri struggled to stand. "I haven't missed a mass in sixty years, lad. Not even the falling Nazi shells could stop me. As long as there's an ounce of life in this tired old body, I'll take my rightful place before the altar."

Alexander was well aware of his uncle's stubbornness. "Very well, old-timer. It's your health that will suffer."

With practiced hands, the young woodsman helped the arthritic priest slip into his alb. This full-length, white linen robe had long sleeves and was gathered at the waist with a cincture. On top of this intricately worked garment he added a stole, a pair of cuffs, and a satin cape.

When the last of his vestments was in place, a new surge of strength seemed to course through the priest's veins. Straightening his shoulders, a look of sudden realization lit his face. With a puzzled stare, he studied the figure of his great-nephew.

"Alexander Sergeyevich, in all my haste to ready

myself for mass, I've completely neglected you. What are you doing here, anyway? I thought that the state had your exclusive services until the end of the month."

Sheepishly, Alexander replied. "They do, Uncle. You see, I've sort of run off."

"What a foolish thing to do, lad," returned the priest angrily. "There's no running from those types. They'll track you down and send you off to the ice and snow of Siberia unless you return at once. What's gotten into you all of a sudden?"

Alexander nervously cleared his throat. "This afternoon at the construction site an artifact was exhumed. It appears to be an exact twin of the sarcophagus that we uncovered in the same woods last fall."

With this revelation, the priest's facial expression softened. Thoughtfully, he crossed himself.

"Well, I'll be. Are you certain that this one's from the same time period, lad?"

Alexander replied more boldly. "They wouldn't allow me a detailed examination, but I was able to get close enough to get a pretty good look. The type of stone and its shape appear to be an exact match, although this particular sarcophagus could have been a bit larger."

"Did the soldiers open it?" the priest asked softly.

"I don't believe so. The last I saw of it, it was being loaded on a truck bound for Moscow."

Before Dmitri could question further, a loud knock sounded on his door. This unexpected interruption broke the priest's intense concentration, and he looked up with an angry glare.

"What is it?" he snapped.

From the other side of the door, a concerned male voice answered. "It's the deacon, Father. I've just come to tell you that we're waiting for the Divine Liturgy."

Suddenly reminded of his ecclesiastical responsibilities, Dmitri responded. "I will be with you in a second, Yuri."

Lowering his tone, he readdressed his great-nephew. "My duty calls me to worship. Please join me and accept Holy Communion. Afterward, we have much to discuss."

Alexander nodded and opened the door for his uncle. Solemnly, he caught the old-timer's glance, then followed him out into the hallway.

During the mass, Dmitri was twice interrupted by a spasm of coughing. The first seizure came as he faced the handful of faithful old women who made up tonight's congregation, and initiated the Great Litany. Straining for bodily control, he was able to complete this series of petitions to the Lord, and somehow managed to continue with the rest of the service.

The second coughing fit came during the Great Entry. So severe was the seizure that Dmitri almost dropped the heavenly oblation that he was carrying to the altar. Only the quick reaction of the deacon kept the chalices upright.

Throughout the mass, whenever Dmitri felt his strength wavering, he merely looked out to the tall, sturdy figure of his great-nephew, who stood in the back pew. The young man had risked his entire future to inform him of the strange find in the foothills of Mount Goverla. Surely he could summon the fortitude to complete his own meager responsibility.

Aware of the frightening consequences if this recently exhumed sarcophagus indeed held the Unholy One, Dmitri surrendered to his prayers with renewed intensity. As he prepared to partake of Holy Communion, St.

John's quotation of the Master's own words took on special meaning.

"I am the bread and wine of life. He that cometh to me shall never hunger, and he that believeth in me shall never thirst. I am the living bread which came from heaven. If any man eats of this bread, he shall live forever . . . and the bread that I shall give is my flesh, which I will give for the life of the world."

Facing the altar, Dmitri uncovered the flat, silver-plated dish on which the Amnos, or blessed bread, was kept. After breaking off a piece of this leavened loaf, he lifted it to his lips. Swallowing this portion, he felt the Master's own essence fill his body with new vigor.

Faith. That was the supreme weapon that the worthy always had at their sides. Evil was impotent against faith. Since Dmitri's heart and conscience were pure, the tempter would not stand a chance of capturing his soul. Now that the Lord's body had been consumed and incorporated, he only needed to sip of the blood to make the transferal complete.

Raising the ornate silver chalice, he drank the symbolic wine. The drink had barely passed his lips when its vile bitterness forced him to spit it back into the cup. Absent was the familiar sweet grape of the Motherland. In its place was a putrid, rancid concoction.

Dmitri fought back his instinctive urge to retch. Flushed and dizzy, he struggled to control himself. Thoughts of disgust, anger, and eventually fear pervaded his inner contemplations.

With the sour liquid still staining his mouth, the priest forced himself to continue the service. Turning from the altar, he faced his flock and lifted up the veiled chalice that held the other portions of the Holy Bread. His voice was strained as he called them to partake of communion.

"With the fear of the one Father, with faith, and with love, draw near."

Leadenly, the faithful rose from their pews to approach the icon-lined altar in a single column. The dozen or so drab babushkas sported familiar, solemn faces. Only in the direst of emergencies did one of these women ever miss a daily mass. To them, receiving communion was as necessary as eating, sleeping, or breathing. Dmitri knew that what his flock lacked in numbers they more than made up in piety.

His great-nephew followed at the end of the line. It was with great relief that Dmitri distributed the last Amnos onto Alexander's tongue. The congestion was making it difficult for Dmitri to breath, while the pain in his chest continued to sap his vitality. It would be impossible for him to stand much longer.

Wondering if the logger could read the torment that was racking his body, the priest met the young man's probing stare with a determined obstinance. Not old age, ill health, nor the Evil One himself had kept him from his appointed duty. Surely there would be time to make the transfer of power. Yet could the lad's soul bear the brunt of the final confrontation?

As the last member of the congregation returned to her pew, the priest again addressed them. "O Father, save thy people and bless thine inheritance."

After returning the chalice to the altar, he turned toward the icon of the dying Master to issue the final prayer of dismissal. Ignoring the shooting pains that coursed through his left arm and shoulder, he spoke out strongly.

"We thank Thee, O merciful Master, that Thou hast this day vouchsafed to give us Thy heavenly and immortal mysteries. Direct us into the right way, on this first day of the season of rebirth. Strengthen all of us in Thy fear. Watch over our life, making our footsteps safe from evil. May your Cherubim, your angels of light, be with us always. For Thine is the Kingdom, and the Power, and the Glory, forever and ever. Amen."

With these words, the mass was over. Relieved that he had fulfilled his obligation, the priest kneeled before the altar while the congregation slowly exited. Try as he did to center his meditations on holy ponderings, he found himself struggling to merely breathe. Alexander discovered his plight and ran up to the altar to help him.

"Uncle Dmitri, please let me call Dr. Korsakov! That congestion is getting worse, and you're burning up with fever."

His lungs wheezing, Dmitri obstinately whispered a response. "No, lad, there's no time for such a luxury. You must hear me out first."

The utter intensity of the priest's stare made any challenge on Alexander's part an impossibility. Reluctantly, he knelt beside his great-uncle.

The church was dark and empty now. Only two altar candles cast their light. Outside, the wind was rising. Alexander sniffed at a current of spicy-sweet incense, as his great-uncle broke the contained silence.

"Lad, I'm not going to be playing games with you. We've been too close throughout the years for me to do otherwise. It looks like this will be one spring that I won't be living to enjoy. Now, I don't want any mourning from you when the time comes. I've lived a good, full life, been close to the one Father, and my heart is clean. But there's one thing that I'm going to need a little help with."

"Just name it," Alexander said. "Anything."

A spasm of deep, throaty coughs shook the priest's upper torso. Spitting up a large lump of bloody phlegm, he continued between gasps of air.

"It regards that sarcophagus you saw earlier today. This particular relic could very well be the same one that I've been searching more than four decades for. Yet I'm too ill now to travel to Moscow to properly identify it. It's ironic, isn't it? I'm relying on you now, Alexander. You will have to convey news of this find to my colleagues.

"Yuri will take you to them. Once you arrive at the monastery, you are to ask to speak to the abbot. Introduce yourself and explain the exact nature of the object that the army engineers have unearthed. Afterward, you're free to do what your conscience deems necessary."

Another violent spasm racked Dmitri's chest. He was so weakened that he didn't even bother to cover his mouth with his handkerchief. A line of crimson spittle drooled down his gray, beard-stubbled chin. Alexander held his uncle tightly by the shoulders. Although he had so many questions to ask he felt ready to burst, his uncle's worsening condition kept him silent.

"Do you understand me, lad?" quizzed Dmitri desperately. "You must swear to me that no matter the obstacles, you will inform the abbot of this find. Swear to me, lad!"

"Easy, Uncle Dmitri!" cautioned the confused woodsman. "Of course I'll swear to it. Now, don't you worry about a thing except getting better. It's time to get you to bed. Then I'm going for Dr. Korsakov, with or without your blessings."

Realizing that he would have to carry the priest to his study, Alexander was just about to lift him up when the candles suddenly flickered. Looking up toward the altar to see what was wrong, the logger caught the scent of something alien and noxious. The vile stench sickened him. It was like decaying flesh, he thought, trying not to gag. A loud rattling movement directed his attention to the chapel's front door. He watched as the two heavy wooden doors swung open. To his utter dismay, no visible form entered. Instead, an icy, all-pervading chill filled the room.

Wrapping Dmitri's gaunt, withered arms around his neck, the lumberjack lifted him with a fluid ease. Halfway across the altar, he registered the impression that there was something in the sanctuary intently observing his progress. Instantly he was reminded of his earlier confrontation in the pine forest, and a wave of terror sent his heart pounding. He rushed past the altar and headed for the room's rear exit, but was abruptly halted by a series of icily familiar, unearthly howls from the direction of the holy altar. With legs heavy and shaking, Alexander reluctantly faced the tabernacle.

As if captured in a hypnotic daze, he viewed what he could only describe as a pair of compact, spiraling balls of fire—fire that hovered menacingly over the chalice holding the sacred Amnos. It proved to be his great-uncle's booming voice that snapped him from his horrified trance.

"Begone with you, Satan! How dare you trespass on the one Father's hallowed ground!"

This mandate served only to incense the balls of light, which began turning in tighter, ever quickening spirals.

"I command you in the name of the Ascended Master to leave this place, foul spirit!" cried the priest, who still hung in his great-nephew's grasp. "Begone, demon! Return to your rightful place in Hell!"

Alexander's entire body was trembling now, as the chill around him increased to a point where he could actually see his breath. Again, a series of bestial howls filled the chapel with a frightening tremor, followed by a tortured series of cries that rose through the sanctuary.

Confusion turned to dread when the two spiraling spheres of fire left the altar and began circling above Alexander and Dmitri. Alexander gasped when a strange vision began to form in the air around him.

First to greet him was a procession of humanlike skeletons. Though formed primarily of bone, this terrifying assemblage sported long, flowing manes of hair, and still had portions of rotted flesh hanging from bony limbs. Most disturbing of all was the fact that the skeletons all had what appeared to be normal eyes staring forth from their bare skulls. In their midst was a large, shaggy, four-legged creature, which had the body of a horse and the head of a hideously deformed, bearded man.

Before Alexander could cry out in horror, he saw an immense, dragonlike beast, carrying a naked man and woman on its broad back. The couple was locked in a noisy and frenzied act of intercourse. Their wild cries of passion were suddenly overcome by an angry, deafening howl that spewed from the mouth of a tall, muscular mortal who followed closely behind them. Only when this figure came closer did Alexander realize that instead of skin, the creature was covered with black scales. Taking in its long tail and the two horns that capped its head, Alexander trembled. When the fearsome beast beckoned to him and let out another horrible howl, Alexander could see its gnashing fangs all too clearly. Its eyes glowed a tortured red.

"In the name of St. John the Pursuer, I order you to leave this holy place at once, damned creatures of Hell!" screamed Alexander's great-uncle, whose voice now projected with powerful force. "Go back to the black pits from which you crawled, and leave this blessed sanctuary in peace!"

Barely aware that he still carried the priest in his arms, Alexander watched as the black-skinned beast broke into a fit of demonic laughter. Yet all this came to an abrupt halt when Dmitri managed to reach into his robe and remove a small vial of holy water. Without hesitation, he uncapped it and flung its contents toward the mocking demon.

There was a loud sizzling sound, followed by a scream of pure agony. A thick cloud of vapor suddenly veiled the horned beast. The scent of burning flesh was everywhere.

Alexander stood completely speechless as the mist cleared and the hellish procession dissipated. He hardly blinked when the doors to the church flung open and the two spiraling balls of fire flew out into the night as abruptly as they had appeared. All that remained of this macabre encounter was the heavy scent of burned flesh.

Alexander turned his attentions back to his great-uncle. "Put me down, lad," Dmitri managed between agonizing gasps. "Please, I implore you."

The logger lowered his great-uncle to the floor. Leaning him up against the altar's rear pillar, Alexander wiped a wide band of glistening sweat from the old man's forehead.

"Don't try to make sense out of that which you just witnessed," said Dmitri. "All that you need to know is that these sights were but an emanation from that black force which we call evil. Now, you must swear to me that you will continue on to the holy monastery. Make certain to tell the abbot there all that you experienced here tonight."

"But what does all this have to do with the sarcophagus I saw being exhumed earlier today?" asked Alexander, who quickly forgot his own concerns when his great-uncle began coughing strenuously once again.

Straining to regain his breath, Dmitri could only whisper. "The Cherubim shall be with you as you initiate your crusade. May the light of the angels of justice guide your every step."

To hear these last words, Alexander had to bend over with his ear practically touching the old man's lips. With the priest's abrupt silence, the woodsman looked up to study his great-uncle's eyes. One glance told him that the elder had breathed his final breath. Gone was the pain that had contorted his kindly features. In its place was an angelic peace, an expression that communicated a final end to all suffering.

It was not grief that caused Alexander to reach out to hug his great-uncle's body. He was inspired instead by pure, unabiding love.

Sitting there, rocking the old man in his arms, the young Ukrainian swore to himself that he would carry out Dmitri's last requests. Even though he would be branded a deserter if he did not return to the dig site, Alexander did not fear the wrath of the Red Army. Now he had other concerns of a much more frightening—and important—nature.

Never would he forget the procession of unholy creatures that had paraded before him. To his dying day he would remember the sickening scent of burning flesh and the cold that chilled his very soul.

4

To the people of the Union of Soviet Socialist Republics, Moscow, their capital city, was known simply as the "Center." This widely used nickname was more symbolic than geographical. Not only did Moscow contain the seat of the Central Committee of the Communist Party, the country's most powerful political institution, but it also was the cultural heart of this immensely diverse republic. World famous museums, symphonic halls, opera houses, and theaters abounded by the dozens. For those fortunate citizens holding internal passports listing Moscow as their hometown, the best that the U.S.S.R. had to offer lay within their reach. In no other Soviet city were consumer goods so readily available. As was so often the case, it usually took an outsider to put these benefits into their proper perspective.

Lieutenant Mikhail Antonov of the Ministry of Internal Affairs, or the MVD as it was widely called, had been stationed in the Center for more than a month now, yet he still found himself marveling at the city's many wonders. This evening's sights proved no exception. The thirty-eight-year-old police detective found himself in the midst of a stakeout in the scenic Arbat district. Together with his new partner, Yuri Sorokin, Mikhail was viewing a part of Soviet nightlife he never dreamed existed. Once again, his impression of the capital city expanded, as he explored a seamy underworld only a few kilometers to the southwest of the Kremlin wall.

The tall, heavyset, blond-haired detective followed his streetwise partner into a cafe frequented by a wild-looking bunch of punk rockers. He had read about such hooligans in *Pravda*, yet until tonight, he had not seen so many in one place. Taking in their multi-colored, spiky hairstyles, strange facial makeup, and weird garb, Mikhail felt as if he had landed on another planet. Although they were working undercover, and dressed in blue jeans themselves, Mikhail still could not help but feel conspicuous. Thus, he breathed a sigh of relief when his partner chose a table in the club's rear.

"What do you think of the Cafe Arbat?" quizzed Yuri lightly.

Mikhail seated himself and somberly shook his head. "If this bunch of freaks is what the next generation is coming to, the Motherland is in serious trouble. I can imagine such a decadent scene in New York, London, or Paris, but how can it be permitted here, in the heart of holy Moscow?"

Yuri wisely smiled. "The sociologists say that this is only a passing stage in their lives. These kids are only bored. We'll make constructive citizens out of them yet, you'll see."

A tired-looking, unkempt waiter approached them, and Sorokin ordered two coffees. As the waiter turned and blended back into the mass of bodies situated near the narrow bar, Yuri continued.

"My comrade from the Far East, you'd be surprised at the powerful families the majority of these youngsters represent. Many are the offspring of ultra-powerful Party officials. I wouldn't be surprised if the sons and daughters of several Politburo members are assembled here tonight."

Genuinely astounded by this revelation, Mikhail Antonov silently scanned the cafe's interior. Immediately before them were approximately three dozen circular cocktail tables. A lighted red candle topped each of these stations, most of which were presently empty. A cramped dance floor lay before a tiny stage, deserted except for a mass of amplifiers, a drum kit, an electronic keyboard, a pair of guitars, and several microphones. The band was on its break.

Lining the room's western wall was the bar area. It was here that the young people had congregated. Mikhail estimated that there were well over a hundred animatedly conversing in this area. How they could possibly hear each other over the pounding, recorded music that blared from the wall-mounted stereo speakers was beyond him.

Veiled by a thick haze of cigarette smoke, Antonov struggled to pick up details of individual faces. Try as he could, the colorful figures merely seemed to blend in with each other.

Mikhail looked to his right and noticed that his partner's attentive glance seemed riveted on this same mass. He wondered how many times the ten-year MVD veteran had had to deal with such personages before. He knew that he was very fortunate to have such an experienced fellow at his side.

The two had been introduced to each other less than a week ago. When Mikhail first set eyes on the thin, balding, beard-stubbled figure of his partner-to-be, he really was not that impressed. The man seemed nervous, a cigarette perpetually at his lips, his dark, beady eyes constantly shifting about the room. It was only later that

Mikhail realized what he mistook for a case of bad nerves was in reality representative of Yuri's overly abundant energy level. The swarthy Muscovite was always on the go. Even when seated, his limbs shook in constant motion.

For the first couple of days, the two detectives had kept their conversation to a minimum. They exchanged little talk of a personal nature. It was not until the night of their first arrest that the ice was broken.

The MVD was in the midst of its annual pre-spring vice sweep of the city. Poised for the arrival of tens of thousands of Western tourists, the city leaders desired Moscow to shine like the jewel of the Communist world it was promoted to be. This meant that embarrassing black marketeers, drug dealers, pimps, and prostitutes had to be dealt with.

The police division that Mikhail had been assigned to was mainly responsible for covering the southwestern section of the city. This included picturesque neighborhoods such as the Arbat district, whose cafes were a haven for drug transactions and prostitution.

Kalinin Prospekt was one of Moscow's most modern avenues, linking the Kremlin with the western reaches of the Moscow River. Near the banks of the river, the twelve-storied Hotel Mir was situated. Adjoining this structure was the headquarters of the Council of Mutual Economic Assistance. It was here that the executive offices of COMECON, the Communist world's equivalent of the European Common Market, was located. Thus, it was only natural that the Hotel Mir housed many Europeans who had business with COMECON.

A recent tip hinted that a well organized prostitution ring was aggressively working the hotel. Since the establishment included many first-time visitors to the capital, the existence of such an operation could prove extremely embarrassing. Mikhail and Yuri's first assignment had been to find out if such a ring existed, and if it did, to break it up.

For three long, uneventful days, they staked out the hotel. A vigilant watch over the bar, restaurant, and lobby areas failed to uncover any hint of impropriety. To see if the establishment's maid staff was engaged in any extracurricular activities other than cleaning, Mikhail even took a room for a night. Judging from his maid's broad girth and an upper lip that sported more hair than his own, Mikhail surmised that not even an Eastern European could be attracted to such a woman.

They were well into the third night of their stakeout, sitting in their battered Volga sedan, while parked on Kalinin Street opposite the hotel, when Mikhail accidentally knocked over their thermos of hot coffee. It promised to be another long, cold evening, and neither of them looked forward to fighting off the chill and fatigue without their blessed fix of sweet, steaming caffeine. To replenish it, Mikhail volunteered to raid the hotel's commissary. It was while leaving the hotel, with the newly filled thermos at his side, that he stumbled upon just the type of action that they had been looking for.

A well-dressed East German preceded Mikhail through the revolving door leading from the hotel's lobby. Something about the man's abrupt manner caught the detective's eye. The German seemed in a hurry to catch a taxicab at such a late hour of the night. Four cabs were parked by the curb. The German opened the passenger door of the first taxi. Peering inside, he seemed dissatisfied, for he went on to check out the contents of the second vehicle. This appeared more to his liking, for he entered and immediately shut the door behind him.

The cab was already pulling out onto Kalinin Prospekt, as Mikhail sprinted across the street, and on a hunch, advised his partner to follow the taxi.

Fortunately, the street was deserted, and Yuri was soon able to catch up with the suspected vehicle. Not really certain what they would find inside the black Chaika limousine, Mikhail recommended that they attempt to secretly tail it. With his headlights turned off, Yuri followed the Chaika southward, down Smolensky Boulevard. This wide, circular thoroughfare made a complete ring around the inner city, yet they found themselves deviating from the boulevard after traveling less than a kilometer. Mikhail could not help but notice the wide grin that lit up his partner's face as they entered a dark, wooded sector, which Yuri identified as part of Gorky Park.

The roadway twisted and turned. It abruptly narrowed, becoming extremely rough. Without the benefits of headlights, they seemed to strike each one of the many potholes that the street was filled with. Yuri alertly guided their Volga to a halt, when the brake lights of the taxi lit the darkness like a flare. Another wide smile crossed his lips as he beckoned Mikhail to follow him outside.

The night was cold and pitch black as they silently crept down the rutted roadway. They spotted the Chaika beside a thicket of gnarled oaks. Not a single interior light was visible. They approached the limousine using the cover of the tree line. At a distance of a hundred meters, Mikhail stifled a chuckle; the rear of the car was bouncing to a spirited rhythm. The sound of squeaking shock absorbers met their ears as they ducked behind the Chaika's trunk.

Mikhail looked on as his partner reached inside his

coat pocket and pulled out a ring holding several dozen keys. After singling out one of them, he directed Mikhail to follow him to the rearmost passenger door. With a steady hand he carefully inserted the key into the lock, gripped the handle with his other hand, then triggered the lock and yanked the door open, all with one smooth, sweeping motion.

Inside the taxi two naked occupants were caught in *flagrante delicto*. Pressing between the open thighs of a gorgeous redhead was the German, whose muscular body stiffened as he turned his head in fear. The detectives identified themselves, and a grunt of relief passed from the man's trembling lips. Rolling sideways, he reached out to dress himself.

An expression of defiant anger glowed from the redhead's eyes. Lying on her back, with her legs still apart, the woman seemed to be daring the detectives to take further action. Both Mikhail and Yuri took in her huge, firm breasts, tight waist, and long, slender legs. Yuri broke the erotic spell. Using a gruff, commanding tone, he ordered the redhead to dress herself, unless she preferred to walk into MVD headquarters naked.

On the way back to the station, the German attempted to bribe them to let him go. Relishing his fear, they pointedly ignored him. After a strict warning, he would be anyway. It was the woman whom they were after.

Though the redhead remained silent and uncooperative at first, she was soon babbling away with her list of accomplices. Sodium Pentothal had that kind of effect on people. All together, more than a dozen women were involved in the taxicab scheme. The pimp responsible for supplying the Chaika's was an elusive, well-known rascal. Though never arrested, or even photographed for that matter, this legendary procurer was simply known as the "Arab" to his women, who described him as being dark and handsome, with a scar lining his cheekbones.

Later that evening, after they had deposited the red-head securely behind bars, Yuri invited Mikhail over to his flat for a drink. Located off two-leveled Sadovaya Boulevard, in the northeastern portion of town, the tiny, three-room apartment was set on the twelfth floor of a huge skyscraper. They sat down to drink their vodkas on Yuri's comfortable couch. As the level of the vodka bottle descended, their tongues began to loosen. Mikhail learned that his partner was married, with his wife and two small children sleeping in the other room. Well before the second bottle was emptied, both men had divulged more intimate details of their lives. From that time onward, they became more than just mere coworkers; now they were friends as well.

Mikhail's thoughts reeled back to the present when a deafeningly loud electronic chord shook the interior of the room he was sitting in. Blinking his startled eyes, he quickly took in the ragged bunch of musicians who were assembling on the stage. Their warm-up also caught the attention of the majority of the cafe's patrons, who streamed from the bar area, to seat themselves at the various candle-lit cocktail tables. Once again, Antonov absorbed this crowd's strange appearance, as a familiar, rough voice broke from his right.

"You really should try some of that coffee before it gets cold, comrade. Though the entertainment has certainly changed here, the Arbat still serves some of the best mocha java in Moscow."

Catching Yuri's wink, Mikhail looked down and noticed that their drinks had been served. Only then did he realize that he had been daydreaming. Such inattention was quite uncharacteristic of him. Yet ever since his transfer, he had been subject to just such periods of mental laxity. Supposing that this was a by-product of his radically new environment, Mikhail nevertheless silently castigated himself. His current line of work made any break in his concentration extremely dangerous. His life, and that of his partner, might depend upon the intensity of his awareness. He had always prided himself on his attention to detail, and now that he was working in the capital, this level of intense concentration would be needed more than ever.

Grasping the clear glass that was set before him, Mikhail picked up his coffee and took a long appreciative sip. He found the brew strong and tasty.

Yuri noticed his enjoyment and commented. "Didn't I tell you that it was pure nectar. Next to a glass of vodka, there's nothing finer."

"I agree," responded Mikhail with a nod. "Tell me, comrade, you have been in this place before? Why? You don't seem like the type who goes in for rock-and-roll."

Yuri's response was masked by a series of booming bass notes and the resonant clash of a cymbal, followed by the sonorous chords of a keyboard, and the twanging tone of a tuning guitar. To be heard over this racket, Yuri had to practically scream.

"Believe it or not, less than two years ago, the Arbat featured the best jazz in the Soviet Union. My wife and I went here on our very first date. Talk about crowds and tough tickets. Why, I had to practically blackmail the owner to get us a decent table. Those were the days, comrade!"

Any further talk proved to be an impossibility as the group initiated its first song. Dressed even more bizarrely than the crowd they faced, the five, skinny, punk musicians pounded out a cacophonous blend of harsh, discordant notes. Above the pulsating rhythm, the vocalist could barely be heard, wailing on about the horrors of nuclear warfare.

Unbelievably, the audience seemed enthralled by this tune. Sitting on the edges of their chairs, many of the onlookers mouthed the vocalist's crude lyrics, while keeping the beat with their hands and feet.

Mikhail could not begin to understand what these kids were enjoying so. If only they would be exposed to some real music, they would hear how shallow this racket actually was. A Tchaikovsky symphony or a suite by Borodin—now that was the type of sound that stirred one's soul! This punk rock could not even scratch the surface.

Angling his line of sight back to the stage, Mikhail tried to sharpen his concentration; yet in pure self-defense, his thoughts drifted elsewhere. Barely thirty days ago, clubs such as the Cafe Arbat could not have even been imagined. In the village of Chabarovsk there could be no time wasted on such nonsense. In the Soviet Far East, survival was the order of the day.

Mikhail had been stationed on the banks of the Amur River for more than five grueling years. Only a few dozen kilometers from the Chinese border raged an actual war. This battle had two distinct fronts. One took place to the southwest. Here, roving bands of Chinese commandos crossed the border whenever they chose. The other front had no boundaries, for the constant struggle with the elements froze the populace in the winter and cooked them in the summer.

Working closely with elements of the Soviet army and the KGB, Mikhail's MVD detachment was responsible for keeping law and order in Chabarovsk. Although it was the principle city in its sector, Chabarovsk was in reality a wild, frontier town. To keep the population in control, Mikhail learned to be a no-nonsense administrator. Even though their very isolation made many state crimes seem irrelevant, he enforced the letter of the law.

For the first few years he was most unpopular. Several attempts were even made on his life. Eventually the situation stabilized, and the citizens of Chabarovsk adjusted to his harsh ways. Then, gradually at first, the previously high crime rate began dropping. Mikhail gained national recognition when these new statistics remained constant after reaching an all-time low.

Mikhail would never forget the morning he received the congratulatory telegram from the minister himself. His superiors in the MVD were not the type who expressed their praise often. To convey his sincere gratitude, the minister was offering to transfer him to Moscow! Here it was hoped that Mikhail's unique investigative qualities could be applied to help stem the unprecedented crime rates currently plaguing the capital city.

Mikhail had been given two weeks to ready his things for the long rail trip westward. After putting the majority of his belongings in storage, he boarded the train and left his past life behind him. Crossing the breadth of the Motherland, he had a better chance to put things in perspective. In these delicate times his country needed him. This was a call that he would not ignore.

It was as the train crossed the Ural Mountains that the reality of his destination hit home. He was being drawn to the Center to give his life new challenge and purpose. In return, he would pledge his total effort.

A gentle hand shook his right shoulder, and Mikhail's eyes again focused. Once more the blaring sound of grinding rock music filled his consciousness. Yet the con-

cerned look on his partner's face was not directed toward
the stage. Instead, Yuri's intense stare was locked on the
bar. Following the direction of this glance, Mikhail saw
for himself what had attracted Yuri's attention.

In the midst of ordering a drink from the bartender
was a tall, shapely young woman, who could not have
been older than her early twenties. A mop of curly,
blond hair framed an exquisitely formed face that did
not need layers of make-up to bring out its natural beauty. Dressed in a mid-length, red-fox coat, she must have
been wearing a very short dress, for her long, lean legs
were completely bare.

Yuri caught his eye and smiled knowingly. The two
detectives did not need to trade words to identify this
personage. Her curly blond hair and red-fox coat were
trademarks exposed by their interrogation of the prostitute arrested only a few nights ago in Gorky Park. The
redheaded one had seemed particularly jealous of this
young woman, for she was supposedly the Arab's current
live-in girlfriend. Per the hooker's suggestion, they had
set up tonight's stakeout, for the young blond never
missed a Friday night at the Cafe Arbat. Now, if only her
boyfriend showed up, the night would be complete.

Both men watched as the blond sat down on a bar
stool, lit a cigarette, then sipped on a long-stemmed
glass of champagne. Her eyes were locked on the stage,
yet a look of bored indifference haunted her expression.

The band was in the midst of a seemingly endless
improvisational jam, when a medium-sized, dark figure,
wearing a camel's hair coat, entered the cafe and
approached the bar area. Mikhail saw Yuri's eyes light up
with excitement as this natty newcomer positioned himself behind the blond's stool. She seemed to jump in surprise when the stranger placed his hands on her

shoulders. As she turned to see who was touching her, a wide smile crossed her face, and soon they were locked in a passionate kiss.

Though the room's thick, smoke-filled haze made viewing conditions far from ideal, both detectives watch-ed breathlessly as the newcomer reached inside his coat pocket and carefully handed the blond what appeared to be some sort of pill. The woman's hand went directly to her mouth, and a quick sip of champagne followed.

After another long kiss, the stranger merely nodded toward the exit. Oblivious to the pulsating music, the blond stood and reached out for her escort's arm. Sec-onds later, they were on their way outside.

Without a moment's hesitation, Mikhail and Yuri left their table. Hurrying past the bar area, they ducked through the padded doorway and found themselves standing on Arbat Street.

The first sensation that Mikhail was aware of was the sudden silence. Next, he noticed the air's icy chill. Yuri spotted the couple half a block away, as they entered the back seat of a black, Chaika limousine. Rushing to their battered, gray Volga, the detectives were soon in pursuit.

Yuri took the wheel as the limo turned northward onto Suvorovsky Boulevard. Since the hour was getting late, the wide thoroughfare had a minimum of traffic on it. Yuri had to proceed carefully so that the occupants of the Chaika would not realize they were being followed.

"Thank goodness that fellow showed up when he did," commented Yuri succinctly. "I don't think that my ears could have stood much more punishment. And they call that music?"

Mikhail nodded in agreement. His own ears were still buzzing. Keeping his eyes glued to the Chaika's tail-lights, Mikhail centered his thoughts.

"Do you think he's the Arab?"

Yuri answered while fumbling for a cigarette. "I couldn't see if he had a scar on his face or not, but that fellow sure dressed like a pimp. That's some coat he's wearing. And I'm certain that he was feeding his girlfriend some kind of pill back there. Hopefully, he'll be leading us right to his lair. I think I'll close a little of this distance between us so that we can do a license check on that Chaika."

Skillfully, Yuri accelerated, guiding the car in behind a Mercedes that was traveling on the lane to the left of the limousine. From this vantage point, Mikhail efficiently jotted down the license number after which Yuri gradually backed away. As they followed the Chaika northward onto Leningradsky Prospekt, Mikhail reached over and switched on the two-way radio. With the transmitter to his lips, he depressed the call switch. In response, a band of throaty static emanated from the radio's speakers. Again, Mikhail clicked the switch that was supposed to give them a clear channel for broadcast. Once more the clash of static indicated that any transmission would be impossible. Worriedly, Mikhail caught his partner's eye.

Yuri merely smiled. Shifting his cigarette to the far corner of his mouth, he reached over with his open right hand and smashed the section of dashboard set immediately above the radio unit. With this, the static abruptly faded, and the heavy strains of a symphony orchestra blared forth from the speakers.

"Ah, it's 'Borodin's Polovtsky March' from *Prince Igor*," said Yuri. "Now this is music. I'm afraid, though, that it looks like we're just going to have to wait on that license check, for it appears that our radio has yet to be properly repaired."

A grin decorated his face as he continued driving down the broad, well-lit parkway which was gradually leading away from the center of the city. Mikhail made certain that the Chaika was in clear view, approximately half a kilometer beyond them. He noticed the dozens of multistoried structures that lined both sides of the street here. Most of these buildings rose more than twenty-five stories high. Many were still under construction, for various cranes and scaffolding could be seen waiting for the dawn's work crews.

The sight of this valley of steel and glass gave Mikhail an eerie feeling. For him the city was still an alien place. Stacked endlessly on top of each other, the people who worked and lived in such structures were a strange breed. How they could thrive without their own plots of earth to nurture was a concept that he was having trouble understanding. He knew that he'd have to learn to cope, for his own cramped, one-room apartment was in a high-rise much like the ones that currently surrounded them.

"We'll be passing Byelorussia train station and the race track soon," observed Yuri. "I wonder where this devil is headed."

"Where does this roadway lead?" asked Mikhail.

"This is the way to Sheremetyevo Airport. From there, the road reaches well past Kalinin and eventually ends up near Leningrad on the Gulf of Finland."

A look of concern crossed Mikhail's face. "Shouldn't we be calling in to headquarters soon? The colonel seemed anxious to know our exact status."

Yuri exhaled a long ribbon of smoke from his nostrils. "Well, I'm afraid that old dog is just going to have to wait. If they'd only give us reliable equipment, things would be so much easier. I don't know about you, but I kind of like being on my own. And besides, one thing about a broken radio is if we can't reach them, they sure as hell can't bother us."

Humming to the strains of the rising martial rhythm that still echoed from the speakers, Yuri carefully steered around a shiny new Zhiguli. When this Soviet-made Fiat was squarely in his rearview mirror, he eased up on the accelerator a bit, as a small knot of traffic was also causing the Chaika to slow. It was while he was mentally charting the course that would take them past this congestion, that a large, green truck, traveling in the opposite direction, turned suddenly in front of them.

"Damn it!" screamed Yuri, as he yanked the steering wheel hard to the left and slammed on the brakes.

The force of this abrupt turn caused Mikhail to be thrown against the door. Instinctively, he braced himself for a collision, yet the truck's rear cargo bay missed their front end by mere centimeters. It was only then that he realized that this mud-stained vehicle belonged to the army.

"That stupid bastard!" cursed his angry partner.

Only years of practice allowed Yuri to quickly regain control. Gliding back into the lane, he glanced into the mirror just in time to see the truck disappear into the driveway of a large, well-lit building. With his face still flushed and his pulse pounding, Yuri fought a rising surge of anger.

"That was a close one, comrade. Are you all right?"

Mikhail merely nodded that he was. He, too, found himself with a racing pulse. Well aware that his partner's driving skill had saved them from certain injury, he exhaled a long breath of relief.

Up ahead, the Chaika's taillights were cutting through a dark patch of deserted roadway. Well out of the central portion of the city now, Mikhail was somehow certain that their trip was far from being over. Yuri stepped on the accelerator and they proceeded farther into the night.

Vasili Pavlinchenko was sadly disillusioned. The portly, fifty-six-year-old watchman had consigned himself to a life of routine and boredom. For two entire decades, his monotonous daily duty at Moscow's Institute of Culture demanded eight hours of his time. Six days out of the week, forty-six weeks of the year, the slow-moving, bald-headed Georgian went about his work with a half-hearted effort. Since little out of the ordinary ever occurred in the course of his rounds, not much additional resourcefulness was demanded on his part. Occasionally he found a door lock or window left open, but this was most often due to neglect rather than intent. He could count but a handful of petty thefts in his years of faithful service.

Twenty years ago, he would have said the tediousness of the job was its worst feature. Yet over the years he had learned to pass the time using all sorts of mental tricks. Eventually, it got so that any deviation from the humdrum was more bothersome than stimulating. No wonder he so enjoyed his present assignment on the late-night shift.

For the last three years, the time from ten at night to six in the morning were all his. Cleared of all but the most assiduous researchers, the multistoried institute was his sole domain. During this time span, Vasili could be practically guaranteed eight hours of total peace and quiet.

To keep himself company, he often whistled as he made the rounds of the various laboratories, storerooms, and offices. Lately, he even found himself singing.

Although he was not known for his vocal skills, Vasili's scratchy, low-pitched bass voice could be heard echoing down the deserted hallways at odd hours, as he slowly shuffled through the building.

Of course, there was always his blessed vodka to fill those empty hours when time seemed to drag unbearably slow. While on duty, Vasili never once allowed himself to become uncontrollably drunk. Rather, he learned to take small sips from his pint bottle, chasing it down with cups of sweet, hot tea. In such a way he was able to extend the spirit's warm, soothing effects throughout his entire shift.

The watchman was proud of this self-control. He had watched too many of his comrades become totally obsessed with their bottles. Many a fine friend had been destroyed in such a manner. Vasili knew that the difference between himself and these unfortunates was that he knew how to pace himself. A little sip once every hour was all that he needed to keep his blood flowing. There would be no need for doctors or pills for him, for he had the tonic of life right there in a clear pint bottle.

Only on the coldest of winter nights did he dare increase his prescription. Yet on this third night of spring, he found himself drawn to his bottle with an unnatural thirst. Try as he could to resist it, he soon had his pint drained, with his shift not even halfway finished.

Vasili supposed this yearning had something to do with the feeling of uneasiness that had possessed him all evening. He first noticed this unusual sensation at dinner. Even though his mother had made his favorite Georgian goulash, he did not have any appetite.

Ever since his father had died, not long after the conclusion of the Great War, his mother had been his only companion. They lived together more like husband and wife than mother and son. Her entire life revolved around him.

In the past, her natural concern for him was accepted and genuinely appreciated. Yet this evening, the look of anxiety that crossed her face when he pushed his untouched bowl of goulash away totally infuriated him. Didn't the woman realize that he had a life of his own? Why, her possessiveness was positively smothering him!

For the first time in years, Vasili had stormed out of their simple, two-room apartment without kissing her good-bye. To regain his calm, he decided to walk the four and a half kilometers to work instead of taking the Metro.

By the time he arrived at the institute, Vasili was repentant. Certainly, his mother was not to blame for his unprovoked outburst of anger. If only they had a telephone in their apartment, he would have called her at once to express his apologies. As it turned out, she would have to wait until he returned in the morning. With this on his mind, Vasili began his rounds.

The arrival of spring meant that the majority of the institute's faculty were presently on their way to their current digs. Thus, he found the building totally without occupants. Starting his initial tour of inspection in the main foyer, Vasili felt somewhat uneasy as he crossed down the wide hallway lined with row upon row of glass display cases. On the shelves of these cases sat an assortment of ancient artifacts, many thousands of years old. Brought from the far corners of the Motherland, these relics were only a tiny portion of the institute's current collection. Intricately carved walrus tusks from the ice fields of Siberia sat next to spearheads from the wilds of Turkmen, pottery shards found beneath the plains of

Kazakh, and colorful spirit dolls unearthed in the Caucasus foothills.

The majority of these pieces were like old friends to the watchman. Over the years, he naturally became very familiar with many of them. Yet tonight, this familiarity was not an amiable one. Instead of inspiration, they promoted dread. As he shuffled down the hall, he got the distinct impression that somewhere close by, someone was watching him. This feeling was enhanced as he passed a row of cabinets holding various human skulls.

Of course, there could not have been a worse time for the building's electrical circuit breaker to blow. The lights snapped out only seconds after Vasili had decided to increase his stride to reach the security of his office as soon as it was possible. This was not the first time that the institute had been thrown into sudden darkness, yet the twenty-year veteran found himself trembling like a scared schoolboy, as he nervously groped for his flashlight. With his pulse pounding in his eardrums, he switched on the torch to figure out exactly where he was. Vasili instinctively jumped, when his flashlight's beam hit smack in the forehead of a particularly ugly prehistoric brute, whose petrified skull sat on the top shelf of the display case on his left. This surge of terror had a sobering effect on the portly watchman. Shaking his head, he addressed himself out loud.

"Easy now, old-timer. Have you finally gone and lost your nerve? They are only your friends. They're certainly in no shape to do you any harm."

These words soothed him, and he realized just how silly he had been. Regathering his nerve, he took off for the central storage room where the suspected circuit box was located.

Ten minutes later, the tripped breaker was reset and

electrical light once more lit the halls of Moscow's Institute of Culture. Though his cramped office was upstairs in the laboratory section, Vasili decided that a little more vodka was much in order. Remaining in the storeroom, he ambled over to the huge, old-fashioned scale that sat beside the loading platform, and reached behind its solid, iron bulk. He smiled contentedly when his hand grasped the familiar glass bottle, stashed there for just such an emergency.

Never before did a drink taste as good! In long, fiery currents, the liquor burned his mouth, throat, and stomach. Its warmth soon seeped throughout his entire body. Nearly half of the bottle was drained before Vasili's mind cleared.

His unjustified fears were merely a reflection of a deep, personal unrest. The pressures of his job must have been greater than he had realized. Perhaps his mother was right, and they should move back to the Georgian countryside where he had been born. Though Moscow was the center of the Motherland, and to live and work there was a privilege beyond comparison, it was still only a city. Man was not meant to live his whole life surrounded by steel and concrete. The trees, hillsides, and fields gave one strength and renewed purpose.

Suddenly, a piercing electronic buzzer broke the quiet. Startled by this shrill tone, Vasili quickly recapped the vodka bottle and set it back in its secure hiding place. Straightening his khaki uniform, he took a deep breath, then calmly strolled over to the black, wall-mounted telephone, placed beside the sealed, corrugated doors of the loading platform. After picking up the plastic handset, he cleared his throat and distinctly addressed the transmitter.

"This is Lieutenant Pavlinchenko of internal security.

May I help you?"

The voice on the other end replied rapidly. "Comrade, this is Corporal Sedov of the Fifth Military District at L'vov. We have a top-priority delivery for you, compliments of our commanding officer, Colonel Sergei Koslov."

Vasili did not waste any time with his icy response. "Corporal, this loading dock will reopen promptly at eight o'clock tomorrow morning. I suggest that you return at that time to complete your delivery."

Without waiting for an answer, the watchman merely hung up the receiver. A few seconds of silence passed, when the telephone once again buzzed. Hesitantly, Vasili lifted the handset to his ear.

"Please, Comrade Lieutenant, our orders are most explicit. The colonel has instructed us to drop off this relic and return at once to the Ukraine. The drive is long, and our commanding officer can be most unforgiving."

Again Vasili cleared his throat. "I'm sorry, Comrade Corporal, but I, too, have my orders. The institute's receiving hours are from 8:00 A.M. to 5:00 P.M. We will be most willing to take delivery of any object that you have for us at that time."

Before the watchman could pull the receiver from his ear to disconnect the line again, he took in the driver's angry reply. "Well, fine, comrade. It looks like we'll be forced to drop the artifact out here on the sidewalk. Can you imagine what the citizens of Moscow will be saying tomorrow morning when they view a stone coffin sitting unattended in the midst of their city?"

"A what?" quizzed Vasili curiously.

"A stone coffin," repeated the driver icily. "Believe me, comrade, this trip has been no joy ride for us. We're exhausted, and we still have many hundreds of kilometers to travel."

Just yesterday, Vasili had talked with one of the institute's research assistants. The young man was excited to be on his way back to Baku, where a promising excavation was rumored to be producing dozens of ancient burial urns. One of the researcher's concerns had been security, for many of these urns had been buried with priceless gems and gold jewelry.

What a waste of valuables, thought Vasili at the time. Now, could such a treasure be waiting for him on the other side of the delivery platform's door? Perhaps he should make an exception to the rules in this instance. After all, procedural instructions were made to bend, especially when dealing with archaeological treasures.

Pulling the handset to his lips, the watchman spoke out boldly. "Corporal, I certainly don't want to force you to leave that artifact outdoors, unprotected. Please give me a second to open the doorway, and you can be off on your journey."

A relieved sigh sounded from the speaker as Vasili hung up the phone and went over to unlatch the delivery entrance. The loud rattle of ball bearings roared overhead as he lifted up the corrugated steel doorway. A blast of chilly night air hit him in the face. Waiting for him on the narrow concrete platform were a pair of soldiers. Parked behind them was their truck with the back end open.

Vasili quickly examined the young man standing nearest to him. Dressed in green fatigues, this tall youngster certainly looked tired and worn, yet an expectant beam lit his face. The fellow greeted him warmly.

"Thank you, comrade, for your help. It's really appreciated. You don't know what a chore it has been getting here. Why only minutes ago, some fool in a Volga almost plowed right into us! Thank you once again."

Vasili nodded. "It's you youngsters that deserve all the thanks. Drove all the way up from the Ukraine, you say? Well, that's really something. Too bad you can't stay to enjoy some of our city's famous hospitality. Now, let's lighten your load so that you can be off."

The two soldiers were happy to accommodate him. Both of them jumped into the back of the truck, whose tailgate was aligned with the surface of the dock. The massive, tarpaulin-covered object located in the center of the flatbed emitted a sickening, ripe scent. Vasili had smelled this putrid odor before as a child, when he had stumbled upon the dead body of a woman in a bombed-out basement during the Great War. He would never forget its source.

"Is there still decaying flesh inside that sarcophagus that you're unloading?" questioned Vasili.

Before answering him, both men took hold of the tarpaulin's edge and pulled it off, revealing a large, rectangular, mud-stained stone coffin. It was only then that the taller of the two soldiers responded.

"No, comrade, that scent is coming from the corpse of one of the unfortunate soldiers who died while excavating this object. He's covered up ahead. The way he's stinking, we'll be getting him to the coroner just in time."

"I thought that sarcophagus looked too ancient to be holding any surviving tissue," commented the watchman. "Has anyone peeked inside it yet?"

The driver responded. "Not to our knowledge, comrade. Who knows how many centuries it's been sealed. Say, you don't happen to have a gurney to help us move this thing?"

"Of course," returned Vasili. "Why strain your

backs?''

Seconds later, he returned with a sturdy, tubular steel stretcher, set on four rubber wheels. With effort, the sarcophagus was lifted onto the stretcher and wheeled into the receiving room.

Since Vasili was able to easily push the gurney under his own power, the two soldiers were quick to excuse themselves. After having him sign a bill of lading, they saluted and wasted no time in returning to the cab of their truck. As they drove off into the night, the watchman pulled down the delivery platform's door and latched it shut. Pivoting, he eagerly set his eyes on the artifact he had just signed for.

The piece was well over seven feet in length, and filled the entire width and breadth of the large, industrial-sized gurney. Completely covered with thick splotches of dried mud, it appeared to be shaped out of a single slab of chiseled gray limestone. Anxious to examine it under the high-powered laboratory spotlights, Vasili hurriedly opened the logbook to officially note the relic's receipt. After filling in the date, time, and a brief description of the object, he knew that proper procedure demanded that he weigh the piece before transferring it upstairs. Since the scale's platform was recessed into the concrete floor, he readily accomplished this act. He recorded the weight, rolled the gurney before the elevator, and depressed the button that would activate the lift.

Seven minutes later, he stood inside the main laboratory, his treasure securely anchored at the room's center. Running his fingers over the smooth, cool stone, Vasili attempted to visualize that which possibly lay inside. Was it merely filled with a dusty pile of some old soul's dried bones, or did a trove of priceless artifacts accompany the deceased to the supposed land of the hereafter?

It was when his fingers chanced upon a strange inscription etched on top of the lid that a pang of guilt possessed him. Did he have the right to pry open the coffin's lid? He had certainly broken enough rules for one night. Yet how could he ignore this once-in-a-lifetime opportunity?

Tired, confused, and very thirsty, Vasili decided that he knew just the thing to clear his weary mind. And besides, he would not have to travel far to reach this solace. In an adjoining room was the cramped space where his shabby, cluttered desk and battered locker were located. Originally designed as a storage area, it had two separate entrances. One led directly into the main hallway. This was the passageway that he normally used. The other door led straight into the lab. Not once had he ever used it.

It took his key several attempts to turn the rusty tumbler of this secondary entrance. When the lock eventually activated, the door swung open with a loud, high-pitched squeal. His few belongings looked different from this new angle. Switching on the light, he positioned himself in front of his desk, kneeled down, and depressed a small, secret panel recessed into the bottom drawer. There, his bottle of vodka awaited him. He grasped it firmly in his hand, then rose to seat himself.

Only after consuming a long, soothing sip did he sit back and put his feet on the edge of his desk. His eyes caught sight of the large, framed photograph of his mother set on his desk top, then glanced off to a clear view of the now-open doorway leading directly into the laboratory. Lighted by the room's powerful spotlights, the massive stone coffin solemnly beckoned. Looking back to the photo of his mother, Vasili lifted the bottle to his lips and consumed a hearty mouthful. With the fire of a thousand suns, the vodka coursed through his being.

Major decisions had never been easy for the watchman. That was one of the reasons he had remained a bachelor over the years. When his father died from wounds experienced on the Western front, no matter the sacrifice, he had sworn to take care of his mother until her dying day.

In the years that followed, life was not in the least bit easy for them. Shelter and food were their major concerns. As the son of a deceased veteran, Vasili had earned the cramped apartment they lived in, as well as a job with a government construction crew. While tearing down the remains of a bombed-out church in the previously occupied city of Kiev, a falling piece of debris had crushed Vasili's hip. Fortunately, he was young and resilient. Transferred back to the capital, he spent a full year recuperating. A slight limp and an occasional arthritic attack were the legacy of that unfortunate incident.

A maintenance position with the Department of Streets followed. When this job proved too physically demanding, he was given his first security assignment with the Museum of Russian Folk Art. Eight years later, he was transferred to the renowned institute where he currently worked.

The times had been hard for the Pavlinchenkos, but at least they had a roof over their heads and some bread in their bellies.

The Orthodox church proved to be his mother's solace. While Vasili surrendered to the monotonous calls of his duty, she spent whatever free time she had, when not in food lines, in the Uspensky Cathedral. There she called upon a savior that Vasili never really could understand.

Although the watchman appreciated the magnificent craftsmanship of the cathedral's icons and other art treasures, the theories of the Church were beyond his comprehension. What need was there for such superstitious nonsense when the founders of their state proved that God was just a foolish fabrication? After all, there was no Heaven or Hell. All one could count on for sure was the reality of the present moment.

Yet Vasili knew that the mass produced a great peace in his mother and the others who attended services regularly. At least for that meager portion of the day they could forget about the worries of everyday life.

Looking once again to the photograph of his beloved mother, and then to the stone sarcophagus in the adjoining room, Vasili wondered if it might be possible to change his destiny once and for all. Opportunities such as this one only came around once in a lifetime.

After taking another swig of the vodka bottle, Vasili's eyes glazed over with an inner vision of gleaming gold and sparkling jewels. Fate had delivered this treasure to his very doorstep! How could he possibly resist its call? It was at that moment that he knew he would not.

Sitting up straight, he recapped the bottle and stowed it back in its hiding place. Next, he stiffly stood, took one last fond look at his mother's photo, then proceeded into the laboratory.

The effects of the vodka he had consumed first became apparent as he approached the gurney. A slight dizziness guided his wavering steps, and for the first time that evening he felt uncomfortably warm. Conscious of a nausea gathering in the pit of his stomach, Vasili attempted to calm his anxieties with a series of deep breaths. Not the type who went against the rules often, the watchman could not help but feel like a guilty schoolboy at the moment.

Upon reaching the side of the sarcophagus, Vasili studied the relic as if seeing it for the very first time. The gray, mud-stained limestone seemed like a long dead entity in and of itself. Massive in length and width, the coffin reeked of great age and importance. Clearly illuminated by the spotlights, Vasili viewed the strange lettering carved into the artifact's lid, and for the first time recognized a dried, red substance caught in the depths of this alien marking.

A sudden thirst parched his dry throat, and Vasili wished that he had brought his vodka along with him. He fought the impulse to return to his desk to retrieve it, for he knew it was now or never. As if hypnotized, he solemnly reached both hands out and carefully gripped the underside of the coffin's cold, stone lid. Inhaling another deep breath, he momentarily closed his eyes, then lifted it up with all of his might. Yet try as he could, the sealed hinge held tight.

Wondering if he ought to force it open, Vasili cursed his bad luck. Committed to going all the way now, he was just pondering which tools would be most effective in breaking the hinge when his fingers chanced upon a tiny metal latch set into the lid's lower lip. Using his right index finger, Vasili depressed this mechanism, which activated with a loud, snapping click.

With his clammy hands slightly shaking, he gripped the lid and felt the hinge give way. Again he inhaled a deep lungful of breath, squeezed his eyes shut, and gently lifted upward.

Vasili Pavlinchenko never really had time to fully comprehend the terrifying series of events that were triggered by his curiosity. Instead, his senses were numbed by a bombardment of paralyzing stimuli. The loud, raspy grating noise of the opening hinge was followed by the arrival of a vile, sour stench that completely engulfed him. Gagging from its rankness, the watchman swayed back dizzily. With tearing, unbelieving eyes, he struggled to focus his line of sight into the coffin's interior. Yet try as he could, all that he could make out was a thick wave of billowing mist that seemed to fill the room with an icy chillness.

Trembling from fear, Vasili wanted nothing better than to slam the lid of the sarcophagus down and run from the lab with all due haste. Though his mind screamed to follow this course of action, his leaden limbs remained inexplicably motionless. What was keeping him from running to safety?

The sudden appearance of two fist-sized balls of fire diverted his shocked attention. Entranced by these glowing spheres, he watched them whip around the perimeter of the lab with lightninglike velocity. With each complete revolution, his heart beat quicker, until its rhythm was twitching in uncontrolled fibrillation.

Oblivious to the sharp stabbing pain that coursed up his left side and left him breathless, he audibly gasped as the swirling red balls of light hovered triumphantly over the top of the now opened sarcophagus. Then they plunged into the coffin's misty depths. A millisecond later, an unearthly, deafening howl rose from this same abyss. Staggered by this cry, Vasili felt his knees crumple, as his last conscious thoughts registered a sight he would carry with him throughout eternity.

Rising from the shadowy interior of the sarcophagus was the tall, dark figure of a man. Unlike no mortal he had ever laid eyes on before, this personage's sallow face reflected a cruelty that was compatible with the two, burning red orbs that made up the centers of his eyes.

Twenty-seven kilometers to the northwest of Moscow's Institute of Culture, detectives Mikhail Antonov and Yuri Sorokin found themselves driving slowly down a narrow, unpaved roadway. Except for the Chaika's taillights up ahead, no other illumination lit the pitch black night. For the last five minutes, not a single human habitation had been visible. Nothing but thick stands of tall birch trees surrounded them. Since Yuri had been forced to turn off the Volga's headlights when they turned off the Leningrad Highway, their progress was rough and extremely hazardous.

It was only after the car bounced over a particularly nasty pothole that Yuri broke the intense silence which had accompanied them the last couple of kilometers. "I just hope our Volga holds together a bit longer. This road can't go on that much longer."

"Where are we, anyway?" quizzed Mikhail anxiously.

Yuri answered while bending forward to peer out of the windshield, as a tree limb scraped against the car's side. "All I know is that the Schodna River is somewhere up ahead. When I was a child, my parents had a dacha nearby. I spent many a summer exploring these woods, and I can personally vouch for their wildness and density."

Again the front axle bounded off a deep rut, and the automobile lurched accordingly. Reaching for the dashboard to steady himself, Mikhail looked forward and excitedly did a double take.

"The Chaika's taillights . . . they've disappeared!"

Instinctively, Yuri pressed down on the brakes, shifted the car into neutral, and turned off the ignition. Rolling down his window, he listened intently. Only the creaking sound of the wind through the tree limbs and the far off surge of flowing water met his practiced ear.

"I certainly don't hear another car engine," he whispered. "Of course, there's always the chance that the road dips down into a hollow up ahead. Such a depression could easily mask their lights and engine noise. Wait here, while I quickly scout ahead."

Before Mikhail could respond, Yuri was out of the door and jogging down that tiny portion of road visible before him. Seconds later, his partner's silhouette was completely swallowed by the encroaching wilderness.

The cool, fresh air that swept over his body from the open window was like a tonic for Mikhail. Though his month in the capital city had been most fascinating, he sorely missed the scent of the woods and the accompanying sounds of the wilds. He was surprised that such a wilderness could be found this close to Moscow.

The muted cry of an owl sounded on his left, and Mikhail was peering curiously into the depths to spot it, when Yuri reappeared. It took Yuri a full minute to regain his breath and make his report.

"Damn cigarettes!" he quietly cursed between gasps of air. "Good thing that we braked when we did. The Chaika's parked around the next bend. Nearby, there's a lovely little wooden dacha. There's a fire going, and it all looks quite cozy."

"Some spot for a love nest," added Mikhail with a wink.

Yuri smiled. "I'll say. I'd just love to have a photograph of that pimp's expression when we break down the door. Any guesses as to what we're going to find in there?"

Mikhail was hesitant with his response. "Don't we need the okay from division headquarters before going in? The colonel seemed most adamant with his initial instructions."

Yuri merely poked his head through the open window and hurriedly replied, "I guess you're right. I seriously doubt that we'll need a backup, but better safe than sorry. Comrade, why don't you see if you can get the two-way working."

Without hesitation, Mikhail reached over and switched on the radio. By the time he had the mike to his lips, the unit was warmed up and ready for a transmission. A familiar line of raspy static crackled as he searched in vain for a clear channel. Catching his partner's concerned stare, he opened the palm of his right hand and smashed it down upon the dashboard. Instantly, the static cleared and a woman's nasal voice came over the speaker.

"In other news today, the Voice of America is proud to report the success of the United States' latest space shuttle effort. The Condor . . . "

Totally disgusted, Mikhail switched off the radio. "It's hard to believe that a society sophisticated enough to put men into space can't produce a two-way radio that works here on Earth. What are we going to do now, partner?"

"Like I said before," returned Yuri lightly, "it's the department's fault that this equipment is faulty. The way I read it, it's now totally our decision whether we go in. What do you say, comrade?"

It didn't take long for Mikhail to make his choice. Reaching into his shoulder holster, he removed a shiny, chrome Kalashnikov pistol. Expertly, he rammed a bullet into the chamber, activated the safety, then returned it to his holster. Briefly catching his partner's hearty thumbs-up, he quietly exited the car. After stretching his long, cramped legs, Mikhail hunched down and began following Yuri farther into the forest.

A cold wind hit the two squarely in the faces as they

rounded a curving stand of tall birches and set their eyes
on a small clearing up ahead. Hastily, Mikhail surveyed
the perimeter. Except for the parked Chaika and the
sturdy wooden dacha, no other signs of human presence
were visible.

"Let's sneak up to the cabin and try to get a peek
through one of the windows," advised Yuri, who still
seemed winded. "I think it's best to know exactly what
we're up against before getting too involved."

Mikhail merely nodded in agreement. The two detectives scurried on toward the log structure, using the cover
of the trees. By the time they reached the side of the
building, a light sprinkle of snow flurries was falling.
Clearly audible was the pulsating bass line of a recorded
jazz quartet.

A single window was set high into the wall's side.
Since Mikhail was the tallest of the two, he was the one
who attempted to peek inside. Standing on his toes, he
barely found his eyes level with the window's lower edge.
Here, a white vinyl shade was pulled down. Unfortunately for the benefit of the privacy of those inside, a
clear space barely two centimeters wide lay exposed. As
his eyes adjusted to the brighter interior light, Mikhail's
stare passed by the room's blazing fireplace and spotted
a familiar-looking man seated calmly at a wooden card
table.

Twisting his head to get a better view, Mikhail's eyes
lit up as he watched this swarthy, dark-eyed, natty figure
in the midst of counting a thick stack of what appeared
to be American dollar bills. Before him, on the table, lay
several fist-sized plastic packets, jammed with a powdery, white substance. This sighting caused the detective's pulse to quicken.

Completing his scan of the room, Mikhail shook his

head in wonder when he identified the blond, curly-haired woman that they had followed from the Cafe Arbat. Seated opposite her escort, she was expertly using a straight-edged razor blade to separate a portion of the white powder into several thin lines. Then she tightly rolled up one of the bills, bent over, and inhaled the powder through the dollar bill and into her nose.

Anxious to share these findings with his partner, Mikhail was just coming down off his tiptoes, when a deep, alien growl sounded from behind. By the time he regained his balance and turned to identify this threat, Yuri was at his side, with gun drawn. Following his partner's line of sight into the stand of surrounding trees, Mikhail set his eyes on the snarling muzzle of a Doberman pinscher. At his side, straining to hold the dog back with the help of a steel leash, was the animal's handler. This stocky, dark-haired young man was dressed in a chauffeur's uniform.

The handler took two steps forward and gave the Doberman several centimeters of additional leash. The dog used this length to close in on the unwanted strangers. Continuing to strain against its leather harness, the dog's eyes brimmed with anticipation.

Ever so slowly, Mikhail met his partner's solemn gaze. Yuri nodded, took a deep breath, and spoke out firmly.

"Pull in that dog and keep your hands where I can see them. We're with the MVD on official state business."

This revelation was all the handler needed to hear to immediately release the dog and then dive for the shelter of a fallen tree trunk. Prompted by this split second of movement, Yuri lurched to his right to try to draw a bead on the handler, while Mikhail crouched to pull out his own weapon. Just as his hand made contact with the cold steel stock of his pistol, the dog was upon him. The

Doberman's snapping jaws kept Mikhail's hand from being able to pull out the Kalashnikov. Knocked on his back, it was all he could do to keep the animal's razor-sharp canines from his throat.

Mikhail let his instincts take command. The musky scent of the dog was full in his nostrils as he struggled to position his hands around the Doberman's neck. With its teeth only centimeters from the detective's exposed face, the dog strained its clawed forelegs upward to dislocate the human's fragile grip. Mikhail vainly attempted to shift his weight so that he could get up off his back. As he scooted backward, the loud, booming blast of a gunshot sounded on his right, followed by the high-pitched explosive whine of an automatic weapon, most likely a lightweight Uzi. Another pistol shot answered, and Mikhail freed his right fist and slammed it down into the side of the Doberman's head.

There was a whimpering cry of protest as the dog reacted to the punch. Taking advantage of this brief pause, Mikhail used the side of the cottage to lever himself up over the top of the animal. He yanked the dog upward by the tough skin of its neck and slammed it down into the earth. There was the loud snap of breaking bone, and the Doberman twitched and then was completely still. As Mikhail watched the life drain from its eyes, the high-pitched whine of ricocheting bullets echoed precariously overhead.

The snow was falling more heavily as he yanked out his pistol and peered to his right to locate Yuri Sorokin. A single tongue of fire exploded from behind a nearby woodpile. Mikhail knew that he would have to find some cover. He decided to move off to his left, to draw the chauffeur's fire and to give Yuri a better chance to finish him off. He scrambled toward a thick tree stump, then leaped to the ground for cover, as a line of bursting automatic shells cut into the earth below him.

Rolling to his left, Mikhail's right hand straightened and he pumped three large caliber shells into that portion of the woods where he had seen the Uzi's muzzle flash. Again the machine gun fired, forcing Mikhail to duck behind the stump. Splintering wood chips stung his cheek, as a single shot boomed out loudly. He heard a pained cry and the sudden crackling of broken underbrush.

The sound of the howling wind, as it whipped past the swaying tree limbs, replaced the bursting whine of bullets. Cautiously, Mikhail peeked over the stump. Through the blowing snow, his partner could be seen slowly emerging from behind the woodpile, his pistol still raised before him. Mikhail managed a single sigh of relief. Then he suddenly heard the starting of an automobile's ignition.

The occupants of the dacha—he had forgotten completely about them! Loudly cursing, Mikhail rose and rushed off toward the cabin's entryway. He was met only by a cloud of dusty exhaust, as the Chaika fishtailed off into the darkness. Seconds later, his partner was at his side.

Disgustedly, both detectives shouldered their weapons. With barely a grunt, they checked on the condition of the man they had shot. Then they would search the dacha, in the vain hope that its occupants had left some evidence behind.

St. Louis, Missouri

The cathedral bells chimed four times, as Dr. Richard Green walked eastward down Lindell Boulevard. It was a typical brisk, early spring afternoon, and the forty-two-year-old professor of linguistics could just make out the rounded top portion of the Gateway Arch gleaming in the distance. The sky was a brilliant blue, with not a cloud visible. He hoped he had seen the last of the ice, snow, and frigid temperatures of winter. Taking a contented pull on the well-chewed stem of his favorite briar pipe, Richard turned onto a walkway that led directly to the campus that had been his home for the last decade.

St. Louis University was one of the oldest Jesuit schools in the country. Founded in 1818, the college offered a well-rounded curriculum, all set in a pleasant, urban environment. One of the university's many lay professors, Richard enjoyed an excellent relationship with the school's clerical hierarchy. He also made good use of the college's excellent Divinity Library, a modern, brick structure that was his current destination.

The university had only recently acquired a rare, Croatian prayer book. Printed approximately five hundred years ago, by the German printer Johann Gutenberg, the text had yet to be completely translated. Since

Richard's specialty was East European languages, the project fell into his capable hands. To accomplish this task, he had been given a sabbatical leave from teaching.

For three months now, he had been working on this project exclusively. It gave him the opportunity of learning more about the Croatian people, who presently lived in the northwestern portion of Yugoslavia. Fiercely independent, the ancient Croats had produced a unique religious vision, free from the influences of both the Roman and Greek Orthodox churches. Since very little was known about the origins of their viewpoints, each day that Richard spent translating the prayer book into English was full of exciting discoveries. Currently he was in the midst of working on a particularly moving psalm, dedicated to the eternal struggle against evil.

"Dr. Green!" broke a familiar, high-pitched voice from behind.

Having just reached the statue of Pope Pius that graced the center of the quadrangle, Richard turned and set his eyes on the petite figure of his research assistant, Maggie Dunn, as she scurried up the walkway. Seconds later, she was at his side. Breathless, she greeted him.

"Thank goodness I was able to track you down, Doctor. A call came in for you seconds after you left the office."

Continually astounded by his assistant's unselfish loyalty, Richard allowed her time to catch her breath. He removed his pipe from his mouth and calmly replied.

"And what call is that, Maggie?"

An incredulous look etched the grad student's freckled, pixielike face. "Why, the call from the Soviet consulate. Have you forgotten about their invitation already?"

Richard absentmindedly grinned. "To tell you the truth, I haven't given it much thought since I was originally contacted. What is the excuse for the holdup?"

Relishing her moment of power, Maggie guardedly answered. "It seems that you were right. The doctor who initially called you is unable to get the manuscripts he spoke of out of the country. Instead, he has invited you to join him in Moscow, where the collection will be available for your complete inspection."

Genuinely surprised by this news, Richard thoughtfully stroked the smooth, golden wood that formed the bowl of his pipe and softly mumbled. "Join him in Moscow, you say? Well, I'll be."

Conscious that she had her employer's full attention now, Maggie continued. "Dr. Yakhut promised that you'd be the personal guest of his institute, which will take care of all of your living arrangements. They've even arranged for your visa and an airplane ticket to Moscow."

After efficiently checking her watch, she added. "I hope you don't mind, but I've already called the travel agency and checked on connections through New York. There's a six-thirty flight out of Lambert that should get you into Kennedy with plenty of time to clear customs. I took the liberty of reserving you a seat."

"And just when is all of this supposed to take place?" quizzed Richard firmly.

Maggie sheepishly cleared her throat. "I know how excited you were when Dr. Yakhut originally called and revealed the collection's existence. Since the Soviets have already flaked out once, by not sending the manuscripts as promised, I thought that you wouldn't want to pass up the opportunity to see them under this new arrangement. So before the Soviets again change their minds, I booked the flight for this evening."

"This evening!" exclaimed Richard, his voice straining. "Why, it's already past four in the afternoon. I can't go flying to the other side of the planet at the drop of a hat!"

Maggie took a deep breath and replied. "I know it's sudden, but if we get going now, I'm certain that I can get you to the airport in time for your flight. Your work schedule here is clear. The Croatian prayer book will be waiting here safe and sound for your return."

Certainly not an impulsive person, Richard's nature rebelled at the very thought of leaving the country on such short notice. Yet he knew that Maggie could cover for him on campus. All that he needed to do was drop by his nearby apartment to gather his clothes, some reference books, and his passport.

Two weeks ago, when the Soviets first contacted him, Richard had been genuinely thrilled. Dr. Felix Yakhut was a renowned archaeologist with a worldwide reputation. His institute, which was operated in conjunction with the University of Moscow, was said to have few rivals.

The collection that Yakhut was so eager to discuss with Richard was originally excavated in Rumania during the past winter. Found sealed in a burial urn, the manuscripts appeared to be hundreds of years old. Because they were composed in a rare Serbian dialect, Yakhut was prompted to call Richard. Both had briefly met a little more than two years ago, during a symposium in Geneva, Switzerland. Since Richard had presented at the conference a well-accepted paper discussing the phonology and syntax of this very Serbian dialect, Dr. Yakhut could think of no more qualified person to help with the initial examination of the collection.

The preliminary arrangement was for the Soviets to send Richard photostats of the original manuscripts. Richard had doubted that the authorities there would let even a copy of such a treasure out of their possession. His assumption had apparently been correct and now the Soviets were asking for his direct personal assistance. Could he refuse such a once-in-a-lifetime offer?

Gazing down at the thin, compact figure of Maggie Dunn, Richard met her impatient stare. As his research assistant, she knew the inner workings of his mind better than anyone on the planet. Confident that he'd grab at this rare opportunity, she seemed to be silently willing him on. Not daring to disappoint her, he took in a deep breath and winked.

"So you think that you can get me on a six-thirty flight. Well, I know your driving's good, yet how are you at packing a suitcase?"

A relieved smile broke Maggie's lips. "I knew that you couldn't resist. Now let's hope you haven't put your winter clothes in storage yet. I believe Moscow's still a bit chilly this time of year."

Taking a last appreciative breath of spring air, Richard pivoted to lead the way back down the walk. A new sense of urgency guided his long stride, and Maggie Dunn needed to increase the pace of her own shorter steps to keep up.

Seven hours later, Richard Green found himself on a Soviet Aeroflot airliner over the Atlantic Ocean. Soothed by a glass of powerful apricot brandy, he leaned back in his cushioned, leather seat and vacantly stared out the nearby window. Outside, the star-filled skies were barely lit by the waxing moon. Unable to view the wide expanse of water that passed below, Richard absorbed his reflection in the windowpane.

To the muted growl of the Ilyushin's four jet engines, he took in his receding mop of curly black hair and a rather narrow forehead that capped a dark, mournful stare. This feature was given additional character by a pair of thick, bushy eyebrows. His aquiline nose was inherited from his father, while his full mouth and square jaw were from his mother's genes. All in all, he was said to have a pleasant face that generally reminded others of actor Elliot Gould.

Closing his weary eyes, Richard recollected the hurried drive to the St. Louis airport. Because of heavier than anticipated rush hour traffic, Maggie brought him to the terminal with only a quarter of an hour to spare. Only the plane's late departure allowed him to reach the gate in time. After leaving Maggie a list of last-minute instructions, he boarded the plane for the two-hour flight to New York City.

This would be his first trip to the Soviet Union, and Richard somewhat anxiously climbed into the shiny Aeroflot jet that was to take him nonstop to Moscow. Soon after leaving Kennedy, he was served a full course Soviet dinner, starting with a bowl of borscht. This tangy beet soup was served along with a spoonful of sour cream. Next came a piping hot serving of beef stroganoff served on top of a bed of browned kasha, or as it was known in the States, buckwheat groats. A wedge of steamed cabbage and a thick slice of black bread accompanied the dish.

Over a glass of sparkling Soviet champagne, which was a bit on the sweet side, Richard got to know a little more about the passenger seated beside him. A salesman by trade, the portly New Yorker worked for an American clothing company that was trying to introduce its line of denim pants to the people of the Soviet Union. He was on his third trip to Moscow that year, and even though the trade authorities there seemed genuinely interested in his goods, they had yet to sign a final agreement.

Frustrated with the red tape that continually shifted the making of the final decision to the next bureaucrat down the line, the salesman was determined to finalize the deal. After sharing with Richard his initial impressions of the bustling capital city, he succumbed to a deep slumber. His even snores continued to sound in the background, and Richard found himself becoming drowsy. Shifting the tilt of his chair backward, he issued a wide yawn and was soon sound asleep.

He awoke to a pulsating electronic tone. Disoriented at first, it took him several seconds to figure out that the stewardesses were preparing the cabin for landing. The wide-bodied airliner was encountering a mild layer of turbulence. With the majority of the passengers still asleep around him, Richard adjusted his chair to its upright position and pulled his seat belt tightly around his waist. He checked his watch and was surprised to find how the hours had quickly passed. He looked out the window on his left, and was greeted with an awesome sight that would stay in his memory forever.

Lighted by the muted Arctic twilight, the ancient woods of Mother Russia passed down below. Completely covered in a blanket of freshly fallen snow, the thick forest of birch and evergreens seemed to stretch in a single expanse to the far horizon. As the plane swung to the south, Richard was afforded an excellent view of the rising dawn sun. Inspired by this magnificent sight, he hardly noticed that the woods below had given way to the first artificial structures.

The grinding sound of the landing gear lowering into place served to divert his attention. It was then that he took in the first passing village. As they continued losing altitude, the individual structures could be made out.

The majority were simple wooden cottages, connected to each other by narrow country roads. He smiled to himself when he spied the gilded, onion-shaped dome of a Russian Orthodox church in the center of one of these compounds. Richard caught sight of a paved highway, a series of railroad tracks, and a collection of concrete, high-rise buildings. Minutes later, the plane touched down with barely a jolt at Moscow's Sheremetyevo Airport.

Richard was one of the first off the plane. Following the covered walkway into the terminal, he was met by a grim-faced customs official. This official's mood soured when Richard revealed that his visa was supposed to be waiting for him at the airport. With his passport in hand, the officer picked up the telephone to verify this crucial fact. It took another quarter of an hour before two figures arrived at the custom's checkpoint to break the impasse. One of these individuals was a tall, uniformed officer, whose rank caused the custom agent to stiffen in attention. At this distinguished officer's side was a familiar-looking, bald-headed gentleman, whose short, thin stature, bright, inquisitive eyes, and baggy gray suit could only belong to Dr. Felix Yakhut.

"Dr. Green, welcome to the Soviet Union!" the sixty-five-year-old professor of archaeology animatedly greeted him in perfect English. "I'm sorry that I was not here earlier to welcome you personally, but I'm afraid that my driving skills are a bit rusty."

"That's quite all right," returned Richard, as he accepted a warm hug and a kiss to each cheek from his host. "Considering the haste with which this whole trip was planned, I'm impressed that you were able to meet me at all."

"Nonsense," retorted Yakhut. "After all, you are my

honored guest. Now, Colonel, what seems to be holding things up?"

The silver-haired officer, who had arrived at Yakhut's side, was all smiles as he approached the junior official and took Richard's passport from him. Without a single question, he opened the document's green cover and stamped its interior. He then handed it back to Richard.

"On behalf of the Soviet government, I would like to officially welcome you to our country, Dr. Green."

Accepting the officer's handshake, Richard looked up when a voice broke from the custom's checkpoint to his right.

"Good luck, Doctor!" cried the salesman, who had been seated next to him on the plane.

Richard waved good-bye to his amiable traveling companion and then turned to follow Dr. Yakhut down the terminal's central walkway. He had to use his full stride to keep up with his elderly host, whose step was more like that of a young man.

"I hope that this last minute invitation hasn't inconvenienced you, Dr. Green."

"Not in the least," returned Richard, as he guided himself around a group of waiting sailors. "But first off, I insist that you call me by my first name."

"Very good, Richard," offered the bald-headed professor. "Only if you agree to call me by mine as well."

"Felix it is," returned the American. "Now, tell me more about this collection of manuscripts that I'm to be examining."

Yakhut smiled. "You Yanks are always in such a hurry to get down to business." Guiding them into a corridor marked, 'Baggage,' he continued. "I'll tell you what. If it's all right with you, I'll be happy to take you past the institute on the way to your hotel. That is, if you're not too tired."

"Actually Felix, I was able to sleep on the plane. Though I could use a shower and a change of clothes, I think it can wait a while. Your discovery has my curiosity aroused. Could you tell me again about the exact location of the burial urn and the circumstances that surrounded its discovery?"

The two men remained deep in conversation as they picked up Richard's bags, oblivious to the blast of frigid air that greeted them as they walked outdoors. Felix Yakhut's black Zil sedan soon sputtered alive and they were off southward into the city.

The Institute of Culture was located in south-central Moscow, some fifteen miles from the airport. To Richard, this trip only seemed to take moments, for he was completely fascinated with not only the conversation, but also the scenery. As they crossed the famous Ring boulevards that circled the city, the traffic grew denser, until they were in a virtual sea of diesel-belching trucks, buses, and passenger automobiles. The early morning sidewalks were filled with an army of bundled babushkas, who expertly used their brooms to clear the pavement of the previous evening's snowfall. These sights painted a picture of a vibrant, alive city that carried on regardless of nature's often harsh, fickle ways.

They crossed the Moscow River, and Richard could just make out a portion of the famed Kremlin Wall in the distance, when his host turned the car abruptly away from the central city. They traveled now on a wide, spacious thoroughfare to the southwest. After passing tree-lined Gorky Park, Dr. Yakhut pointed toward a huge, column-lined building that lay directly before them. Identifying this as the university, he wasted no time in guiding the battered sedan up to the entrance of an adjoining structure.

Dr. Yakhut parked in a space reserved for the institute's director. A short, brisk walk took them to the base of a wide stairway. Just as they were about to begin their climb to the building's entrance, a single figure came dashing at them from the parking lot. This individual wore a thick fur coat and sported a full head of shiny red hair. With blue eyes gleaming, this attractive young woman approached them and exclaimed.

"Good morning, Dr. Yakhut!"

The bald-headed professor seemed surprised. "Yelena Lopatin, what in Lenin's name are you doing here? Aren't you supposed to be in the Carpathians?"

While exchanging a warm hug, she answered. "Ah, so I see that my telex never reached you. I should have figured as much. The reason I've returned early is to personally examine a sarcophagus dug up by an army engineering unit working in an adjoining valley. All the initial evidence shows it to be Scythian in origin, possibly belonging to one of their warlords."

Felix Yakhut grinned. "You don't say. My, that should be exciting. May I ask when this relic is scheduled to arrive here?"

Yelena only now eyed the stranger who stood beside the institute's director. "The army was handling the transfer. It was expected here sometime late last night."

Noticing her preoccupation, Felix winked. "Well, let's just hope that our comrades in the military have upheld their part of the bargain. Oh, by the way, I'd like you to meet Dr. Richard Green, who has joined us all the way from the United States. Richard is a most distinguished linguist, and will be helping us examine the Orinsky manuscripts."

The two shook hands while Dr. Yakhut continued.

"Yelena here is one of our top field workers. She is also one of our prettiest."

"So I've noticed," remarked Richard Green smoothly.

Yelena turned toward the institute's entrance, her chapped cheeks blushing. "Shall we see if my treasure has arrived yet?"

Beckoning her onward, Dr. Yakhut followed her up the stairs. Close behind was Richard Green.

Inside, the warmth was most welcome. Richard found himself in a spacious vestibule. Except for the large, crimson, hammer-and-sickle flag that hung from the ceiling, the room could belong to any natural history museum back in the States. Large, glass display cases lined the walls. Inside were stored objects ranging from fossilized bone of all sizes, to an assortment of ancient pottery, jewelry, clothing, and farm implements. Though he would have loved to examine this collection more closely, Richard continued following his hosts up another interior stairway.

Waiting for them at the top of the steps was a single, uniformed watchman. From his concerned look, Richard knew that he was the bearer of bad news.

"Dr. Yakhut, I was just going down to try to find you. I'm afraid there's been a tragedy here. Only a few minutes ago, while initiating my morning rounds, I chanced upon the body of Vasili Pavlinchenko in the main examination theater. The poor fellow's stone-cold dead."

The institute's director grimaced. "Are you certain that he's expired, comrade? Perhaps we should call an ambulance."

The watchman shook his head. "It will be the coroner's van that we'll be calling to pick up our coworker, Doctor. Why, already he's stiff as a board. Come on, I'll show you."

Somberly the watchman pivoted and led the way down the tiled hallway. Richard followed at the rear of the group, silently admiring the series of wall-mounted photographs that showed the staff's workers at various dig sites. When his escorts turned into an adjoining room, Richard did likewise. He took a single step inside and then halted to survey the tragic scene that awaited them.

Dominating the room was a large, tubular-steel gurney. On top of this device sat the object that Yelena Lopatin had mentioned, a seven-foot-long, carved stone sarcophagus. The whole scene was lighted by a powerful surgical lamp, and Richard focused his attention on the crumpled body that lay immediately beside the gurney. Dressed in a guard's uniform, this pasty-skinned, corpulent figure was sprawled out on the linoleum floor, his face frozen in horrified pain. Quick to his side, Dr. Yakhut felt for a pulse and then grimly shook his head.

"I'm afraid Comrade Pavlinchenko has indeed expired. From the degree of rigor mortis that has already set in, I'd say that he's been dead for several hours now."

"What appears to be the cause?" questioned Yelena.

"From the grimace on poor Vasili's face, I'd say that he died from a heart attack," returned the institute's director. "Such seizures are known to be extremely excruciating."

Taking a second to close the guard's eyelids, Felix Yakhut stood and absentmindedly stroked the cold stone of the sarcophagus. "So this is the relic found in the Carpathians."

Yelena joined him. "This is it, all right. It was found buried vertically, only several kilometers from the Scythian village site that we were exhuming."

Nodding with this revelation, Dr. Yakhut set his eyes

on the alien-looking inscription carved into the coffin's lid. As he traced the outline of this strange etching with his fingers, Yelena spoke out.

"If it is indeed the burial vault of a warlord, perhaps that inscription identifies him. Yet for the life of me, I still can't make any sense out of that etching."

"Well, perhaps our esteemed colleague can help us identify it," replied the director. "What do you make of this scribbling, Richard?"

The American uncomfortably picked his way around the corpse of the fallen guard. As he eyed the engraving in question, his expression turned to one of confusion.

"It doesn't appear to be of Serbo-Croatian origin. In fact, it doesn't look like anything I've ever seen before. Why don't I make a tracing and then see what my reference books make of it?"

"That would be most appreciated," said Felix Yakhut, who caught the expectant glance of Yelena Lopatin. "Yet before getting started with such a task, what do you say about opening the lid to see what awaits us inside?"

"But what about Comrade Pavlinchenko?" countered the watchman.

Felix Yakhut turned to face the guard and answered. "Unfortunately, there's little we can do for Vasili now. Why don't you go and find a tarp to cover him with? Then you had better call the police and have them dispatch the coroner's van to make a pickup."

Nodding obediently, the watchman pivoted and left the room, leaving the three scientists alone. Somewhat anxiously, Yelena Lopatin positioned herself at the vault's side. With her director and their American guest close by, she carefully stroked the vault's upper surface.

"This is something that I've looked forward to for several days now. You don't know how much I desired to break this seal back at the dig site."

"I can imagine," offered Felix with a wink. "Yet in the interests of science you waited for more stable viewing conditions. I commend your patience, my dear. I seriously doubt that I could have done likewise. Now, enough of this chatter. Let's see what is inside."

Gripping the lid, Felix vainly attempted to open it. When Richard's efforts also failed to budge it, Yelena circled the underside of the vault's seal with her fingers. Beside the corpse of Vasili Pavlinchenko she suddenly halted.

"I believe there's some sort of latch mechanism here," she excitedly revealed. "Let's see if I can trigger it."

With a good deal of effort, she activated the lock, which opened with a loud, metallic click. All eyes were on Yelena as she grabbed hold of the lid and lifted it upward.

A sour, musky scent instantly met her nostrils, and Yelena backed away dizzily. Straining to peer into the interior of the open sarcophagus, her shocked expression filled with disbelief. For the coffin was completely empty.

"I don't believe it!" she cried. "I could have sworn that this seal had yet to be broken."

"That may very well be," offered Felix Yakhut. "Yet it's very unlike the Scythians to be so wasteful. Maybe it was looted by grave robbers."

"I doubt that," returned Yelena. "I witnessed this relic's exhumation myself, and I can assure you that it was buried deep in the earth. Besides, the sarcophagus didn't show the least sign of having been tampered with."

"Well then, maybe that inscription can help clear up the mystery," offered Richard Green, whose mouth suddenly stretched in a wide, uncontrollable yawn.

Seeing this, Dr. Yakhut solemnly shook his head. "Perhaps it can, but right now, I'm afraid you've done enough for today. It's time to get you settled into your hotel room and get a good Russian meal in your belly. Then, after a shower and a nap, there will be plenty of time to lose yourself in work."

With the exhausting aftereffects of his long journey finally catching up with him, Richard let loose another yawn. Realizing that a little rest would surely do him no harm, he somewhat hesitantly backed away from the sarcophagus. Good-byes were exchanged, and the last thing that the American remembered, as he followed Felix Yakhut out of the examination room, was the look of puzzled concern that continued to mask the pretty face of Dr. Yelena Lopatin.

Two and a half kilometers to the northeast of the Institute of Culture, in the shadow of the Kremlin wall, stood the gray, nondescript brick building housing the headquarters of the MVD. As the internal police force, the MVD was responsible for the daily administration of law and order throughout the Soviet Union. Nowhere did this force face a greater challenge than here in the capital city.

Like any cosmopolitan center worldwide, Moscow was home to a plethora of criminal activity. Murder, robbery, rape, and other assaults were a daily occurrence. When added to a constantly growing drug culture and an active black market that dealt in everything from foreign currency to blue jeans, the urban crime problem took on epidemic proportions. Constantly underbudgeted and understaffed, the MVD did its best to keep the criminal element in check, permitting Moscow to shine as the jewel of socialism that it was intended to be.

Colonel Yakov Kukhar had been with Moscow's police force for the last thirty years. A former naval commando, Kukhar joined the MVD as a lowly traffic cop. Two years later, he was a full-fledged detective. The portly, big-boned Ukrainian was proud of his achievements, which reached their pinnacle a year ago when he was finally made chief of the major crimes section. This unit was designed to handle Moscow's most vile criminal transgressions, and thus was made up of the force's toughest cops.

To handle his men, Kukhar organized them along the lines of the military. Discipline was the order of the day, and he did his best to instill strict virtues into all who worked for him. That was why he was particularly upset on this spring morning as he faced two of his most aggressive investigators, who had been called before him for a major rules infraction.

Lieutenants Mikhail Antonov and Yuri Sorokin had only been working as a team for a couple of weeks now, yet surely they knew better than to attempt a major drug bust without any backup. Though Antonov had only arrived in Moscow recently, his partner was a ten-year MVD veteran, who had lived in the capital city all of his life. Having worked with the major crimes section for the last two years, Sorokin could not be excused. As the chief riveted his hard gaze on the thin, balding detective, he slapped his hand on his desk and vented his anger fully.

"Your actions disappoint me, comrades! Not only have you wasted a good two weeks work, but you've let the Arab know that we're on to him as well. That weasel will be extra cautious in the days to come. Why, I wouldn't be surprised if he even leaves Moscow altogether."

"I seriously doubt that," dared Yuri Sorokin. "The Arab isn't the type who scares so easily. If Mikhail's observations are correct, the Arab presently has a major stash of cocaine on his hands. I'll bet my pension that he's already on the streets peddling it."

"What about the man you gunned down?" questioned the colonel. "Could he be one of the Arab's suppliers?"

Yuri shook his head. "He was only a two-bit thug that was hired as a driver and bodyguard. He's got a long arrest record, yet it's all for petty stuff. Most likely he was involved only as a lackey."

"I think that we should concentrate our investigation on that woman we followed from the Cafe Arbat," offered Mikhail Antonov eagerly. "If she hasn't skipped town, she'll be moving through every hooker in Moscow."

Again Colonel Kukhar slapped the face of his desk with his open hand, this time with enough force to make the two detectives nervously jump. "Enough of your impertinent foolishness! Because you failed to go by my rules, one of the most dangerous bastards in all of Moscow is once more on the streets. I thus have no choice but to reassign you to another unit."

Sitting up straight in the hard chair that faced the colonel's desk, Yuri Sorokin's beard-stubbled face reddened. "But it wasn't our fault, Chief! If our radio had been working, you'd be issuing us medals instead of transferring us elsewhere."

"A broken radio is no excuse!" screamed Kukhar. "You know perfectly well that a raid of this magnitude required backup. Being so-called intelligent men, surely you could have figured out a way to get word to me. No, comrades, I have no other choice but to reassign you to the coroner's department."

"Not the corpse squad!" complained Yuri, his words tinged with disbelief.

An exasperated expression painted the colonel's face. "Get out of my sight, both of you, before I transfer you to refuse collection where you rightfully belong!"

Taking this as the final word, Mikhail Antonov and Yuri Sorokin rose from their chairs and left the office. Immediately outside was a large, open area, where the detective's desks were situated. With six of the dozen or so desks currently occupied, the shrill sound of ringing telephones and pecking typewriters provided the backdrop as Yuri nervously reached for a cigarette. Seconds later, he was drawing in a deep lungful of smoke.

"This reassignment can't be for real," observed Yuri, whose cigarette now seemed glued to his lips. "It wasn't our damn fault that they give us equipment that won't work. Curse the luck!"

Mikhail Antonov answered while seating himself heavily behind his cramped desk. "Easy now, partner. What's done is done, and now we have to pay the piper. We knew the risks when we went into those woods and it's certainly not Colonel Kukhar's fault that things didn't turn out as we would have liked them to."

Yuri shook his head and walked over to his own desk. Here he picked up a half-filled glass of milk. Removing his cigarette, he took a sip from the glass before spitting its contents back disgustedly.

"I can't believe that this damn milk is sour already!"

Just as he was putting his cigarette back between his lips, his phone rang. Wincing at the shrill sound, he picked up the receiver.

"Detective Sorokin here."

A painful expression crossed his face as he reached out

for a pencil and paper. Silently, he jotted down a single address before hanging up and speaking to his partner.

"Don't get too comfortable, comrade. That was our new supervisor, the coroner. It seems that they have a fresh corpse for us to check out on the south side of town. He says if we hurry we might even get there before it starts to stink."

Not really concerned in what manner he served the state, Mikhail Antonov accepted his new call to duty without complaint, for at least dead bodies couldn't fight back. Reaching out to hastily finish off the cheese sandwich he had been in the midst of consuming when they were called into the chief's office, Mikhail rose and grabbed his coat. With Yuri leading the way, he climbed down the two flights of stairs that led to the parking lot.

Outside, a warm morning sun greeted them. The snow that had fallen during the previous night had long since turned to slush. Stretching his cramped frame, Mikhail took in the blue, cloudless sky. A gentle wind blew in from the west, its gusts fragrant with a hint of the coming spring. This was his very favorite season, when life itself seemed to be renewed.

How very ironic it was for them to currently be assigned to the coroner's department, thought Mikhail. Dead bodies had always been repugnant to him. He had examined his share of corpses through the years, yet he never got over his feeling of revulsion. He was certainly in no hurry as Yuri climbed into the car and took his place behind the steering wheel.

There was unusually heavy morning traffic. Annoyed with both their slow pace and the nature of their new duties, Yuri Sorokin seemed ready to explode in frustration. Quick to use the Volga's horn, the Muscovite seethed in anger. Since he was at the wheel, Mikhail vainly attempted to make the best of their situation, before Yuri wrapped their car around a telephone pole. His tales of country life back in Chabarovsk eventually served to calm his chain-smoking partner. By the time they passed the Cathedral of the Archangel, Yuri was almost his old self once again.

This was to be Mikhail's first visit to the famed Institute of Culture. Though he would have liked to enter its column-lined portals under different circumstances, his pulse quickened as he subconsciously took in the cathedral's gilded, onion-shaped domes.

"Have you had a chance to visit the Cathedral of the Archangel as yet?" quizzed Yuri unexpectedly.

Mikhail shook his head.

"Well, when you get a chance," Yuri said, "you just have to make a stop there. Its icons and frescoed walls are nothing short of breathtaking."

Mikhail grinned. "You know partner, I never took you as the religious type."

"Spectacular artwork and architecture can't be ignored no matter what the subject matter may be," countered Yuri. "Besides, even Ivan the Terrible was enchanted by the building. Why, three hundred years ago, he ordered the original designer's eyes gouged out so that he could never create an edifice of such beauty again."

"You don't say," mumbled Mikhail, who was aimlessly watching an individual enter the church.

He was wondering absently from what far corner of the Motherland this pilgrim was drawn, when a bus cut suddenly in front of them. Stomping on the brakes in just enough time to keep from colliding, his partner expressed his displeasure with the shrill ringing of the horn and a series of rude hand gestures. Though the bus driver's thoughtless turn indeed almost caused an accident, Mikhail couldn't help but laugh as Yuri screamed out, questioning the legitimacy of the driver's parenthood. Quick to realize the ridiculousness of the situation himself, Yuri was infected by his partner's mirth, and soon both of them were laughing uproariously, the tension of the morning at long last relieved.

6

The footpath sloped downward into a broad valley
filled with massive evergreens. Alexander Sergeyevich
followed several paces behind his guide. He had first visited these woods more than a decade ago with his Great-
Uncle Dmitri, with whom he had been searching for
archaeological treasures. Alexander had returned to the
valley twice since then, each time at the prompting of his
great-uncle.

A stream gurgled in the distance. With each step,
Alexander was acutely aware of Dmitri's absence. The
old man would never walk this path again. They had
buried him in Vorochta's main cemetery earlier that
same day.

When Alexander had informed the deacon of his
great-uncle's last request, Yuri Sobolev had instantly volunteered to lead Alex to the secret monastery Dmitri had
spoken of. They left right after the last shovelful of dirt
was deposited on the priest's grave.

Alexander had kept an extremely low profile since his
great-uncle's death. After he failed to return to his army
unit, he was classified as an official deserter. Thus he was
grateful to leave Vorochta, where at any moment he
could have been arrested. He welcomed the relative ano-
nymity of the highlands as he and Yuri traveled farther

south.

They stopped for a quick lunch of bread and cheese upon reaching the banks of the Prut River. Here they turned to the west, and after quickly fording the river, began their way over the path that led them to the ever-green forest.

Throughout their journey, Yuri had set a blistering pace. This was fine with Alexander, who could not wait to contact the abbot mentioned by his great-uncle. Alex had not realized that there was a monastery hidden somewhere in these woods, and was surprised that Dmi-tri had not mentioned this fact during their past wander-ings.

The air temperature seemed to drop as they reached the floor of the valley. The rush of current was all-encompassing, and Alexander soon caught sight of the narrow, twisting stream, whose meander was shaped by an assortment of boulders and fallen tree trunks. Leafy ferns and fist-sized clumps of clover gripped the stream's banks, covering it in a lush, green carpet.

Even though there were still several hours of daylight left, the sun was all but blotted out by the thick canopy of overhead limbs. The evergreens towered above, their very scent rich and intoxicating. From the sheer thickness of their trunks, Alexander knew that many of these trees were hundreds of years old. So far the isolation of the forest had protected them from the logger's axe, but Alex doubted that such a valuable stand would remain untouched for much longer.

The path was flat and easy to follow as it wound its way through the primeval forest. To a harsh chorus of squawking ravens, they penetrated deep into a portion of the wood that Alexander had yet to visit. He was soon passing through some of the largest trees he had ever seen. Like ever-watchful sentinels, these silent giants reached hundreds of meters into the sky, with trunks so thick that it would take the combined reaches of at least three large men to encircle them.

As the trail snaked around a particularly massive stand of trees, Alex picked out the sound of water tumbling nearby. The sound intensified as Yuri led him through a thicket of ferns, and then over a fallen tree trunk that bridged the stream. The trail began climbing here as it faithfully followed the brook's meander.

The sound of falling water rose to an almost deafening intensity. It was not until Alex passed around yet another grouping of immense evergreens that he spotted the source of this commotion. Some fifty meters above the forest's floor, a waterfall cascaded downward from a solid shelf of fractured limestone. Alex stood quietly for a moment and absorbed this spectacular sight. Then he noticed that the path they were following seemed to end at the pool of water that lay before them. What now? he thought. Are we supposed to swim? "Now where, Comrade Sobolev?" he called out above the crashing water.

The deacon turned to respond as he reached the edge of the pool. "Have faith, my friend, and don't let your eyes deceive you!"

With this he pivoted and began approaching the shelf of rock from which the falls were created. Alexander looked on with eyes wide with disbelief as his guide proceeded to duck down and begin walking directly into the solid wall of cascading water. Only when he had disappeared completely from sight did the young woodsman sprint over to the pool's edge.

Ignoring the fine mist of icy water that constantly sprayed from above, Alex positioned himself as close as he could to the limestone wall. As he reached this vantage point, he spotted the narrowest of passageways lying between the rock shelf and the waterfall. Carved out of solid stone, the passage appeared just wide enough for a man to squeeze through. Since this had to be the way Yuri had just gone, Alex ducked down and rushed forward.

After the briefest of soakings, he found himself in a narrow tunnel. The waterfall sounded with a hollow roar as he turned to view it. A curtain of falling water veiled the forest beyond. Alex was beginning to feel a little claustrophobic when a deep voice echoed from behind him.

"Come on, lad, we don't have all day!"

Alex immediately turned to make his way farther into the tunnel. Yet all too soon the direct light faded and the darkness forced him to an abrupt halt.

"Comrade Sobolev, where are you?"

As his words echoed in the distance, a blindingly bright shaft of compact light suddenly caught him full in the face. Covering his eyes to deflect the unexpected illumination, Alex breathed a sigh of relief when he heard Yuri's voice.

"I want to be at our destination by nightfall, so let's move it, lad! Now, stay close on my heels and we'll be safely out of this tunnel before you know it."

The deacon angled the shaft of his battery-powered torch forward and began to walk with careful steps. Alex wasted no time joining him. The passageway that they now traversed was carved out of solid limestone and was just wide and high enough to allow them passage. The sound of the waterfall soon faded in the distance, to be replaced only by the hollow echoes of their footsteps.

In one section of the tunnel, the passageway suddenly

merged into a vast subterranean chamber. Pointed stalagmites and stalactites projected from the cavern's floor and roof. Though Alex wished he could explore the site more completely, the deacon hurried through the chamber and ducked into yet another narrow tunnel. The going was a bit more difficult, as the grade increasingly steepened.

Alex was drenched with sweat and wheezing for breath by the time the tunnel leveled out. The deacon seemed oblivious to any fatigue, and pushed on without stopping to rest. Alex let out a sigh of relief when they rounded a wide bend, and he spotted a patch of bright light in the distance. As he had hoped, this illumination led them once again above ground.

Alex ducked through the passageway and found himself on the edge of an oak forest. The trees were large and bent with age. Set on a steep hillside, the oak grove glistened with life in the falling light of late afternoon.

The deacon returned his flashlight to his pack and pointed toward the hill's summit. "We'll be able to see Mount Goverla from that vantage point," he observed.

"How much farther is the monastery?" Alexander asked. He wanted nothing better than to rest his weary body.

Scanning the deep blue, cloudless sky, Yuri answered. "If those legs of yours can hold out, we should be there within the hour."

"Something tells me that you're no stranger to such journeys, Comrade Sobolev," Alex retorted, massaging his cramped calves. "Surely you didn't get into such excellent shape by merely working around the church."

The deacon wisely winked. "Though your great-uncle certainly kept me busy around the cathedral, your observation is most astute, Alexander Sergeyevich. As it happens, I have been making this hike every month for the last fifteen years. The monks rely on me to bring up supplies such as flour, tea, and sugar—things their holy community cannot produce."

"Exactly what is the nature of this community, comrade?" probed Alex. "Until my great-uncle mentioned it, I had no idea that such a place existed."

Beckoning Alexander forward, the deacon answered. "All that I know for certain is that they are a most revered, holy order. They are dedicated to scholarship and prayer, and are very devoted, humble men. One look at their abbey, and you'll know this fact for certain."

Alex was curious to know more, yet the climb forced him to hold back his questions and instead concentrate on his progress. He reached the hill's summit completely winded and drenched in sweat. While struggling to regain his breath, he joined his guide, who was scanning the surrounding countryside.

Before them, filling the entire southern horizon, was majestic Mount Goverla. More than two thousand meters high, the mountain glowed in the gathering light of dusk. Conscious that the night would soon be upon them, Alex looked on as the deacon pointed toward the nearby foothills.

"We don't have far to go now, lad. In fact, you can just see a portion of the abbey over there, beyond the jagged outcropping of rock above the tree line."

Alex intently followed his guide's gaze and soon spotted the collection of structures that Yuri was speaking of. Looking more like a medieval castle than a holy enclave, the community was situated at the base of a sheer rock face. A stone wall surrounded a series of interconnected buildings whose central structure was capped by a gilded, onion-shaped dome.

Alexander was anxious to at last convey the message that his dying great-uncle had entreated him to deliver. He gratefully followed his guide down the narrow footpath. Their course was now due southward.

"Brother Nikolai, what are you still doing out here? The vesper bell will be ringing any second now!"

The portly monk's words seemed to have absolutely no effect on the bare-chested young man. With the sweat glistening off his muscular chest and arms, Nicholas merely placed another log on the chopping block, lifted his axe high overhead, and swung it downward. There was a loud "whop" as the blade split the log cleanly in half. Tossing the resulting kindling aside into a rapidly growing pile, the man was about to place another fat log on the block when he was interrupted again.

"What's gotten into you, Nikolai? Have you gone deaf? Now, put down that axe this instant and come indoors with me. Why, the abbot himself will be delivering this evening's sermon!"

As if to underscore this last observation, a bell began tolling nearby.

"There's the vesper bell now," the monk commented, wincing as Nicholas split yet another log. Realizing that the deep, pealing tones of the bell failed to have their intended effect upon his associate, the monk cried out desperately, "For the love of the one Father, stop this pigheaded nonsense of yours at once, Nicholas! You've been working nonstop at this woodpile since morning prayers, and it's time to both spiritually and physically refresh yourself."

Only when the bell tolled its final time did the bare-chested penitent finally respond. Guiding the blade of his axe firmly into the chopping block, he turned to regard the heavyset, brown-robed figure who stood before him.

"Why, I don't believe it," the other monk said. "If you've indeed finally come to your senses, then you'll dress yourself and follow me to the chapel. If we hurry, we should just be able to make it in time."

As he mopped his brow with a handkerchief, a sudden look of understanding registered in the young monk's eyes. "I'm sorry, Brother Konstantin. I didn't realize how late it was getting to be. There's no reason for you to be tardy because of me. So be off, and I'll join you in a minute."

"You won't be getting rid of me that easily, Nikolai Andreivich. I won't budge until you don your robe. Then I'll have the honor of personally escorting our youngest initiate into the holy sanctuary."

Well aware of his hefty associate's obstinacy, Nicholas shook his head. "I don't know why you even bother with me, Brother Konstantin. I am unworthy of your attention."

"Sometimes I wonder myself," retorted the husky monk, whose eyes were soft with kindness. "Yet there's something about you that reminds me of my own youth. You know, I was something of a misunderstood rebel myself."

Nicholas bent over and picked up the brown, homespun robe that lay neatly folded on the ground beside the waist-high pile of newly cut kindling. He pulled the garment over his shoulders and frowned.

"So you think that I'm a misunderstood rebel," he said, smoothing down his long, blond hair. "That's certainly not how I see myself. For what you perceive as rebelliousness is actually spiritual weakness on my part."

"So you spend all day here at the chopping block to

do penance for your sins," observed Konstantin softly. "As I've told you before, you're much too hard on yourself, my friend. Stop thinking so much, and surrender yourself to a greater calling. Prayer is the way to tap this peace. If we hurry, perhaps your salvation can begin this very evening, during vespers."

Shrugging his broad shoulders, Nicholas beckoned the stout monk to lead the way. As he moved toward the arched doorway that would take them indoors, Nicholas contemplated his associate's words of advice. There could be no ignoring the fact that he had been feeling depressed and self-critical lately. In fact, he had even considered leaving the order to prove his self-worth in the outside world.

In his twenty-seven years of life, Nicholas had known little else but the hallowed, stone hallways that he was presently traversing. Brought to the abbey at the tender age of seven after his parents were killed in a fire, Nicholas had spent the next two decades in the company of the monks of the Order of St. John the Pursuer. Such was the nature of his adopted family as he grew into manhood, and finally he became an actual initiate of the order on the eve of his sixteenth birthday.

As Nicholas passed by the cavernous stone room where the abbey's well-stocked library was located, he fondly remembered the day of his initiation. He had been looking forward to this event for months on end and, as the youngest member of the community, he desired to prove himself as a man. Thus he spent as much time as possible in the library, studying the Latin, Greek, and ancient Slavic texts whose mastery would be tested in the initiation exam. As it turned out, he passed successfully, but not without spending many a sleepless night immersed in the manuscripts on which the holy order was founded.

A Latin chant sounded in the distance, and Nicholas breathed in the rich scent of frankincense. This pleasing aroma became stronger as he followed Brother Konstantin into the candlelit chapel. The icon-lined room was filled with six rows of simple, wooden pews. At the moment, only the first row was occupied. Here ten brown-robed monks knelt before the central altar, their drawn hoods all but veiling their individual visages.

A single figure stood in front of them. The abbot's flowing white hair and beard perfectly matched the color of his ankle-length robe. Though well into his eighties, the abbot stood straight and firm, his crystal blue gaze riveted on his flock, who were soon joined by two latecomers. Only when all twelve of his brethren were assembled before him did he solemnly greet them.

"Welcome, brothers of St. John, on this sabbath of rebirth. We kneel before the one Father, with our hearts pure and our efforts united in shared purpose. For we shall never forget why we are gathered in this holy community.

"Almost two thousand years ago, our spiritual guide gathered the twelve chosen ones together on a stormswept clearing on the island of Patmos. Here he announced his Divine Revelation and confronted the hordes of the Evil One. Soon afterward, the twelve left the island on a handmade raft. Once back on the mainland, they quickly scattered to the far corners of the planet, to await that fated moment when the Beast is destined to reawaken.

"Our abbey was founded as a bastion of light. For countless decades, the brothers of St. John the Pursuer have existed on this site, ever ready to do battle with our despicable foe. To give us strength in the period of waiting, those who have preceded us have recorded the last time the Evil One was confronted, here in these very hills, one thousand years ago. We must be ever vigilant, for the time of the reawakening is near. And above all, we must never doubt our purpose, for we are all that stands between the world of man and the black pit of Hell itself.

"Now, stand and join me in the celebration of our faith. And after the body and blood of the Ascended Master have been shared by all, then I will read from the divine book of our predecessors."

Nicholas was one of the twelve hooded monks who rose to their feet with this command. Though his back and his raw, calloused hands ached after his long day at the chopping block, he felt a strange peace course through his weary body. And for a rare, blessed moment, he completely forgot the spiritual concerns that had led him to the woodpile in the first place.

Nicholas was last in line to receive a drink out of the large silver chalice the abbot handed to each monk. Next, a delicate wheat wafer was distributed. Like the wine, this was a symbolic host, designed to represent their master's body. After he had distributed the last wafer to Nicholas, the abbot backed away and instructed the monks to kneel once more. As they did so, his voice rose in prayer.

"Blessed Father, holy and strong, have mercy upon us. And may the blessed gifts of your blood and body deliver us from all tribulation, wrath, and danger."

To this the monks sang out in unison, "Lord have mercy."

The abbot positioned himself behind the altar's pulpit. This raised platform was shaped from solid limestone, and had a life-sized icon carved on its face. Nicholas had always been particularly fascinated by the design of this icon. It showed a winged archangel dressed in armor. The angel was thrusting a spear at a serpentlike beast that lay coiled beneath his feet. Even as a child, Nicholas had always identified with this warrior-angel, whose muscular frame was much like his own.

It proved to be the deep, bass voice of the abbot that brought the young monk's attention back to the pulpit. He listened as the elder spoke out passionately.

"The reading is from the divine record of those who came before us. Written a millennium ago, the passage tells of the time when the Beast last walked among us."

Looking down at the rostrum, the abbot opened a thick red book and began reading out loud. "From the Orthodox priests of the surrounding villages we learned that a bloodthirsty demon was loose in our midst, a demon whose insatiable hunger craves human flesh above all other. To investigate this startling report, Brother Nikolai was sent into the outer world, in order to determine if this beast and the Reawakened One were one and the same.

"Nikolai was armed only with his great faith when he left the abbey and entered the realm of man. Here he tracked down the families of each of the half-dozen victims who had already been sent to early graves. In each instance they were young women whose bodies were found drained of blood and partially devoured.

"It was during a chance meeting that Nikolai encountered the beast responsible for these atrocities. A group of barbarian Tartars had been reported in the region, and our holy representative had been guided into the village of Vorochta just as this savage band was completing one of its infamous raids.

"At the outskirts of the burning village, Nikolai observed a single individual dressed in the buckskin clothing of the Tartars. Yet from his vantage point, hidden at the edge of the surrounding woods, Nikolai could see that this figure was not from the east. For he had fair skin, long, black hair, and deep green eyes that bored into one's very soul. It was obvious that he was riding with the horde, for he was carrying several bagfuls of loot, recently expropriated from the sacked village. One of these canvas bags, draped over the haunches of his horse, held an object of particular interest. For wrapped inside was a young girl who was little more than a child.

"Thinking that he was alone in the clearing, the tall, black-haired raider proceeded to unwrap his prize. Laying the limp corpse of the child on the ground before him, he ripped off her clothing and began ravenously feeding. Like a half-starved wolf, the stranger tore at the raw flesh, lapping at the blood to quench a thirst formed in Hell.

"Sickened by this sight, Nikolai could only watch as the beast finished his meal and rode off into the forest. He knew without a doubt that this bloodthirsty stranger was none other than the creature he had dedicated his entire life to hunting down and destroying at all costs. Yet because he was improperly armed to do battle, Nikolai was forced to return to the abbey to prepare for the inevitable confrontation.

"For six days we surrendered ourselves to nothing but holy prayer. Then as the sabbath dawned, the altar stone was removed, and the blessed spear exhumed from its subterranean crypt.

"As the youngest and most physically capable amongst us, Nikolai was chosen to carry the spear into battle. He did so without flinching, and eventually the Beast was cornered near the headwaters of the Prut. A violent conflict ensued, during the course of which our dear Nikolai lost his life while planting the sacred spear deep into the Beast's chest. I was personally there to witness this event and will take to my grave the tormented screams of anguish that spewed from the Evil One's vile lips as the black life force ebbed from his cursed body.

"A specially designed sarcophagus was built to house the Beast's remains. It can be recognized by the numerals 666, which are carved into its lid. This numerical sequence was conveyed to us by our holy founder, and is known as the Mark of the Beast. Woe to those who come upon this holy relic, for before the sarcophagus could be properly interred, it was spirited off by the returning Tartar horsemen, who supposedly buried it somewhere in the surrounding woods. The exact location is unknown to us. And thus began the time of waiting once more."

Closing the book at this point, the abbot looked up to address his spellbound audience. "Thus saith the words of Abbot Nikon, as written ten centuries ago. Know them as the gospel, and take strength in their essence. For it is written that the Evil One is destined to walk the earth once again. And if it should be during our earthly existence, we shall go to our graves gladly in order to wipe this vile poison from the face of the earth!"

These last words were delivered with unusual force, and the order's youngest member found himself completely enthralled. Though Nicholas had heard this reading before, it never failed to stimulate him. Filled with new purpose, he looked out to the icon that was carved into the face of the pulpit, and knew very well that he had been named after this same monk, who had so nobly sacrificed his life a thousand years ago.

Nicholas continued to study the intricate icon as the abbot initiated the prayer of departure. It was during the closing hymn that he became aware of an unusual disturbance taking place at the back of the chapel. Strangely enough, two outsiders had just entered and were now in their midst. He recognized one of these individuals as the fellow who faithfully brought in their monthly supplies. At his side was a tall stranger, dressed in the simple garb of a woodsman, who appeared to be about the same age as Nicholas. The young man appeared confused and extremely nervous, and Nicholas instinctively sensed that he was the bearer of grim tidings.

"Alexander Sergeyevich, welcome to our humble abbey," said the abbot. "I want to personally convey my condolences. Your great-uncle was a fine man. His presence will be missed by all those his faith touched. Now, exactly what is the nature of the business that brings you here?"

The abbot sat forward and waited while his unexpected guest cleared his throat to respond. Calmed by the private confines of the abbot's office, the nervous woodsman managed to find the words to express himself.

Alexander told him of the discovery that had prompted his trip to Vorochta. After describing the sarcophagus, he did his best to relate the terrifying confrontation that took place inside his great-uncle's sanctuary. Alexander's voice was trembling as he recreated the demonic procession of phantoms that Dmitri had managed to exorcise.

The abbot absorbed this fascinating story with great interest. There was no doubt in his mind that his visitor was telling the truth. Yet one part of the woodsman's incredible tale was particularly significant, and the abbot carefully probed him further.

"You can relax now, Alexander Sergeyevich, for your obligation has been fulfilled. Like Father Dmitri, I, too, am most interested in this relic that you saw the soldiers pull from the earth. Were you able to see if there was any unusual writing carved on the coffin's lid? And what kept the soldiers from opening it?"

"The sarcophagus had already been loaded into the back of a truck when I arrived," replied Alexander. "And I only got a chance to examine it briefly. Since most of its stone face was still stained with mud, I wasn't able to see if the lid had any identifying marks on it. As to what kept the soldiers from opening it, you can blame a group of Moscow-based archaeologists for that. They have been digging for relics in an adjoining valley and somehow heard of the discovery. They talked the army into conveying the sarcophagus back to the capital for a complete scientific study."

"A group of archaeologists, you say? Why, that's incredible!" returned the abbot.

"But what does all this mean?" Alexander asked. "The finding of an ancient relic is one thing. But what does it have to do with the horrifying vision I encountered back in Vorochta? I swear to you that those demons were real!"

"Easy, lad," advised the abbot. "The unholy procession you witnessed was not from this earthly sphere. As there is a Heaven above, so is there a Hell below. From time to time the door to this black pit is unlocked, and the horde of evil is released into the world of mortals. By the grace of the one Father, your great-uncle met the challenge and sent the unholy ones back to the abyss from which they crawled.

"It is quite possible that the discovery of the sarcophagus that you witnessed had something to do with the release of this evil. The purpose of the Order of St. John the Pursuer is to properly investigate such incidents. We exist to make absolutely certain that the gates of Hell are securely locked, and that the unholy spawn of evil is contained in the black depths to which it belongs."

The young woodsman seemed confused by this explanation, and the abbot added, "The concepts that I speak of are indeed perplexing. Yet to those of us who dedicate our entire lives to such ponderings, they are as clear as night and day. Thus I do not expect you to understand all that you have witnessed these last couple of days. Just know that you have fulfilled your obligation, and that the one Father is thankful for your assistance. As of this moment, the great burden that you have been carrying is transferred to the Order of St. John the Pursuer. Now tell me lad, will you be returning to your army unit?"

Though Alexander was anxious to know more about the nature of the relic that had led him on this strange journey, he shrugged his shoulders. "If I do return, I'll be facing certain arrest. The penalty for desertion is very severe, and it will most likely be off to the gulag for me."

"Do you have any family that can shelter you?" the abbot asked.

Alexander grimly shook his head. "My great-uncle was all that I had left."

An idea occurred to the abbot, and he sat forward expectantly. "I realize that we don't have many comforts to offer, but the order would be honored to take you in. We are a humble, holy sect, dedicated to scholarship and prayer. Yet these ancient walls are thick enough to keep out the cold, and we manage to keep our bellies full with the crops that we grow. This abbey also contains a superb library, whose contents will help you further understand our divine purpose. It should serve to clarify the great mystery that you have managed to stumble upon."

Alexander gratefully accepted the abbot's gracious

invitation, for he was sincerely anxious to know more
about the Order of St. John the Pursuer, and he knew
that he had nowhere else to turn. Feeling like a great
weight had been lifted from his shoulders, the young
woodsman prepared to meet his new destiny.

As was his habit, Nicholas spent most of the evening
studying in the library. After consuming only a heel of
black bread and some borscht for dinner, he surrendered
himself to his current research project.

The library occupied a large, drafty room that was
overflowing with a vast collection of volumes. Books
were everywhere, lining the walls, and even stacked on
wooden pallets on the floor. Interspersed among these
volumes were several tables, only one of which was currently occupied.

By the light of a single, flickering candle, Nicholas
read from the pages of one of the library's more recent
acquisitions. The book was entitled *Mein Kampf* and
was written by Adolf Hitler. In reality, Hitler had dic-
tated this work to his secretary, Rudolf Hess, when he
was imprisoned in 1923 after failing to gain control of
the Bavarian government in Munich. It was a comprehensive work, in which Hitler laid down not only his
plans for making Germany strong internally, but also of
conquering all Europe and eventually the entire world.

Nicholas found that the book offered a fascinating
glimpse into the twisted mind of the man who was to be
known as Der Fuhrer, or supreme leader of the German
people. Particularly interesting to the young monk were
those passages in which Hitler expounded his vehemently anti-Semitic beliefs. Of course, all of this had later
come to fruition when the Nazi gas chambers extermi-
nated millions of Jews, Catholics, and other individuals

deemed undesirable by the Fuhrer and his cohorts.

To Nicholas, this tragic holocaust was an example of unconstrained evil at its worst. The rise of the Nazis had occurred less than five decades ago, proving that modern man was still very much susceptible to the malevolent callings of the Fallen One.

An earlier study had brought Nicholas to the writings of Joseph Stalin. Like Hitler, the Soviet premier was a ruthless leader who was responsible for the untimely deaths of millions of innocent people. Though many of his bloody purges were subsequently covered up by the government, Stalin unquestionably stood alongside Hitler as one of the most despicable figures the world had ever known.

Both individuals fit in well with the young monk's belief that throughout history, certain mortals had been chosen to be vessels of the Evil One. Possessed by the great deceiver, these figures brought suffering and death to millions.

Strangely enough, the order that Nicholas currently served practically ignored men such as Hitler and Stalin, labeling them mere fanatics. The more Nicholas read, the more he saw such mortals as the Devil incarnate. The young monk could not help but wonder if such men were not in fact the true enemy their spiritual founder had warned of two thousand years ago.

Nicholas often had trouble understanding the exact nature of the Beast he had sworn to vanquish at all costs. Readings such as the one included in the evening's vesper service only served to confuse him that much more. The creature his fellow brethren had hunted down a millennium ago was responsible for but a handful of deaths. How could this be compared to the likes of a Hitler or Stalin, whose direct orders literally sent millions to their graves? Were not such individuals the true representatives of the Evil One on Earth? Perhaps their order had somehow become misdirected through the years and was now focusing on the wrong enemy.

Diverting his glance from the page that he had been skimming, Nicholas focused on the flickering candlelight. A familiar, gnawing tension formed in the pit of his stomach, and once again he felt the bitterness of spiritual doubt.

He was wondering what harsh penance he should impose upon himself this time in an attempt to return to the path of obedience, when a bell began tolling in the distance. It was fast approaching midnight, and a call to worship at this late hour was unprecedented. Nicholas pushed himself away from the table and hurried toward the chapel to see what the mysterious commotion was all about.

The torchlit corridor was empty as he proceeded toward the cathedral. The sound of his footsteps echoed off the passageway's stone walls and floor. Only a few decades ago, such a call to worship would have sent dozens of monks scurrying from their beds to the chapel that he was quickly approaching. Yet today, only thirteen disciples remained. The majority of them were at least seventy years of age. Like the abbot, these monks were reaching the end of their lives on Earth and would all too soon be able to serve in the spirit only.

Nicholas was the only member of the order under fifty years of age. It was up to him to make certain that the abbey was infused with new blood and that the tradition of St. John the Pursuer was perpetuated, a great responsibility to a person whose own spiritual doubts had lately made him question the order's very existence.

The aroma of frankincense greeted him as he rounded

a bend in the corridor and saw the closed wooden doors of the chapel. Before entering, he dipped his fingers into the font beside the door and traced the outline of a cross on his forehead with holy water. This symbolic act reaffirmed his belief in the sanctity of the one Father; his son, the Ascended Master, who lived among mortals and was sacrificed on the cross; and the spirit that linked man with the divine afterlife to come. Thus fortified, Nicholas pushed open the heavy wooden doors and stepped inside.

The young monk was surprised to find the sanctuary lighted by hundreds of flickering white candles. Waves of billowing incense veiled the air as he peered at the altar and found that some sort of strange ritual was taking place. His fellow brethren were already gathered before the pulpit. Each figure was dressed in a white robe and had his hood pulled up. They stood in a straight line, facing the abbot. Beside their spiritual leader stood a figure dressed in the orange robes of a neophyte. Only as Nicholas drew closer did he identify this stranger as the mysterious young man who had arrived earlier that evening during vespers.

Nicholas joined the line of eleven monks who stood before the altar. As he did so, the abbot beckoned them to kneel. Positioning himself behind the pulpit, the white-haired elder spoke out forcefully.

"I have called this special mass to introduce Alexander Sergeyevich, who has decided to join our order as an initiate. Alexander is a native of Vorochta and brings with him news of a most distressing nature.

"Three days ago, a Soviet army engineering unit near the Prut headwaters pulled a sarcophagus from the earth. It may very well hold the remains of the Unholy One. Unfortunately, this relic was spirited off to Moscow before Alexander could have a chance to see if its lid held the three numerals that would positively identify it as the Beast's final resting place.

"To learn this fact for certain, I have decided to send a representative of the order to the capital. Once in Moscow, this individual will track down the relic and determine if our greatest fears have indeed finally been realized."

Stepping off the dais, the abbot walked over to the edge of the altar and halted before Nicholas.

"Brother Nicholas, you have been chosen to travel to the capital city. Because the time of release is near, you will not go unarmed. Two thousand years ago, our order's beloved founder received a weapon cut from the very cross on which the Ascended Master was crucified. The divine spear has been kept in our midst for a millennium, when the Beast last walked among us. Protect it well, for it is the only device on Earth that can do injury to the unholy creature, whose flesh is impervious to mortal weaponry."

Walking over to the front edge of the pulpit, the abbot bent over and depressed a latch that was recessed beneath the rostrum's lip. In response to his touch, the front portion of the pulpit slid open to reveal a hollowed-out interior compartment. A solitary spear was mounted here on a cushion of deep blue velvet. The abbot grasped it carefully and pulled it out for all to see.

Nicholas found his heart pounding away wildly in his chest as he took in the relic whose previous existence had been but hearsay. The slender weapon resembled a javelin and was carved out of a single piece of highly polished, dark wood. When the abbot placed the spear's butt on the floor beside him, its pointed tip extended well past the elder's hip. All in all, it appeared to be a formidable weapon, which, even without its legendary powers, would be a deadly instrument in the hands of a trained attacker.

Nicholas's mind was still reeling over his surprise assignment. He watched as the abbot lifted the spear high overhead and cried out passionately.

"In the name of St. John the Pursuer, I beseech thee, one Father, to bless this holy crusader! Protect your earthly proxy, and guide him by the light of righteousness. For if the Beast indeed walks the Earth sphere once again, our chosen disciple shall be all that stands between this despicable creature and the world of mortals."

Nicholas almost cried out when he saw that the elder's spear had begun to pulsate with an unearthly golden glow. The abbot lowered the glowing weapon and lightly touched Nicholas with it on each of his shoulders. Each time the spear touched the young monk, a tingling current, much like a mild electric shock, jolted through his body. Conscious now of his destiny, Nicholas listened as the abbot cried out to the heavens.

"Glory be to the one Father, to whom no miracle is too great! And blessed be your servant Nicholas, who has donned the spiritual armor of the warrior-priest to protect your holy interests. May your light always be with him, Lord of all, as he initiates this greatest of crusades. For thine is the Kingdom, and the Power, and the Glory, forever and ever. Amen."

7

It was rapidly approaching noon when Mikhail Antonov and Yuri Sorokin finally pulled up before the Institute of Culture. Their late arrival was due mainly to the heavy traffic and the fact that, while crossing Smolensk Boulevard, they were involved in a minor accident. Though no injuries or major damages were sustained, the detectives were forced to pull off the roadway by the driver of the car whose fender they had clipped. In normal circumstances they would have ignored this gesture, but the shiny Zil limousine they had hit carried the license plates of a Politburo member. As it turned out, one of the ultra-powerful men who virtually ruled the entire Motherland was indeed waiting for them in the back seat of the limo. He took several minutes to properly admonish the detectives for their careless driving habits. After making certain that his secretary had taken their names, he ordered them to see what they could do about straightening the dented bumper. With the help of a tire iron, they managed to accomplish this repair, and forty-five minutes later, they were on their way southward once again.

Mikhail and Yuri had decided earlier not to let the morning's calamities upset them. Though their confrontation with the loud-mouthed Politburo member stretched their patience to its limits, they shrugged off their misfortune with a joke and soon forgot all about it. Awaiting them outside the column-lined Institute of Culture was a large white van with *Coroner's Department* printed neatly on its paneled side.

"Oh swell, our first morning on the job and it looks like the meat wagon has already beat us to our corpse."

Yuri Sorokin shrugged his thin shoulders. "What's the hurry, anyway, hotshot? It's not like the stiff we've been sent to check out is in a rush to get anywhere, except maybe to his coffin."

Mikhail could not help but chuckle as he led the way outside. Behind him, Yuri followed with their worn leather evidence bag.

The day was turning out to be a beauty. The deep blue sky was accented by a bank of high-flying, powdery white clouds. The winds gusted gently from the southwest, and the temperature was well above freezing. Spring was in the air, and even a flock of passing ravens seemed to be noisily discussing its arrival.

A grim-faced watchman directed them upstairs. Once they ascended the stairway, the strobelike pulse of a photographer's flash unit beckoned from an adjoining room. Assuming that this camera belonged to the coroner's team, the two investigators entered a doorway marked Examination Theatre I.

What appeared to be a massive stone funeral vault sat in the center of the brightly lighted room. Two members of the coroner's pickup team were kneeling in front of it. They had their collapsed gurney at their side and were in the process of wrapping a full grown man's corpse into a heavy plastic body bag.

The flash of a camera's strobe light broke to their left, and Mikhail and Yuri both turned their heads when a high, nasal voice shouted. "Smile, comrades!"

Another photo was triggered, and this time the strobe temporarily blinded the two newcomers. Yuri cursed, while Mikhail's hand went instantly to his eyes. It took a full thirty seconds for his eyesight to return to normal. Finally he was able to identify the photographer, who was a trim, middle-aged man dressed in a khaki safari suit. He seemed to be smirking at them.

"Sorry if I caught you off guard, comrades. Believe me, it wasn't intentional."

"Don't feed me that line, Pavl Serafimov," countered Yuri Sorokin. "Everyone knows that you'd photograph your own mother on the crapper if there was a rouble in it for you."

Lowering his camera, the photographer looked hurt. "Come now, Yuri, is that a proper greeting for a long lost comrade?"

The bald-headed detective softened his tone. "Well, at least you caught my good side. Make certain that you send me a decent print."

With this remark, both men smiled as they stepped forward and hugged each other warmly.

"Has it really been a year since I've seen that ugly face?" teased Yuri.

The photographer nodded. "Indeed it has, my friend. And believe me, all of it wasn't spent at a Black Sea resort, either. For six long months, I was assigned to the front in Afghanistan."

Realizing that he had yet to introduce his partner, Yuri beckoned him to join them. "Mikhail Antonov, I'd like you to meet the best photojournalist in the Soviet Union, Pavl Serafimov Barvicha."

As the two shook hands, Yuri continued. "What brings you back to the Center?"

"A welcome change of orders," responded the keen-eyed cameraman. "When the good folks at *Pravda* complained one too many times about the realistic nature of my combat shots, the next thing I knew it was back to Moscow for me. I got this assignment with the coroner's staff two weeks ago. Although it's a bit dull, at least I don't have incoming mortar rounds to constantly contend with. What about you, Yuri? Are you still keeping our city safe with the MVD?"

Yuri caught his partner's glance before replying. "Actually, all of us seem to be in the same boat. Our transfer orders lending us to the body squad hit us only this morning. Believe it or not, this is our first official case. Speaking of the devil, what do we happen to have here?"

The trio approached the two kneeling attendants, who were in the process of zipping up the body bag.

"It looks like a routine heart attack victim," reflected Pavl casually. "The deceased was a watchman who apparently succumbed to the fatal seizure sometime in the early hours of the morning. The victim was in his mid-fifties, and a good forty pounds overweight. From what I gathered from his coworkers, he had a genuine passion for his vodka as well."

As Pavl signaled the attendants that he wanted to take one last photo of the corpse's face, Yuri addressed his partner. "Well, comrade, it appears that our job has already been completed for us. Does that inquisitive country mind of yours sense any possibility of foul play here?"

Before answering, Mikhail studied the face of the deceased, which was just visible through the unzipped folds of the body bag. During the course of his official duties, he had come across many a coronary victim, and this one certainly seemed no different. Too much fat and not enough exercise could take a man to his grave just as quickly as a bullet. The frozen mask of pain that was locked in the fallen guard's pasty face certainly indicated that he had met his death in just such an excruciating seizure.

Mikhail looked up and took in the massive relic that was positioned immediately above the corpse. The vault was cut from a solid piece of stone and seemed to be of great age. Since its lid was closed, he had no idea what its contents were, but he wondered what, if anything, the sarcophagus had to do with the guard's unfortunate heart attack. His partner's voice prodded him on.

"Well, partner, shall we let the lads here complete their job? After all, our esteemed coroner is anxiously waiting."

Mikhail blushed. "I'm sorry, comrade. I see no reason to delay removing the corpse. Go ahead and get on with it."

The attendants took this as the final word and finished zipping up the bag. After hoisting it unceremoniously onto the gurney, they wasted no time in exiting, leaving the trio of investigators alone in the examination room.

With the body now removed, they were free to circle the stone sarcophagus. Clearly awed by its size, none of the men said a word. It was Yuri who broke the silence first.

"Do you think that this coffin scared that poor guard to death?"

"I was thinking the same thing," returned Mikhail, who looked on as his partner cautiously touched the relic's surface.

"Any guesses as to this thing's age and origin?" ques-

tioned Yuri. "For the likes of me, I've never seen anything quite like it."

"The vault was exhumed in the Carpathian foothills,"
broke the crisp voice of a woman from behind them.
"Our initial estimate is that it is more than nine hundred
years old."

The men turned as the woman approached them. Her
long red hair cascaded over her laboratory smock, and
her blue eyes seemed to snap with intelligence.

"Good morning," she said. "I'm Dr. Yelena Lopatin
of the institute's field research staff. Can I be of some
assistance?"

Yuri stepped forward to greet her. "As a matter of
fact, you can, comrade. I'm Lieutenant Yuri Sorokin,
and my colleagues here are Mikhail Antonov and Pavl
Barvicha. We have been dispatched here to investigate
the demise of your night watchman, and we were wondering if this stone funeral vault could have had anything to do with his death. You must admit that the
piece is most imposing and could give one quite a shock,
if stumbled upon. May I ask what lies inside?"

Yelena walked briskly to the side of the vault. "Actually, it's empty. Would you like to have a look?"

Without waiting for an answer, she reached under the
lip's edge, and after triggering some sort of latch, lifted
the lid upward. Each of the investigators were quick to
look inside.

"No one was as disappointed as I was when its contents were found missing. Since I personally saw it being
pulled from the earth, we can only assume that grave
robbers beat us to it."

"That is indeed unfortunate," commented Yuri. "Yet
surely this magnificent stone vault by itself must be
worth something. Incidentally, when did it arrive here?"

"We believe it was sometime last night. I only arrived from the dig site early this morning. In fact, I was just on my way upstairs to see if the vault had arrived when I was informed of Vasili Pavlinchenko's untimely death."

Yuri's brow tightened. "Surely you must have some record indicating the exact time that this piece arrived here. Doesn't your receiving department have a bill of lading?"

"It apparently arrived after normal receiving hours," Yelena shrugged.

"Yet if that is so," Mikhail Antonov asked, "who would have been here to accept an object as large as this?"

Yelena seemed a bit irritated by this line of questioning. "We're still checking to make certain, but it appears Vasili Pavlinchenko was alone here for most of the night. That would make him the only one available to accept the shipment."

"Is such a practice normal?" continued Mikhail.

Yelena's patience hit its breaking point. "Of course it's not, but exceptions happen! What are you getting at, anyway?"

Mikhail instinctively lowered his voice. "Please excuse my harsh tone, Doctor, but it's our job to help figure out what triggered the watchman's heart seizure, if such an attack indeed proves to be the cause of his death. You know, back in Chabarovsk, I investigated the death of a postal worker who died of a coronary after handling a back-breaking load that was way beyond his strength and endurance. Maybe this is what happened to the guard."

"I believe you may have hit the nail right on the head," added his partner with a wink.

Pavl Barvicha suggested that the four of them proceed

to the loading dock to look for evidence of the vault's arrival. As it turned out, the sharp-eyed photojournalist was the one who spotted Vasili Pavlinchenko's clipboard hanging beside the receiving room's massive scale. They quickly noted the late hour of the vault's receipt, and Mikhail Antonov's simple theory seemed substantiated.

It was only later that afternoon, after the investigators had long since left the institute, that Yelena Lopatin's curiosity got the better of her. On a whim, she gathered together a muscular group of grad students and had them wheel the sarcophagus downstairs to be weighed once again. Much to her surprise, she learned that the piece was one hundred sixty pounds lighter than it had been when Vasili originally logged it in late last night.

Had the inexperienced watchman merely read the scale incorrectly? Though this was most likely the case, Yelena found it hard to ignore such a conspicuous discrepancy. She made a mental note to share this information with the institute's director during their next meeting together.

Two blocks due north of the institute, an overweight, heavy-legged dutywoman struggled with her afternoon chores. Olga Tyratam always prided herself in being a self-sufficient, tough old woman, yet the winter that was just passing had drained her like never before. Even the simplest task was difficult now. She was constantly out of breath and fatigued, and it was hard for her to even find the stamina to do her own marketing and prepare her meals. With the additional responsibilities of her managerial position, she was just barely making it through the day.

Olga attributed her worn condition to old age. Not really certain of the exact date of her birth, she could pretty well account for seventy-three years of life. Never a believer in doctors and pills, she decided long ago that when this day inevitably came, she would do her best to stick to her routine to the very end. There would be no hospitals or nursing homes for her, not if she had anything to say about it.

For almost three decades now, she had been the manager of a three-story, thirty-unit apartment building. Built before the Great War, the sturdy, old, brick structure was one of the few brownstones left standing in Moscow. Most buildings of this size had long since been replaced by more efficient, high-rise complexes. Such multistoried, concrete and steel monstrosities were soulless to Olga, who constantly thanked the fates for keeping the demolition teams far from her familiar walls.

As Olga bent over her dustpan in the building's lower hallway, she recollected the day when she had first moved in. At that time the worn black-and-white linoleum tile of this corridor had sparkled like the floor of a palace. How very proud she had been to keep it polished to a mirrorlike luster.

Of course, her beloved Konstantin had been alive in those exciting days. Fresh out of the navy, he had been sent to Moscow to work in one of the giant steel mills that Stalin was building. With this assignment came their very own two-room apartment. Before that time, she had shared a cramped apartment with her husband's family back in Kiev. To think that they would have a place of almost the same size for just the two of them was mind-boggling. It only went to prove that their people's years of selfless toil and sacrifice were finally beginning to pay off.

Since they were the first to move in, Olga was named dutywoman. It was her job to keep the structure in tip-

top shape. She was responsible not only for its maintenance, but for the tenants' proper behavior as well. Constantly aware of their comings and goings, she got to
know them better than her own family. She learned to
appreciate the good individuals, and make certain in her
weekly police report to note any deviant activities such as
alcoholism or black marketeering.

She had been young and full of energy in those innocent days, and she had handled her tasks with ease. Just
knowing that her husband was available to counsel her
on any difficult maintenance problems made her job
that much easier. Yet as the fates so cruelly willed it, less
than a year after arriving in Moscow, her Konstantin was
crushed to death in a horrible industrial accident that
took seven others to early graves as well. She had been
alone ever since.

Merely thinking of that day made Olga's eyes sting
with tears. Konstantin! she thought, rubbing her cheeks
clumsily with the back of her hand. She was not ordinari-
ly one to cry. For years she had pushed self-pity to the
back of her mind. I'm just so tired today, she thought, so
very tired. With no energy left to spare for wasteful tears,
she willed her arthritic limbs onward to finish the sweeping. Then she would only have one more task to complete before returning to her apartment for her evening
rest.

With a superhuman effort, the old woman whisked
the last clump of dirt from the hallway. Not stopping to
put down the broom, she turned stiffly and slowly made
her way to the rear of the corridor, where the door leading to the basement was situated. She fumbled to unlock
this stained wooden portal, whose rusty hinges always
seemed to squeal in protest. A descending stairway composed of a dozen wooden steps now faced her. Beyond

this was a solid wall of darkness.

Since electric lights had never been installed in this portion of the building, Olga had to use the kerosene lantern that hung on the wall beside the top step to illuminate her way. To light its wick, she removed her late husband's prized Zippo lighter from her apron pocket. Though it took several tries, her stiff fingers soon had the lantern glowing with light.

Her final chore of the day was to check the fuel level of the building's oil-powered furnace. Despite the fact that spring was officially upon them, Olga knew that they had yet to see the end of winter weather. The snows would once again fall before the final thaw arrived, and a furnace without diesel oil would be dangerously useless. As had been her habit for the past thirty years, she would check the furnace's fuel level one more time before the return of the warm weather made such a responsibility unnecessary.

Before descending the stairway to get on with this unpleasant task, Olga took a series of deep breaths to gather both her physical strength and her nerve. The basement had never been one of her favorite places. It was dark, dirty, and a natural home to roaches, spiders, and rats. She had a particular aversion to this last species, and thus carried the broom along to keep the perpetually hungry rodents at a distance.

Ever mindful of the fact that in their very neighborhood, only three weeks ago, a pack of rats had crawled into a baby's crib and bitten a newborn infant to death, she cautiously proceeded into the cellar's black depths. She was trembling with exhaustion by the time she finally cleared the last step.

Olga allowed herself a few moments to catch her breath before moving on to the furnace. A heavy, musty smell permeated the air, and she picked out the shadowy shapes of discarded furniture and boxes of all sizes. Holding the lantern out in front of her, she bravely began picking her way forward. Well aware that the treasure of the czars could be stored down here without her knowing it, she promised herself to see to the basement's proper cleaning one day. If the end did come for her soon, at least she could go to her grave in peace, knowing that her building was in order from top to bottom.

Halfway across the room, she struck her shin on an exposed wooden plank. As the pain shot up her leg, she could not help but curse the fool who had left the obstacle there. For a moment Olga felt a strong urge to return upstairs and send one of the younger tenants down in her place, but then she set her jaw in determination. It was her job, after all, and what she'd started, she could finish.

She was limping rather badly by the time she finally reached the furnace. Proud of her accomplishment, she set the lantern on the floor and wasted no time unscrewing the cap to the fuel storage tank. As she was reaching for the wooden measuring stick that was kept on top of the tank, an alien, scurrying noise sounded out behind her. Olga's pulse quickened as she picked up the broom she had carried along with her. She swung it wildly and smashed it against the tank, filling the basement with a resounding metallic clash.

Olga felt proud of herself as she put the broom down and picked up the measuring stick. No group of stupid rodents would keep her from her appointed state task. A new sense of confidence possessed her, and even her stiff, arthritic fingers seemed more supple.

Plunging the stick deep into the tank, she pushed it down until she heard it hit bottom. Then she pulled the measuring stick back out and placed its tip up against the lantern. The tank was bone dry, just as she'd figured.

Olga knew that the new breed of younger apartment managers would not have bothered to take a heating oil measurement this late in the season. Deceived into thinking that spring had indeed arrived, their fickle thoughts would be elsewhere. Yet pity their poor tenants when the next northerly inevitably arrived! The first thing in the morning, she would call to request a fuel delivery. This shipment would surely see them well into the real thaw.

Olga sighed, wondering if her tenants appreciated her resourcefulness. She screwed the cap back in place and put the measuring stick back on top of the tank. As she bent over to pick up the lantern, the sound of scurrying feet again broke from behind her.

Olga wasted no time whacking the head of her broom up against the empty fuel tank. But this time, as the racket produced by this concussion faded, the alien scurrying sound was still audible. Never one to underestimate the bravado of a hungry rat, Olga's limbs trembled in both revulsion and fear. Sweat beaded her flushed forehead, and her heart pounded with a painful intensity. She knew that she had to get out of there at once, yet her leaden legs refused to cooperate.

The sickening patter of tiny feet seemed to be intensifying, and Olga could only close her eyes in response. Like before, she thought, it's going to happen like before. It had been forty years now, but she remembered the horror of it as if it were yesterday. Nazis. An air raid. She and her sister Lena had taken shelter in a basement—a basement like this one. At first they had not been overly frightened. They could hear the first detonating bombs like thunder in the distance. But the bombs got closer and closer, and suddenly a tremendous explosion engulfed them. Deafened by this concussion, Olga was thrown off her feet and knocked temporarily unconscious. When she eventually awoke, she looked out to find the basement in utter shambles. Thankful for her own survival, her next thought was of her sister. She pawed through the rubble, frantically searching. That was when the nightmare really began.

Olga would always remember the moment she first spied Lena's inert body partially buried beneath a pile of fallen bricks and mortar. Already covering her broken figure were dozens of fat, brown rats, in the midst of a feeding frenzy. Somehow she managed to knock the rodents off the bloody, torn corpse. Then she collapsed in shock. When the rescue teams pulled her out only minutes later, she emerged from the debris with a new understanding of death's hideousness.

More than four decades later, the trauma of that fated afternoon was still fresh in her mind. As she stood in the dark basement with her eyes tightly closed and limbs trembling, Olga knew she would share her sister's fate if she did not get control of herself. As it turned out, it was the loud sound of a crate overturning nearby that served to tear Olga from her trance. Not even the largest of rats could create such a racket, she realized. She opened her eyes and vainly searched the blackness. The padded sound of footsteps echoed in the distance, and a new concern crossed Olga's mind. Filled once more with the will to live, she cleared her dry throat.

"Hello, who's out there?"

Goosebumps formed on her skin when no one answered. She could no longer hear the sound of footsteps, but she could have sworn that there was definitely someone out there. Though this unknown party could be one of the neighbor kids trying to give her a fright, she instinctively thought otherwise. Most likely she had chanced upon some sort of transient who had chosen her basement for a crash pad. Never one to take kindly to such intruders, Olga bravely lifted up the lantern and again addressed the blackness.

"I know that you're out there, comrade. So whoever you are, identify yourself, before I go and call out the militia."

Again there was no answer, and Olga's arthritic grasp on her broomstick tightened. "I'm issuing you one last chance, comrade. Show yourself this instant!"

As if in response, a distant rumbling noise was suddenly audible. It got increasingly louder, and Olga knew that it was only a passing Metro train. Built beneath the adjoining streets in the days following the Great War, the subway was an old familiar friend to Olga, who decided that the time for twenty questions was over. Gathering her nerve, she began making her way toward the stairwell as quickly as her tired legs could get her there.

Halfway to her goal, the kerosene lantern at her side went abruptly dead. The blackness quickly encompassed her, and she cursed angrily. But her annoyance all too soon turned to fear as she contemplated her precarious position. Alone in the basement, with a possible intruder hiding in the shadows, she had to get the lantern relit and get upstairs with all due haste. Quickly she knelt on the floor and placed the lantern in front of her. Her hand was shaking as she reached into the pocket of her apron and extracted her late husband's lighter. The worn lid opened with a click, and a flame soon graced the lighter's wick. Blessing American industry for creating such dependable devices, Olga attempted to relight her lantern. Much to her disappointment, it failed to ignite. This meant that she would have to find her way across the rest of the basement with only the flickering lighter for illumination.

Pain shot through her knees as she stood and gradually reinitiated her perilous journey. The light was just enough to renew her confidence. Olga had almost made it to the stairway when a gust of cold, noxious air hit her full in the face. A sickening rank scent met her nostrils, and she was again overtaken by a wave of sheer panic. The hairs on the back of her neck rose as her ears picked out a dreaded sound behind her. Over the distant roar of the passing Metro train could be heard the heavy, ponderous shuffling of approaching footsteps.

Somehow she summoned the courage to turn and confront this intruder head on. With the flickering flame of the Zippo lighter held out like a beacon in front of her, Olga's voice quivered with fear.

"All right, comrade, you've succeeded in nearly scaring this old woman to death. Now will you stop being such a spineless coward and show yourself?"

Another wave of tainted air passed over her, and in the speed of a single heartbeat she got her wish fulfilled. A man's face suddenly appeared before her. Shock turned to pure fright as Olga's will collapsed under the sheer power of the stranger's evil stare. Staggering as if a knife had been plunged into her breast, she found herself swallowed by a glance whose pupils seemed to be formed by tongues of crimson flame.

Olga's knees weakened, and she was only barely aware of the stranger's sharply etched cheekbones, his hairless, pointed jaw, and thin, cruelly pursed lips. Yet she instantly knew of his intentions when his mouth opened, exposing a ruby red tongue and a set of pointed, yellowish teeth that looked more like a wolf's than a man's.

No words of introduction were needed. Olga knew that this stranger was none other than the king of the rats himself. Called from the black sewers of Moscow, his only purpose was to feed. Having seen his subordinates at work on her own sister, Olga shuddered in awareness. For a fleeting second anger overcame her panic and she valiantly raised her broomstick overhead. Yet quicker than she could lower it, the beast was upon her. Swallowed by the rumbling roar of the passing Metro train, the dutywoman's screams for help went unanswered, and all too suddenly her time of earthly life was over.

The stranger with eyes of fire perched triumphantly beside his fresh kill. With the mortal's limbs still twitching, he bent over and hungrily bit into the sagging skin of his victim's inner thigh. A warm, salty spurt of blood met his parched lips, and he sucked into the torn tissue with a frenzied intensity. Only after gulping down several mouthfuls did he lean back and issue a loud belch. His gaunt face was satisfied, for a thousand-year-old thirst had at long last been satiated.

With this feeding came renewed strength. Already he could feel the nerve sensation returning to his previously numb limbs. Tissues that had lain dormant for a millennium awakened like an early spring blossom opening to the sun. As the nourishment pumped deeper into his body, even his consciousness was affected. For the first time in countless centuries, memories, long since forgotten, rose in his mind's eye, and he remembered what it was like to truly live again.

Since even dreams were unknown to him during his years of sleep, his mental stimulation was at first alien to him. His thoughts jumped randomly, and it was a struggle to control them. He finally did so by regulating his breath. Pulling in deep ribbons of air through his nostrils, he filled his lungs completely before emptying them and then repeating the process. By concentrating solely on this simple procedure, his mental focus sharpened and his confusion gradually lessened. As he gazed out into the darkness, he mentally recreated the path that had led him here.

He had awakened only recently and found himself in some sort of strange castle. The startled mortal who had served to break the seal provided him his first blood feeding, enough to give him the strength to make good his escape. Though the events of the first couple of hours went by in haze, he remembered reaching the castle's catacombs. It was by way of this maze of tunnels that he was drawn to the room in which he currently knelt.

Ever so slowly his eyes returned to the body on which he had fed. Plump and disease-ridden, the old woman's corpse lay like a side of spoiled pig meat. There was a time when the mere idea of such a meal would have repulsed him. But like a young animal, he would have to gain his strength first before initiating a hunt for the prey that satisfied him the most. This meant that he would have to find a lair far away from mortal reach. Since exposing himself to the light of day was far too dangerous, he decided to return to the catacombs. There he would rest and grow strong.

Satisfied with this plan, the reawakened one pushed away the torn body of the old woman and attempted to stand. For a moment he swayed back dizzily, but he quickly regained his balance and stood erect. He yawned with contentment, and a sudden realization came to him. His name—he knew it now. "My name," he announced with pride, "is Vladimir!"

8

Moscow's main morgue was located on Pirogovskaya Street. It was situated in a four-story brick building, only a block from the Jaroslav rail terminal.

Dr. Albert Stura was the facility's director. At fifty-six years old, he was known as a competent administrator and an excellent physician. With his thick, flowing mane of white hair, movie-star good looks, and a tan he managed to keep even during winter, Stura was somewhat of a legend to his staff. They also appreciated his superb sense of humor and his insistence that everyone—himself included—share equally in the workload. In addition to his full schedule of administrative duties, Stura still found time to do his fair share of autopsies.

Today was no exception. After meeting with the budget board all morning, he returned to his office only to find it in complete chaos. He looked around in disbelief. His personal assistant looked a bit shaken as she rushed forward to explain.

Sasha had only recently joined his staff, yet already her intelligence and ability to get things done had made an impression on Stura. Usually cool under pressure, the lanky, twenty-three-year-old Georgian's voice nervously quivered as she took her boss aside and explained just what was going on.

Since he had left for the budget meeting, all hell had broken out at the morgue. It all began when a midmorning fire at a preschool sent in the charred corpses of seven innocent youngsters. At approximately the same time, a drunken sailor plowed his stolen automobile into a crowded downtown bus stop. As the dozens of injured were carted away in ambulances, the bodies of three babushkas, two metal workers, and a French citizen were somberly loaded into a line of coroner's vans. As if this was not enough to keep them occupied, they also had three separate homicides, a suicide, two stroke and three heart attack victims arriving at the same time.

Sasha's first job had been to find enough refrigerated storage space for all of these corpses. Once this was accomplished, she began the somber task of trying to identify each of the lifeless children. Fortunately for her, Albert Stura arrived just as she was about to brief the grieving parents. Without a moment's hesitation, the director insisted that he personally handle this most delicate of assignments.

Though he had been with the morgue for more than two decades, Stura could not help but be affected by the series of emotional confrontations that followed. Since several of the corpses were burned beyond recognition, dental records were needed to guarantee an exact match. Yet because the victims were so young, such records were practically nonexistent. After explaining the predicament to each parent, he excused himself to return to his office. There Sasha was waiting with a compassionate smile and a bottle of brandy.

The drink did much to calm him down. His assistant's expert hands were in the midst of relaxing the knot of muscles that had contracted at the back of his neck when the shrill ring of the telephone broke the temporary quiet. The voice of Colonel Yakhov Kukhar of the MVD rang out excitedly. He had just learned that a French national had been killed in their city, and he was insisting that an autopsy be carried out with all due haste.

Albert Stura employed his most diplomatic tone to assure the esteemed colonel that he would see to this task himself. As he hung up the receiver, he noted that his assistant had refilled their glasses. He also could not help but notice the devilish gleam in her dark green eyes. He had been attracted to the long-legged Georgian from the first time he met her and only now realized that the attraction was mutual. As he wondered if they could get to know each other on more intimate terms right here in his office, a loud knock sounded on the door. Sasha's face fell.

"You may come in," Stura called, shaking his head in resignation.

With this, the door opened and three men walked in. Stura immediately recognized the khaki-suited leader of this trio as his new staff photographer, Pavl Barvicha. Behind him followed two strangers who were a study in opposites, to say the least. The taller of the two was muscularly built and had short blond hair and a deep blue, no-nonsense stare. Beside him stood a thin, balding figure. He was badly in need of a shave, and was clenching an unlit cigarette between his lips. He surveyed the room nervously as Pavl Barvicha stepped forward.

"What the hell is going on out there, Chief?"

Albert Stura somberly shook his head. "I forget that you're still a neophyte at this game, Comrade Barvicha. Days like this do occur, and you just have to take things as they come. I'll never forget back in 1971, when we had two unconnected plane crashes within the city limits on the same day. Why, on that evening we had to literally stack the bodies on top of each other to get them in the cooler. Though it might take a bit of work, we'll manage, as we always seem to. Now, how can I help you?"

The photographer gestured at the two men who had followed him into the office. "Sir, I would like you to meet two of your newest investigators, Lieutenants Yuri Sorokin and Mikhail Antonov."

"Ah, the MVD detectives," reflected Albert Stura. "You know, I just had the honor of speaking to your former supervisor, Colonel Kukhar. Is that man always so obstinate?"

Instantly pleased with the director's tone, Yuri Sorokin grinned. "The secret's not to take him personally, sir. The attitude I believe you've detected is just his way of getting things done."

"Well, I do hope that the chap has a lighter side," Stura said dryly. "As you'll learn if you hang around here, life's short enough as it is. Now, I see that our ace photographer has been showing you around. When will you be getting started?"

This time it was the muscular blond, Mikhail Antonov, who answered. "We already have, sir. We're just returning from the Institute of Culture, where we picked up the body of the night watchman."

"It appears to be a routine heart attack, chief," added Pavl. "We cased the place thoroughly and noted no signs of foul play."

Albert Stura pushed his chair back and stood up. Only then then did he remember the assistant who stood behind him. "Excuse me, Lieutenants Sorokin and Antonov, but in all the excitement, I forgot to introduce my personal assistant, Sasha Litvov. As you'll soon learn,

Sasha here is the real genius behind our little operation."

Blushing at this introduction, Sasha nodded in greeting. "Now," Stura added, "is there anyone here who'd like to join me for lunch?"

The others politely refused this offer. Stura shrugged his shoulders and gave Sasha his order, instructing her to serve it in the main operating room. As she left the office, the director followed her into the tiled hallway, with the trio of investigators on his heels.

"Have you showed our comrades here our little work room, Pavl?" he questioned.

"I'm afraid that I haven't had a chance yet, chief."

"Well then, comrades, allow me to be your tour guide," offered the suave, white-haired physician. Without another word, he made his way briskly down the well-lighted, spotlessly clean corridor. When he reached the end of this hall, he turned to his right and ducked through a closed doorway.

Mikhail Antonov was the last one to follow him through the door. He could not help but marvel at the size of the room they were entering. As large as a gymnasium, the immense chamber was brightly lit by a series of surgical lamps that were suspended from the vaulted roof. A dozen operating tables were spaced evenly throughout the room. Each of these platforms were surrounded by at least two gowned attendants, who were busily working on the bodies laid out before them. A hushed, somber chatter filled the room, and Mikhail breathed in the sharp, distinctive odor of formaldehyde.

Like butchers at a meat market, the coroners went about their macabre business. Mikhail had never been a squeamish person, but he felt a bit queasy as he watched one female attendant calmly lop off the upper portion of an old woman's skull with a handsaw. Mikhail quickly diverted his glance to the next table down the line. Here, a heavy plastic body bag had just been laid out. He looked on while this bag was unzipped and saw the stiff corpse of the watchman they had been responsible for delivering.

"Well, I'll be," said his partner. "There's the poor stiff that we brought in from the institute."

With this observation, the morgue's director halted his advance and joined his colleagues around the corpse of the late Vasili Pavlinchenko. While one of the attendants undressed the guard, Albert Stura carefully examined the body from head to foot. Only then did he speak.

"So you believe that a coronary took this fellow down, comrades. It may very well be, but I'll bet my pension that our friend here suffered from liver disease as well. Shall we take a look?"

The director smiled and skillfully donned a surgical robe and gloves. As he was about to pick up a razor-sharp scalpel, his personal assistant arrived at his side. Sasha carried a silver serving tray, on top of which sat a pair of sandwiches. Upon seeing her, Albert Stura's eyes widened.

"Sasha, my dear, as always you got here just in the nick of time. Why, I feel faint from hunger. What treats did you bring me?"

"I managed to track down a tongue on black bread, and some herring, onions, and sour cream on rye."

"The herring shall do for now, my dear," said the director.

Mikhail Antonov could not believe it when the handsome doctor picked up the herring sandwich in one hand and the scalpel in the other. Without hesitating, he took a bite out of his meal and slit into the belly of Vasili

Pavlinchenko at the same time. While thoughtfully chewing his snack, Stura began to cut a Y-shaped incision. He started at the tip of each shoulder and worked his way down over the sternum, ending at the pubic bone. As the blade cut through the abdomen, the flesh parted to reveal a thick layer of yellow fat.

The coroner took another bite from his sandwich, and Yuri Sorokin abruptly excused himself and took off running for the nearest restroom. Mikhail was able to control his own nausea, as Stura bent over the incision and began peeling back the layers of skin. Mikhail was captivated by the various internal organs that were soon displayed before him.

Suddenly, the room's paging system activated. Mikhail looked up as a high-pitched, nasal voice echoed through the rafters.

"Investigative team Able, please pick up line six. Investigative team Able ... . "

As the message was repeated, Pavl Barvicha commented dryly, "I believe that's you, Comrade Antonov."

Pavl led him to the nearest telephone. Here Mikhail recorded an address on Moscow's south side, where the body of a woman who had supposedly been attacked by a pack of rats was waiting for them.

As Mikhail ducked into the bathroom to check on Yuri Sorokin and get on with this new call to duty, the coroner continued with his autopsy. Confusion etched Albert Stura's face as he peered into the corpse's body cavity. He shook his head in disbelief. In a normal autopsy, there would have been a considerable seepage of blood in the abdominal area. So far, there had been no signs of bleeding whatsoever. The same puzzling results were obtained when he pried up the rib cage and exposed the pericardium and lungs.

Sasha rejoined him as he was cutting into the scalp in preparation for opening up the guard's head.

"I don't understand it," muttered the coroner as he expertly worked the blade of the power saw through Vasili Pavlinchenko's skull. "Believe it or not, this corpse hasn't produced a single drop of blood so far!"

"But that's impossible," exclaimed Sasha. She watched breathlessly as Stura removed the top portion of the guard's skull and began probing into the exposed brain.

"See for yourself," he said. He pointed at the large vein that ran along the membrane at the top of the brain. "Even the superior sagittal sinus is collapsed and dry."

After absorbing this strange fact, Sasha watched closely as Albert Stura began an examination of the corpse's jaw and neck regions. As it turned out, she spotted the two alien holes in the guard's neck just as Albert Stura did.

"That's odd," he whispered. "They seem to be located right over the right carotid artery."

"Could it be a dog bite?"

Stura shook his head solemnly. "Right now, I just don't know, but I think that it's best if we keep this thing to ourselves. Cover the body and return it to storage. We'll come back to it as soon as I've relayed our findings to the Ministry of Justice."

Ignoring the remains of his lunch, Stura returned to his office, leaving his puzzled assistant the task of returning Vasili Pavlinchenko's remains to cold storage.

Richard Green spent a good portion of his first day in Moscow sleeping. This had not been his intention, but once he settled into his hotel room, showered, and lay down for what was to be but a half-hour nap, his jet lag got the best of him. By the time he eventually woke up, it was well past five o'clock.

His thoughts were a bit hazy as he sat up in his bed and scanned the room's simple furnishings. He spied the wall-mounted desk that held his briefcase. At that moment he remembered the etching that he had promised to translate for the institute.

He rose and went straight to the desk. There he sat down and reached into his briefcase to remove the flimsy, translucent piece of paper on which the tracing had been drawn. In an effort to establish the origin of the symbols copied there, he pulled out a thick, scholarly volume entitled *Languages of the Ancient World*. With stubborn determination, he began leafing through its pages.

A quarter of an hour later, he spotted an obscure entry that seemed to match the mysterious etching almost exactly. It belonged to an extremely rare dialect, Moldavian Greek, which had not been used for a thousand years. Drawn to represent numerals, the symbols corresponded to the Latin numbers 666.

Instinctively, Richard reached out to grasp his ever-present pipe. As he positioned its scarred bit between his lips, he could not help but associate this particular series of numerals to a passage in the Revelation of St. John.

He reached into his suitcase again and pulled out his Bible. After a moment, he found the passage he was seeking in the last verse of Chapter Thirteen, in the Divine Revelation of St. John. It read, "Let him that hath understanding count the number of the Beast, for it is the number of a man; and his number is six hundred and sixty-six."

Richard was stimulated by this correlation and picked up the telephone to call the institute. His call found Dr.

Yakhut at a banquet, where he was the guest speaker. With his host unavailable, Richard asked to speak with Dr. Yelena Lopatin, the woman who was responsible for bringing the sarcophagus up from the Carpathians.

As it turned out, Yelena was busy carbon-dating a portion of the vault and could only speak for a few seconds. Though Richard had not consciously planned it, he found himself asking the attractive field researcher to dinner at his hotel that same evening. He was pleasantly surprised when she accepted his invitation.

Only after he hung up the receiver did he realize that he had forgotten to tell her of his findings. Deciding to wait for dinner to do so, he rose to unpack and see how his travels had treated his clothing.

The call directing Mikhail Antonov and Yuri Sorokin to the city's south side for the second time that day arrived in just enough time to strand them in the middle of rush-hour traffic. Even though Moscow's central planners had attempted to move as much major industry as possible to the outskirts of the city, the streets were still packed with scurrying commuters. Stalled in a virtual gridlock, the traffic belched tons of sooty diesel fumes and moved at a snail's pace.

Happy to have his partner at the wheel, Mikhail took in the surrounding mass of humanity. Though the Metro subway system was able to accommodate some five million people a day, this still left an inordinate amount of surface traffic. Before being transferred to the capital, the largest city that Mikhail had ever lived in was Charbarovsk in the Soviet Far East. Moscow's population of approximately eight million was more than sixteen times larger. He was only just now grasping what it was like to live in a place with so many people.

Life seemed so much less complicated in the country. Mikhail's father had always argued that it was against the very nature of humanity to grow up knowing only concrete and steel. A man needed to have contact with the soil to understand his true place in the scheme of things. The longer Mikhail lived in the city, the wiser the observation seemed.

A muted snore broke out behind him, and Mikhail turned and found their backseat passenger fast asleep. Though he had only met him a few hours earlier, Mikhail had already formed a genuine liking for the photographer, Pavl Barvicha. His worldly knowledge and cosmopolitan ways were like a breath of fresh air. They were fortunate indeed when Dr. Stura absent mindedly assigned him to their team.

As Mikhail shifted his line of sight to include his other partner, he could not help but stifle a laugh. Yuri still looked a little green around the gills as a result of the episode in the morgue. This had been the first time Mikhail had seen the streetwise detective lose control, and he found it somewhat reassuring to know that Yuri was only human after all.

Yuri caught Mikhail's amused glance and nervously shifted his unlit cigarette from one side of his mouth to the other. "Something on your mind, partner?" he said.

"Well," said Mikhail, "I was just thinking about that mess back at the morgue. Why, in Chabarovsk, the coroner doesn't see that much action in a month."

"That's a hell of a place," observed Yuri grimly. "I wonder how the staff can take the grind day after day."

A baton-waving traffic cop suddenly signaled Yuri to halt, and the beard-stubbled investigator was forced to jam on his brakes to obey. A frustrated truck driver began wildly honking his horn behind them, and Yuri angrily struck the plastic steering wheel with the palm of his hand.

"Easy now, partner," cautioned Mikhail. "You know, in a lot of ways, I wonder who has the more stressful job. At least back at the morgue, they don't have to constantly fight this damn traffic."

Yuri grinned in agreement as he put the car into gear and proceeded across the intersection. The traffic was a bit lighter here, and soon they were passing by tree-lined Gorky Park. At this point, Pavl Barvicha sat up in the back seat and yawned.

"You wouldn't happen to have a cup of hot tea around, would you, comrades?" he asked sleepily.

Mikhail reached into the cluttered glove compartment and removed a shiny silver thermos. "Would you settle for some day-old coffee?" he countered.

The photographer could hardly believe his ears. "Did you say coffee, my friend? Where in Lenin's name did you scare up some of that precious brew?"

"Actually, we lifted a pound during an arrest last week," returned Mikhail, sloshing some coffee into a plastic cup. "I hope you don't mind, but it's a bit luke-warm."

Pavl was quick to reach over the seat and grasp the cup, which he sniffed appreciatively. "That's quite all right, comrade. I'll manage just fine."

Like a true connoisseur, the photographer took the smallest of sips, savoring the precious drops that passed his lips. "Why, it's absolute nectar! My friends, you don't know how long it's been."

Mikhail could not help but smile at Pavl's exuberance. As he capped the thermos and put it down at his side, Mikhail noticed that his partner was also grinning. Looking more like his old self once more, Yuri guided their battered Volga in and out of the surrounding traffic lanes. Oblivious to a chorus of honking horns and angry hand gestures, he whipped them around the slower traffic and into an outer lane reserved for VIP traffic only. Here the going was much quicker, and soon they could see the massive, column-lined building they had visited earlier in the day.

A quarter of a kilometer north of the Institute of Culture, Yuri slowed down and guided them onto a substantially narrower side street. Barely the width of a single automobile, this pothole-filled thoroughfare was lined with ancient brick tenements. When he found the address he wanted, Yuri pulled the car right up onto the cracked sidewalk and turned off the ignition.

Pavl Barvicha insisted on finishing his coffee. "Boy, this neighborhood is a real gem," he observed as he readied his camera. "It's as if we've gone back in time fifty years."

Yuri nodded. "Moscow's like that, comrade. Why, I can take you to a place only a few kilometers from here that you'll swear is right out of the pioneer days. There are folks living in log cabins."

"What's so amazing about that?" protested Mikhail. "In Chabarovsk, such crude habitations are as common as snow in the winter. Even I lived in a log cabin for a while."

Yuri shook his head. "But this is the Center, partner! Everyone knows that the homes here are the most modern steel and glass structures in all the Motherland. All I'm trying to say is that the mere fact that neighborhoods like this one still exist shows that our dear city still has some character left after all."

"Amen," added the photographer, who was ready for action. Swinging the strap of his 35mm camera over his neck, he pointed to a nearby three-story brownstone building.

"I believe that's the place, comrades. Are you ready to see what manner of death awaits us?"

Yuri and Mikhail followed Pavl to the apartment's entrance, where a distraught-looking, middle-aged woman sat on the narrow stoop. She seemed confused, and it was obvious that she had been crying.

Suddenly aware of their presence, she wiped her face dry, took in a deep breath, and greeted them somberly. "Thank the heavens that you finally got here. You are from the police department, aren't you?"

Yuri nodded and pulled out his shield. "Lieutenant Sorokin at your service, comrade. My partners and I would have been here forty-five minutes ago, but the cross-town traffic was impossible."

"At least you got here before the children returned from school," she grimly reflected.

"Are you the one who discovered the body?" probed Yuri.

She nodded. "I had just returned home from work and noticed that our dutywoman was not in her apartment, as was her habit. Since the poor dear hasn't been feeling well lately, I thought it best to check the building for any signs of her. That's when I discovered that the basement door had been left open."

With this thought, she was possessed by uncontrollable sobs. Mikhail Antonov sensed the enormity of her upset and tried to calm her down. "We're here now, and there's nothing more for you to worry about."

"That's easy enough for you to say," she managed between sobs. "In my entire life, I've never seen such a horrible thing!"

Caught in a renewed fit of emotion, she again burst

into tears. This time, Mikhail looked to his colleagues for help. Yuri shrugged his shoulders, while Pavl tried a different tactic.

"Excuse me, Ma'am, but I'm with *Pravda*. Do you mind if I get your photograph for our paper?"

The bluff showed almost immediate results as the witness's hands went straight to primping her kerchief-covered hair. Somehow she summoned the emotional control to speak.

"*Pravda*, you say? Why, to think that because of such a tragedy, I'll finally be in the papers. And just look at me, a total mess! Do you mind if I run off to my apartment so that I can put on my face and at least look presentable?"

Pavl slyly smirked. "Not at all, comrade. In fact, take your time. While you're at it, my colleagues and I will be down in the basement to check out this tragedy firsthand."

Once the emotional witness was safely out of their way, the trio of investigators entered the building. They had little trouble locating the entrance to the basement.

Each of them pulled out a standard-issue flashlight Yuri Sorokin led the way down into the pitch-black cellar. Pavl Barvicha followed behind him, and Mikhail Antonov took up the rear.

Not really knowing what awaited them, Yuri halted on the final step and hastily scanned the room with his torch. The beam of light cut through the darkness and revealed several pieces of old furniture and dozens of dust-covered storage crates. A narrow walkway penetrated this assortment of odds and ends and Yuri cautiously began his way over it.

Barely aware of his colleagues who followed close behind him, Yuri concentrated on his beam of light, which he angled immediately before him so as to not bump into any of the crates. As he made his way around a cobweb-covered sofa, he halted when a high-pitched squeaking sound broke from up ahead. Taking a deep breath, he raised his light and soon spotted the source of the noise. His skin crawled with revulsion, and he stopped in his tracks. Hundreds of madly scurrying rats were feeding on an object that lay sprawled on the basement floor. Yuri gasped as his flashlight illuminated the torn stump of a human foot sticking up in the midst of this pack of frenzied rodents.

Madly he reached out to pick up the nearest convenient object, which turned out to be an old, bulky tube radio. Lifting it above his head, he flung the radio forward, hitting the rat pack squarely in its center. A deafening chorus of squeals filled the air as the rats scurried off. After a single glance at the remains of their feast, the seasoned detective doubled over and began to vomit.

Pavl Barvicha and Mikhail Antonov were quickly at his side. They angled their flashlights to illuminate the floor several meters in front of them. Both spotted the torn remains at approximately the same time. As Mikhail turned to empty his own stomach, the photographer looked on, seemingly spellbound by what he saw.

Pavl had only seen one other human corpse in such a pitiful condition. He had been a day's hike out of Kabul at the time and had discovered a Soviet tank commander splayed out on the highway, his upper layer of skin completely torn off by the Mujahedeen. He had left Afghanistan shortly after that, with the hope of never again seeing such an atrocity. Now he was reliving the horror right here in the heart of Moscow.

Ever mindful of his duty, Pavl raised his camera and reluctantly began snapping off photographs of what was left of the dutywoman. The camera's strobe cut the blackness with an eerie intensity, clearly revealing the bits of torn ligament and chewed bone that only hours ago had belonged to a living human being. He finished off the roll of film as quickly as he could and joined his dazed colleagues at the stairway's base.

"Not a very pleasant sight, is it, comrades?"

Pavl's grim observation was met by Yuri. "It's one thing to see such a sight at the morgue, where the coroners ply their trade. Yet to know that an innocent old woman was stripped to the bone in this lonely place by a crazed pack of rats completely sickens me. I've heard of babies being attacked in their cribs by such rodents, but never a full grown adult!"

"I agree," Mikhail said. "Even in the wilds of Siberia, where the winters can drive an animal crazy with hunger, I have never heard of a rat being responsible for the death of a woman—or a man, either. Didn't the witness mention something about the old woman not feeling well lately? Perhaps she had a bad spell and fell to the floor here unconscious. Sensing an easy meal before them, the rats then sealed her doom."

"Sounds logical to me," agreed the photographer. "Yet we must be open to the possibility of foul play."

Yuri nodded. "Comrade Barvicha is right. Though it will be far from pleasant, we must completely comb this basement for evidence. But before we begin, how about helping me cover the old lady's remains?"

While Yuri and Mikhail searched for a tarp or blanket to accomplish this somber task, the photographer began exploring the cellar's recesses. Carefully picking his way around the cluttered junk that seemed to cover the room from wall to wall, he halted before the building's massive furnace. Sighting the beam of his torch down to the

ground here, he picked out a collection of fresh footprints, clearly left behind on the soot-covered floor. Certain that this meant that the dutywoman had been here
in the first place to check on the furnace, Pavl beamed.

He was just about to inform his colleagues of this fact
when he spotted another set of footprints leading off
into the basement's depths. As he began to follow this
trail, a deep-throated sound caught his attention. This
gradually rose in volume and seemed to get even louder
as Pavl reached the cellar's outer wall. Seconds later, he
found an actual opening in this wall. Formed at a spot
where the wallboard had long since decayed, this crack
provided the inquisitive photographer just enough room
to squeeze his body through.

The chugging sound that had drawn him here grew to
a crescendo, and he found himself in some sort of tunnel. It was completely lined with wet cobblestone and
extended well to the horizon in both directions. It was
just large enough to allow him room to stand erect. Hurriedly, he reloaded his camera and snapped off several
pictures of this exciting find. Only then did he squeeze
back through the cracked wall and call out loudly.

"Over here, comrades! You'll never believe what I've
stumbled onto!"

It took some time before the two investigators were
able to join him.

"What in the hell are you carrying on about?" asked
Yuri, his tone soured by his solemn duty.

Pavl shined his torch on the hole he had just crawled
through. "Go ahead and look inside. It leads to some
sort of tunnel."

In no mood for games, Yuri somberly eyed the photographer before allowing his curiosity to get the better
of him. Hurriedly, he poked his head through the crack.

Only when he saw what was on the other side did he bother to squeeze the rest of his body through the opening.

Mikhail had a bit more trouble than the others fitting his muscular figure through the narrow opening, but soon all three of the investigators were standing in the tunnel. The beams of their torches clearly illuminated the stained, stone walls as Pavl's animated voice echoed forth eagerly.

"Didn't I tell you that I had stumbled upon something truly amazing! I was just poking around the cellar and had found what I believe to be the dutywoman's footprints beside the furnace, when I chanced upon another set of tracks leading toward the wall we just crawled through. That's when I heard a strange, distant roar. It seemed to be coming from this direction, too."

"We heard it also, comrade," interrupted Yuri. "I'll give you odds that there's a Metro tunnel nearby."

Absorbing this observation, Pavl continued. "But what do you make of this place, comrades? Surely it's not of modern construction."

Again it was Yuri who answered. "What we most probably have here, my friend, is a portion of the ancient catacombs that still undercut this section of the city. Incidentally, much of our Metro system follows this route, first hollowed out by our ancestors. Now, all of this is genuinely fascinating, Pavl, but hadn't we better be getting back to our jobs? The attendants will be here any minute now, and if it's all right with you, I'd like to get out of this hellhole by nightfall."

Guilt etched the photographer's face as he realized that the detective had a good point. "You're right, comrade. I'm sorry that I allowed my curiosity to lead us away from the job at hand. I, too, have a family waiting for me, so let's get on with it."

Beckoning Yuri to lead the way, Pavl followed the scrawny detective as he ducked through the cracked wallboard. This left Mikhail Antonov momentarily alone in the tunnel. He could not help but wonder where the catacombs led. Shrugging his massive shoulders, he was about to return to the cellar when his ears picked out the faraway bark of a single dog. Assuming that this was coming from one of the rat terriers that the underground Metro workers were known to favor, Mikhail pivoted to return to work.

From an adjoining alcove, the recently awakened Vladimir also heard the distant bark of this canine. As he lay on a narrow ledge of flat stone, his long, lean body curled in a tight, fetal ball, Vlad subconsciously absorbed this far-off sound. Satiated by his recently completed meal, his dreams had filled him with a vision of the past that seemed just as real as life itself.

He was a child again, filled with a boy's passion and innocence. At his side romped his ever-faithful terrier pup, Pasha. Together they joined Vlad's father, Prince Yuri Dolgoruki, and his *kudesnik* (soothsayer), on an outing to the banks of the river known as the Moscow. Here the prince hoped to establish a village that would take advantage of the site's excellent position on the already established, north-south trade route.

It was a crisp, clear day and the spring equinox had just passed. Happy that the worst of the winter weather was over, Vladimir ran through the thick birch wood that lay on each side of the river. Only when he reached the stream's edge did he halt to silently admire the magnificent countryside that now encompassed him.

Pasha's playful yelps signaled the arrival of Vlad's

father and the sour-faced *kudesnik* named Igor. It was Igor who set the outing's serious tone. With exacting precision he set up a number of candles and incense holders. He lit them only after muttering a long, complicated incantation. All of this was undertaken to appease the spirits of the river, for it was said that an evil creature dwelled beneath these very waters.

Vlad had always been one who took such superstitions lightly. Yet all of this quickly changed when the noon sun was mysteriously blotted out of the crystal blue sky, only seconds after the last candle had flickered out in the gentle wind. This was followed by Pasha's growls of warning and Yuri Dolgoruki's sudden shout to take cover. Though Vladimir's memories were hazy at this point, he remembered looking up into the sky, which was just barely colored with an ethereal twilight, and viewing some sort of huge, soaring bird overhead. The youngster's pulse quickened when this creature abruptly swooped down at him, revealing the astonishing fact that it had two heads, with eyes seemingly formed of fire! A sharp pain coursed through his neck, and Vlad fell to the earth unconscious.

The next thing that he remembered was waking up in his bed several days later. Pained fever drenched his brow in sweat, and he could barely manage to open his eyes and take in a scene that would stay with him forever. For there was his dear family standing about him, their sobs of sorrow clearly ringing out with the prayer of the dead. Straining with all of his might, he struggled to inform them that he was still very much alive. But his voice would not speak, and his heavy limbs lay unmoving. Was this not his deathbed? And if it was indeed, then how could he still be living?

The loud, shrill barking of that dog interrupted Vla-

dimir's macabre vision of the past. Like one who had
awakened from the portals of death, he stirred uneasily.
He opened his eyes and focused them on the cramped,
stone alcove in which he lay. Memories of his realistic
dream quickly faded. All he could think about now was
sheer survival—for he was in a time and a place that he
had absolutely no knowledge of! All that he knew for
certain was that the blood of life still coursed through his
weary veins.

It was pure instinct that guided him as he cautiously
peeked his head out of the dark recess in which he had
sought shelter. There, in the direction from which the
incessant yelping emanated, two pinpricks of advancing
light were visible. Taking in the tunnel that encompassed him, Vlad knew that escape was impossible. This
left him with but one alterative.

Anatoly Kirinsk and Viktor Chimki had each been
with Moscow's subway system for the last twenty years.
Both had been army engineers before that, and both
were expert surveyors. Used to working underground for
the better part of the day, they knew each meter of the
immense system that twisted beneath the capital city like
a snake.

Dressed in hard hats and rubberized, hip-length wad-
ers, they were exploring an ancient section of catacombs
that adjoined the tracks in this portion of town. With
the aid of their powerful flashlights, they were in the
midst of a feasibility study for future expansion of the
ever-growing system.

The passageway that they had been following for the
last hour was new to them. Not shown on any official
map, it was discovered only when a portion of the
adjoining Metro tunnel had collapsed after a major sewer

break. So far, it appeared to be very well preserved, considering its great age.

The tunnel was completely lined in stone and shored up by sturdy wooden timbers. Only a few centimeters of water covered its floor. Other than the usual spider webs and rat droppings that one would expect to find down here, the passage was remarkably free of debris, allowing the two engineers to make excellent progress.

As usual, Bambi, their loyal rat terrier, was pointing the way. Her lead was kept in check by the stout leash that Viktor Chimki held onto. Otherwise, the barking canine would be off on her own, in search of the furry rodents she was trained to track down. Both engineers knew that her mere presence kept the packs of blood-thirsty rats that abounded here deep in their burrows. Without such vermin to worry them, there was little down here to fear, except the possibility of a cave-in or an encounter with a pocket of poisonous gas.

Viktor had been Bambi's exclusive master for three years, and he could not help but notice how excited she had been all afternoon. Her unusual behavior was especially apparent this past hour. During this time her yelps were particularly agitated, and it took a genuine effort on his part to keep her from getting too far ahead of them.

"I tell you, Anatoly, this bitch of mine must be in heat," observed the heavy-framed surveyor, as he allowed himself to be tugged forward. "She hasn't acted this way since she was a pup."

Anatoly Kirensk was a good six inches shorter than his partner and had to walk almost at a trot just to keep at Viktor's side. "That might very well be, comrade. But listen, it's time to turn back now. It's getting late, and we've given the state our fair share of work already."

Viktor did not show the least inclination to stop. "But Anatoly, old friend, the river can't be far off now. I've just got to see for myself how far this passageway really extends."

Anatoly was used to his partner's headstrong ways. "Then for the love of Lenin," he panted, "if you insist on going on, will you at least slow down this exhausting pace? What's gotten into you, anyway? You act like you're in a race with the Devil himself!"

Anatoly's words reverberated sharply off the tunnel's walls, and Viktor immediately pulled back on his dog's leash. "I'm sorry, my friend. I'm afraid that I was allowing Bambi to set the pace. She'll have to remember who's master now, or she'll have an awfully sore neck in the morning."

The leash still strained tightly, but their frantic pace began to lessen. Anatoly was catching his breath, when Bambi let out a particularly shrill series of loud, whining barks.

"My heavens, Viktor, perhaps she's cornered the king of rats himself!"

"What in the world would the General Secretary be doing down here?" Viktor returned with a grin.

Despite his attempt at humor, Viktor was beginning to feel real concern. He had never heard his dog behave this way before. He was seriously considering his partner's suggestion to turn back, when Bambi's mad barking abruptly ceased. Seconds later, the leash went slack.

"What in the hell is going on up there?" cried Viktor, shooting his flashlight beam into the darkness.

Since Bambi had been at the end of a twenty-five-meter tether, he could view only that portion of the catacomb's stained walls that lay immediately before him. Unable to see his dog, Viktor's voice trembled nervously.

"I think you're right, Anatoly. It's time that we headed back. Let's just get that hound of mine, and we'll be off. Here, Bambi!"

Viktor tugged sharply on the leash. Though it was made of sturdy canvas, he felt it snap, and when he pulled it in, he could see the frayed portion where it had broken off.

"That's impossible!" observed the startled engineer. "She could have never chewed through this material. I tell you, Anatoly, something damned unusual has happened up there. Let's get to the bottom of it and get out of here."

Viktor did not wait for a response, but strode forward, his jaw set in determination. Anatoly followed a bit more hesitantly, then picked up his pace so that he could catch up with his partner, whose hefty frame had disappeared around a distant corner.

The five-foot, four-inch native Muscovite did not like their situation in the least. His intuition warned that there was danger up ahead, and his gut tightened in anticipation. With his footsteps echoing hollowly, Anatoly began his way around a curve in the tunnel. Then he heard a strange whimper up ahead. Quickly, he twisted his flashlight down to see where this sound was coming from.

The beam of his torch cut through the blackness, illuminating the kneeling figure of his partner. In his arms was what appeared to be the limp body of Bambi. It was only as Anatoly continued his approach that he saw that the dog's head had been torn off.

"What in Lenin's name happened here?" he cried out.

Viktor was on the edge of tears. "God only knows, my friend. But whatever sick beast is responsible for this atrocity has to be close by."

Anatoly nervously scanned the surrounding portion of tunnel with his torch. "Perhaps it's another dog, or maybe even a wolf. Whatever, I think it's best if we return to the station and come back tomorrow, properly armed."

He was about to redirect his light when a sudden movement caught his eye. "I see something, Viktor! Over there, by that indentation in the wall!"

Following Anatoly's pointed finger, Viktor put down the carcass of his dog and picked up his flashlight. He moved the beam upward and caught sight of an object that lay on a wide ledge, halfway up the wall. He shivered with revulsion upon identifying it as Bambi's severed head. Anger quickly overcame his shock, and he began to make his way toward the alcove.

"What in the world do you think you're doing?" Anatoly yelled. "Let's come back here when we're better prepared!"

Viktor did not even look back. He was driven solely by the thought of revenge. When he reached the shoulder-high alcove, he directed his torch's beam to illuminate its wide expanse. His dog's head stared back at him with unseeing eyes. It lay in a pool of fresh blood. The flesh of its neck was ripped open, with the underlying veins and connective tissue clearly visible.

Rage filled his being. When an icy hand touched his shoulder, he turned his head angrily, expecting to set his eyes on his partner. What he saw instead caused a wave of pure terror to overcome him. His entire body shook with fright. This tall, gaunt figure did not belong to Anatoly Kirensk. He looked more like a creature from a horrible nightmare. Viktor took in the stranger's ghostly white skin and blood red, snarling lips. Then he dropped his flashlight in shock. Unable to call out in warning, he looked on powerlessly as the stranger's hypnotic gaze bored into his own. When he saw the two spiraling balls of fire that lay encapsulated in the creature's pupils, Viktor lost all will to resist.

A dozen meters behind him, Anatoly tried to make some sort of rational sense out of the confrontation taking place before him. Anatoly looked on impotently as Viktor suddenly went down to his knees. His partner was a bear of a man who always held his own in a fight, yet he seemed to be groveling at this stranger's feet like a frightened schoolboy. Surprised at Viktor's total silence and submission, Anatoly decided to find out what the hell was going on.

His heart was pounding in his chest as he approached the alcove. He angled his flashlight to illuminate the mysterious man's gaunt figure. It took only one look at his ghoulish face to assure Anatoly that his own life was in peril. Oblivious to the fact that he was leaving his partner behind, Anatoly turned and sprinted madly down the passageway, his only concern being to put as much distance as possible between himself and that loathsome demon.

9

The dining room of the Hotel Ukraine occupied a cavernous hall dominated by massive, gilded arches and a single huge, crystal chandelier. Well-known for its elegant Victorian atmosphere, the restaurant catered especially to tourists, foreigners, and those Muscovites who could afford its steep prices. These diners were drawn not only by a lengthy menu of Soviet delicacies, but an excellent floor show as well. This evening's entertainment was a folk orchestra from Kiev.

Richard Green had always had a particular fondness for the sound of the *balalaika*. Even so, he had never seen one of the triangular-bodied, three-string instruments played in a live performance. When he mentioned this fact to his redheaded dinner companion, Yelena Lopatin made certain that the maitre d' seated them as close to the stage as possible.

Over a glass of rather sweet Soviet champagne and an order of beluga caviar, they sat back and listened as the band completed its first show of the evening. Richard found the music delightfully refreshing. He enjoyed its wild harmonies, irregular rhythms, and invigorating tonal qualities. Though many of the pieces were new to him, he did recognize an excellent rendition of *Midnight in Moscow*, and Rimski-Korsakov's stirring *Flight of the Bumble Bee.* Immediately after this selection, the orchestra took its break.

Yelena lifted her glass and toasted. "To the music of the Motherland. May its rich melodies bring peace between our peoples."

"I'll second that," returned Richard as he raised his own glass and clinked it against Yelena's. After taking an appreciative sip of champagne, he added, "You know, during the concert I couldn't help but think that if the American people only had more exposure to Soviet culture, especially its music, they'd understand what a rich heritage you have here. Too many of my countrymen have absolutely no idea of what life in the Soviet Union is really like."

"We're not all cold, ruthless warmongers, are we, Dr. Green?" observed the archaeologist, a smile crinkling the corners of her mouth.

"That's Richard to you. Now help me out with this caviar. It's really delicious."

Yelena needed no more prompting to reach for a piece of sliced bread, to which she added a coating of cream cheese and a spoonful of black caviar. She took a bite and savored the rich, slightly salty taste. Richard did likewise and lightly commented, "One benefit of being a Soviet is being able to enjoy such a treat every night of the week."

Yelena shook her head. "If that were only the case, comrade. To tell you the truth, I haven't had a bite of real beluga since my sister's wedding, eight months ago. Most of it is prepared for export, and the precious little that stays here is priced far beyond the average citizen's means."

"Well, then," said Richard. "I guess that means we'd better not waste a single bite."

As both of them finished off the caviar, the waiter arrived with their soup. The bowls were filled to the rim with piping hot broth. Richard stirred it to reveal thick slices of carrots, celery, onions, potatoes, cabbage and sausage.

"Are you finding your accommodations comfortable?" asked Yelena between bites of sausage.

Richard wiped his lips with his napkin before answering. "Actually, I'm afraid the mattress was a bit too inviting. What was intended as a half-hour nap lasted the entire afternoon. You see, I had planned to get to that translation much earlier."

"Well, at least you got some rest, Richard. The vault I brought up from the Carpathians has waited for us for at least a thousand years. Surely a proper unraveling of its mysteries can wait another day or two."

With this, the waiter arrived with their entrees. Both had selected tonight's house specialty, chicken Kiev. Prepared perfectly, the tender breast oozed pure butter when it was sliced. Accompanying this dish were ample side orders of brown rice and steamed mixed vegetables.

"Everything is marvelous, Yelena," Richard exclaimed, after both had feasted in silence for several minutes. "Now tell me, how did your radiocarbon dating test go?"

Yelena put down her fork. "The results are still inconclusive, but we can be pretty sure that the vault was originally buried in the tenth or eleventh century. We still have no idea what happened to its original contents, though."

Polishing off the last bite of chicken, Richard pushed his plate away and took a sip of champagne. "Well, perhaps this information will help. It took a bit of searching, but it appears that the writing carved into the coffin's lid is Moldavian Greek in origin. The translation corresponds to the numerals 666."

Yelena finished her meal and thoughtfully sipped her drink. "That's certainly peculiar. Could it be a date?"

"Either that or a symbolic code of some sort," Richard said guardedly.

Yelena leaned forward to speak just as the band began to tune their instruments beside them. "This all sounds fascinating, Richard. Do you mind if we continue this discussion elsewhere? My apartment is only a few blocks away, and at least we can talk there without having to shout."

Richard patted his stomach and nodded. "That sounds fine with me. After all that food, stretching these legs will be most appreciated. I'll just take care of the check, and then you can lead the way."

To a resounding chorus of *balalaikas* they left the restaurant and exited the hotel. It was rather chilly outside, and Richard gratefully ducked into Yelena's awaiting Lada automobile. This compact vehicle was sparse on accessories, but its heater worked well and was soon spewing out a welcome current of warm air.

The traffic was light and Richard sat back to enjoy the ride, which proved to be a short one. Yelena's apartment complex was a modern, multistoried affair and one of the few in Moscow to offer heated garage parking to its tenants. Though all of the building's four elevators were currently out of service, Richard did not mind the climb to the seventh floor. By the time he reached the doorway to her apartment he was a bit winded but none the worse for wear.

While Yelena went into the kitchen to prepare tea, Richard remained in the living room. Comfortably furnished, the room contained a large couch, two upholstered chairs, and a large glass cabinet that immediately caught Richard's attention. Lining its shelves were an assortment of objects. He identified a pair of intricately carved walrus tusks, a miniature jade elephant, several jagged arrowheads, and a collection of ancient burlap dolls. While he was marveling at their hand-painted features, the voice of his hostess issued from behind him.

"Those are spirit dolls, Richard. I came across them while on a dig in Turkmenistan. They were sealed inside a burial urn and are approximately four hundred years old."

"It looks like you have a whole family here," observed Richard.

Yelena reached his side. "You are quite astute, comrade, for this is indeed representative of the family of the deceased. The dolls were buried along with the corpse to accompany it into the afterlife. When the body was later transferred to the institute to be dissected, I felt that it was my responsibility to adopt the nine figures you see before you. They've been in my possession ever since."

"If those fellows could only talk, think of the tales they could tell." Richard smiled.

Yelena grinned. "Sometimes, when I'm alone here at night, I swear I can feel something from their presence. It's nothing malevolent or anything, just a distinct sensation that I'm not so alone after all."

"Now, how about joining me on the couch for some tea?" Richard seated himself beside his hostess, who wasted no time in renewing the conversation. "You mentioned earlier that the numerals 666 might have a symbolic meaning. What did you mean by that?"

Richard cleared his throat and took a sip of tea. "In the last book of the Bible, the numerical sequence 666 is said to be representative of the Devil. It is also known as the Mark of the Beast."

"Ah, so it has origins in Christian mythology," sighed Yelena. "I have read both the Old and New Testaments and find them somewhat remarkable historical chronicles. Are you a very religious man, Richard?"

Not certain what the archaeologist was getting at, he answered as honestly as possible. "I was raised in a devout Roman Catholic family, and even though I'm presently on the staff of a Jesuit institution, I haven't actively practiced my religion since I was a teen-ager. Why do you ask?"

"I don't mean to be nosy," Yelena said softly, discerning his sensitivity. "I just wanted to know a bit more about your background. You see, my own mother was a devout believer herself. She made certain that I was baptized and that I had an elementary religious education. I, too, strayed from the Church soon after entering upper school."

This revelation caused Richard to beam with surprise. "You don't say. And here I thought that I might be in the company of a hard-line Communist agnostic."

Yelena shook her head. "No, I'm not even a Party member, though I must admit that I've been fully indoctrinated. Our Socialist forefathers had some brilliant economic theories, but I'm afraid that their spiritual values left a bit to be desired. You see, from the beginning, Lenin held that religion was basically opposed to the materialistic world outlook that was so essential for Communism to be successful. Since the Church preached that the good life would come not as a result of revolutionary effort, but in Heaven through divine grace, Lenin feared that Church followers would be satisfied with their lot in life. Thus they would accept their station rather than seek to change it at the expense of their masters. In this way not only was religion hostile to science and materialism, but supportive of a privileged class as well."

Richard continued. "I read once that Communism is a religion all in itself, which sees the state as God, work as worship, and social order as the promised land. It even has its own holy trinity: Marx, Engels, and Lenin."

"That very well may be," reflected Yelena. "In fact, that train of thought is probably what kept me from surrendering my soul to Communism in the first place. I don't believe that I could ever exist thinking only of this life, planning only in terms of my physical needs. Though the Communists say any belief in God is an indication of a self-deluding inferiority complex, I couldn't exist without God. Just think how drab and dull life would be without the mystery of creation to ponder!"

Richard grinned and took a sip of his tea. "I take it that you keep these beliefs to yourself."

"Most certainly," replied Yelena. "Though times here have changed somewhat, this sort of talk will get you nothing but trouble. Archaeology is my passion, and I wouldn't like to find my area of exploration limited to a patch of Siberian permafrost. Now, what is your expert opinion as to why the numerals 666 have been so carefully carved into the lid of that sarcophagus?"

The American decided to express himself fully. "Though this is all mere speculation, I'd say that whoever was buried in that coffin was an enemy of the Church. Most likely it was under Church auspices that the remains were interred and the lid thus inscribed for all eternity."

"I can't help but wonder who this mystery person could be," said the frustrated Soviet. "My first guess was that we had chanced upon the tomb of a Scythian war-lord. I could have sworn that it would be intact as I watched it being pulled from the earth. Since someone else has apparently beaten me to the remains, all that I can do is try to investigate the numerals further. Perhaps I'll be able to learn more about its original contents that way.

"But enough of my selfish concerns. More tea?"

Richard patted his stomach. "No, thank you. But do you mind if I smoke?"

"Of course not, comrade. Would you like a cigarette?"

Richard politely declined, and instead pulled out his trusty Canadian and a soft leather pouch full of tobacco. After carefully loading the bowl of the pipe and tamping the tobacco down, he put a match to it. The room soon filled with the sweet aroma of vanilla and rum.

"By the way, Yelena, do you happen to know anything about those Serbian manuscripts that prompted Dr. Yakhut to invite me here?"

Yelena paused to refill their tea cups. "Well, I was in the Carpathians at the time of their initial discovery," she said, "but since then I've heard from the professor whose expedition chanced upon the find. Not only have they proved to be genuine, but several centuries older than originally assumed. Altogether, there are dozens of separate documents. Dr. Yakhut feels that they may have been part of an ancient library. Because of the complexity of the dialect in which they were recorded, they have only managed to translate a few pages. Thus, the bulk of the project is awaiting your most capable attention."

Richard took another draw on his pipe and then yawned. "Speaking of the project, I believe I still haven't quite recovered from jet lag. I'd like to be at the institute bright and early. Could I impose on you to call a taxi for me?"

"I'll do nothing of the sort," said Yelena. "Come, my own humble limousine awaits you below."

Realizing that she was not about to take no for an answer, Richard acquiesced. As they made their way downstairs, he accepted her offer to pick him up first thing in the morning. He had genuinely enjoyed her company and found himself looking forward to his first full workday on Soviet soil.

By the time Mikhail Antonov and Yuri Sorokin left the morgue and their paperwork behind them, it was well past eight in the evening. Yet before they could return to their homes for a well-deserved rest, they found themselves with one more job to complete. This task took them back to MVD headquarters, where they had been ordered to clear their lockers of all personal belongings. This order merely served to finalize their abrupt change of assignments.

Up to this time, Yuri had been certain that their transfer to the coroner's department was only temporary. Now he was beginning to wonder if his ten years of hard work for the MVD had all gone for naught. His partner could not help but share his concern.

The two men were silent as they began to empty their lockers. Mikhail had but a few pieces of clothing, magazines, and toiletries to contend with, while his partner had ten years' worth of personal effects to handle.

Several cardboard cartons had been set aside to help them with their packing. Fortunately for them, the locker room remained empty of other detectives, and they were able to proceed without having to explain themselves. Though the entire staff was surely well aware of their reassignment by now, the thought of facing them at this moment was not at all appealing.

It took just less than fifteen minutes to complete their unpleasant task. With their cartons in hand, they left the locker room through a side exit that led directly to the parking lot. Quickly now, they headed for the shelter of their rust-worn Volga. Halfway across the lot, they were illuminated by the headlights of an approaching vehicle. Yuri cursed and hurried toward the Volga as a black-paneled police van pulled up beside him. He was fumbling for the trunk key when the driver of the van emerged and greeted him.

"Well, good evening, Comrade Sorokin. What brings you here at this late hour?"

"Hello Anton," returned Yuri dully, "my partner and I were just moving out our things."

Detective Anton Valerian had joined the MVD not long after Yuri and his tone rang out with sincerity. "I still can't believe that the colonel is handing you over to the coroner so readily. At least your new boss is a likable enough chap. In fact, I hear that Stura is quite the ladies' man."

"That may very well be," responded Yuri, as his hand went to his breast pocket to pull out a smoke.

Anton Valerian was quick to pull out a matchbook and light his colleague's cigarette. "Well, look at it this way: at least you won't have to deal anymore with the type of nut case that sent us out this evening. You wouldn't believe what this lunatic has been rambling on about."

With this, Valerian's partner went to unlock the van's side door. Cautiously, he beckoned their prisoner to join them. Seconds later, a small, thin-framed figure climbed hesitantly out of the van. Yuri could tell from the man's rubber boots and helmet that he was a Metro worker. With his face and coveralls stained with dirt, he looked out with wild eyes.

"Please, you've got to go back there and save Viktor! After what that hideous creature did to our poor Bambi, he won't stand a chance!"

Conscious that no one was paying serious attention to his rantings, the Metro worker turned abruptly and attempted to flee. He only managed to go a few steps before running into the iron grasp of Mikhail Antonov.

"I'm sorry, Comrade Antonov," offered Detective Valerian, who quickly stepped to Mikhail's side to take possession of his prisoner. "We should have cuffed him and put the leg irons on him the moment we apprehended him back at the Universitet station."

"What was he doing down there?" questioned Mikhail.

Anton Valerian was quick to answer. "Believe it or not, this fool had crawled out onto the tracks and was threatening to stop all train traffic with his body, if need be. He seems to think that there's a monster down in the Metro system. The monster supposedly attacked both him and his partner before he managed to escape."

Yuri Sorokin stepped forward. "Has he been drinking?"

Anton shook his head. "It doesn't appear that he has. I'd say that it's more likely his had a nervous breakdown."

"Has anyone checked out his story yet?" asked Mikhail.

"No, but I imagine that the colonel will most likely have us follow it up," answered Anton disgustedly. "That's just how I want to spend the rest of my shift, crawling around some damp, musty Metro tunnel, all because of a lunatic's ravings."

Remembering that his colleagues had their own problems, Anton's tone softened. "Well, we'd better get on with it. Good luck to you, comrades."

As the MVD veteran ambled off toward the station house with his whimpering prisoner in tow, Mikhail commented, "Isn't the Universitet Metro station near the underground tunnel we found earlier today?"

"I believe they're less than a kilometer apart," Yuri said lightly. "Why do you ask? I hope it isn't because you suspect this man's monster was also responsible for the death of our poor dutywoman."

Mikhail smiled. "No, not that, comrade. I just couldn't help but marvel at the coincidence of it all."

"It's a small world, all right," Yuri said, yawning. "Now, how about us loading up our belongings and getting out of here? I don't know about you, but this old-timer is beat!"

Looking forward to a hot shower, a good meal, and a comfortable mattress, Mikhail turned back to the Volga. His partner was close by his side.

Deep beneath the streets of Moscow, Vladimir Dolgoruki lay his bloated body on the damp, stone floor of the alcove. He had fed well, and a comalike drowsiness was calling him to sleep. After he positioned his limbs in a tight, embryonic ball, his dreams returned.

He was a lad again, lying on his deathbed after succumbing to the bite of the fiery-eyed, flying demon. Through his feverish gaze he could see his family gathered around him, their eyes wet with mourning.

Beside his weeping mother stood a black-robed stranger who was muttering some sort of incantation. It was only later that Vlad learned that this mysterious, dark-eyed elder had been summoned to Vlad's bedside by his father. His father had desperately scoured the region in an effort to find a physician who could cure his ailing son. Vlad's condition continued to deteriorate. A bargain was struck, and the so-called miracle worker pledged to bring the boy back from the portals of death in exchange for a future say in the rule of the prince's new village, which was to be known as Moscow. Three days later, Vlad's fever miraculously broke, and he awoke from his coma like one who had risen from a sound night's sleep.

The months passed, and Vlad grew strong and smart. It was on the eve of his sixteenth birthday that a messenger arrived with horrifying news. Approaching the young village of Moscow from the east was an army of crazed, yellow-skinned horsemen, known as Tartars. Ferocious and cruel, they spared no one in their path. Vlad's birthday was spent preparing the town's defenses, and a week later, the Tartar hordes attacked.

It was during the initial siege that Vlad first tasted human blood. This fated event came when the lad's broadsword sliced into the neck of a charging cavalryman. Some of the Tartar's blood spurted onto Vlad's parched lips. Strangely enough, he was not repulsed, but instead found it stimulating. In the days that followed, he was to find himself secretly slaking his thirst on the corpses of friend and foe alike.

Eventually, the Tartars withdrew. Yet as life returned to normal, Vlad's craving for blood intensified. This desire was especially strong with the arrival of the full moon. At such a time, his thirst rose unbearably. At first he tried to satisfy it with the blood of small animals such as rabbits, cats, and dogs. When these sources failed to stimulate him, Vlad sneaked out into the countryside and began abducting his first human victims. He soon learned that virgin blood was the most powerful and ever after he sought young females in particular.

It was almost a year to the day of the first Tartar attack that Vlad was exposed. Upset with the rash of strange deaths that had taken an unusually high number of maidens to early graves, the suspicious townspeople set a trap. One of the local *boyars* sent for his daughter, who had until that time been living in Kiev. Well known for her comeliness, she was allowed to set up house for herself in the deep woods, with only a single maid in attendance. Vlad took the bait, and on the night that the moon rose full, he stalked her. Unbeknownst to him, a band of locals had hidden in the surrounding woods, waiting to see what the night would bring.

They chased him all the way back to his father's castle, where he took shelter in the catacombs. Yet even there he was not safe, for the townspeople brought their hunting dogs to sniff him out. With this pack on his heels, he sprinted down the narrow, winding maze of tunnels and eventually made it to the banks of the underground river that lay beneath the castle. Exhausted, he let the current pull him northward.

Dawn was just breaking over the eastern horizon when he scrambled out of the river and climbed into the surrounding hills. Just when it appeared that he had indeed made his escape, he heard the sickening sound of barking dogs in the distance. Running again for his life, Vlad entered a section of the forest that he had never before explored. A thick mass of birch trees encompassed him, and above him the ravens called out harshly. His lungs were heaving in exhaustion. The sound of the ever-approaching pack seemed to be intensifying when he emerged into a clearing. Waiting for him there was a man whose appearance chilled the roots of his dark soul.

Well into his seventies, the white-robed elder sported a full head of silver hair and a thick beard to match. His vibrant blue stare locked with Vlad's as he lifted a wooden spear high over his head and spoke out distinctly.

His words were confusing, for he identified himself as Father Nikon the Pursuer, whose sole purpose in life was to hunt the likes of Vlad. Though Vlad was certainly younger and stronger than this mysterious elder, the spear that he held above him sent waves of terror streaking down Vlad's spine. Without a doubt in his mind, he somehow knew that this weapon was the only instrument that could truly harm him.

Vlad cringed with horror as the old-timer took a step forward. Vlad's total attention was locked on the pointed spearhead, when a sudden commotion broke from the woods behind him. He remembered hearing the mad barking of dogs and the thumping, pounding sound of horses' hooves. Seconds later, a detachment of Tartar calvary rushed into the clearing. One of the horsemen grabbed him by his shoulders, and Vlad was soon holding the warrior's waist with a snorting stallion now beneath him. Both confusion and relief guided his thoughts, as the powerful voice of the white-haired elder screamed out that he would wait to finish his mission for all eternity if necessary. Vlad remembered how the sound of yelping hunting dogs quickly faded, replaced solely by the sound of the galloping horses that had rescued him.

Vlad's realistic vision of the past was broken by—of all things—the barking of distant dogs. He awoke from his sound slumber groggily at first, but it did not take his reawakened senses long to sharpen.

Once again, he found himself in an unknown time

and place. Stimulated by his recent feedings, his thoughts urged him farther into the dark catacombs that had sheltered him so far. There he could feed safely, away from the pathetic mortals that were forever attempting to track him down. For he knew now that once he attained his full strength, there was only one object that he need fear. And once this spear was in his possession, his safety would be insured for all eternity!

10

The ringing of his bedside telephone woke Mikhail Antonov from a sound slumber. It took several confused seconds before he emerged from deep sleep. He groped for the receiver and a single glance at the alarm clock showed it to be half past four in the morning.

"Antonov here," mumbled Mikhail groggily. The voice that greeted him was Yuri Sorokin's. "Sorry about the early wake-up call, partner, but duty calls once more. We've been ordered back to the morgue with all due haste. Can you be downstairs in twenty minutes?"

Mikhail looked at the clock again. "I'll be waiting for you. Drive carefully."

Only after he hung up the phone did he wonder what was calling them back to work so damned early. He wearily sat up in bed, yawned, scratched his chin, and reached over to turn on the lamp. The light struck him like a flare, and it took another thirty seconds or so for his eyes to adjust to the brightness. To awaken fully, he decided to head straight for the shower.

Since the hot water in his apartment building did not flow until six in the morning, he was forced to bathe in a torrent of icy water. It might as well be a Siberian stream, he thought grimly. Mikhail finished his shower, wrapped a towel around his waist, and walked over to the kitchen counter to switch on his electric coffee percolator. Made in America, he had confiscated it during a recent arrest and adapted its current. As was his habit, he had loaded the percolator before going to bed, and thus would have a piping hot cup ready in less than three minutes. He walked back to the bathroom to brush his teeth and shave while the coffee perked.

His gums were bleeding heavily as usual, and he knew that he ought to make an appointment with the dentist. He had been putting this visit off for the better part of a year. Now that he had the best oral surgeons in the Motherland available to him in Moscow, he knew that his only excuse was cowardice.

After he had gargled, and spit the bloody rinse into the stained basin, Mikhail reached over for his can of shaving cream. Another item that seemed to be available only here in the capital, he had expropriated the can from the stash of a black marketeer. At least he would not have to whip up his own foam today, Mikhail thought and carefully spread the thick white cream onto his cheeks, jaw and neck.

A week ago, Yuri had given him a package of American razor blades. Not about to ask where his partner had obtained such a treasure, Mikhail was able to enjoy a smooth, cut-free shave, even without the benefit of hot water. As he wiped the leftover cream from his face, he studied the reflection that stared back at him in the mirror.

Sucking in his slight paunch, he knew that he was at an age when his belly could quickly get unmanageable. Though he would like to spend more time at the gym, his frantic schedule just would not allow it. At least his shoulders, arms and chest were still solid with muscle, the result of a decade of weightlifting.

Mikhail could see the evidence of thirty-eight years on his face. Crow's-feet were just beginning to form at the corners of his dark green eyes. His facial skin seemed to be stretched tightly over his pronounced cheeks and square, dimpled chin. Fortunately, his mop of blond hair was intact. It was this feature, plus his large build, that had earned him his boyhood nickname—the Swede.

The scent of coffee diverted him from the mirror and into the kitchen. Still clothed in only a bath towel, he poured himself a full mug of the aromatic, dark brown brew. It was a rarity even here in the capital. Too hot to drink, he decided first to dress himself.

Mikhail's current position demanded that he supply his own uniform. His working wardrobe consisted of five brown, Polish-made suits. Identical in cut, he had bought them last fall in Chabarovsk. At the same time he had also purchased a dozen white dress shirts, three pairs of brown loafers, and several ties, all in varying shades of red. He found that having such a simple selection saved him time in the morning, for he could just grab any garment that was clean and not have to worry about coordinating a new outfit. Thus he was able to dress himself in a matter of minutes and have some time left over to enjoy his coffee before heading downstairs.

He had moved into Moscow with a minimum of personal belongings. As luck would have it, the three-room flat to which he had been assigned came with an assortment of well-used furniture.

The table was covered with groceries. It also held the remnants of his last three nights' meals. Looking beyond the open tins of canned fish, the empty milk bottles, and chunks of stale bread, he surveyed the adjoining living room. It could sure use a cleanup. A narrow sofa, two end tables, and a pair of hard, straight-backed chairs were the limits of his furnishings. At the end of the room, a solitary double-paned window looked out to a high-rise built exactly like the one he occupied. He could almost see a portion of clear sky from this window.

In an effort to give the room a bit of character, he had purchased a large poster that showed the magnificent, wooded shores of Lake Baikal. He had tacked it to the far wall, and usually found his gaze captured by its tableaux whenever he sat down at the dinette to eat or drink. This morning proved no different. Mikhail appreciatively sipped his coffee and surrendered his gaze to this photograph of one tiny portion of the world's largest freshwater lake.

It was nearly thirty years ago that Mikhail's father had first taken him to the shores of Lake Baikal. Almost two thousand kilometers west of Chabarovsk, the lake was accessible only by train. The ride itself proved a great adventure for Mikhail, who until that time had never been out of the town of his birth.

His father's position as a senior customs official allowed him the luxury of being able to frequently satisfy his one great passion in life: fishing. And nowhere did the trout, salmon, and pike grow more monstrous than in Lake Baikal. More than a mile deep in places, it was fed by thousands of Siberian tributaries, all rich with minerals and nutrients. Several of these were of volcanic origin and fed into the icy waters of Baikal, trailing bubbling wisps of steam in their wake. Near these warmer places the seals tended to gather. Such graceful creatures had been unknown to eight-year-old Mikhail before his first trip, and he had watched in wide-eyed wonder as they frolicked. Soon afterward, he proudly pulled in his first pike, its narrow, skinny body almost longer than

Mikhail's own.

He and his father had returned home several days later with their ice chest filled to the brim with freshly caught fish, many of trophy size. Mikhail could not help but feel that his father treated him more like a man after their outing together.

They were only able to visit the lake together five more times. Shortly after his thirteenth birthday, his father was killed by a group of Chinese commandos during a border skirmish. Since then the fishing excursions to Lake Baikal had held a special place in Mikhail's heart, for as long as their memory remained bright, his father would always be with him.

Mikhail often wondered what his father would say about his son's life. His father had many friends in the military, and he had hoped that Mikhail would become a career officer. Forced on his own when his mother passed away a week after he graduated from upper school, Mikhail had immediately enlisted in the army. He left the armed forces a decade later, having worked his way up to the rank of first lieutenant in the military police. Because of his superb record, the MVD offered him a position back home in Chabarovsk.

Then he met Lara and, three months later, Mikhail found himself engaged. His intended bride had thick brown hair, flashing dark eyes, and no love for police work. She found it overly dangerous and immediately began to pressure Mikhail to seek safer employment after they were married. He genuinely enjoyed his work, and when it came down to choosing between the MVD and marriage, he was forced to issue his fiancee an ultimatum—either accept his chosen profession or the engagement would end. Lara left Chabarovsk three days later, to return to her parents' home in Kiev. And

Mikhail remained a bachelor.

In the weeks and months that followed, Mikhail's work became almost an obsession with him. He gave up his social life to bring law and order to the wild frontier settlement. His sacrifice showed results, as the crime figures fell during three successive quarters. And when the orders arrived transferring him to Moscow, his coworkers looked at him with envy.

The Center had almost a mystical quality to it, especially to those who lived in remote areas like Chabarovsk. Somehow Mikhail had thought that his life would be less empty in the capital, and for the first couple of weeks it had been. Now the novelty was wearing off, and Mikhail knew that Moscow was far from being a Socialist utopia.

Just as in the Soviet Far East, the capital was now in the midst of a war against crime. Violent homicides were at an all-time high, and transgressions like armed robbery, rape, and aggravated assault were occurring with an unprecedented regularity. When Mikhail considered the active black market and rapidly growing drug culture here as well, it seemed to him that the Center was fighting for its very existence.

Mikhail emptied his mug and saw that it was time to be off. He grabbed his hat and coat and left his apartment to begin the twisting climb down the thirteen flights of stairs that would bring him to ground level. It was still so early that the dutywoman, who acted as the building's concierge, had yet to take up her position behind the front desk. Alone in the darkened foyer, he put on his overcoat and quickly ducked outside.

It was a raw, frigid morning. A stiff wind blew in from the northwest, bringing with it freezing cold and just a hint of icy drizzle. Mikhail pulled up his woolen collar, and was considering whether or not to wait indoors, when a familiar gray vehicle turned down the deserted street. Though the Volga's windows were veiled by steam, he knew in an instant that the driver was Yuri.

"Good morning," he called, as he gratefully vaulted inside.

Yuri gave him a withering glance. "My, aren't you the bright-eyed one! I don't have to tell you what my sweetheart and I were in the middle of doing when that call from the department arrived. And here I thought that our new assignment would at the very least give us some decent hours."

Mikhail reached out to buckle his seat belt when the Volga hit a slick patch of newly formed ice and slid to the left. Yuri steered into the unexpected skid and soon had the car back under control. Reaching over to downshift, he observed, "So this is the early spring that everyone was talking about for the last couple of days. I wouldn't be surprised if this front brings a major snowstorm in its wake. That'll bring those dreamers back to reality soon enough."

"Back in Chabarovsk, we had snows well into June," returned Mikhail. "Even with the arrival of summer, we always had a sweater close by, in case the northern winds decided to blow. By the way, do you have any hint of why we've been called back on such short notice?"

Yuri steered them off the side street where his partner's apartment had been located, and directed the Volga onto a wide, six-lane thoroughfare that was practically empty of traffic. Only then did he answer.

"Actually, I have no idea. I believe it was Dr. Stura's assistant who placed the call. Now there's a looker for you. Do you think Stura's played doctor with her yet?" he asked with a wink.

Mikhail grinned. "If Pavl Barvicha is to be believed,

Stura has bedded practically every woman on his staff by now."

The mere mention of the good-natured photographer seemed to lighten Yuri's spirits. "Comrade Barvicha has certainly been known to tell his share of tall tales," he said. "Still, in this instance, I've got to believe him. Our esteemed coroner has the eye of a wolf, and his assistant is too much a woman to ignore."

"Why, I heard that Albert Stura has been happily married for the past twenty years," Mikhail said.

"Now you know why they say *happily*," Yuri returned.

Mikhail chuckled and reached forward to switch on the radio. A blast of static emanated from the speaker, and he hit the dashboard hard with the flat of his hand. Almost instantly, the interference faded, to be replaced by the mournful strains of a symphony that Yuri was quick to identify.

"Ah, Tchaikovsky's *Symphony Number Six in B Minor*, the infamous *Pathetique*. You know, it is said that Tchaikovsky wept continuously while composing this score. Since he died of cholera only nine days after the work's first performance, perhaps it was a premonition of death, a self-written requiem. Whatever, this music certainly fits the sullen mood of Moscow on a gray, frigid morning like this one."

A powerful gust of wind struck the car head-on, and the battered automobile seemed to shudder in response. The icy draft prompted Yuri to turn the heater's fan to full, but even then it was barely able to counter the sudden drop in temperature. Used to such trivial discomforts, the two veteran investigators merely pulled their overcoats closed a bit tighter. Surrendering themselves to the music, they sat back, each man silently absorbed in a foreboding chorus of violins.

A quarter of an hour later, they turned onto Piro-govskaya Street and pulled up to the nondescript brick building where Moscow's main morgue was situated. A light snow shower was falling, and Yuri cursed when he could not find a decent parking place. Since he was in no mood to walk, he pulled the Volga onto the snow-covered median strip that was located immediately in front of the entrance and parked. The symphony that had captivated them for most of their trip was just com-ing to a sorrowful conclusion as they exited the car and crossed the street on foot.

Inside the morgue the air was stifling, heavy with the scent of disinfectant. Both men removed their coats and signed in at the reception desk. Then they proceeded straight for the coroner's office. Waiting for them in the anteroom were Pavl Barvicha and Anton Valerian, the heavyset detective whom they had encountered just last night in the parking lot at MVD headquarters. The vet-eran investigator was somber-faced and appeared exhausted, his baggy suit smeared with grime and soot. As he met his colleagues' inquisitive glances, his voice crackled alive.

"During all my years on the force, I've never seen any-thing quite like it before. To think that another human being could be responsible for such a thing!"

With this, Valerian began to tremble and Pavl Bar-vicha reached out to calm him. Yuri could sense how shaken his coworker was and addressed his question to the photographer instead.

"What in the hell is he talking about, Pavl?"

Before the photographer could reply, Anton Valerian answered in a quivering voice. "You both remember that crazed Metro worker we were bringing in last night? Well, just like I said, Colonel Kukhar sent me and my partner underground to check the man's story out first-hand. I could have sworn that it was all going to be a wild-goose chase, but I accepted the Metro department's offer to send along a pack of terriers to escort us, anyway. No use in exposing ourselves to a needless rat bite. So off we went down through the Universitet station and into the bowels of the system itself.

"It's funny, but I was still thinking that this whole thing was a complete waste of time, even as our dogs chanced upon an opening in the Metro wall that was not on any map. The barking mutts led us straight into a portion of the ancient catacombs that still undercuts the south side of Moscow to this day. Considering its age, the passageway was in amazingly good shape, so I decided to go on, at least as far as it appeared safe to do so.

"I was just beginning to reconsider my decision when the dogs really began barking up a storm. It took all of our effort to restrain them, and minutes later, we saw what was causing their upset.

"I can still see it in my mind's eye, as clear as the moment I first stumbled upon that poor fellow's torn body. What kind of maniac could be responsible for such a demented thing?"

Once more Valerian's body began trembling uncontrollably. He started sobbing, and Pavl Barvicha vainly tried to calm him.

This time it was Mikhail Antonov who probed. "What in the world did he find down there, Pavl?"

The photographer looked up. "Comrade Valerian here and his partner discovered the remains of a Metro worker and his dog. The terrier had been cleanly decapitated, while the engineer's corpse was found partially devoured."

"Was it rats again?" asked Yuri.

Pavl shook his head solemnly. "This is the sick part, comrades, for it appears that the bites were caused by another human being. Dr. Stura is completing the autopsy as we speak."

There was a moment of silence as the two newcomers absorbed this shocking revelation.

"Perhaps it was the other Metro worker who did this despicable thing," Yuri observed matter-of-factly. "He certainly didn't appear to be in his right mind when we confronted him last night."

"I agree," added Mikhail.

The photographer sighed. "The man you speak of is currently in this building, where tests have just been conducted to see if he's the one responsible."

"And if he's not?" dared Mikhail.

Pavl nervously cleared his throat. "I really didn't think that it was important to share this with you, but the more I contemplate it, the more I believe otherwise. Yesterday afternoon, right after we discovered the duty-woman's body, I found a trail of footprints left in the soot beside the furnace. This track led right to the crack in the wall where we found the underground passage-way. That passage could very well be the entrance to the same catacombs that Anton and his partner were search-ing late last night. What if those footprints don't belong to the old woman as I presumed, and what if the rats weren't really what caused her death in the first place?"

Mikhail seemed astounded by this train of thought. "Are you saying that some third party, with a taste for human flesh, could be responsible for both the dutywo-man's and the Metro worker's deaths?"

Before Pavl could answer him, the door to the office flew open and in walked Dr. Albert Stura, his assistant Sasha, and Colonel Yakov Kukhar. The coroner nodded

grimly at Anton Valerian. Sasha took this as her cue and
walked over to the hefty detective's side, where she
addressed him compassionately. "Come now, detective,
how about coming with me for a nice cup of tea? Then
we'll see about getting you a clean change of clothes."

In no condition to resist her offer, Anton meekly nodded his head. Sasha smiled, then took him by the arm
and slowly led him out of the room.

Once the door shut behind them, Dr. Stura led the
remaining group into his inner office and sat down
behind his cluttered desk. Colonel Kukhar sat down in a
chair facing him, while the three investigators remained
standing.

The coroner turned to Mikhail Antonov and Yuri
Sorokin. "Well, comrades, I'm certain that you've heard
all about our gruesome find from your big-mouthed
coworker. The results of the initial autopsy are still not
final, but it appears that the Metro worker indeed died
from shock induced by a massive loss of blood. We discovered dozens of bite marks that were particularly dense
near the region of the victim's carotid artery. In the surrounding tissue, we found evidence leading us to believe
that the body was then chewed on, for much of the flesh
was torn from the corpse and is missing.

"Could these bites be caused by rats?" Yuri asked.

The coroner looked to the impassive face of Colonel
Kukhar before answering. "No, Comrade Sorokin, this
time the bites appear to be human."

Yuri took a second to absorb this macabre revelation.
"Was it his partner who did this?" he asked as calmly as
he could.

"We're still testing, but it appears that the bites don't
match up," said Stura coldly. "The . . . individual
responsible for this atrocity had unusually long and

pointed canine teeth. In fact, the only similar pattern of teeth marks that I can compare them to are that of a wolf."

"Well, maybe that's your culprit," Yuri said.

"That's preposterous!" boomed the authoritative voice of Colonel Kukhar. "There's no time for such outlandish statements, Lieutenant Sorokin. I'd appreciate it if you'd keep such idiotic comments to yourself."

Albert Stura was quick to interject. "I think what the colonel is trying to say is that we are absolutely certain that the suspect is human. We've got a description of the bastard. Colonel, I believe you still have the transcript. Why not share it with our associates?"

A bitter scowl flashed across Kukhar's face as he intently eyed the three investigators. While silently appraising them, he reluctantly reached into his breast pocket and removed a leather-bound notebook. He flipped open the cover and began to read aloud.

"The suspect is a middle-aged, white male. Unusually tall and thin, he was last seen wearing what is described as a frayed and stained, full-length brown robe, similar to those worn by Orthodox priests. Since the Metro engineer's corpse was found stripped of his white coveralls, there is a chance that our suspect has changed costume.

"Though the lighting inside the subterranean tunnel was poor, the surviving engineer was able to give us a somewhat detailed description of the suspect's face. When the engineer calms down sufficiently, I'll get him together with the department's sketch artist. From what he initially described of the killer's facial features, this portrait should give us an excellent idea of just what the maniac looks like.

"He's reported to have long, scraggly, black hair, with a rather gaunt, angular face. His skin is pale, and he has a pointed, clean-shaven jaw, pursed, reddish lips, a thin nose, and highly defined cheekbones. The eyes are described as dark and piercing, with pupils glowing with a fiery red tint."

"Did the surviving Metro engineer actually see this person attack his partner?" Mikhail asked.

Meeting the blond-haired detective's inquisitive gaze, the colonel responded. "Right now, we believe that he ran off only seconds before his partner was murdered."

"Why didn't he try to intercede?" asked Yuri.

"The man was simply terrified," offered the coroner. "We've presently got him upstairs, where we took an impression of his bite. He's still greatly affected by the confrontation. One thing that is most apparent is that whatever he saw, he really believes is real."

"And there's more," the colonel added. "It now looks as if this same person could be responsible for two other homicides, both of which, by coincidence, you initially investigated."

"Do you mean the security guard and the dutywoman?" asked Pavl incredulously.

Nodding his head, Kukhar solemnly looked to the coroner, who continued. "Like the Metro engineer, both individuals died from shock, induced by a massive loss of blood. They also sported similar puncture wounds."

"But what about the rats that we saw feeding on the dutywoman's body?" countered Yuri. He fumbled anxiously for a cigarette. "Surely they were the cause of her loss of blood."

The coroner responded firmly. "That indeed appeared to be the case upon initial examination of the corpse. But as I further studied her remains, I found two anomalies. The normal human body contains up to ten pints of blood. Even taking into consideration the frenzied feeding of the rats that you witnessed, some of this blood should have remained in the dutywoman's system. Yet we found it nearly dry, as if it had been siphoned out of her body with a tube.

"The second aberration was the bite marks that lined her inner thigh. Set along the femoral artery, these distinctive wounds proved to be an exact match to those found on the necks of the security guard and the Metro engineer. I have to believe that the same person was responsible for all three homicides."

"That's incredible!" exclaimed Yuri. "I've come across some perverted crimes in my time, but this one wins the prize."

"For once I agree with you, Comrade Sorokin," reflected the colonel. "That's why we're relying on you to rid the streets of this maniac before he strikes again. Dr. Stura has kindly agreed to release the three of you. As of this moment, you're officially working for the MVD. Find this person, and perhaps we'll talk about making this transfer a permanent one."

Dr. Stura added, "I don't have to remind you that your cooperation in keeping this matter secret is crucial. If the public were to learn about the hideous nature of these crimes, a panic would surely ensue. Your discretion is a number-one priority."

"I think you can rely on us to keep our mouths shut, doctor," Pavl Barvicha said. "As it turns out, I know the perfect place to begin our investigation."

11

Far below the streets of Moscow, Vladimir Dolgoruki continued down the dark, cobblestone-lined passageway. Since his last feeding, he had seen absolutely no evidence of humanity, and this suited him just fine. In the safety of solitude he hoped to grow strong.

To protect his sensitive skin from the cold, damp atmosphere of the catacombs, he had dressed himself in the strangely designed, one-piece garment that his last victim had been wearing. It was formed from a mysterious, lightweight material that was surprisingly resilient. He had left his own tattered clothing back in the alcove.

As Vlad picked his way forward, he reflected on the extraordinary torch that the owner of this garment had been carrying. Oddly enough, it did not appear to need a flame to illuminate the darkness. Even when this torch fell into a puddle of stale water, its light continued glowing. Surely it must have been designed by a warlock!

He had also seen strange things when he escaped from the castle in which he had woken. He could only surmise that he was captive in an alien land, far from the hills of his birth.

The one familiar feature that he could take some comfort in was the tunnel in which he found himself. Designed much like the catacombs that lay beneath his father's cas-

tle, this winding, narrow passageway gave him a feeling of
security.

No torches lined its walls, but Vlad could pick out his
course regardless of the lack of illumination. This unusual ability seemed to be a result of his last feeding. Like an
animal that hunted the midnight woods, his eyes had
somehow adapted to the blackness. His father had once
told him that only a wolf had such an ability. Now, to
think that he had such a unique gift only puzzled Vlad.

He knew that the time would soon come when his
awakening would be complete. When his full strength
was restored, he would actively explore this strange, new
world. For only one mortal object could do him harm
here, and once this weapon was his, he would be not
only beyond fear, but death itself!

With this goal in the back of his mind, Vlad began his
way down a sloping portion of passageway. Thick, intricately shaped cobwebs blocked the tunnel here, but he
burst through them, heedless of the dozens of huge spiders that soon crawled over his head, shoulders, and
body. Oblivious to their angry bites, he flicked the
insects off with the back of his hand. As he reached the
bottom of the slope, the catacombs flattened out. Here
the floor was covered in raw sewage. Knee-deep in this
filthy, stinking muck, he continued forward.

Above him, millions of spawning roaches hung on the
rough-hewn stone roof, while a family of squealing rats
crawled on the ledge beside him. Vlad had a genuine
affinity for these red-eyed, brown-skinned rodents. Like
he, they lived only to feed. Glad for their company, he
watched them nibble on the ripe effluvium that stuck to
the tunnel's slimy walls, and he found his own hunger
growing. Instinctively, he quickened his pace.

Just as it seemed that these catacombs would go on

forever, the tunnel turned upward. Soon the floor beneath him was completely dry. Vlad halted when the passageway before him split into two separate routes. Both looked promising, but he chose the one to his right. He traveled in this direction for what seemed like an eternity, when suddenly he hit a dead end. He cursed angrily, for his appetite had grown to enormous proportions.

Just as he turned to retrace his steps, a distant, muffled roar sounded. Vlad listened intently to trace its source. He then caught sight of an enormous rat squeezing its fat body through a crack in the dead-end wall. A pinprick of light penetrated the seam in the mortar where the rodent had emerged. Hurrying to the spot, Vlad reached out to dislodge the surrounding cobblestone and found it unbelievably easy to remove. Minutes later, he had dug a hole of sufficient size to squeeze his own body through.

Vlad found himself inside a passageway that was more than twice the size of the tunnel he had been previously traveling. As the mad roaring sound he had heard earlier intensified, Vlad looked out and saw that the catacombs here were lined with what appeared to be smooth tile. Four thin iron rails were laid out side by side on the floor, their lengths stretching out to the horizon in both directions. What looked like a narrow stone pathway stretched along the opposite wall. Vlad was just about to drop onto the tunnel's floor, to cross over, when a blindingly bright light issued from his left.

The monstrous device arrived with an ear-splitting clamor. Unlike any object he had ever seen before, it seemed to be a series of linked iron carriages. Its grinding wheels traveled on two of the floor-mounted rails. Unbelievably, there seemed to be no horses providing its rapid propulsion!

Vlad had to cover his ears with the palms of his hands as the vehicle whipped by him at a speed faster than even the most skilled Tartar cavalryman could approach. His heart pounded wildly as he realized that there were windows cut into the sides of this device. Inside the carriages were dozens of strangely dressed mortals! Mesmerized by this sight, he watched as the last cubicle shot by him. With this, the deafening roar that had accompanied the exotic vehicle began to fade. And soon, blessed silence returned.

Vlad vainly sought to make some sense of the strange scene that he had just witnessed. His father had once told him that there were said to be ancient cities lying to the west of their homeland. Here humans lived with a variety of wondrous inventions that made their daily lives easier. The greatest of these cities was called Rome.

While riding with the Tartars, Vlad had actually traveled upon one of the amazing stone roadways that the Romans had built throughout Europe. Formed of smooth rock, this pavement allowed for speedy travel even during the wettest of springs. The Khan had even showed him a portion of the incredible system that the Romans called aqueducts. These aboveground, stone channels were used to convey water to places that would otherwise go dry. Thus a farmer would not lose his crop because of a lack of rainfall.

Vlad could only surmise that the iron carriage he had just seen whip by him was but another extraordinary Roman invention. Who knew—perhaps he had even been transported to the city of Rome itself! That would explain the strange design of the castle that he had just escaped from and the peculiar dress of his victims. To make certain of this fact, and to appease the gnawing hunger that still rose from the pit of his empty belly, Vlad decided to follow the walkway that lay on the tunnel's other side. By doing so, he was bound to come across another mortal sooner or later. Perhaps then he would be able to find the quickest trail back to his homeland.

New confidence guided Vlad's steps as he dropped down onto the tunnel's floor and crossed over the smooth, iron tracks. After climbing a low wall, he found himself on the path that he desired. With quick strides, he began walking in the direction the iron carriage had been headed.

For sixteen-year-old Anna Markova, this morning was surely one of the most exciting moments of her young life. Today was her long-awaited birthday. Not only was a new rabbit coat waiting for her at breakfast, but a new set of privileges as well. No longer would her parents look at her as a mere child. At sixteen years of age, she was now well on her way to womanhood and would be treated accordingly.

Anna's father had been the one to inform her that for the first time ever she would be allowed to take the Metro to school without her grandmother accompanying her. Certainly this was but the first of many steps toward her ultimate freedom. Why soon, she would even be able to go on a real date! She gloated over this stimulating thought while chewing her breakfast blintzes.

The Park Kultury Metro station was only a few blocks from their apartment, and Anna looked forward to the walk as never before. She could not help but notice the tears that wet both her parents' eyes as they bundled her up in her new rabbit coat and kissed her good-bye.

The morning was crisp and invigorating. Though not

as warm as the previous day had been, the air had just a hint of spring in it. This was Anna's favorite season, when the earth itself seemed to celebrate a rebirth.

After wishing the baker and the poultry man a spirited good morning, she crossed the street and decided to cut through the park. Her grandmother had never liked this route, even though it was an excellent short cut. Anna noticed that a trace of dirty snow still lay in patches on the ground. A few weeks ago this accumulation had been so thick that the path she was crossing now had been completely buried. Surely any day now, the first tulips would shoot up through the previously frozen soil. Then she would know for certain that spring had arrived.

On the other side of the park she faced a wide boulevard filled with traffic. To a chorus of honking cars and diesel-belching trucks, she positioned herself at the closest intersection and joined the throng of bundled pedestrians waiting to cross to the other side. Most of these people were bound for the same Metro station as she. The majority were adults on their way to work. Anna could not help but feel their equal.

The policeman's whistle sounded, and the mass of traffic reluctantly ground to a halt. Two short whistles followed as the policeman gave the all-clear signal for the pedestrians to cross. Anna joined this mass of humanity, walking across the wide boulevard and turning toward the bright red, neon "M" that hung above the sidewalk about a block away. Another minute later, she began her way down the wide set of steps that led directly into the Metro station.

The waiting platform was situated in the midst of a cavernous hall. This immense room always reminded Anna of the interior of a royal palace. Crystal chandeliers hung from the tiled roof, and the walls were formed from a series of gilded arches. In the center of these arches were dozens of mosaic representations of historical scenes from the Middle Ages. Anna's favorite scene was that of a mounted knight in shining armor. It graced the wall across from the southern portion of the platform, and it was here that the youngster decided to wait for her train.

Detached from the throng gathered near the platform's center, Anna breathed a sigh of relief. Crowds were definitely not to her liking. She would much rather find herself in the pastoral setting so expertly expressed in mosaic tile before her. The thick woods that the knight was emerging from reminded her of the forest that surrounded their holiday *dacha*. She knew that in only a few short months she would be off to the cottage, which lay several hundred kilometers west of the capital city.

Some of Anna's favorite memories were of this peaceful, rustic place. Her parents seemed to enjoy it as much as she did, and she could not figure out why they did not live there the whole year through, instead of just a couple of weeks in the summer.

Anna blushed as she remembered the young man she had met there only last year. She had chanced upon him while hiking through the woods, looking for mushrooms. He was fishing at the time. Standing on the bank of the river with the warm sun reflecting off his bare shoulders and chest, he turned and spotted Anna just as she emerged from a line of gnarled oaks. Her heart beat wildly as his deep blue gaze met hers. When he smiled, she thought she would almost faint.

They introduced themselves, and Anna learned that he was a lordly eighteen years of age, also a Muscovite, who was staying in his parent's nearby summer *dacha*. A mysterious heaviness filled her throat as she talked. Her cheeks felt as if they were on fire. The two of them conversed for the better part of the afternoon, and Anna found herself being scolded by her mother when she returned home late.

That night, she dreamed she was in his muscular embrace. Yet when they bumped into each other several days later, he treated her distantly, as if she were merely a child. Perhaps that would all change in the coming summer, for she was sixteen and officially a woman. Now if her breasts only continued to fill out and her pimples disappeared, maybe the boys would look at her with new eyes.

Smiling at this thought, Anna's attention was drawn by the faraway sound of an approaching train. She took one last look at the mosaic knight and turned her head to survey the nearby Metro tunnel. Though the subway train was still not visible, she did spot the tall figure of a single man. He seems to be approaching her from the walkway that lined the tracks here. The light was dim, but she could just make out that his lean figure was clothed in the white coveralls of a Metro engineer, though he was not wearing the customary red helmet.

Something about this stranger aroused her curiosity. To get a better look at him, she decided to walk over to the platform's edge. This should still give her plenty of time to get back to her train once it arrived.

Anna found herself far removed from the other passengers. Proud of her adventurous spirit, she watched as the engineer continued his approach. When he was still a good two dozen meters distant, he abruptly halted. Then, of all things, he beckoned her to him.

The light was just sufficient for her to make out the man's face. As she studied his dark features, she found

RICHARD HENRICK

236

her heart fluttering with the same excitement that had possessed her when she first spotted her boyfriend last summer. Yet the engineer was far more attractive. With thick, wavy black hair falling down to his shoulders, he reminded her of the great ballet star, Rudolph Nureyev. He had the same intense stare and sharp, hollow cheekbones.

When he continued to beckon, Anna briefly turned to make certain that no one else was behind her. Since there was not another soul even close by, she realized that his signal must indeed have been meant for her. With her curiosity now piqued, she decided to walk over to see what he wanted.

Two peculiar things struck her as she continued her approach. The first was the ripe, musky scent that seemed to grow stronger with her every step. And second was the heavily soiled stain that marked his pant legs, plus the fact that he wore no shoes. That was odd, Anna thought. Why would a Metro engineer be dressed that way?

Fearing that he was in some sort of trouble, Anna was about to speak when the overhead light exposed a new dimension to the stranger's face. At first she had thought he was only in his early twenties, but now she wondered otherwise. For there was a harsh cruelty to his expression that reminded Anna of a much older person. Seeing this, she hesitated. But she couldn't seem to stop herself completely. Something about him drew her closer.

Anna shivered in awareness when she saw the two balls of fire that swirled in the center of his pupils. Fear rose inside her, and she trembled uncontrollably. If only she could stop moving forward. The musky scent that emanated from the stranger's pores sent her swooning back dizzily, and it was his icily cold grasp that kept her from falling. Like one caught in a nightmare, she vainly tried to scream for help, but her vocal cords were frozen by sheer terror. The stranger pulled her farther into the dark recesses from which he had just emerged. Locked in her abductor's vicelike embrace, she found herself powerless to resist.

Anna's last thoughts were of the subway train that was soon whipping by them and the grim fact that she would never live to see another summer arrive after all.

The trip from the Abbey of St. John the Pursuer to Moscow took Nicholas the better part of twenty-four hours. Not even waiting for daybreak to depart, the blond-haired, twenty-seven-year-old monk left for Vorochta soon after receiving his surprise assignment. Accompanied by the man who delivered the abbey's monthly supplies, Nicholas left the foothills of Mount Goverla and proceeded straight into the pine forest that filled the valley below.

As they approached Vorochta, the brown-robed monk anxiously realized that he was about to enter a world far removed from that of the monastery. Though Nicholas was no stranger to such towns, and had even traveled to Kiev on a previous occasion, he could not help but feel that he was from another realm when they finally reached the village. His guide led him to Vorochta's tiny train station.

Still dressed in the homespun brown robes of his order, carrying an elongated, oaken case and a knapsack filled with some personal effects, Nicholas boarded a northbound freight train. He arrived in L'vov five hours later, after a brief stop at Ivono-Frankovsk. To get to Moscow, he had to travel by way of Kiev. Fortunately, he made each of his connections and arrived in the capital just as a new day was dawning.

This was the monk's first visit to the Center, and he found himself genuinely excited as he anxiously climbed up the steps of Moscow's Kievskaja train station. The great city had already awakened, even though the sun had just pierced the cloudless horizon. A brisk current of morning air, heavily tinged with diesel smoke, greeted him. As it turned out, it did not take him long to spot the traffic responsible for this pollution. Beyond the scurrying mass of pedestrians was a wide boulevard. Visible here were hundreds of cars, trucks, and buses. Caught in a virtual gridlock, this tangled line of commuter traffic gave Nicholas a much better idea of the great size of the city he had just entered.

To the west he saw many high-rise buildings. He knew that somewhere beyond this wall of multistoried buildings was the legendary Kremlin. Located in the geographic heart of the city, the Kremlin governed the entire Soviet Union. Chagrined that he did not have enough time to visit the historical sector he had read so much about, Nicholas sought directions to the monastery where he would be staying.

He hired a cab to convey him to the Convent of the Virgin. Located several kilometers south of the train depot, this monastery was now part historical museum and part convent. By prior arrangement, the members of St. John the Pursuer stayed in this holy enclave on the rare occasions when they traveled to Moscow.

Nicholas was quite happy to temporarily escape the frantic rush of commuting Muscovites as he crossed over the parklike cemetery that surrounded the convent. Many of the tombstones were beautifully carved and appeared to have been designed in the Baroque period.

Dozens of stately oaks also occupied this grassy plot, and beyond it he could see the distinctive red walls and onion-shaped domes of a large cathedral.

It was a grizzled groundskeeper who escorted him to the Mother Superior's office. To get there, Nicholas passed down a wide, brick corridor filled with expertly crafted icons. Most of these painted panels showed scenes from the lives of the saints and appeared to be many centuries old.

His white-haired escort silently led him through the building and directly into a large anteroom. Here he left Nicholas in the capable hands of a middle-aged nun. She was dressed in a gray habit and was obviously fulfilling her role as a secretary. Looking up from her typewriter, the sister smiled.

"Welcome to the Convent of the Virgin of Tikhvin, Brother. How can we help you? Are you a pilgrim, perhaps?"

Nicholas nodded, conscious of the knapsack he still carried on his back and the precious load he held at his side. "That I am, Sister. I hail from the far-off Carpathians, and I bear a letter of introduction from my abbot to your superior."

Setting down the oaken case, Nicholas removed his pack and pulled out a parchment envelope, which he handed to the secretary. She had only to glance at the red wax seal that graced the back of this document to realize its authenticity.

"If you'll just wait here one moment, I'll give this to the Mother Superior," she replied, disappearing into an inner office.

Nicholas barely had time to study a superbly rendered crucifixion scene beside the secretary's desk before she abruptly returned.

"Sister Katrina will see you now."

Thankful for her efficiency, Nicholas reshouldered his pack and entered the doorway. The office in which he now found himself was quite large, and its walls were lined with icons. In the center of the room was a cluttered desk, and seated behind it was a kindly eyed, white-haired sister, who also wore a gray habit and appeared to be well into her seventies. She set the abbot's letter on her desk top and smiled.

"So you're from the Order of the Pursuer, Brother Nicholas. Welcome to Moscow. I am Sister Katrina, the Mother Superior here. How is my good friend, the abbot?"

Feeling instantly at ease, Nicholas answered. "He is quite well, Sister, considering his advanced age."

"You don't have to remind me of that," said the Mother Superior. "I can remember him when he wasn't much older than you are."

The nun thought for a moment. "You must be exhausted after your long journey," she said, "and I imagine you're starving as well. Why don't I show you to your quarters, and then you can rest before the afternoon meal is served."

"That sounds most enticing, Sister Katrina, but I'm afraid there's no time for such a luxury right now. You see, my mission here is quite urgent."

"What else would prompt the surprise visit of a member of one of the most hermetic holy orders in all the world?" observed the Mother Superior. "Can I help you with this mission, my son?"

Nicholas solemnly nodded. "Actually, you can. I'm searching for a certain sarcophagus that was recently exhumed in the Carpathians. We believe this same relic was conveyed into Moscow by a group of archaeologists.

It is my task to track these individuals down."

"And I happen to know just the place for you to start," returned the grinning elder. "Only a few kilometers from this spot lies the Institute of Culture. If it's an archaeological treasure that you're after, the institute is where you'll find it. Dr. Yakhut, the institute's director, is a personal friend of mine. He's supervised many an excavation right on these very grounds."

"Whatever for?" asked Nicholas.

"Don't let these modern quarters fool you," replied the elder. "In reality, this monastery was founded by Boris Godunov in the latter part of the sixteenth century. Dr. Yakhut determined that it was constructed on the site of the Soviet army's position during a decisive battle with the Tartars in 1591. This proved to be the last time that the Tartar hordes advanced as far as Moscow, and it signaled a turning point in our people's history.

"I don't suppose you know the story of the wonder-working icon of the Mother of God of the Don. This relic supposedly contributed to the Soviet victory, and it was Dr. Yakhut himself who rediscovered this priceless treasure buried beneath these walls. We will be forever in his debt for finding this object, which has been responsible for many a documented miracle since."

Entranced by this narrative, Nicholas quickly returned to the job at hand. "The institute sounds like a good place to start. Do you think that I'll encounter any difficulties in gaining entrance to this institution?"

"Why, of course not," the elder said. "I'll personally call Dr. Yakhut and set up an appointment."

"That is most kind of you, Sister."

Already reaching for her intercom, Sister Katrina wasted no time in asking her secretary to telephone the institute. Fortune was with them, as this call found Dr.

Yakhut at work in his office. Nicholas was granted an appointment with the institute's director that very morning.

"You can get to the institute by way of the Metro," instructed the white-haired sister. "The entrance to the subway is only two blocks east of here. Four stops away is the Universitet Metro station. Exit there and follow the underground tunnel all the way to the institute."

"I don't know how I can properly thank you," said Nicholas.

"Just complete your mission successfully, and that will be thanks enough," answered Sister Katrina, whose tone hinted that she understood the significance of the young monk's presence in her office.

"Now, you'd better get going if you don't want to be late," she added.

Nicholas left the convent grounds with a new sense of confidence. Having stashed his knapsack in the Mother Superior's office, he covered the two blocks to the Metro station quickly.

A large neon "M" led him underground by way of a fast-moving escalator. Caught up in a press of grim-faced commuters, he managed to find the proper platform on which to wait for the southbound train. Nicholas was surprised to find the main concourse elegantly decorated. The roof was formed from a series of domes with huge chandeliers suspended from the roof's stucco ribs. Between these crystal fixtures were a variety of monumental mosaics showing different scenes from Russian history.

Feeling more like he was in a museum than a train station, the young monk was in the midst of studying one of the mosaic panels when he heard a brusque male voice.

"Excuse me, comrade, but I would like to see your papers."

Nicholas quickly turned around to see a single, uniformed policeman, who wore the distinctive blue epaulets of a militia officer. Though the monk's internal passport was current, his pulse nevertheless quickened as he reached into the folds of his robe and pulled out the necessary document.

The officer studied the passport's contents and curtly commented, "It seems that you are a long way from home, Comrade Andreivich. May I ask what sort of business calls you to Moscow?"

"I am a religious scholar doing research into our country's past," replied Nicholas, doing his best to meet the militia officer's stare without flinching. "I am currently on my way to the Institute of Culture, where I hope to speak with the institute's director."

"Is this your first visit to Moscow?" quizzed the officer.

"Yes, it is," Nicholas said evenly.

The policeman momentarily diverted his icy glance to study the monk's clothing and the strangely shaped, elongated case that he carried at his side. "So," he said, "when did you arrive in town, and where are you staying?"

The grinding sound of an approaching train broke in the distance. "I've only been in the capital a few hours at most. I'll be staying at the Convent of the Virgin."

The sound of the train increased, and just as Nicholas was wondering if the officer would keep him from boarding the vehicle, his interrogator waved him on. "Good luck with your research, comrade. And please, be careful during your stay here."

Nicholas felt a great sense of relief as the uniformed

policeman smartly wheeled to continue his rounds. As it turned out, he had little time to further contemplate this confrontation, for the subway train pulled up to the platform seconds later.

The interior of the car he entered was immaculate. He seated himself by a window and looked out as the train left the station. It picked up speed quickly and soon entered a dark tunnel, speeding southward beneath the crowded streets of Moscow.

Four stops later, Nicholas exited the car along with a group of book-toting students. As he crossed the platform, he was once more intercepted by a uniformed policeman. Again, he was forced to display his internal passport, and he wondered if such tight security measures were standard procedure here in the Metro. Nicholas made the best of this inconvenience by asking the young militia officer the quickest way to the institute.

His papers checked out, and Nicholas was soon on his way down a narrow, subterranean passageway that was completely lined in white tile. This route led him straight into the basement of a large building. Here a marble stairway carried him up into a central foyer, which had dozens of brightly lit display cases. These contained objects ranging from intricately painted pottery to fossilized bone. After registering at the information desk, he began climbing yet another marble staircase. This brought him to a wide hallway whose walls were lined with photographs of archaeological excavation sites.

Halfway down this hall was the director's office. Nicholas entered and approached a gray-haired secretary who was busy leafing through a file cabinet. Nicholas cleared his throat and interrupted her.

"Excuse me, but is Dr. Yakhut in?"

Though the secretary had been concentrating on her work, she calmly looked up and took in the handsome young newcomer. "Why, I'll bet you're the fellow Sister Katrina called about."

"That I am," returned Nicholas. "I hope that Dr. Yakhut is still available."

The secretary smiled. "Of course he is, comrade. Why don't you just have a seat while I buzz him?"

Nicholas watched as she went to activate the desk-mounted intercom. "Dr. Yakhut, Sister Katrina's colleague has just arrived."

A husky male voice came from the speaker. "Very good, Petra. I'll be right with him."

Not thirty seconds later, a short, thin, bald-headed gentleman emerged from the inner office. Well into his sixties, he wore a loose-fitting gray suit. His face looked kind and inquisitive.

"So you're the young fellow who prompted Sister Katrina's call. I'm Dr. Felix Yakhut, and I'd like to welcome you to our institute."

Nicholas smiled. "I'm Brother Nicholas Andreivich. My order is located in the Carpathians, near the Rumanian border. Several days ago, a stone sarcophagus was pulled from the earth by an army engineering unit near the headwaters of the Prut River. One of our abbot's great passions is archaeology, and before he was allowed to get a detailed description of this relic, it was reportedly transferred to Moscow for further examination. I have been sent here to track down the sarcophagus, and if possible, record a firsthand description of it."

Noting the young monk's intensity, Dr. Yakhut responded. "It seems that the fates have brought you to the right spot, Brother Nicholas, for the object that you speak of has indeed found its way to this institute. In fact, it's only a few doors away. Shall we take a look at the treasure that has brought you these hundreds of kilometers?"

Nicholas beamed. "Never in my wildest dreams did I guess that I would be able to find it so quickly."

"Have you no faith, comrade?" the director joked, turning toward his secretary. "Petra, why don't you call Dr. Lopatin and let her know that she will soon be having some visitors?"

As his secretary picked up the intercom handset to carry out this request, Dr. Yakhut once again addressed his young guest. "By the way, comrade, what is the name of this order that you serve?"

"We are known as the brothers of St. John the Pursuer."

"I don't believe I've ever heard of your order," returned the director. "May I ask just who or what your order pursues?"

Not certain how to respond to this question, Nicholas paused.

"Dr. Lopatin doesn't seem to be in her office," the secretary reported. "She must still be in X-ray."

"Then I bet that's where we'll find the sarcophagus," reasoned Dr. Yakhut. "If you'll just come with me, Brother Nicholas, your search will soon be over."

Hoping that this would indeed be the case, the young monk followed the director out into the hallway.

On the floor immediately above, Dr. Richard Green settled into his own cramped cubicle to get down to work. As promised, Yelena Lopatin had arrived at his hotel bright and early to pick him up. Richard had been surprised to find himself looking forward to this drive, for it would allow him more time with one of the bright-

est, most attractive women he had ever met. The trip
went too quickly. Before he knew it, they had arrived at
the institute, where Yelena showed him to his office.

Her own work space was only a few doors away, and
she left him with an invitation to join her for lunch.
With this delightful thought in mind, he began to orga-
nize his desk. He was in the midst of this chore when a
freckle-faced research assistant arrived with a sealed cardboard carton. The young man introduced himself and
informed the American that inside the box were the
manuscripts that Richard had been waiting for.

The linguist wasted no time in stripping the packing
tape and lifting off the carton's lid. Inside was a thick
pile of papers. The collection appeared to be composed
of at least a dozen individually bound parchment manuscripts. Richard recognized the paper stock as a type used
by Church chroniclers during the Dark Ages. The intricately formed script confirmed his suspicion that the collection had originated in an Eastern European monastery
approximately eight centuries ago.

Before beginning a page-by-page translation, he
decided to separate the manuscripts so that he would
have a better idea of just how much work was facing him.
Since the parchment was extremely brittle, he had to
proceed very carefully. As he pulled each of the bound
volumes from the carton, he hastily scanned their title
pages. All in all, the ink had been preserved remarkably
well, and he was able to identify manuscripts dealing
with a variety of Church affairs. Several appeared to be
theological treatises. These rare volumes would be of
special interest to his colleagues back at St. Louis University. Other texts referred to various historical narratives,
and a particularly thick manuscript appeared to be a
library catalogue. As he was leafing through this fasci-

nating document, his telephone began to ring. Richard carefully set the manuscript down on his desk and reached for the red plastic handset.

"Richard, this is Yelena. Listen, I know that you've only just gotten started, but something incredible has just happened. Can you join me right away in the X-ray room?"

"Why, certainly," replied the American. "How do I get there?"

"Just exit your office and turn to the right. X-ray is in Room 313."

"I'm on my way," said Richard.

Though he had been looking forward to an uninterrupted morning of work, he could not ignore Yelena's invitation. He headed straight for Room 313.

Inside, he found Yelena and the institute's director huddled beside the recently exhumed sarcophagus. Standing next to them, peering into the coffin's hollowed-out interior, was a blond-haired young man dressed in the long brown robes of a monk.

"Are you absolutely certain that this vault was empty?" demanded the stranger passionately.

Noting the American's arrival, Yelena answered. "That it was, comrade. I personally witnessed the original exhumation and can attest to the seal's integrity."

"But were you there to break this seal yourself?" continued the monk.

"Unfortunately, I wasn't," replied Yelena. "You see, one of the institute's guards received the sarcophagus during an after-hours delivery. Since the lid was found open the next morning, it is assumed that the same guard was responsible for unsealing it. In any case, we have uncovered no evidence that would lead us to believe that anything was inside. Whatever it held must have been removed at an earlier date."

The young monk looked up sharply. "And may I speak with this guard?"

This time it was Dr. Yakhut who answered. "I'm afraid not, comrade. You see, he died on the very night that the sarcophagus arrived here. In fact, the poor fellow was found slumped beside the relic, the apparent victim of a heart attack."

The monk seemed shaken by this revelation. Yelena was quick to interject. "Brother Nicholas, I'd like you to meet Dr. Richard Green, an American linguist who is currently working with the institute. It was Dr. Green who translated the inscription on the relic's lid."

Richard stepped forward to exchange handshakes and found the monk's strong grasp cold and clammy.

"Good morning," greeted the American in perfect Russian. "I take it that you are in some way familiar with this sarcophagus?"

Nicholas met the American's glance. "The order to which I belong has sent me here to examine this artifact firsthand," he said. "Since it was originally discovered not far from our abbey, we were hoping that it would help fill in a portion of our region's history."

"I had similar hopes," added Yelena.

Sensing that the young monk was holding something back from them, Richard cautiously probed. "I myself have the honor of working for a Jesuit institution. May I ask who you're affiliated with?"

"My order is St. John the Pursuer," returned Nicholas. "We are a small sect, dedicated to scholarly research and prayer."

Feeling a bit uneasy with the American, Nicholas turned to address the institute's director. "Dr. Yakhut, in order to be assured that the deceased guard did not have an accomplice, would you mind if I spoke with the officials investigating your man's death?"

"Though I find such a possibility highly unlikely, if it will make you feel better, it's fine with me," said the bald-headed director. "Dr. Lopatin here can help you reach them."

Yelena fumbled in the pocket of her lab jacket and pulled out a business card. "The investigator's name is Mikhail Antonov," she said. "He's assigned to the coroner's office, and can be reached at the number that's here on the card."

While the monk scanned this information, Richard Green could not help but vent his curiosity. "I know it's none of my business, but just what were you expecting to find in this coffin? Does it have anything to do with the inscription carved on its lid?"

"This might be the case," Nicholas said. "Why do you ask?"

Once again, Richard had the impression that the young monk knew more than he was revealing. "My translation of this inscription proves it to be a most enigmatic one."

"And just what do you mean by that, Doctor?" countered Nicholas.

"Do the numerals 666 mean anything to you?" Richard asked.

So, thought Nicholas, the American knew the translation of the Moldavian Greek numerals that he himself had seen only minutes ago. The young monk could only wonder if Dr. Green also knew of their significance. He therefore gave a guarded reply.

"The numerical sequence that you mention is rumored to have several symbolic meanings, one of which is mentioned in the New Testament. I would be happy to discuss this fascinating subject with you at a later date, but right now, my holy obligations force me to excuse myself. Dr. Yakhut, may we return to your office? I would like to telephone this investigator from there."

"Why, of course," replied the director, who beckoned the blond-haired monk into the hallway.

Yelena and Richard stood alone in the X-ray room.

"I'm sorry I had to interrupt you earlier, Richard, but I thought that you'd be interested in meeting our brown-robed visitor."

"I'm glad you called," said the American. "What exactly was the young man doing here, anyway?"

Yelena gently closed the coffin's lid. "He apparently traveled all the way up here from the Carpathians to have a look at this artifact. He arrived here, along with Dr. Yakhut, only moments before I telephoned you. The look on his face when he first saw the inscription prompted my call. Why, he turned white as a ghost, and for a second I thought he might faint from shock. I'm certain that he was able to translate those numbers and was somehow affected by their presence, almost as if he were expecting to find them here. He seemed to regain control of himself when he learned that the sarcophagus was empty. And then he started questioning. That's when you arrived."

"I wonder what he was expecting to find inside the coffin?" reflected Richard.

"Who knows," added Yelena. "Perhaps he was sent here just to corroborate the presence of the inscription. Yet surely he could have done that with a single phone call."

"I'd like to know more about the order that he represents," said the American.

"I'll access the university library and see what I can

come up with," offered Yelena. "And if I draw a blank, perhaps you could telex your associates back at St. Louis University.

"Now, I'd better be letting you get back to the work that originally brought you here. Have you gotten a chance to examine the manuscripts yet?"

Nodding that he had, Richard added, "They appear to be in remarkable shape for their age and could very well have been written more than eight centuries ago. The script indicates a most definite Eastern European origin. One of the most exciting documents looks like a monastic library catalogue. There's no telling what books the listing will reveal."

"It sounds very exciting, Richard. Why don't we have lunch together later on, and you can brief me more fully."

"I'd enjoy that," responded the American, who could not help but notice the warm smile that turned up the corners of Yelena's mouth as she extended her invitation.

12

The three investigators arrived on the south side of Moscow just before the early morning commuter traffic was at its worst. Following Pavl Barvicha's suggestion, they decided to initiate their investigation in the catacombs directly adjoining the slain dutywoman's basement.

Yuri Sorokin was the first to crawl through the hole in the wall and enter the subterranean passage. With a cigarette between his thin lips, the hairless detective scanned the black depths with his flashlight, then reached into his pocket and pulled out a compass. He studied it for a moment as his partners joined him.

"Well, comrade, which way should we go?" asked Pavl. His camera hung ready around his neck.

Yuri scratched his jaw. "I think we should do our best to head north. If the three homicides are indeed related, that appears to be the direction in which the perpetrator is traveling. What do you think, Misha?"

The blond-haired investigator tested his flashlight by shining it on the passageway's roughly hewn stone ceiling. "Your guess is as good as mine, comrade. How much farther can this tunnel go, anyway?"

"For all I know, it could extend all the way to the Kremlin and beyond," returned Yuri, who pocketed his compass. "I've been told that no one really knows the true extent of these catacombs, many of which were originally excavated hundreds of years ago."

"Well, let's get on with it," prompted Pavl. "This place gives me the chills, even without knowing that a murderer could be hiding in the shadows."

Turning to his right, Yuri began his way down the narrow passageway, followed closely by the photographer. Mikhail Antonov brought up the rear.

For the first quarter of a kilometer, the tunnel was relatively dry and flat. This allowed for rapid progress, even though their flashlights provided the only light.

Not really certain what they hoped to find, Mikhail took in the large pieces of gray cobblestone that formed the walls. He occasionally saw a cockroach darting for cover. All was silent except for the hollow sounds of their footsteps and the monotonous sound of dripping water.

Mikhail silently cursed as the passageway began to descend and the thick air filled with the stench of raw sewage. As the grade gradually evened out, the source of this sickening smell became all too apparent. The sour muck that they were forced to travel through extended halfway up Mikhail's shins, and his stomach was churning.

Mikhail's skin tingled with revulsion when his light caught the bulbous shape of a huge rat swimming in the sewage before him. When a chorus of excited squeals sounded to his right, he redirected the angle of his light and took in a revolting sight that almost made his knees buckle. Completely lining the walls here were hundreds of swarming, brown-skinned rodents. Fighting off the sensation to scream in horror, Mikhail concentrated on lengthening his stride. He hardly noticed it when the grade gradually increased. With this ascent, the tunnel floor was soon almost dry.

He had little time to celebrate, for blocking their progress ahead was a series of immense silken cobwebs. Both Yuri and Pavl had stopped to study the first of these webs when Mikhail arrived at their side.

"I guess this is where we turn back," said the sullen, blond-haired detective.

Redirecting the beam of his flashlight into the black depths before them, Yuri answered. "Why do you say that, comrade? Surely you're not afraid of a few spiders. Besides, as Pavl here was just pointing out, the webs that extend all the way across the tunnel's width seem to have been recently broken. That can only mean that someone else has been through this passageway not long ago."

"But how do we keep from getting bitten?" Mikhail asked.

This time it was the photographer who replied. "We'll take off our jackets and drape them tightly over our heads, necks, and shoulders. Then we'll move through this section of tunnel like an express train."

Though he would have liked to argue otherwise, Mikhail watched as his coworkers removed their jackets. Realizing that it was useless to protest, he reluctantly joined them.

"I'll run interference, while you two light the way from here," offered Yuri. "That'll clear a path for you to follow. Just remember not to stop until you pass the last web. Now let's get on with it. My gut tells me that we're close to something important!"

Without wasting a second, Yuri spit the cigarette butt from his lips and covered himself with his wrinkled suit jacket. Then he lowered his head and started sprinting down the tunnel's web-covered length. When the flee-ing figure was all but indiscernible in the distance, Pavl turned and winked at Mikhail.

"Don't look so grim, comrade. After all, how much do you think one of those little eight-legged buggers can eat?"

Mikhail grinned weakly as the photographer added, "That's more like it, Antonov. Now, shall I lead the way, or would you like to do the honors?"

Beckoning him to go on, Mikhail felt his nerves tingle as Pavl Barvicha dashed out into the gossamer blackness. Mikhail scrambled down the passageway himself.

His legs were heavy and his lungs heaved with exhaustion when he finally passed by the last discernable web. He slowed to a halt only after spotting his coworkers, who watched anxiously several meters in front of him. Yuri's excited voice broke through the stillness.

"Drop it, Misha! Drop your coat and stand aside at once!"

Not knowing what all this commotion was about, Mikhail followed this puzzling command anyway. He dropped the woolen jacket onto the ground and rather calmly stepped to the side. Only when he looked to the ground did he understand. He swayed dizzily when he saw the collection of large, furry black spiders that graced the back of his coat.

"It appears that they picked you for their dinner," Pavl said, smiling.

Mikhail was still collecting his nerves when Yuri Sorokin casually popped another cigarette between his lips and pulled out his compass. "Good," he said, "we're still headed north. That should put us not far from the spot where that Metro engineer was killed."

"Do you really think that the same person responsible for murdering that engineer also killed the dutywoman and the security guard?" asked Pavl.

Yuri pocketed his compass and answered. "If the coroner is correct and the three did die from blood loss, I'd say that it's extremely likely that the deaths were committed by the same individual. Why, we've just about established the fact that the killer could have used these catacombs to travel from victim to victim."

"But what kind of person could be responsible for such a horrible thing?" Pavl persisted. "And why drain the victim's blood?"

Yuri lit his cigarette and exhaled a ribbon of smoke "I'm not so certain that it's a human we're after. These attacks still sound like they were committed by either a wolf or a pack of dogs."

"Unfortunately, Dr. Stura and Colonel Kukhar don't concur," Mikhail said. "If you ask me, a human is very capable of such an atrocity. Who knows, we could even be up against some kind of drug-crazed cult that uses blood in its rituals. Such things are not unheard of in the Far East."

Pavl shook his head. "But for such a thing to occur in Moscow?"

"Even the Center is not immune to senseless crime," reflected Mikhail.

"We shouldn't be far from the river now," Yuri said, pointing to the blackened portion of tunnel that lay beyond them. "And the Metro runs somewhere nearby. Let's move on, and if we don't come up with any evidence by the time we reach the river, we'll go back to the car."

They continued down the passageway for another quarter of an hour before they heard the distinctive sound of cascading water in the distance. Not long after, the three investigators smelled a horribly rank scent. It was so vile that even Pavl Barvicha's iron-clad stomach began to churn in protest.

Vladimir Dolgoruki heard the distant sound of running water long before he actually saw the underground river itself. Lured by the bubbling current, he lengthened his steps and, minutes later, spotted a muted light at the far end of the passageway. After hours of traveling in pitch blackness, this illumination at first blinded his oversensitive eyes. As he came closer, however, his pupils gradually adjusted.

He soon found himself standing on a narrow, mud-covered riverbank. Though its wide channel was partially covered by a thin layer of ice, Vlad could just make out the swiftly moving water visible beneath the translucent icy coating. The mere sight instantly calmed him.

He looked across to the opposite bank and was amazed to see that the river had cut this underground channel through solid rock. Upstream, the light continued to shine. There, approximately an eighth of a kilometer distant, was what appeared to be a patch of open sky. Before walking over to investigate, Vladimir decided to indulge in yet another feeding.

Vladimir had been carrying the girl's limp body at his side since abducting her near the spot where he had first seen the extraordinary horseless carriage. She had come to him most willingly, proving that his long-dormant powers were already returning. Many years ago, while riding with the Tartars, he learned the trick of calling his victims to the very portals of death, where he left them with just a spark of life. After giving them ample time to recuperate, he would strike once again, continuing the process until his weakened prey lost all will to go on living.

In one village, Vlad was able to feed himself on three

different girls for an entire moon cycle. Of course, this was at a time when he was at the peak of his strength. By alternating his attacks with each changing moon phase, his unsuspecting victims provided him a feast of virgin blood. Their parents only knew that their children were bedridden with a mysterious, energy-sapping disease. Unfortunately, thirty days proved to be the limit of his prey's endurance, and each of the girls expired soon afterward. With this convenient food source abruptly shut off, Vladimir was forced to continue his hunting elsewhere.

When he had first spotted the girl standing alone on the underground platform, he knew that he had an excellent chance to feed on her in just such an extended manner. His first priority was to snatch her away without being detected. To accomplish this task, Vlad employed a unique ability that he had discovered soon after being bitten by the flying demon on the banks of the Moscow River. By merely focusing the direction of his subconscious thoughts, he could control the will of even the most stubborn individuals.

He first put his mesmerizing skills to use on his parents. Whenever he was about to be scolded, he merely projected his thoughts into the minds of either his mother or father, and before he knew it, they would see things his way. Not long after learning of his strange new ability, he found himself cornered in a dark section of the forest by an angry boar. Just as the wild pig lowered its razor-sharp tusks and was about to charge, Vlad looked the enraged beast in the eyes and willed it to be gone. Seconds later, it loudly squealed and ran off, never to be seen again.

Aware that he had a unique gift, Vladimir put it to use when he began his time of blood-feasting. Although controlling the minds of a group of adults could be most difficult, hypnotizing his favorite prey proved to be hardly a challenge. For the most part the girls he encountered were weak-minded and usually thought only of themselves. They could be mentally lured without the least difficulty. His latest victim had proved no exception.

The girl with the long brown braids had put up the feeblest of struggles. Vlad had no trouble whatsoever pulling her back into the shadows before she attracted the attention of the strangely attired mortals waiting on the nearby platform. Scarcely voicing a whimper of protest, she allowed herself to be dragged back into the shelter of the catacombs. It was here that he initiated his first feeding.

The smooth skin of her neck was soft and warm. Her jugular vein was pulsating. Vladimir carefully pierced the skin with his needlelike canine teeth. He was cautious not to make the cut too deep before he succumbed to his insatiable hunger and began gulping her life's fluid. The rich blood was hot and slightly salty. So pure was its virgin essence that he felt its effects soon after it began trickling into his belly.

As her blood merged with his own, a surge of adrenalin coursed through his body. Just as if he had been struck by lightning, his newly energized limbs trembled as his senses overloaded with bliss.

Along with this sudden surge of strength, new purpose rose in his fully awakened consciousness. He carefully picked up the girl, who had lapsed into a coma. Lifting her under his arm like a limp rag doll, he eventually made his way toward the riverbank. Before he left the dark, protective, womblike depths of the catacombs, another feeding was surely justified. He would need every available ounce of strength for the confrontation that would inevitably be upon him.

As the underground river surged beside him, Vlad knelt and gently embraced the still-warm body of his prey. Though the girl's eyelids were tightly closed, he could see her eyes moving beneath them. The dream was accompanied by the barest of whimpers from her dry, parted lips. Vladimir could not help but wonder what pictures the dream was painting as he bent over her smooth neck. Two pinpricks of dried blood guided his lips downward.

Her soft skin was easily penetrated, and once again he thirstily sucked out her precious life's fluid. As its powerful essence merged into his bloodstream, a wave of sheer ecstasy caused him to sway.

Never before had he felt so totally alive! Never had his senses been so finely tuned!

Though he hungered for more, Vladimir forcibly restrained himself. He knew that he would have to limit the amount of blood that he took from her body. Such a convenient source of nourishment could be of great use to him now. Who knew in what corner of the world he had awakened?

Vlad breathed a sigh of relief upon noting that the barest of fluttering pulses was still visible beneath the pale skin of the youngster's neck, proof that she would live to be his once again. Like a father lifting his sleeping child, he gently picked her up and stood.

It was then that he heard the approaching footsteps and saw the three flickering pinpricks of light. A feeling of revulsion settled upon him as he realized he was once again the hunted. The flying demon's bite had cursed him with the blood hunger, and even now mortals would not allow him a moment's respite. Thus he had no choice but to toss aside the tiny body that he had been carrying and turn to defend himself.

Yuri Sorokin was the first to spot the tall, lanky figure that stood beside the roaring underground river. Dressed in white coveralls, this individual spun to face them and let out a deafening, mournful howl that was unlike anything Yuri had ever heard. Yuri dropped his cigarette as his jaw opened in astonishment.

"Over there, comrades!" he managed to sputter, shakily pointing toward the riverbank.

Still not certain what type of life form they had cornered, Yuri struggled to regain his self-control. Pavl Barvicha knelt down beside him. Seconds later, the photographer's bright strobe lit the black depths like a flare. Barely conscious of the motorized whine of his associate's camera, Yuri reached into his jacket and pulled out his pistol. By the time he had unholstered his 9mm Kalashnikov, Mikhail Antonov had positioned himself on Yuri's left, his pistol also drawn.

"Halt, or we'll shoot!" cried Mikhail forcefully.

Heedless of this command, the long-haired stranger took a step forward. Lifting his forearm to shield his eyes from their lights, he let loose another bloodcurdling wail.

"I said freeze, comrade!" shouted Mikhail, who almost gagged over the rank scent that was particularly strong in this portion of the passageway.

When their suspect took yet another step forward, Mikhail clicked off his pistol's safety and rammed a bullet into its chamber. "Halt now, or we'll shoot!" he repeated.

Growling in protest, the stranger momentarily stopped his advance, giving the detectives a chance to get a better look at him. Using their flashlights to scan his long, lean body, they saw that he was wearing no shoes or socks. His stained coveralls barely extended beyond his bony white shins, and it was obvious that this outfit was a borrowed one.

The suspect was covering his eyes with his arm, yet Mikhail was able to make out his pointed jaw, hollow cheekbones, and long, scraggly black hair. Certain that this was the same man he had heard described in the coroner's office, Mikhail addressed his partner.

"It's him, all right. He's even wearing the slain Metro engineer's clothing!"

Having finally gathered his nerves, Yuri responded. "This arrest should sure serve to prove our worth to the colonel. You keep a bead on the bastard, while I put the cuffs on him."

Mikhail watched as his partner pulled out a pair of shiny steel handcuffs from his jacket pocket. Holding them in the same hand as his flashlight, Yuri cautiously moved forward, his gun still raised before him.

Even though the suspect did not appear to be carrying a weapon, Mikhail felt uneasy. Unable to forget the look of terror that had filled the surviving engineer's eyes as he described his own encounter with this maniac, he did his best to provide Yuri with adequate cover. With his gun barrel pointed squarely at the stranger's chest, Mikhail listened as Yuri's voice rose over the constant surge of cascading water.

"Get those hands over your head, and move up against the wall!" ordered the veteran detective.

While Pavl Barvicha continued to photograph the entire scene, Mikhail felt his apprehension increase as the suspect failed to respond to Yuri's commands. Once again, Yuri cried out forcefully.

"I said, get those hands over your head, comrade! What's the matter, are you deaf?"

Yuri was only a few steps away from the suspect when the stranger finally lowered his arm. He stared back at his would-be captors. Yuri had a particularly good vantage point, and he could see the two pointed teeth that protruded from the sides of the suspect's upper jaw as he drew back his lips and snarled. The hostile, terrifying growl sounded like the noise a wild animal would make. Yuri felt the hair on his neck stand on end. His horror intensified when he saw the strange, flickering, crimson flames that seemed to be centered deep in the suspect's dark gaze. Yuri could barely breathe. His limbs shook so badly that he actually dropped his flashlight and the handcuffs.

As these objects clattered to the floor of the passageway, his partner interceded. Mikhail arrived at Yuri's side just as the suspect pounced forward and pulled Yuri into his grasp. Barely able to react to this lightning-fast move, Mikhail instinctively crouched down and raised his gun to fire. Yet he found himself unable to find a clear shot.

Mikhail watched as the suspect held Yuri in front of himself like a shield. He must have been incredibly strong, for the wiry detective lay limp and unmoving, powerless to resist, in the man's arms.

Sensing that the stranger could snap Yuri's neck with the least bit of effort, Mikhail reluctantly lowered the aim of his pistol and spoke out cautiously. "All right, comrade, you've made your point. No one is going to harm you. Just let Detective Sorokin loose, and you'll be free to go on your way."

Strangely enough, these conciliatory words seemed to have absolutely no effect on the suspect, whose bearlike grasp on Yuri continued to tighten.

"Maybe he doesn't understand Russian!" shouted Pavl Barvicha. He proceeded to convey Mikhail's offer in expertly spoken English, French, and German.

"I'm afraid those are the only languages I'm fluent with," the photographer said weakly.

Since it did not appear that they would be able to negotiate their way out of this predicament, Mikhail decided to attempt to break the impasse with one more show of force. Once again he lifted his pistol, this time setting its sights squarely in the center of the suspect's forehead.

"Now let Detective Sorokin go this instant!" he exclaimed. "I'm warning you, comrade. I could easily break this stand-off with a single shot."

This threat only seemed to aggravate the suspect, for he let loose yet another unearthly wail. As the terrifying shriek faded, Mikhail fought to steady his aim. Known as an expert marksman even under the most trying of circumstances, now he found his right hand shaking so badly that he didn't dare chance a shot. Sweat poured off his forehead as he tried to calm himself with a long, slow breath.

What followed happened so quickly that the blond-headed detective could react only by instinct. He was steadying the butt of his pistol with the palm of his left hand, when the suspect flung Yuri with an unbelievable ease into his kneeling partner.

Mikhail bore the brunt of the concussion with his upper chest and arms. Though he dropped his flashlight, he was able to hang onto his gun. Pushing Yuri's limp body aside, he scrambled to one knee and fired at the suspect at point-blank range.

The blast of the 9mm shell exploded with a deafening retort, and Mikhail could have sworn that he heard the hollow sound of the bullet as it smacked into the solid flesh of his target. But the stranger kept on moving, oblivious to any injury. Without the benefit of his flashlight, Mikhail could barely see the suspect as he whipped past Pavl and disappeared into the black depths of the catacombs, leaving only a vile stench in his wake.

A muted, painful groan kept Mikhail from initiating a pursuit. Holstering his pistol, he turned his attention instead to his prostrate partner.

"What in the world hit me?" mumbled Yuri groggily, his face bruised and badly cut above the right eyebrow.

Mikhail helped him sit up. "Don't worry, my friend," he said. "I'm almost certain that I managed to get a slug into the bastard. He won't be going far."

Suddenly mindful of his duty, Yuri protested. "Don't worry about me, Antonov, go after him!"

Just then Pavl Barvicha called out behind them. "Quickly, comrades, over here by the riverbank!"

Without a moment's hesitation, Mikhail grabbed his flashlight and turned to join the photographer beside the underground river. Lying on the muddy bank was the limp, naked body of a girl. Pavl felt for her pulse, while Mikhail took in her long brown braids and the two clearly distinguishable bite marks on the side of her neck.

As Yuri shakily joined them, Pavl observed breathlessly, "She's still alive! Come on, we've got to get her to a hospital at once!"

Mikhail caught his partner's concerned gaze. Both men looked out into the black depths of the catacombs, where the one responsible for this atrocity was last seen fleeing.

Again it was the anxious voice of the photographer that commanded their attention. "There seems to be some sort of light emanating from downstream. I bet that's where this portion of the Moscow River flows aboveground. That should put us just south of the Kremlin, near the Repina clinic. Come on, comrades. If we hurry, we might be able to save this poor child's life!"

While Pavl covered the girl with his jacket, Mikhail solemnly addressed his partner. "Comrade Barvicha is right, Yuri. Let's do what we can to save this girl's life. Then we can return to finish off this bastard once and for all. Besides, it looks like you could use some medical attention yourself. That cut on your forehead is a nasty one."

Yuri wiped the blood off his brow with the back of his hand. "For the life of me, I've never encountered anyone like that brute. Why, he had me completely under his spell. It was almost as if he had hypnotized me!"

Conscious that he, too, had temporarily fallen under this mysterious stranger's spell, Mikhail compassionately patted his partner on the back, then turned to help Pavl carry the unconscious child down the slippery riverbank.

It had not been fear that sent Vladimir running for the protective depths of the catacombs. Rather it was an instinctive urge to keep as far as possible from the mortals' disgusting presence. Contact with the outside world, except for purposes of feeding, still sickened him.

By his very nature, he was a creature of solitude. Humanity simply bored him with its selfish, petty concerns and weak, foolish aspirations. The three strangely attired men whom he had just faced were perfect representatives of humanity at its worst. Though Vlad failed to understand their words, there could be no ignoring their hostile intentions. When one of them actually had the nerve to step forward and dare to constrain him,

Vlad reacted instinctively.

How very weak was this mortal's will! It only took a single look to cause him to tremble like a scared old woman. Then, once he was psychically debilitated, Vlad merely had to attack as a wolf would a cowering fawn.

Vlad would have loved to drain this pitiful mortal of his life's essence. But his belly was full, and since he was in no mood to play foolish games, he could think of no better course than to get as far as possible from the three mortals.

Though he hated to leave his newly captured prize behind, Vlad sprinted off into the catacombs. He did not halt until he was certain that he wasn't being followed.

The girl's blood had refreshed him in a most satisfying way. Unlike his earlier meals, her essence was pure and free of disease. Since his strength had returned, he could afford to be selective in his choice of future victims.

Vlad squatted to rest against the passage's cold, stone wall. The catacomb's floor was partially covered with water here, and he could just make out a couple of fat rats wallowing in the stale liquid before him. All was quiet except for the high-pitched whine of these rodents and the distant sound of dripping water.

Vlad contentedly yawned, then fingered the newly formed hole in the lower right portion of his rib cage. This painless wound was created when one of the mortals attacked him with some sort of strange, hand-held stick. A fiery tongue of flame had erupted from the object's hollow barrel, accompanied by a thundering boom and a rapidly advancing projectile that was smaller than a spearhead, and which shot through the air, finally embedding itself in his cold flesh.

Such a fantastic weapon could be extremely potent on

the field of battle. Vlad shuddered to think what his friends, the Tartars, could do with such a remarkable object. Surely the projectile it fired could penetrate even the thickest of armors. Freed from their crude spears and bulky bows, the horde could complete its sweep of Europe until the whole world surrendered to the Tartar throngs.

Some of Vlad's fondest memories harked back to the time that he had spent with these brave, resourceful warriors from the east. Unlike normal men, the Tartars were a breed apart, and no European was their equal. They proved to be excellent riding companions, never questioning Vlad's need for privacy or his thirst for the blood of their vanquished.

He would never forget the time he first confronted the brown-robed mortal after one of these raids, the man who was responsible for the years of confinement from which Vlad had just reawakened. This despicable individual had been armed with a single weapon—one far more effective than any exploding firestick.

The spear the man carried was unlike any other weapon Vlad had ever faced. Though it appeared ordinary enough, the lance affected Vlad in the strangest of ways, and it was this weapon alone that led to his first death.

Now that he had been reborn, Vlad knew that only one device on Earth could do him harm. Without this weapon, even the mightiest of mortals could not endanger him.

Somewhere in the world, this lance awaited him. And once it was his, no power in this universe could wrest it from him. Only then would he be not only beyond all fear, but death itself!

Shivering at the thought of such a blissful possibility, Vlad decided to return to the spot beside the river where he had confronted the three mortals. Then he would continue downstream, to the place where the bare light of day beckoned. Here he would wait for the protective cover of night before emerging again into the world. Maybe then he could identify the strange land in which he had awakened. And he would feed to regain his full strength. It was time to prepare for the inevitable confrontation that destiny itself had willed at the beginning of time.

13

The Repina clinic was a two-hundred-bed, full-service hospital, located due south of the Kremlin on the banks of the Moscow River. Only recently renovated, the forty-year-old facility contained one of the capital's most modern trauma care centers. Here, all sorts of problems could be dealt with, ranging from serious injuries, to heart attacks and strokes.

The emergency room staff was well into its morning shift when the three MVD investigators entered carrying the limp body of the girl. The attending physician efficiently determined the sixteen-year-old's condition and immediately began treating her for shock while a blood transfusion was prepared.

Genuinely relieved to hear that the youngster had a fighting chance to survive, Mikhail, Yuri, and Pavl gathered in the lobby of the emergency room.

"Well, comrades, it looks like we made the right decision after all," observed Yuri as he pressed a blood-soaked handkerchief against the open cut above his eyebrow. "The ultimate tragedy would have been to lose her now."

Reaching for the camera that still lay strapped around his neck, Pavl added, "At least I've got the one responsible for this barbarity on film. If it's all right with you two, I'd like to get over to the lab at once and get to work developing it."

"Of course, Pavl," Yuri said. "We'll join you back at headquarters."

"At least we'll have something to hand out to the other investigators," reflected Mikhail. "So make certain you make plenty of duplicates."

"Will do," returned the photographer, who wasted no time in leaving the clinic.

Yuri took a seat in the lobby and beckoned his partner to join him.

"I never got a chance to ask what your impressions are of our suspect," whispered Yuri. "I'll lay odds that he's a complete psychopath who's on the run from an asylum."

"That could very well be," said Mikhail. "Yet I can't help but feel that there's something beyond madness operating here. Of course, he could be high on dope. That could account for his unusual degree of strength and his apparent fearlessness."

"But how and why in the world is he draining the blood of his victims?" Yuri persisted. "That's the really sick part."

His partner thought a few moments. "He could be doing it for some kind of ritualistic purpose. I've read about such organizations existing in Rumania. They use blood in their religious ceremonies."

The doors to the emergency room swung open. Out walked a stout, middle-aged woman, dressed in a white lab coat. She scanned the lobby and approached the detectives.

"Good morning, comrades. I'm Dr. Primorsk. I thought you'd like to know that the girl you brought in is responding to treatment. Though the poor thing remains in critical condition, it looks like you got her here just in time.

"Those two bite marks that appear to have been cut into her carotid artery—was the youngster attacked by some kind of dog? If so, the animal must be captured, or we'll be forced to begin preventive treatment for rabies."

Yuri grimly shook his head. "All that we can tell you, Doctor, is that her wounds were not caused by any dog. The beast responsible is human—we think."

The doctor gasped. Noticing the severe gash on Yuri's brow, she changed the subject. "That's a nasty wound you have there, comrade. Are you going to let us take a look at it, or do you want to needlessly risk infection?"

Yuri grimaced. "It's only a scratch. I'll live."

"Nonsense," scoffed the portly physician. "That cut is deep and will require stitches to heal properly. When's the last time that you had a tetanus shot? Lockjaw is a most painful way to die, my friend."

Aware of his partner's trepidation about doctors, Mikhail interceded. "The doctor is right, Yuri. Go ahead and let her treat you. I'll use the telephone to report back to headquarters, and then I'll finish completing the girl's admittance papers. Now, quit being such a coward. Good partners are hard to come by, and I don't want to lose you just yet."

"All right, if you really think it's necessary," muttered Yuri, allowing the doctor to lead him by the arm through the swinging doors of the emergency treatment area.

Stifling a chuckle, Mikhail rose and headed toward a nearby telephone booth. He deposited two kopecks and dialed Colonel Yakov Kukhar's private work number. Three rings later, a gravelly bass voice answered.

"This is Deputy Assistant Saratov speaking."

"Comrade Saratov, this is Mikhail Antonov. Is the colonel there?"

"I'm afraid the colonel has just left. Where in the world have you been anyway, Antonov? The chief's been waiting for your call all morning!"

Mikhail cleared his throat. "Is there somewhere that I can reach him? It's extremely important that I talk to him as soon as possible."

"That will be impossible for the time being, Antonov. He's sequestered in the Kremlin, and left orders not to be disturbed. By any chance does this have to do with those three corpses that were found drained of blood recently?"

Surprised that Saratov had been briefed on the details of this case, Mikhail cautiously probed. "Why do you ask?"

The assistant deputy answered directly. "Because if it does and you have any pertinent information, there's a slim chance that I can manage to relay it to the colonel before he begins his meeting."

Mikhail decided to trust the deputy, who was Kukhar's closest associate. "Very well, comrade. Tell the chief that we actually confronted the suspect in the catacombs near the Moscow River, as he was in the process of carrying off victim number four. Though he subsequently escaped us, Pavl Barvicha was able to capture our man on film. I'm calling from the Repina clinic, where the victim we rescued is currently fighting for her life."

"Why that's an incredible report, Antonov! If what you say is true, the colonel will be most interested. I'll do my best to try to reach him at once."

"You do that, Comrade Saratov. I'll be checking in personally just as soon as my partner's wounds are treated."

Still excited by Mikhail's news, the deputy assistant added, "By the way, comrade, you received a phone call earlier. Hold on while I get the message."

Mikhail patiently waited for Saratov to return. He scanned the lobby and saw that a very pregnant woman had just entered the clinic. From the way she held her bulging belly, she appeared to be in labor. Mikhail was impressed by the manner in which she managed to calmly waddle over to the admittance desk. Abruptly his attention was called back to the deep voice of the deputy assistant.

"Here we go, comrade. The party identified himself as Nicholas Andreivich. Dr. Lopatin at the Institute of Culture referred him. Say, isn't that where the first blood-drained corpse was found?"

"So it was, comrade. Now, how do I reach this party?"

"The number he left is 2.52.24.51."

"Very good, Comrade Saratov. Thanks for your help."

Quick to disconnect the line, Mikhail dropped another two kopecks into the telephone and dialed the number that the deputy had just relayed to him. He was surprised when a female voice answered.

"Convent of the Virgin."

Mikhail asked to speak to the party that had called him, and found himself once again put on hold. While waiting to converse with this mysterious person, he looked out to the lobby and again pondered the pregnant newcomer, who was patiently filling out a thick pile of admittance forms.

"This is Brother Nicholas Andreivich." said a relatively young-sounding male voice.

"Comrade Andreivich, this is Lieutenant Mikhail Antonov. I believe you called my office earlier today."

"Why, yes, Lieutenant. Dr. Lopatin at the Institute of Culture gave me your number."

"So I understand," replied Mikhail. "Now, how can I

help you?"

A bit guardedly, the young monk responded. "I was hoping that we could talk face to face, Lieutenant."

"I wish that I had time for that, comrade, but my schedule is a hectic one. Can I ask what this is regarding?"

"It concerns the recent death of a security guard at Dr. Lopatin's institute," answered Nicholas. "I have an idea that this man did not die from natural causes."

He instantly gained Mikhail's full attention, for the details of the guard's death were yet to be released to the general public.

"It's more than a hypothesis," continued the monk, "for I am certain that the man was murdered."

Mikhail's curiosity was now completely piqued. "You don't say. And I suppose you just happen to know who this murderer is."

"As it so happens, I do," stated the monk. "I am staying at the Convent of the Virgin, on Moscow's south side. Can you be here within the hour?"

Distracted, Mikhail muttered, "I suppose I could manage."

"Good," said Nicholas. "I'll be waiting for you in the convent's library."

With this, the line went dead, and Mikhail hung up the receiver. He peered down at his watch absentmindedly, then looked up to scan the lobby. On his way out he stopped at the front desk and scribbled out a note to his partner, informing him to rendezvous at headquarters. Then, with his steps guided by a new urgency, he left the clinic to hail a taxi and find out precisely what this mystery caller was talking about.

Deputy Assistant Saratov managed to reach his boss

just as he was about to enter the hall where his morning meeting was scheduled in less than three minutes. Although he was determined not to be late to this all-important gathering, Colonel Yakov Kukhar nevertheless allowed a secretary to guide him to the telephone where his assistant anxiously waited on the other end of the line.

With one eye on his pocket watch, the colonel listened as Saratov relayed to him the details of his phone conversation with detective Mikhail Antonov. By the time Saratov concluded his report, the colonel hardly noticed that the heavy oaken doors to the conference room had already slammed shut.

Leaving his assistant with orders to phone him should any further encounters be reported, the colonel hung up the receiver and took a second to pull himself together. It was not often that he was called inside the walls of the Kremlin. Waiting for him on the other side of the sealed doorway was an assemblage of the Motherland's most powerful individuals. Known as the League of the Godless, this organization primarily dealt with matters that touched upon the spiritual core of the Soviet Union.

This afternoon, the league had summoned the colonel to brief its members on the three unusual homicides that had recently taken place in the capital. The veteran MVD officer was thankful that his deputy had managed to reach him when he did. For now he would be able to promise the league that the perpetrator would soon be behind bars.

Taking a deep, calming breath, Kukhar walked up to the oaken doors and knocked three times. A uniformed guard opened the door and beckoned him to enter.

The room was huge. Its walls were covered with gigantic canvasses of Soviet landscapes. Hung from the center of the ceiling was a magnificent crystal chandelier, positioned directly above the room's only furnishing, a large, circular mahogany table. Seated around this table were seven grim-faced men, all of whom were at least sixty years old.

It was obvious that the meeting had already been called to order. Kukhar inferred this fact when a white-haired elder, who had been in the midst of some passionate speech, suddenly halted his discourse. Looking down to meet this elder's icy glance, Kukhar sheepishly nodded and seated himself in the remaining vacant chair.

The elder scanned his captive audience before resuming his speech. Known simply as the Chairman, his captivating stare displayed a force that betrayed his frail appearance. Though his white hair was thinning and his veined cheeks were shrunken, his pale green eyes gleamed with life. He puffed out his chest, which displayed a variety of the Motherland's highest decorations, before solemnly continuing.

"Now that our esteemed colleague from the MVD has given us the honor of his presence, it appears that we can get started once again. As I was saying in my opening statement, today the Motherland faces its greatest challenge, not from outside its borders, as has been the case in the past, but from within. For the first time since the revolution, angry crowds walk the streets of our cities, their chants filled with hatred and frustration. It is their mistaken belief that the Communist system has somehow failed them.

"There are those in the Politburo who directly lay the blame for this show of civil disobedience on the people's spiritual dissatisfaction. It seems that our masses are no longer content to sacrifice material comforts for the good of the country as a whole. Yet the imperialists continue to force us to divert most of our funds into the defense of our country. This trend shows no sign of changing and, thus, it is up to us to come up with alternative ways to channel the people's interests away from materialistic consumer goods and services.

"The Soviet people must be re-educated. No sacrifice should be too great for them. They must learn to understand that only one thing matters. They must recognize that the integrity of the Motherland must always come before the selfish, bourgeois needs of the individual.

"This is the spiritual sickness that is threatening our very existence! And it is against this subtle enemy that we must focus our forces. Otherwise our great Socialist experiment will go for naught.

"With this said, it is now time for the secretary to read the salient points of last week's meeting."

Seated to the chairman's right, a hefty, nattily dressed gentleman leaned forward and shuffled his notes. Colonel Kukhar recognized him as the Minister of the Interior, Dmitri Gnutov. Only after putting on a pair of bifocals did the minister begin to speak.

"During our last meeting we sketched out a campaign to root out the various organizations responsible for the social strife that has swept over the Motherland this past winter. It was unanimously agreed that our first target should be the religious institutions that have been directly sponsoring this unrest.

"The league ordered Marshal Obolensk to step up his organization of paramilitary units, whose task it will be to discourage public prayer meetings and baptisms. These elite units are to be made up of select members of the armed forces. They are to be sworn to secrecy and will be accorded bonuses according to the amount of religious literature and Bibles that they are able to confiscate.

"Marshal Obolensk was also chosen to select those individuals needed to carry out the assassination of various Moslem fundamentalist leaders. The elimination of these troublemakers is a number one priority, as the unrest along the Motherland's southern border continues to increase.

"Minister of Education Ramenki was then commissioned to draw up an outline of a new program of agnostic studies, which is to be instituted in every public school within the month. A similar program is to be taught at all weekly Komsomol meetings and in every factory in the nation.

"With this assignment, a debate ensued concerning alternative methods of rooting out religious dissidents. No concrete proposals resulted from this discussion, and the meeting was subsequently adjourned."

Putting down his notes and removing his bifocals, the minister of the interior nodded silently at the chairman.

"Thank you, Comrade Gnutov. Before hearing more about the spiritual redirection assignments, I would like to introduce this afternoon's special guest. Colonel Yakov Kukhar has been with the Moscow branch of the MVD for more than four decades. He is a respected criminologist and brings with him today a report of a most disturbing nature.

"The facts that you are about to hear are classified. Only a select handful of individuals know of their existence. Because of your position in the league, it has been decided that they are also to be shared with you, in order that a plan of action can be mounted.

"As you will soon see for yourselves, a situation of the utmost delicacy has presented itself. Listen carefully to the facts involved, and then we will open the topic for general discussion. Colonel Kukhar . . . "

Solemnly nodding in response to this introduction, the colonel cleared his throat and began to speak. "Esteemed comrades, two days ago the body of a security guard was found in a laboratory at the Institute of Culture. Upon initial observation, it appeared that the man was felled by a coronary, and he was routinely conveyed to the city morgue for an autopsy. It was at this time that our coroner, Dr. Albert Stura, discovered that the real cause of death was shock, induced by a radical blood loss. The corpse was completely siphoned of blood, and two human bite marks were subsequently found on the guard's neck. It was through these puncture wounds that the bodily fluids were supposedly extracted.

"When the blood-drained body of a dutywoman was brought in the next day with similar bite marks, Dr. Stura informed my office, and an intensive investigation was begun. This led to the discovery of yet another corpse with matching wounds. This time it belonged to a Metro engineer who was apparently attacked by another man while exploring a portion of the catacombs that lay in the vicinity of the Universitet train station. The engineer's partner witnessed this attack, and it was from his shocked lips that we derived our first description of the perpetrator.

"Per municipal statute 97571, which instructs the MVD to notify the league should it encounter any crimes of a ritualistic nature, I immediately telephoned Marshal Obolensk to fulfill my obligation. As a result of this call, I was invited to speak to you today. Little did I realize that I would have yet another incident to relay to you.

"Only minutes before I entered this hall, I was informed by my deputy that this very morning three of my men actually confronted the one responsible for these horrible crimes. This encounter apparently took place in still another portion of the catacombs, near the Moscow River. There my men chanced upon the beast as he was in the process of carrying away a fourth victim, a sixteen-year-old girl. Fortunately they interceded in time to save this youngster's life, though the suspect was able to escape. Like the others, the child was also severely bitten, with a great deal of blood gone from her body."

"Why, that's remarkable!" gasped the league's secretary, who was busy scribbling down notes.

A murmur of nervous chatter swelled, quelled by the banging of the chairman's gavel.

"Quiet down, comrades!" ordered the feisty elder. "Show some respect, and allow our guest to conclude his briefing before rudely interrupting him."

With the floor once again his, the colonel continued. "I just wanted to add that one of my men, who encountered the suspect this morning, is a photographer. I understand that he's presently in the laboratory developing the film he was able to shoot. Thus I hope to be able to distribute actual snapshots of the murderer within the hour."

Once more the members of the league could not help but vent their amazement, and again it was the chairman who quieted them down. "Come now, comrades, control yourselves! Now, you've all heard the colonel's report, yet one all-important question remains unanswered. Colonel Kukhar, were any of the unsavory details of this case released to the public?"

All eyes were on the veteran detective as he nervously formulated his reply. "Though departmental policy is strict in such matters, I regret to inform you that rumors did begin to circulate soon after the first autopsy was completed. The stories were centered around the peculiar manner in which the victim was murdered. A technician in the coroner's department was reported to have shared these facts with his fiance, who happens to be a secretary at MVD headquarters. By the time the rumor reached my office, it was blown completely out of proportion."

"How so?" the chairman pressed.

It was obvious that the colonel was uncomfortable as he replied. "The rumor implied that the three victims were killed by a blood-sucking demon with supernatural powers. I believe that the word used to describe this monster was 'vampire.' "

Again the members of the league audibly expressed their reaction. Yet this time the chairman seemed to be in no hurry to quiet them down. When he finally did speak out, his forceful voice was just as effective as his gavel.

"We all know the power of rumor," he reflected. "So often, we ourselves use such idle hearsay to our own benefit. Yet in this instance, it will produce only needless panic.

"Fortunately for us, it sounds as if Colonel Kukhar and his men are close to apprehending the cold-blooded maniac responsible for these despicable crimes. But until this madman is safely behind bars, we can take nothing for granted.

"Considering the current mood of the city's populace, such a wild rumor is all that is needed to produce chaos. An exaggerated monster myth circulating at this moment will create needless fears and anxieties, which could easily lead to further insurrection and lawlessness.

"All of us know that such monsters only exist in fairy tales. As a lad growing up in the western Ukraine, I was exposed to all sorts of native superstitions. To my grandmother, vampires, werewolves, and hobgoblins lurked in every dark wood. She even used garlic and thorns to keep such beasts far from our cottage.

"The arrival of the Communist age showed our citizens how foolish such infantile beliefs were. Lenin proved without a doubt that the Christian god was but another of these moronic superstitions. There is no omnipotent Father sitting in the sky, pulling the strings of his mortal puppets, just as there is no devil, God's evil counterpart here on Earth. Since the creature known as the vampire is a supposed spawn of this evil one, Lenin proved that such a beast could not possibly exist.

"It's as simple as this—Christianity teaches that God is the creator of both good and evil. Yet we know for a fact that there is no God, and that good and evil exist only in the hearts of men. There are no avenging angels from Heaven or flesh-eating demons from the bottomless pit!"

"Well said, Comrade Chairman!" interrupted a deep bass voice from the far end of the table. "But I think we need to take precautions against the possible failure of the MVD."

All eyes turned to face the youngest member of the league, Marshal Viktor Obolensk, the assistant director of the KGB. "Even as we talk, a bloodthirsty maniac is loose in our beloved city. If this beast continues his atrocities, it will prove impossible to stem the panic of the masses. And the news that a so-called vampire is loose in the capital of atheism will prove a bit embarrassing, to say the least. Just think how such a story would play in the Western press. Even though we in this room know that such a creature could not exist, we must act. As it happens, I know the perfect person to call upon. Since we have employed his expertise before, all of you know how effective this individual can be. So, if I have your blessings, I'd like permission to call in Comrade Igor Strellnikoff."

"But I feel that such a move is unwarranted," Colonel Kukhar said. "My men are close to breaking the case and bringing in an outsider now will be but a waste of valuable time."

"I disagree," countered Obolensk. "With all due respect to the colonel, it's obvious that a case such as this deserves special treatment. That is why we must bring in Strellnikoff. He will track down the murderer and in the process debunk the ridiculous rumor that will soon be spreading through the city like wildfire."

"But Comrade Chairman, my department is more than capable of ridding the streets of Moscow of this killer!" pleaded the colonel.

Conscious that Kukhar's pride was at issue, the chairman cautiously interceded. "The MVD is a most competent organization, but in this instance, we cannot be too careful. I think that the marshal's suggestion is a good one. Strellnikoff and his detachment of Spetsnaz commandos will be able to sweep the catacombs and root out this maniac. It will be comforting to have these forces on the streets of the capital should we encounter any civilian unrest.

"To ensure that the rumors concerning the so-called vampire are put to a halt, I hereby authorize Colonel Kukhar to have his men round up all individuals who have firsthand knowledge of these crimes. They are to be placed in protective custody at MVD headquarters and released only on my say-so. The militia will also halt further investigation into this matter, with all files to be transferred to Major Strellnikoff's command with all due haste."

Yakov Kukhar knew that he had been defeated, but he dared not argue his case further. He rose when the chairman politely excused him. The veteran investigator was hardly aware of what the members of the league were vehemently discussing next as he turned toward the doorway to reluctantly carry out the chairman's orders.

14

After returning from the institute, Nicholas sequestered himself in the convent's library. Here he attempted
to resume the research project that he had originally initiated back at the Abbey of the Pursuer.

The young monk was in the midst of reading William
Lawrence Shirer's *The Rise and Fall of the Third Reich*.
Even though the book gave substance to his own theory
that Adolph Hitler was the true representative of the
Fallen One in the modern era, Nicholas could not concentrate on this superbly documented history. His
thoughts were riveted on the relic he had seen with his
own eyes only hours before. For if the writings of his holy
predecessors were to be believed, in this very sarcophagus Satan's legitimate spawn had been imprisoned for
one thousand years.

There could be no denying the three Moldavian Greek
numerals carved into the coffin's stone lid. Known as the
Mark of the Beast, they were put there by Nicholas's
brethren a millennium ago as a warning to all humanity.
Now it was up to Nicholas to determine exactly where
the Beast was located, and then to hunt him down with
the only weapon that could destroy the hellish creature.

Time was of the essence. If the Beast was indeed stalk-
ing the streets of Moscow, countless lives would be

endangered.

Diverting his glance from the pages of the book he had been reading, Nicholas focused his attention on the life-sized icon mounted on the library wall. It was a beautiful representation of the Virgin Mother wearing a bright blue robe. Her fair-skinned face seemed to glow with inner life, and Nicholas felt a deep spiritual peace course through his being. Gone were the doubts that had once left him cold and confused. In their place was a warm, glowing sensation that filled him with new purpose and direction.

The abbot had chosen him to undertake this all-important holy mission to Moscow. Surely this was a great honor. The significance of this assignment was enhanced now that he had set his eyes on the sarcophagus and had seen the three numerals that were cut into its lid.

As the unraveler of a mystery recorded two thousand years ago, Nicholas was but an extension of his spiritual mentor, St. John of Patmos. Confident that he would not let his master down, the young monk silently reaffirmed his vows, his glance still locked on the magnificent icon of the Ascended Master's virgin mother. So deep were these ponderings that he did not realize that he was no longer alone.

A delicate female voice bade the monk's attention. "Excuse me, Brother Nicholas, but you have a guest."

Pulled abruptly from his deep reverie, Nicholas turned his head and took in the figure of a blond-haired man who had followed one of the sisters into the library. As the sister humbly excused herself, this brown-suited newcomer directed his full attention to the seated monk.

"Lieutenant Antonov, I presume," greeted Nicholas. "Thank you for your promptness."

Mikhail took several steps forward. "I was fortunate to get here before the evening rush hour. As I said over the telephone, my schedule is an extremely tight one, so could you get to the matter that necessitated my presence?"

Instantly sizing up the detective as an honest, hardworking man, Nicholas replied, "I appreciate your candor, Lieutenant, and I promise to waste as little of your precious time as possible.

"I originally called you to inquire about one of your investigations. Several days ago, the body of a security guard was found inside the Institute of Culture. It was reported that this man died of a heart seizure. I have reason to believe that his death was not caused by natural means."

"I am not in the habit of discussing such matters with strangers," Mikhail said. "Even if this is indeed the case, how is it that you learned of this information?"

Nicholas sighed. "As I said before, I'll try to waste as little of your time as possible, so please excuse my directness. The order that I serve has historical knowledge of the sarcophagus beside which the security guard was found. We believe that a creature was buried in this same coffin a thousand years ago. This cursed being was not dead, but instead lay in a state of dormancy. My sole purpose on Earth is to wait for the moment when the seal to this vault is broken and the creature reawakens to kill once again."

Mikhail's first impression was that he was listening to the rantings of a lunatic. Yet the monk's intensity was sincere.

"Did you say kill, comrade? And just how does this so-called creature do away with his victims?"

"By sucking out their lifeblood," said Nicholas.

The detective's eyes opened wide.

"And if it turns out that the security guard's death was caused by just such a mysterious blood loss, I have one other question for you, Lieutenant. Have there been similarly mutilated bodies found in the city since then?"

Genuinely amazed by the monk's intuition, Mikhail fought back the urge to reveal all he knew. "Once again, I'm not at liberty to share such information with you."

"Oh, come now, Lieutenant! I understand your vows of secrecy, but these are human lives we're talking about. No matter how foolish and irrational I may sound to you, you've got to trust me. Otherwise, there's no telling how many more victims will fall to this bloodthirsty fiend."

Mikhail remained skeptical. "What is the name of this order that you belong to?"

"St. John the Pursuer," said Nicholas curtly.

"Can the legitimacy of this institution be corroborated?"

"Why, of course," the monk said. "You need only ask the Mother Superior of this convent. I believe that Dr. Lopatin at the Institute of Culture can also vouch for the Order of St. John the Pursuer."

Though he did not care to admit it, Mikhail, too, had disturbing questions about the murderer's mortality. He could have sworn that his aim had been true earlier in the catacombs. He was almost positive that he had shot the suspect cleanly in the chest. A hollow-point, 9mm bullet had incredible stopping power, but the man had escaped without leaving so much as a drop of blood on the ground behind him.

Still hesitant to divulge all that he knew, Mikhail's response was guarded. "I must admit that you have touched upon several elements that are most intriguing, comrade. Before I can open up to you completely, however, it's absolutely necessary that I know more about this so-called order of yours.

"If you don't mind, I'd like to continue this discussion back at the Institute of Culture. Once your legitimacy is confirmed, I believe we'll have more to talk about."

Richard Green and Yelena Lopatin broke for a late lunch. The redheaded archaeologist chose a cozy little cafe only a few blocks from Red Square. To properly celebrate Richard's first full morning of work, they started off with a bottle of champagne and a platter of *zakooski*. The appetizers included a tart potato salad with chopped pickled gherkins, some freshly sliced cucumbers, and several pieces of a delicious cooked sturgeon known as *osyotr*.

Next, they were served piping hot bowls of *schchee*. Made with a salted cabbage that Richard thought tasted like sauerkraut, the soup had several pieces of stewed beef in it and was topped by a dollop of *smetana* (sour cream).

For their main course, they both ordered the house specialty, chicken *tabaka*. This dish reminded Richard of fried chicken, though it was rather heavily seasoned. Yelena explained that the main spice he was tasting was coriander. According to Yelena, Armenians swore that coriander would help one live to be at least a hundred years old. Richard toasted this folkloric wisdom and ate heartily.

Both turned down desert and instead finished off the champagne. In no mood to immediately return to the institute, they decided to walk to Red Square. It was a gorgeous day, and Richard got his first close-up view of the Kremlin wall and the brightly painted, onion-shaped domes of St. Basil's Cathedral.

Because of Richard's status as a working tourist, they were allowed to advance to the front portion of the long line of people waiting to see Lenin's tomb. As they entered the mausoleum, Yelena related to him the interesting fact that the preserved body of the founder of Communism was for the most part formed of hardened wax. Only the head, hands, and feet were once real.

After this rather solemn tour, the bright lights and animated crowds of GUM department store were most welcome. Organized around a central fountain, the store was in reality three separate shopping arcades occupying two different levels. Though Richard was expecting otherwise, he spotted a wide variety of consumer items for sale here. He was especially impressed with the menswear available. Though it was not necessarily stylish by American standards, there appeared to be plenty of shirts, trousers, suits, and jackets to choose from. There were long lines of customers as well.

Yelena gave him a quick lesson on how the system worked here. First the consumer had to wait in a line to get a salesperson to make out a proper bill. Then he was forced to wait in another line to pay the bill. Yet another line awaited the customer near the exit, where their purchases were wrapped and picked up.

Shopping in Moscow required great amounts of patience, and after some browsing Richard followed his guide outside. They noticed that the sun had sunk low in the sky, but still finding themselves in no mood to return to work, they slowly walked back to the car, enjoying the temperate winds that blew from the south.

They finally returned to the institute refreshed and ready to resume working. Richard was eager to show Yelena the library catalogue that he had spent most of the morning translating, and he invited her to accompany him to his office. As they entered his cubicle the American noticed a sealed envelope sitting on the top of his desk. His name was typed on the front, and he opened it and quickly skimmed its contents.

"Well, I'll be. It's a response to that telex that I sent to Saint Louis University before we left for lunch."

Taking a moment to read this document, he proceeded to share its contents with his guest. "It appears that my Jesuit colleagues have indeed heard of the order our mysterious brown-robed visitor mentioned earlier. It seems that the Order of St. John the Pursuer goes all the way back to the days of the New Testament. It supposedly got its start on the island of Patmos, not long after the crucifixion. St. John the Divine was the founder. And are you ready for this? It says here that not only is it one of the most secretive religious sects in all of Christianity, but that it is composed of warrior-priests, dispersed throughout the world, whose sole purpose is to await the coming of the Antichrist."

Looking up from the telex, Richard's face was flushed with excitement as he continued in a trembling voice, "My god, Yelena, those numbers carved into the lid of the sarcophagus! 666 is not only known as the Mark of the Beast, but as a symbol for the Antichrist!"

Linking her gaze with the American's, Yelena suddenly paled. "You don't really think that such a beast actually exists, or that we might have been responsible for digging it up and unleashing it on the streets of Moscow? Because if you do, there's one detail I think I'd better share with you.

"I realize that this may be an insignificant observation, but on the same day that we found the dead security guard, I noted a one-hundred-sixty-pound discrepancy between the weight of the sarcophagus when it was originally logged in by the deceased and its actual weight as recorded later that afternoon. Maybe the difference can be attributed to the fact that someone truly was sealed inside and was released sometime during the night by that poor sentry."

"I think we had better share this information immediately with Dr. Yakhut," Richard said. "Then I guess a call to that monk is in order."

Richard was about to pick up the intercom to contact the institute's director when a knock on his door temporarily diverted him.

"Come in!" he called.

The door swung open, and in walked Lieutenant Antonov of the MVD and the very same brown-robed monk.

"Good afternoon," said the detective. "I realize that we're barging in here without an appointment, but Dr. Yakhut told us that this is where we'd most likely find the two of you."

Trying hard to conceal his excitement, Richard replied, "As it turns out, your visit saves us a phone call."

"Were you trying to contact me?" asked Mikhail.

Richard shook his head. "No, actually we were seeking Brother Nicholas."

The young monk nodded. "How can I help you, Doctor?"

The American was uncomfortable with the detective's presence, and he expressed himself carefully. "I just wanted to inform you that my Jesuit colleagues back in the United States have sent me a brief description of the order to which you belong. I believe that we now know why you've made this long trip to Moscow from the Carpathians."

Nicholas exchanged a long look with Mikhail Antonov before answering. "I see. Since it appears that you know all about my background now, would you mind sharing this information with the lieutenant here? You see, he seems to doubt the legitimacy of the holy order that I serve."

Richard handed Mikhail the telex he had just received. "It's all there," he said. "The Order of St. John the Pursuer has graced this planet for almost two thousand years."

The blond-haired investigator gave this document but a cursory examination. "This is all very fascinating," he said, "but these are modern, enlightened times. Surely such organizations are anachronisms now."

"Anachronisms, Lieutenant?" echoed Nicholas. "I can prove otherwise.

"Since it's apparent that you have some knowledge of the purpose of my order, it's time for me to be completely honest with you. Yes, I came to Moscow to see if the three Moldavian Greek numerals were carved into the coffin's lid. Now that I have seen this inscription with my own eyes, an even greater responsibility beckons me. It is my sworn duty to track down and destroy the creature locked inside that sarcophagus for the last thousand years."

"You're saying that this creature is the Antichrist?" asked Yelena.

Nicholas nodded. "Yes, Dr. Lopatin, he is known by that name and many others."

"But all of this is foolishness of the first degree!" interrupted Mikhail Antonov. "Creatures such as this only exist in fairy tales or bad dreams."

There was compassion in the monk's tone as he

responded. "When will you quit your own childish game-playing and admit that the institute's guard did not die of a coronary, as initially suspected? Come to terms with yourself, Lieutenant, and share with us your findings. Otherwise, countless others will needlessly suffer."

Yelena broke in. "Did Vasili Pavlinchenko die at another's hand, Lieutenant? Please, you've got to tell me! I'm the one responsible for bringing that infernal sarcophagus to the capital in the first place."

All eyes were on the detective as he rubbed his forehead meditatively and answered her. "To tell you the truth, I don't know what the hell is going on here! All I know is what my gut tells me. I should just walk right out of here. But for some damned reason I'm going to tell you what you want to know. Who knows, maybe you can help me make some sort of sense out of this whole ugly mess.

"Vasili Pavlinchenko did not die from a coronary as was originally assumed. It wasn't until his autopsy that we found two bite marks on his neck and learned that he died from shock induced by a massive blood loss.

"Strangely enough, two more bodies were brought in that had succumbed to similar wounds. And if that wasn't enough, my partners and I actually interrupted this so-called monster of yours while he was attempting to suck the lifeblood out of yet a fourth victim, only a few hours ago. Unfortunately, the bastard managed to elude us."

"You actually laid eyes on the Beast?" the astounded monk asked.

Mikhail nodded, "Not only that, comrade, but we've got the photographs to prove it."

"Where did this confrontation take place?" prodded

Nicholas.

Realizing that he had said too much already, Mikhail sighed. "You might as well know all of it. We came across him in a portion of the catacombs that undercuts the southern portion of the Kremlin, near the Moscow River."

"I should have known that he would be drawn to that part of the city," reflected Nicholas. "Not only will it provide him shelter, but it is familiar territory as well."

"What do you mean by that?" asked the detective.

The monk's eyes opened wide. "Don't you understand, Lieutenant? The Evil One has explored those subterranean passageways before, when they were originally built almost ten centuries ago!"

"Oh, come now, that's unbelievable!" said Mikhail.

"No more so than a being who craves human blood," returned the monk.

"Lieutenant Antonov, in all honesty I must admit that I can't help but question the rationality of such a creature's existence," interjected Richard Green. "Yet in my years of church research, I have come across several events whose outcome can only be labeled miraculous. So perhaps we should all listen carefully to what Brother Nicholas has to say, without being too judgmental."

"I agree," added Yelena. "I've come across some strange myths in my own line of work. And who's to say which tale is fact and which is fantasy?"

Even though his mind rebelled at the thought of accepting the existence of a supernatural demon, Mikhail forced himself to at least consider the possibility. "Okay, Brother Nicholas, say that your monster really does exist and is responsible for the three homicides. Precisely who is this creature, and how can he be killed?"

"His mortal name is Vladimir Dolgoruki," said the

monk. "He was born ten centuries ago, in a small village not far from here. Vlad's father is credited with having founded the town of Moscow. It was during an excursion to the river, on whose banks the first Kremlin was constructed, that Vlad succumbed to the bite of a legendary, two-headed flying creature, whose representation was later to grace the heraldic emblem of the czars.

"This bite infected Vlad with a dark essence that has stalked the earth since the beginning of time. As a slave of evil, Vlad was given the gift of immortality. In reality, this was a curse, for his eternal youth demanded a single and constant food source—mortal blood.

"Only one weapon exists that can harm the Evil One. By the grace of the one Father, this divine spear was given to my order's spiritual founder and has been passed down through the centuries. The Order of St. John the Pursuer exists solely to hunt down the Beast, whenever or wherever he should awaken. As a representative of this order, I was sent here with the holy lance at my side, to see if the time of reawakening was upon us.

"One thousand years ago, an initiate of our order successfully confronted and defeated the Beast in the body of Vlad, and the Evil One was subsequently buried in a specially designed sarcophagus. Now you people have taken possession of the sarcophagus, and its accursed occupant is once again loose upon the earth.

"I am relying upon you to help me track down this unholy creature. We can contain the Beast by using the sacred lance against him. Only then can he be sealed back inside his sarcophagus for the next thousand years of sleep."

A jarring telephone ring interrupted the monk's spirited discourse, and Richard Green reached out to pick up the receiver, his thoughts far from the mundane world.

"Hello, this is Dr. Green. . . . Yes, as it so happens, he's right here. Hold on while I get him for you."

Looking up, the American caught the glance of the blond-haired detective. "It's for you, Lieutenant."

Mikhail took the handset and heard the animated voice of his partner.

"By the grace of Lenin, at last I finally tracked you down. As it turned out, I survived my medical treatment, and after reading your note, returned to headquarters."

"Have you gotten a chance to see Pavl's photographs yet?" Mikhail asked. The others in the room were staring at him as he spoke.

"I've seen them, all right," returned Yuri. "But that's not why I'm calling. The chief wants to see all of us at once. It's about our current assignment, and from what I've been led to believe, this meeting is most urgent. When can you get here?"

Mikhail glanced at his watch. "I'm on the south side now. By the time I grab a cab, it'll probably be six."

"I'll send over a squad car for you," offered Yuri. "And please get here as soon as you can. Kukhar's been screaming his head off all afternoon, and I don't relish the idea of having to face him alone."

Mikhail hung up the phone and spoke quickly. "I'm afraid that I have to return to headquarters, comrades. This discussion has been most fascinating, and I'm looking forward to continuing it at a later date. But right now, there are two things I have to ask of you. First of all, I must order you to keep all of the information that I shared with you to yourselves. If I learn of any leaks, I will have no choice but to order your arrests. And most importantly, it's imperative that you don't take any direct action without my approval. This includes you, Comrade Andreivich. I realize that you've been sent here for a distinct purpose, but right now, you've got to trust the authorities. We are most prepared to track down this beast that you are pursuing, whatever its manifestation. By proceeding on your own, you'll only be getting in the way. Do I make myself clear in these matters?"

Nicholas solemnly nodded, and Mikhail turned toward the doorway. "Very good, comrades. I'll be in touch with you as soon as possible."

With this he departed, leaving Richard, Yelena, and Nicholas together in the cramped office.

"I want to thank both of you for your patience," said the monk, after an awkward stretch of silence. "It was wrong of me to involve you in this whole affair, and if you'll excuse me, I'll be on my way."

"Now hold on a second," said Yelena. "If what you say is true, it's in our best interest to assist you in your effort to destroy this creature."

"Yelena's right," said Dr. Green. "Besides, we're not about to let you go, now that our curiosity has been aroused by your tale. Tell us more about the history of this unearthly beast, and let us plan our next move together."

Nicholas felt bolstered. "I think an excellent way to get started would be to get the map of the catacombs the lieutenant mentioned. Are such charts available?"

Yelena beamed. "As it so happens, the institute was responsible for undertaking the only comprehensive study of the catacombs, which run extensively beneath the city. With a bit of digging, I believe I can find the diagrams."

"Then what?" asked Richard.

"Why, our next move is only too obvious, Doctor," said the monk. "Then we prepare for battle!"

Noting the peculiar gleam that sparkled in the young monk's eyes, Yelena diverted her gaze to meet that of her American coworker. Richard Green nodded in awareness, and only then did the full extent of their involvement finally dawn in his consciousness.

15

It was pure hunger that eventually drove Vlad from the catacombs. The mortal scent still hung thick in the heavy air as he crept down the pitch black passageway. Soon the rushing sound of cascading water broke in the distance, and Vlad knew that he was close to the banks of the underground river.

Much to his dismay, the girl's body was not where he had left it. Various footprints were imprinted in the mud where the child had last lain. This could only mean that the other mortals had carried her away.

Feeling angry and ravenous, Vlad knew where his course would now lead him. To appease his growing appetite, he was forced to stalk his prey in the streets of the strange village in which he had awakened.

Instinctively, he looked downstream. He could see only the faintest light flickering in the distance, so he knew that night must have fallen. Thankful for this, he began his way down the riverbank and only then noted the three distinct sets of footprints traveling in the same direction.

A gust of fresh air greeted him as he walked. The cool, exhilarating breeze blew his hair away from his face and triggered long-forgotten memories of his youth.

A heavy feeling of despair settled upon him. The

accursed bite had set him apart from other mortals. The fates had drawn the flying beast to his throat, and now Vlad was condemned to pay the ultimate price of living a life that knew no death.

Vlad consoled himself with the thought of his sole earthly pleasure: feeding. The warm body of a fresh victim in his grasp, the sweet essence of blood as it dripped down his throat and filled him with new strength—for this purpose only he walked the earth without family or friends, guided by an insatiable hunger that knew no appeasement.

Vlad's stride faltered as he reached the tunnel's opening and he carefully peeked outside. Dusk had just fallen, and he looked out to the river as it continued to flow downstream. As the current emerged aboveground, its channel widened, the banks now formed by two tree-lined ridges. To get a better idea of his whereabouts, he decided to climb to the top of the ridge to his right. Little was he prepared for the view that awaited him.

Stretching for as far as his eyes could see was an unbelievable city. Formed from a collection of what appeared to be immense castles, this town was unlike anything he had ever witnessed. Its immense size and scope stirred the roots of his imagination.

Beyond the surging river, a constant, muted roar rose in the distance. As he continued downstream, he viewed the panorama of a gigantic bridge barely illuminated by a line of flameless torches and holding hundreds of individual carriages. Vlad was incredulous that, like the underground chain of carriages, none of these vehicles had horses or oxen pulling them! This snakelike mass of traffic proceeded over the bridge with a grinding rumble. Belching forth thick clouds of smoke, it seemed like an entity unto itself.

On the opposite bank of the river he spotted a huge, brick tower whose spiraled roof was topped by a brightly glowing, five-pointed star. Connected to this structure were the walls of what appeared to be a formidable fortress. Known as a kremlin to the Tartars, such a bastion could easily withstand the most ferocious enemy onslaught.

While Vlad was studying this fort, he noticed a single figure standing immediately in front of the tower. Even from his vantage point on the other side of the channel, he could see that she had blond hair and was dressed in a full-length fur coat. Though a roadway followed the riverbank in front of her, only an occasional carriage roared down its narrow length. Since no other pedestrians were visible, Vlad knew that this woman could very well provide him with sustenance without needlessly compromising his safety. He would have to cross the river first, however.

On impulse, he sprinted down the ridge that he had been following and plunged into the water. An icy chill greeted him, and he had to begin swimming immediately to counter the river's swift current.

Vlad's stroke was powerful. Taught to swim at an early age by his father, he had spent many a summer frolicking in the Moscow River. Those were innocent, blissful days, and Vlad's mind was filled with pleasant memories as he established a steady pace.

Could he ever forget that glorious summer when his father first chose the site for their new village? Called Moscow for the river that it overlooked, this town was to be greater than any yet gracing the region. Since several important trade routes naturally crossed at this point, it would be a perfect commercial settlement.

How excited his father had been when he led Vlad

down to the river to picnic and swim! His father's eyes had been filled with dreams, and Vlad, too, had been overcome with enthusiasm.

His powerful stroke now brought him to the other side of the channel. A stone wall formed the bank here. Vlad pulled himself out of the icy current and began to climb the new obstacle. He could only hope that his tempting prey was still waiting on the other side.

Katya Morozova was chilled to the bone and seething with anger. Even though she was a prostitute by trade, she had not been forced to work the streets like this since originally arriving in the capital more than a year ago from Minsk. If she had wanted such humiliation, she would have stayed in the Ukraine!

Katya had hoped that things would be better in Moscow, and for the first couple of months indeed they had been. She had often wondered what magical force had been at work on that momentous afternoon when she first arrived at the Center and departed the train at Kievskaya station. Armed only with her aunt's internal passport and her own good looks, Katya immediately went to work.

Word of mouth called her to the Arbat district, where a woman like herself had the best chance of success. With her long, thin legs, she was able to make the most out of her homemade miniskirt. Why, that very night, she had found herself with a purseful of newly acquired roubles. That night she also landed a pimp and a penthouse apartment.

Katya's live-in boyfriend was named Aram Kazakov, but he was more commonly known simply as the Arab. This nickname made reference to his swarthy good looks and his Armenian ancestry. A man of many talents, he made his living with his wits and his nerve. Most of his self-made wealth was accumulated in trafficking black market goods. Blue jeans, athletic shoes, Japanese stereos, and cocaine were his specialties. He also offered his managerial skills to a select group of attractive young women who, like Katya, happened to make their living by selling sexual favors to the highest bidder.

Most of Katya's clients were wealthy businessmen who learned of her unique services from their network of contacts. She had made it a practice to take on no strangers without a solid reference, and thus managed to keep her arrest record to a bare minimum.

Aram had promised her that she could retire soon and that they then would get married. Lately she had begun to wonder if this was just another of his lies. Why else would he insist that she walk the streets tonight like a common whore?

Though Aram had claimed that the extra duty was necessary to help finance her unmanageable coke habit, Katya was certain that he had an ulterior motive. Most likely his motives centered around a big-breasted red-head from Sverdlovsk, whom he had only recently taken under his wing. Katya could clearly see the way the red-head played up to Aram, and she could sense his interest in her as well. Why else would he give her the profitable taxi concession, while Katya was tossed out onto the freezing streets of Moscow to earn her day's keep? Why, those two were probably making it even as she stood here beside the Kremlin wall, waiting for the next horny client to drive by! This thought infuriated Katya, and she swore to herself that she'd kill that damned redhead the next time she caught her making eyes at her man.

Katya disgustedly reached into her bag for another cigarette. She flicked open her gold-plated Dunhill lighter and considered her alternatives. She could always pack up and leave Aram. But what would that get her? She had no money of her own to get an apartment, and besides, who else would supply her with the ever-increasing amount of cocaine that she needed just to make it through the day?

One thing she was certain of was that she could never return to Minsk. Her parents had always stifled her, and now that she had lived in the Center for a full year, she was completely spoiled. No, there was only one solution to her predicament, and that was to teach a certain some-one a lesson in humility. Once the big-chested redhead was out of the way, the Arab would realize how much Katya really meant to him, and once more she would be in his favor. Then there would be no more evenings like this one, freezing her tail off for a stranger who might very well be working for the MVD.

Taking a deep drag on her American cigarette, Katya scanned Kremlovskaja Street and wondered when she would have enough money to return to the apartment. Her current take was almost fifty roubles a day, and so far, she had earned barely half that much.

The last time she had worked this location, good for-tune had certainly been with her. No sooner had she tak-en up her position beneath the water tower when a black Zil limousine pulled up and its occupant beckoned her to join him inside. Katya assumed he was a Kremlin big-wig, for he was clothed in an exquisitely cut French suit, and even had several medals pinned on his lapel. She received a fifty rouble note for her services, and because she had pleased him so quickly, she was back out on the street before she knew it, her purse thirty roubles even fuller and her day's work all but over.

Today was a vastly different story. So far, she had had only one customer, and he was just a lowly bureaucrat who had consumed too much vodka at lunch. Katya had taken him to a nearby flat, where he proceeded to satisfy himself at her expense for a good hour. He had promised her forty roubles, but had only come up with twenty-three of them. In no mood for arguing, Katya took the cash and returned to her perch beneath the Kremlin walls, the stench of alcohol still clinging to her.

The one good feature of her current location was its magnificent view. Even the Center was no stranger to urban blight, and the Moscow River was one of Katya's favorite places to get away from the endless concrete and steel. In a way, this portion of the city reminded her of her rural birthplace, on the banks of the Dnepr. Though the capital had plenty of action, the one thing she missed was the tranquility of the pine forest in which she had been raised. Thus the line of evergreens that graced the river's opposite bank was a welcome sight.

It was while Katya was gazing downriver at this stand of trees that she noted a man climbing the grassy embankment toward her.

As he crossed the street she saw that he was dressed in a pair of white coveralls. The Metro personnel wore similar outfits, so Katya assumed that he was on his way to or from work. Katya took in his tall, slim frame and suddenly noticed that he was wearing no shoes. For some reason, this strange fact upset her, and her apprehension intensified as she viewed the long black hair that fell to his narrow shoulders. Surely he was unlike any Metro worker that she had ever seen!

Soon Katya got a good look at the man's face. He had dark, angular features that some would consider ruggedly handsome. Yet Katya thought otherwise. She sensed something cruel and evil in the stranger's expression. His cheekbones were sharply etched, and his black eyes were piercing.

Katya toyed with the impulse to flee. Though this seemed like a most prudent course of action, for some reason her limbs would not respond. She could only stand there, her eyes wide with panic, her pulse beating wildly, as the mysterious, long-haired stranger continued his approach.

Katya managed to gather her nerve and timidly voiced a salutation. "Good evening, comrade. Nice night for a walk, wouldn't you say?"

The stranger was only a few meters from her now, and Katya was aware of an unpleasant, musky scent that seemed to accompany his approach. She realized that her words of greeting had somehow escaped him.

"I said good evening, comrade," repeated Katya, her tone a bit stronger. "Are you all right, my friend?"

The stranger suddenly halted and took a moment to appraise her face and figure with his piercing glance. Katya's entire body shivered uncontrollably, and she felt her will weakening. When his icy gaze met hers directly, his lips turned up in the slightest of sneers. Somehow with this mere look he had managed to violate the innermost portion of her being. Once more she found herself fighting the urge to flee. Yet as before, her limbs would not obey.

Katya gasped when she saw the crimson spheres of fire that suddenly formed in the stranger's eyes. The hairs at the nape of her neck rose when he pulled back his lips to reveal a set of elongated, pointed teeth. Then he let out a long, terrifying hiss that seemed to well from deep inside his throat.

Katya swooned dizzily and was saved from falling to the ground by the stranger's strong grasp. His scent was now overpowering.

The last thing that she remembered before drifting off into blessed unconsciousness was a series of shrill, whistling blasts that penetrated the night air like the cries of a demon.

"Stop this instant!" ordered the young sentry from the Kremlin's nearby ramparts. "I'm warning you, comrade, put her down now, or I'll fire!"

The guard concentrated the beam of his flashlight on the two figures that stood among the trees beneath him. He had been intently admiring one of these individuals for a good portion of his watch.

This section of the Kremlin grounds was a notorious hangout for prostitutes, and the tall, fur-coated blond who worked the territory this evening was a real looker. The young sentry had considered propositioning her himself until he noticed the white-coverall-clad newcomer. Something about this man's appearance bothered him, and he watched as the stranger approached the woman. They seemed to briefly converse, and then she mysteriously fainted. The wiry stranger caught her in his arms and was about to carry her off when the sentry decided it was time to intervene.

"I'm only going to warn you one more time, comrade!" cried the sentry, but the suspect ignored him, draping the woman over his shoulder, then sprinting for the cover of the nearby tree line.

"Damn you!" cursed the guard, and his free hand went once more to his whistle. He let out a series of warning blasts as he madly raced down the narrow ramparts. The suspect was still illuminated by the beam of the sentry's flashlight, but seemed oblivious to his warnings.

The stand of pines that the stranger was following graced the entire southern wall of the Kremlin. If he continued traveling in the direction he was headed, he would eventually come to Moscow's central concert hall, with Red Square close behind.

Though the guard carried a revolver, he did not dare use it for fear of hitting the woman. As he chased the stranger, he was joined by two police agents who had been alerted by his whistle blasts. These two burly, plain-suited KGB operatives were assigned to the Kremlin's exterior security detail.

"Over there, in the trees beside the river!" managed the exhausted sentry between gasps of air. With the aid of his flashlight, he was able to illuminate a portion of the parkway, and for a second, the back of the fleeing figure, still bearing the prostitute, was visible.

"I was in the midst of my rounds and had just reached the water tower when I saw him abduct a young woman—I think she's a prostitute. I ordered him to put her down, but he just kept running."

Sharing a brief, concerned look with his partner, one of the agents pulled out a large flashlight and directed it into the trees. This beam was more powerful than the sentry's torch, and it illuminated the surrounding area. Soon the suspect was clearly visible. This time when the light hit his back, he suddenly stopped and turned directly toward the wall.

The two KGB officers and the out-of-breath sentry had no trouble making out the suspect's tall, gaunt figure, which was clothed in a pair of white coveralls. The fur-coated, blond woman was tossed over his shoulder like a sack of flour. Shading his eyes from their light, the stranger stood facing them, almost as if he were taunting them to take further action. Noting his long, dark hair and distinctive facial features, one of the KGB agents exclaimed, "It's him, all right! I'll use the two-way to notify Marshal Strellnikoff. Now for the love of Lenin, we mustn't let him out of our sight!"

No sooner were these words spoken than their suspect took off running. This time his strides were long and powerful, and his pursuers could barely keep up with him. They had just passed the Annunciation Tower when he suddenly disappeared from sight.

The muffled roar of an advancing helicopter became audible as they anxiously scanned the now-vacant tree line with their flashlights. Seconds later, a blindingly bright shaft of light penetrated from above, illuminating the parkway as if a new day had dawned. Yet even with the assistance of the hovering helicopter, the suspect and his victim failed to materialize.

A truckload of armed soldiers was dispatched onto Kremlovskaja Street. With the helicopter still hovering above, they made an intensive sweep of the parkway that lay between the southern walls of the Kremlin and the neighboring Moscow River. In spite of all their efforts, the only piece of evidence that they were able to come up with was a full-length fox coat, found carelessly tossed upon the ground beside a lofty evergreen.

The thrill of the pursuit had an intoxicating effect on Vladimir. As he carefully picked his way down the steep, stone stairway, he smiled as he thought about the men's clumsy efforts to capture him. The hands of fate had miraculously led him to the secret doorway that was cut into the brick tower's base.

The mortals had discovered him from the top of an adjoining rampart. Like the woman he still carried over his shoulder, they had spoken to him in a vaguely familiar, but nevertheless incomprehensible tongue. Soon afterward, they triggered some sort of magical torch that clearly illuminated him, even from the great heights of the wall. Though he had next expected to hear the deafening, explosive bursts of their firesticks, they had failed to attack, and Vlad had been able to escape by heading directly toward one of the large towers that was set into the wall.

His father's kremlin had been similarly built, and when Vlad felt along the base of the tower he had chanced upon this entrance, which was designed to permit those inside the fortress secret access to the outside world. The doorway led straight into a cramped, musty chamber. It was dark inside, and from the cobwebs and dust that had collected, it was obvious that the room had not been visited for many years. A stone stairway was cut into the floor, and though Vlad was anxious to satisfy his ravenous hunger, he readjusted his precious load and made his way into the pitch black confines of the depths below. Vlad welcomed the solitude, for he had no desire to have any more encounters with the mortals, at least until he had completed feeding.

Vlad looked down to make certain that his next meal was still unconscious. Satisfied, he reached the base of the stairway and found himself in yet another portion of catacombs. This passageway had a low stone shelf set in its center, and an assortment of bleached white bones littered the floor. Vlad noted the presence of quite a few human skulls interspersed with the dusty debris. Such remains were most likely deposited during a time of siege, when a proper burial would have been impossible.

Feeling at home in these hushed surroundings, Vlad carefully laid his victim on her back on the flat, rock shelf. The coat that she had been wearing when he first confronted her had since fallen off, and she was clothed only in a skimpy, one-piece garment that barely covered her shapely thighs.

Vlad silently admired the long, curly, blond hair that framed her exquisite face. He could not help but notice that her lips, cheeks, and eyes were covered with a substance that seemed much like paint. This coloring was especially apparent on her lips, which were coated with an oily, pinkish substance.

The pulse still fluttered beneath the smooth, white skin of her neck. Before feeding, Vlad took a moment to examine more closely the rest of the attractive mortal's body. He ripped off the flimsy garment she wore and took in her slender figure, which sported a perfectly shaped bosom, compact hips, and long, shapely legs. As he touched her smooth skin, Vlad found his own pulse racing madly with excitement. For the first time in a millennium he felt the stirrings of true desire. A primal need, even greater than that of his bloodthirst, overcame him. He trembled as he tore off his own awkward garment and swore that this woman would be his.

Only after he was completely spent and had satisfied his primal longings was he possessed by another hunger. Still entwined in the unconscious woman's embrace, Vlad licked the glistening skin of her neck, and it was at that very moment that she awakened.

Katya Morozova's dream had been most vivid and upsetting. In this vision, she found herself re-exploring the forests of her youth. She had just stumbled upon the corpse of a recently slain deer, when a huge, shaggy wolf suddenly showed itself. Startled, Katya turned to flee, but found that her heavy legs would not respond. She could only stand there in terror as the wolf cautiously moved in closer.

Katya screamed as the creature snarled, displaying a

pair of yellowing fangs. Yet no one was close enough to hear her as the wolf sprang forward, knocking her flat on her back.

She remembered the beast's unpleasant, musky scent as he positioned himself on top of her. Unable to scream out in horror, she could only watch as the creature began stroking her bare skin with its cold paws. Her dread turned to sheer revulsion when the wolf began to rape her.

The pain was indescribable. It was only after it had spent itself that she remembered looking up into the beast's gaze. In the center of the creature's dark pupils were two, swirling crimson spheres of fire. This was no ordinary animal, she realized, but one dispatched from the black bowels of Hell.

With this shocking realization, Katya snapped back into consciousness. She found herself in a dank, pitch black chamber, lying naked on a hard, stone ledge. A vile, musty odor seemed to emanate from the man kneeling above her.

Katya struggled to orient herself. Looking up at the man's face, she absorbed his cruelly handsome features and the long, stringy mop of dark hair that fell over his shoulders.

It was then that she remembered the man she had seen walking along the Moscow River. He had been approaching her when her memory had suddenly gone blank. Such lapses of consciousness had plagued her ever since she had started using cocaine, and Katya supposed that he had subsequently propositioned her. Yet where had he taken her, and why was she filled with such revulsion and dread?

Anxious to be on her way, Katya nervously cleared her throat. "Well, comrade, now that you've enjoyed yourself, how about paying up and letting me go? How many roubles did we agree on, anyway?"

When the man did not respond, Katya tried again. "Did you hear me, comrade? I said get off of me, and let me be on my way!"

This time when he did not respond Katya tried to push him off. Yet he proved stronger than he appeared. Unable to budge him, she could only plead her case.

"What is it, comrade, don't you think you've gotten your rouble's worth? If anyone in the Center can give you a better time, just let me know, and I'll be glad to give you your money back."

To prove her case, Katya began to grind her hips seductively. Yet this only seemed to infuriate the stranger, who slapped her hard on the side of her face.

"Hey, no rough stuff, comrade!" screamed Katya.

Completely ignoring her words of protest, the stranger let loose a loud, hissing sound and proceeded to strike her once again. This blow broke a blood vessel in Katya's nose, and a torrent of blood was soon streaming down her neck. The stranger was quick to lick up this flow with his tongue.

"So that's what you're into," Katya said breathlessly. "I'm warning you, comrade, this is going to cost you!"

Grabbing her by the jaw, the stranger lifted up his head and met Katya's gaze directly. As she returned his glance, she was aware of only one shocking fact. Her nightmare had come to life. Just like the wolf's eyes in her dream, the stranger's eyes were now formed of two spiraling spheres of crimson flame. Unable to scream in panic, she could only stare silently as a new vision began forming inside the flickering flames.

First to greet her was a procession of human skeletons, complete with flowing manes of hair and portions of rotting flesh still hanging from their bones. Following them was a large, shaggy, four-legged creature with the body of a horse and the head of a hideously deformed man. Next came a monstrous dragonlike beast, which carried a copulating man and woman on its broad back. And close behind was something tall and muscular. Completely covered with black scales, it sported a long tail and two pointed horns. This last beast beckoned to Katya and let out a loud hiss, displaying a pair of frightening, pointed fangs.

In a heartbeat, the hellish vision dissipated. Yet to her utter horror Katya found that these same fangs now graced the mouth of the stranger who had abducted her. Blood stained his thin lips as he roughly jerked her head aside and lowered his mouth until it touched the skin of her neck. Two sharp pinpricks of pain followed, and soon afterward, Katya stopped her struggling. As the strength ebbed from her body, she was distantly aware of a muted slurping sound and a gathering lethargy that signaled a sleep from which she would never awaken.

Vlad fed on the blond-haired mortal until not a drop of blood was left in her body. He had originally intended to prolong her final demise for as long as possible. In such a way, he could have obtained nourishment from her for days on end. He had lost all control when she had unexpectedly awakened, however, and now he would have to return to the mortal world to hunt again. But for the time being, his belly was full and his appetite satiated.

Vlad looked at the woman sprawled beneath him. Though her corpse would soon be cold, there were many others around who could satisfy him just as well. Content with this thought, Vlad rested his head on his prey's full bosom, and he closed his eyes to sleep.

16

Lieutenant Mikhail Antonov arrived back at MVD headquarters just as the evening shift of militia squad cars were leaving for their patrol sectors. Upstairs, behind the doors marked "Detective's Bureau," a thin, bald-headed man puffed nervously on a cigarette as he sorted through a pile of photographs. Mikhail spotted this familiar figure as he entered the room to a cacophony of ringing telephones and clanging typewriters.

"Good evening, partner," he called.

Looking up from the picture he had been studying, Yuri Sorokin smiled in relief. "Thank goodness you made it, Misha. There's no telling how much longer the chief's patience would hold."

Noting the large bandage on Yuri's forehead, Mikhail said, "I see the doctors at the clinic had a look at your cut. Was it serious?"

Yuri snuffed out the cigarette he had been smoking. "It was nothing, my friend. After a few dozen stitches, I'm as good as new. I wish that I could say the same for that poor girl we brought in for treatment. At last report, she was still alive, but just barely."

"Is she conscious?" Mikhail asked.

"It seems she's still in a deep coma," replied Yuri. "Some present for her sixteenth birthday."

"So you were able to at least identify her?"

Yuri solemnly nodded. "Her name is Anna Markova. She was last seen at the Universitet Metro station on her way to school. When she didn't show up there, her parents were informed, and they contacted the department. They made a positive identification at the clinic less than an hour ago."

"It's comforting just knowing who she is," said Mikhail, who only then turned his attention to the photos his partner had been sorting through. "Are those the shots that Pavl took earlier?"

"That they are, my friend. Feast your eyes on the bloodthirsty bastard responsible for these crimes. If I have my way, this psychopath won't be walking the streets of Moscow for long."

Mikhail leafed through the stack of photographs. Though the majority of them were badly blurred, the man was clearly discernible in several of the shots. He appeared to be middle-aged, with long, flowing, black hair and distinctly etched cheekbones. His gaze was dark and piercing, and his pupils glowed a puzzling shade of crimson.

"Could Pavl have made a mistake while developing these shots?" asked Mikhail. "It almost looks like this guy's eyes are on fire."

"So it does," reflected Yuri. "Pavl is downstairs in the lab right now, reprinting another set of negatives. We should have the results any minute, but from what he says, some people just photograph this way."

"Well, at least we've got something concrete to share with the others," offered Mikhail. "And if the information I learned today pans out, we might very well have the bastard's name, too."

Yuri's telephone rang. "Sorokin here," he barked into

the handset.

Mikhail listened as his partner talked. "As it so happens, he just walked in this instant, Colonel. We'll be there within the minute."

Yuri hung up the phone and reached out to light yet another cigarette. "I'm afraid we're in for it now, Misha. The chief sounded absolutely furious."

"So, what else is new?" said Mikhail, flipping through the stack of photos one last time.

Yuri closed the top button of his shirt and pulled tight his frayed tie. "At times like this I wish I would have become a farmer like my grandfather. At least he only had to contend with the fickle ways of nature. Now, will you put those damned photographs down and join me, comrade? Our entire careers could be at stake here!"

Mikhail returned the stack of pictures to Yuri's desk and followed him into an adjoining anteroom. Deputy Assistant Saratov was waiting for them there.

"He's expecting you, comrades," he said somberly. "Go right on in."

Yuri and Mikhail entered the inner office to find Colonel Kukhar sitting behind his cluttered desk, with the phone cradled to his ear. The tension showed on his face as he silently beckoned the men to take a seat. They could not help but overhear as the colonel spoke into the handset.

"Why, of course, Marshal. You can rest assured that you will have my complete cooperation in the matter. If you should change your mind, though, please don't hesitate to ask for our assistance."

With this, he hung up the receiver and took a second to massage his forehead before addressing his officers. "That, comrades, was news of a most distressing nature. It seems that our blood-hungry maniac has struck again.

This time he was seen just south of the Kremlin, near the Annunciation Tower, where he abducted a suspected prostitute."

Yuri sat forward and spoke excitedly. "That's not far from the spot where we confronted him earlier! We can be down there in less than ten minutes."

Yuri was already standing when the colonel spoke angrily. "For the love of Lenin, sit back down, Sorokin! This is one pursuit that you won't be participating in."

Yuri was bewildered. "But the sighting?" he asked anxiously. "Surely our efforts can best be spent tracking the beast down."

"So now you've become an expert administrator as well," snapped the colonel. "As of this moment, the MVD is no longer on the case. The powers that be feel there are other organizations better able to handle this matter."

"But that's ridiculous!" burst Yuri. "As keepers of law and order in the capital, the MVD has the best resources available for such a pursuit."

"Your loyalties are noted, Lieutenant Sorokin, but unfortunately there's absolutely nothing I can do to alter this directive. Unlike some people, I have learned not to question the chain of command."

Mikhail cleared his throat and dared to express himself. "Where is the suspect now, Colonel?"

"He was last seen running along the south wall of the Kremlin, headed toward Red Square. Special elements of the armed forces have already sealed off the area, and an extensive search is currently in progress."

Before he could continue, there was a knock on the door, and in walked Pavl Barvicha. The photographer was dressed in a white lab coat and held a stack of newly developed negatives in his hand. Pavl meekly nodded to his coworkers.

"I'm sorry I was late, sir, but I thought you'd want to see this latest series of prints."

Pavl handed them to the colonel and stepped back beside Mikhail.

"But I thought you were going to try another process on these pictures?" Colonel Kukhar said gruffly.

"But I did," returned Pavl. "And just like before, I got these results."

"This red glow in the suspect's eyes must be a fluke of some sort," muttered the colonel. "You say that certain people reflect the light of the strobe in such a manner?"

"Yes, but it's rare for such a thing to occur in more than one photograph. You see, the strobe has to hit the subject's pupils at just the right angle to obtain that effect."

"Well, I guess all of this really doesn't matter much now," Kukhar said. "The way it looks, the army will have our man before the next sun rises."

"What do you mean?" Pavl said, shaking his head.

It was Mikhail who answered this question when it was obvious that the colonel was wrapped up in his own introspection. "There's just been another sighting, Pavl. This one took place immediately south of the Kremlin, where our man abducted yet another victim."

"Then what are we waiting for?" said the wild-eyed photographer. "Come on, comrades! Let's be there to finish off the bastard."

"We'll be going nowhere," Yuri said somberly. "The authorities have taken it upon themselves to pull the MVD off the case."

"Surely you're joking," returned Pavl. "Is such a thing true, Colonel?"

The veteran investigator nodded.

"I am coming close to actually figuring out our suspect's identity," Mikhail pleaded.

"What do you mean by that?" asked the colonel.

Mikhail sat forward. "Earlier today, after escorting our young victim to the hospital, I received a call from a certain party who said that he had some information concerning the homicide that took place at the Institute of Culture. Since this incident had not been reported to the general public, I decided to meet the man and interview him. You wouldn't believe what I learned. Not only did he know that the guard was found drained of his blood, but that there had been other murders as well.

"Even stranger were his suspicions that some sort of legendary demon was responsible for the crimes and that a religious cult held the only weapon that could do this creature any harm. Needless to say, I was prepared to write him off as a kook. Then the existence of the cult was corroborated by members of our very own Institute of Culture."

Colonel Kukhar's eyes were wide with concern as he walked over and stood directly before Detective Antonov. "You didn't tell him anything about the murder of the guard and the others, did you, Lieutenant?"

Mikhail braced himself for trouble. "I'm afraid I did, sir. I am certain that he isn't just some screwball. I was hoping that he could help us track down the madman responsible for the bloodlettings, no matter from what ungodly world."

A look of pained disgust shot across Kukhar's face. "I don't believe it, Lieutenant! Tell me what I'm hearing isn't true and that you didn't really share confidential departmental information with an outsider."

"Actually, there were three of them involved," Mikhail confessed sheepishly.

Stunned into silence, Kukhar closed his eyes and
rubbed his forehead as if he were in excruciating pain.
When he finally vented himself, his tone bordered on
hysteria.

"I will deal with your insubordination at a later date,
Lieutenant Antonov! Right now, it's imperative that
these outsiders be placed under protective custody with
all due haste. So take your two associates here, and if any
of you value your future service to this branch of government, deliver to me these three individuals as soon as
humanly possible. Do you understand me, comrades?"

Taking in Kukhar's strained tone, beet-red face, and
bulging eyeballs, the three investigators nodded meekly.

"If you do, why in the world are you still sitting
there?" cried the colonel, who appeared close to losing
control.

Yuri and Mikhail stood up immediately and almost
tripped over each other as they hurriedly followed Pavl
out of the room.

Marshal Igor Strellnikoff gazed down at the scene
from his vantage point in the observation seat of the helicopter. The entire south wall of the Kremlin was visible.
With the aid of a powerful spotlight mounted beneath
the chopper's nose, he could pick out the seven individual towers. He could also see the hundreds of scurrying
ground troops that combed that portion of the tree-lined
parkway between the wall itself and the nearby river. The
elusive quarry had last been sighted there.

Though he had supreme confidence in his men,
Strellnikoff still could not figure out why they hadn't
uncovered their prey's trail by now. Surely one man
shouldn't be that difficult for naval commandos to flush
out. Yet they had been searching the grounds for more

than two hours now, and so far, they had not chanced upon even a footprint.

Patience was not one of Strellnikoff's virtues, and he restlessly pulled down his helmet's transmitter to contact his second-in-command. His trusted captain was currently on the ground with the rest of the men, and Igor had gotten off the line with him less than five minutes ago.

"Captain Vorkuta!" barked Strellnikoff, practically shouting in order to be heard over the deafening grind of the helicopter's rotors. "Have you spotted anything yet?"

There was a moment of static, and then a crackling voice came over his headphones. "That's a negative, Marshal. We've combed every centimeter of ground as far as the Water Tower, and so far we haven't found a trace of him."

Strellnikoff responded gruffly. "I think that it's time to get some sappers to work, digging into the bases of those towers. Start at the water tower and work your way eastward. Maybe we'll find a secret tunnel or something. At the same time, I want you to commence dragging the river. Who knows? Perhaps our suspect fell into the water while trying to escape."

"I will do so at once, sir," returned his subordinate.

"You do that," said Strellnikoff. "And this time, instruct the men to keep their eyes open. He's got to be close!"

With this comment, Igor disconnected the line and peered out the helicopter window. To enhance his view, he used one of the dashboard instruments to readjust the angle of the helicopter's spotlight. Soon the powerful beam was centered solely on the Kremlin's southernmost tower.

Known as the Water Tower, the structure was originally built in 1488 and, like the other corner towers, was circular so that its guns could cover an entire field of fire. In
recent times, a characteristic five-pointed star had been
mounted on its pointed steeple. Strellnikoff knew that
the tower had acquired its present name in 1633, when a
pump was installed in it to convey water up from the
Moscow River.

Strellnikoff watched as a flurry of activity became visible around the tower's base. Here dozens of men were
arriving with picks and shovels. Glad to see that his
orders had been carried out so efficiently, Igor slowly
scanned the entire south face of the Kremlin with the
spotlight. Only after he completed this intense reconnaissance did he order the pilot to move the helicopter
farther downstream to hover almost directly over
Beklemishev Tower, the Kremlin's easternmost point.

From this vantage point, Red Square was clearly visible. Strellnikoff could make out the distinctive, onion-
shaped domes of St. Basil's Cathedral, and beyond, a
squat, elongated structure whose smooth granite walls
were illuminated in red floodlights: Lenin's mausoleum.
Only a few dozen meters from the eastern face of the
Kremlin, the mausoleum housed the remains of the
republic's beloved founder. The roof of the building was
used for a reviewing stand, and it was here that the
Motherland's leaders gathered to celebrate various state
occasions.

Strellnikoff had been part of the May Day parade, and
he had led his crack squad of commandos before this
reviewing stand regularly for more than two decades
now. May Day was always a special event, and he felt
honored to be part of the annual festivities.

Red Square was practically empty now, but on parade

day it was packed to capacity with curious onlookers and participants. It was thrilling beyond belief to be a part of the mass that gathered to celebrate the nation's independence. Strellnikoff lived for the moment when he ordered his men to direct their eyes to the right, toward the mausoleum's roof, where the premier and the other members of the Politburo waited. For in that single glance, they reaffirmed their loyalty to the republic, pledging their very lives if necessary to keep the Soviet Union free from foreign dominance.

Yet strangely enough, on this fated evening, they found themselves facing a threat from within. Upset that a single man could cause them so much trouble, Strellnikoff decided that for safety's sake, he had better call up some armor that could block off Red Square if necessary. He would deploy these forces on nearby Oktabra and Kuybyshev streets.

Since the suspect had last been seen fleeing in that direction, Strellnikoff had already taken the precaution of covering the square with various undercover and uniformed agents. Though he doubted the killer had been able to get this far, he could not be too prudent. If the suspect was able to penetrate Red Square, the surrounding city awaited to further shelter him, and detection would become even more difficult.

Strellnikoff continued to gaze out the cockpit window and momentarily caught his own reflection in the shiny glass. Staring back at him was a grizzled face, given character by a square, dimpled chin, and a full, black mustache. His closely cropped hair was a mix of salt and pepper, and a distinctive black patch covered his right eye. Though well into his fifties, he was in superb physical shape and could still hold his own in the boxing ring, even against the freshest teen-aged opponents.

When he had first joined the armed forces at the age
of eighteen, the Great War had been over for more than
a decade. Yet the Motherland's wounds still ran deep,
and today a united effort on the part of Soviet citizens to
face the Western imperialist threat was sorely needed.

Strellnikoff had risen through the ranks of the military
quickly, and by his thirtieth birthday he was already a
full captain. Special operations were his forte, and he
gained notoriety as one who could be counted on for the
impossible assignment. Within the last five years, his
unit had been increasingly called in to face various
threats from within the Motherland's borders. These
included border uprisings, ethnic disputes, and other
problems that were not conducive to a smooth-running
state. Lately he had become somewhat of an expert on
the numerous dissident religious organizations inside
the Soviet Union.

Only recently he had been called into the Caucasus
region, where a group of Christians were undermining
the state by promoting baptisms and prayer meetings.
The cult was rapidly growing in size, and Strellnikoff was
instructed to eliminate its organizers. He did so by dis-
guising several trusted officers as potential church
recruits. They infiltrated the church, and soon not only
had a list of its entire membership, but also the location
of its printing presses and its precious supply of Bibles.

With such inside information, Igor had no trouble
arresting the church leaders. Subsequent raids netted
reams of Christian literature, which Strellnikoff did not
hesitate to put to the torch. When he and his squad left
the region, the Caucasus cult was all but obliterated.

Religion was a deceptive evil. Like a cancer, it might
look innocent enough from the outside, but inside was a
different story. The philosophies that the Christians pro-

moted ran counter to those of the state. Their promise of a blessed Heaven to come after this life spread like wildfire among the gullible peasants and babushkas, who feared death more than anything else. Thus they became Christians in an attempt to ease their anxieties.

Good Communists had their Heaven right here on Earth, Strellnikoff believed. They had no need for foolish rituals, which were not only a waste of precious manhours, and were energies that could be better applied to labor, but they were a drain on resources as well.

Strellnikoff and his men had put the citizens of the Caucasus back on the right path to socialist redemption.

A blast of static from his helmet-mounted headphones interrupted Igor's thoughts. He peered anxiously at the portion of the capital visible below.

Once this presumed psychopath was successfully captured, Igor was promised a full month off at his Black Sea dacha near Sevastopol. The warm sun and gorgeous women of this region were known throughout the Motherland, and Strellnikoff gloried at the idea of a real opportunity for rest and relaxation.

But first, a killer had to be tracked down. Only after this seemingly simple task was completed could he begin seriously planning how to spend this most anticipated vacation in the sun. With this in mind, the veteran officer activated the helicopter's two-way radio to call in the armor.

The evening traffic was light as Yuri guided the battered gray Volga down Universitet Prospekt and into the institute's parking lot. His fellow investigators had been unusually uncommunicative during the fifteen-minute trip from militia headquarters, and Yuri passed the time listening to the opening movement of a Rachmaninoff symphony on the radio.

He found a parking space close to the building's entrance. It was a cool, overcast night, with just a hint of spring in the air. Stopping briefly to light a cigarette, Yuri had to proceed at full stride to catch up with his coworkers, who had continued briskly toward the building without him.

He found himself wheezing for breath as he clambered up the endless succession of concrete steps that led to the institute's gilded entranceway. He arrived inside in just enough time to hear Mikhail greet the uniformed guard seated behind the reception desk.

"We're here to see Dr. Lopatin."

Intently scanning the faces of the three newcomers, the sentry shook his head. "I'm afraid that could be rather difficult, for you see, the doctor signed out more than an hour ago."

"Damn it!" cursed Mikhail. He reached into his suit pocket and pulled out his identification card. "We're with the militia. Is there any way we could learn exactly where she went?"

The white-haired guard flipped through the pages of his clipboard. "So you're with the MVD. Why, that's an excellent organization, and you should be proud to serve the state in such a way. If only I were a little younger, I'd join you."

Suddenly finding the entry he had been searching for, he added triumphantly, "Ah, here's the good doctor's signature, now. Yep, just as I thought, she left her destination blank, like she almost always does. That one's sure a beauty. If she had any sense, she'd be out looking for a husband. Say, why don't you see if Dr. Yakhut knows where she took off to? He's working late tonight, and you'll find him in Room 212. In fact, I'll call him now and tell him you're on your way."

Thankful for the old-timer's cooperation, Mikhail led the way up the marble stairway situated to the right of the reception desk. Yuri stubbed out his cigarette in the guard's ashtray. Even so, he was still wheezing for breath by the time he joined his colleagues on the second floor landing.

Yuri had been here once before, while investigating Vasili Pavlinchenko's untimely demise, and he was thus somewhat familiar with the building's layout. He followed his coworkers down the broad, tiled hallway and finally came to a halt in front of the door marked *212*. Immediately beneath these engraved numerals was a stenciled placard that read "Dr. Felix Yakhut, Director of Operations."

They entered without bothering to knock. Inside they found a deserted anteroom. The secretary's desk was vacant, but a spirited voice called out to them from an inner office.

"I'm in here, comrades!"

Sitting behind his cluttered desk, with a pile of work before him, was the institute's bald-headed director.

"Do come in, gentlemen," said Dr. Yakhut amiably. "I just got off the intercom with security. Glad to see that my man wasn't napping. Now, if I remember correctly, it's Lieutenants Antonov, Sorokin, and Barvicha. How can I be of further assistance to three such esteemed members of our militia?"

Mikhail got right to business. "We're here looking for Dr. Lopatin, and I understand that she has signed out. Do you have any idea where she's gone?"

"I certainly do," said the director. "Though I can't say precisely where you'll find her. The last time I saw the good doctor she was rummaging through the chart files, looking for the maps of Moscow's ancient catacombs. The next thing I knew, she was pulling hip-boots and flashlights out of the storage room, and then she stormed right out of here without even telling me what she was up to."

"Was she alone?" asked a worried Mikhail.

Dr. Yakhut shook his head. "I should say not. Do you know that she had the nerve to pull one of my very own researchers away from an important translation? And to think that I had invited him all the way from America to assist us with this project.

"Yelena has certainly done some impulsive things during her tenure here, but this one tops them all. She hasn't gone and gotten herself in trouble, has she, Lieutenant?"

"That remains to be seen," muttered Mikhail. "By the way, Doctor, was there a tall, blond-haired fellow accompanying her as well?"

"Oh, you mean the monk," said the director. "I'm sorry to have left him out. He was with her, all right. He said that he belonged to some obscure order in the Carpathians and was interested in taking a closer look at the sarcophagus Yelena was responsible for bringing to us."

Having heard all that he needed to hear, Mikhail prepared to exit. "You've been most helpful, Doctor. Thank you for your cooperation."

While Mikhail beckoned for his two coworkers to lead the way outside, Dr. Yakhut's voice rose with concern. "Now hold on a minute, Lieutenant! What's this whole thing about, anyway? Both Dr. Lopatin and Dr. Green are my direct responsibilities, and if anything has happened to them, you've got to tell me."

"As far as we know, you have nothing to worry about," said Mikhail sympathetically. "We only wanted to question her, and I would most appreciate it if you'd have her call MVD headquarters and ask for me the moment you hear from her."

"Does this have anything to do with those charts of the catacombs I caught her searching through earlier?" continued the doctor.

Ignoring his questions, Mikhail guided his two colleagues into the hallway and headed straight for the stairs. Though it was obvious that Yuri and Pavl were just as puzzled as Dr. Yakhut had been, Mikhail fended off their questions by establishing a blistering pace. It wasn't until they were outside the institute that they were able to catch up with him.

"What in the world was that all about?" managed Yuri between gasps of breath.

"I'll wager my pension this has something to do with those catacombs," offered Pavl.

Mikhail said pensively, "As it happens, you're correct, comrade."

"But what does all this have to do with finding the outsiders the colonel ordered us to take into protective custody?" Pavl asked. "My entire career's about to be ruined, and I still don't know why!"

Conscious of his partner's frustration, Mikhail softened his tone. "Yuri, if you'll drive us as quickly as possible to that portion of the tunnel where we found Anna Markova, I'll tell you everything I know along the way."

Mikhail knew that he should have kept his big mouth shut. Why had he ever told the civilian trio where the suspect had been encountered? Now, it seemed, the two scientists had actually joined the monk on his fabled quest. Did they really believe in the existence of the Evil One the monk spoke of, and did he really have a weapon that could stop the mysterious murderer? Wondering

what his coworkers would say when he told them about
the Order of St. John the Pursuer, Mikhail ducked into
the MVD car with Yuri and Pavl, and together they
began the long trip across town.

17

Try as he might, Vlad found himself unable to slip into a sound sleep. His encounter with the blond-haired woman had left him restless and fidgety. In an effort to compose himself, he began monotonously pacing from one end of the darkened chamber to the other.

The touch of the woman had triggered new longings, and for the first time in centuries, he tasted the bitter essence of real loneliness. He would never live to have a human mate who really cared for him and from whose loins offspring would be born. The flying demon's bite had set him apart as a race unto himself, and he was condemned for all eternity to be rejected and forlorn. The cold realization angered him, and Vlad cried out in the darkness.

"Father! Why did you bother to save me when I was stricken by the Evil One? If only you had let me die in peace!"

A shiver of dread coursed through Vlad's body, and he furiously beat his fists upon his own chest in an effort to rid himself of the fiendish spirit that reigned inside him. Where others knew love and attachment, he would only know the joy of blood-feeding. This, and only this, was his sole purpose!

A gradual calm descended upon him, and Vlad

momentarily stopped his pacing to pick up the white, one-piece garment he had snatched off the body of his male victim. With a single goal in mind, he slowly began to dress.

He left the chamber and walked through a narrow passage that took him away from the mortals who were trying to hunt him down.

The tunnel he chose was musty, its dank floor partially covered with fallen debris. But these obstacles were minor, and he followed the passageway for a long time. Finally, the barest of flickering lights beckoned in the distance. An expectant smirk turned the corners of Vlad's mouth, and his pace instinctively quickened.

Once again it was a crumbling stone stairway that conveyed him up into the base of an immense tower. As before, this structure was empty, and Vlad wasted no time locating its secret doorway. Carefully crawling through the portal, he soon found himself standing in front of yet another section of the enormous, red-brick kremlin.

This time, however, no cascading river greeted him. Laid out before him was a low-lying, elongated building that seemed to be constructed of glowing red granite. Some sort of tiered reviewing stand was set into its roof, and Vlad scrambled to the front of this structure to see what it overlooked.

He audibly gasped when he saw an immense, cobblestone square. Large enough to house the entire Tartar horde, this spacious portion of open ground was surrounded by an assortment of strangely shaped structures. Though the dark of night kept him from examining these buildings more closely, they were certainly unlike anything he had ever seen before. The structure on the right side of the square was particularly fascinating, and it was in this direction that Vlad allowed himself to be drawn. Traveling in the shadows of the great wall, Vlad reached his goal with mouth agape. Not even in his wildest dreams did he think that mortal men could be capable of designing such an amazing edifice!

What impressed him most were the variety of brightly colored, onion-shaped domes that rose from the building's roof. Several of them looked like they were designed to imitate a sultan's turban, while others appeared to be monstrous, gilded teardrops.

While wondering what such a remarkable structure could possibly hold, Vlad glanced down at one of its many entrances. There he spotted a fresh prey.

It appeared to be a young woman, also dressed in a long coat, and seemingly alone. Vlad could hardly believe his good fortune, and he decided to approach her directly. After he had rendered her unconscious and carried her back to his subterranean lair, he would once again taste the forbidden fruits of primal pleasure denied him for a thousand lonely years.

Lieutenant Svetlana Nikulin had just returned from a two-week-long exercise in the Ural Mountains and was looking forward to enjoying three days of rest and relaxation in the capital, when she was suddenly called back to duty. As one of the few female members of the Spetsnaz, she dared not express her displeasure. Surprisingly enough, she found herself chosen for an undercover operation, which was to take place right in the heart of Moscow, in Red Square itself.

After a cursory briefing, she was ordered to take up her current position, standing near the entrance to St. Basil's Cathedral. It had not been necessary to change into her uniform, and she was allowed to keep on her civilian clothing. Of course, hidden within the folds of her long, woolen greatcoat was a loaded 9mm automatic and a police whistle, which she was to use to call in reinforcements should she spot the suspect.

Not really certain what crimes this individual was accused of committing, Svetlana had no trouble memorizing his distinctive description. Tall and slender, with shoulder-length black hair, the suspect was last seen in the area less than two hours ago, dressed in white coveralls. He was supposedly armed and extremely dangerous, and she was authorized to use her gun on him should that prove necessary.

Svetlana was an expert shot. In the course of her official duties, she had killed other men on several occasions. Once in Afghanistan, she had cut down several rebel Mujahedeen with a single burst of automatic weaponfire. And that same night, she had slept as soundly and innocently as a newborn baby.

She supposed that her current assignment had something to do with the recapture of an escaped criminal. Yet this individual must have been responsible for quite a heinous crime if the Spetsnaz had been called in to apprehend him.

From what she had gathered, Marshal Strellnikoff himself was directing the operation. Svetlana had personally met this respected officer on the day that she graduated from boot camp. He had looked larger than life as he stood there on the podium, handing each of the new officers their hard-earned commissions. Well over six feet, five inches tall, he towered over most of those present, and his distinctive black eye patch and salt-and-pepper hair gave him a most distinguished appearance. It was rumored that he had never been married. Svetlana could not help but wonder what it would be like to bed a man like Strellnikoff. Surely it would be the experience of a lifetime!

Chuckling at this idle thought, Svetlana readjusted her woolen muffler and pulled up her coat's collar. The night air was moist and chilly. She had no idea how much longer she would be forced to remain at this post, and was mentally visualizing a cup of steaming hot tea, when a sudden movement caught her attention. Turning to her left, she looked in the direction of the Kremlin and saw someone approaching her from the great wall's shadows. She felt her pulse flutter as she took in the man's tall, slim frame and scraggly, black hair. It had to be him. The white coveralls he wore confirmed it.

Svetlana's first impulse was to reach into her pocket and remove the police whistle. Then she merely had to blow three short blasts to guarantee the arrival of adequate reinforcements in a matter of seconds. Yet as the suspect continued his approach, Svetlana wondered if it would not be possible to capture him on her own. He certainly did not appear to be armed, and from his slight physical build, she imagined that she could easily get the better of him with a few well-placed karate blows.

Such a capture would earn her certain commendation. How ironic it would be for her, the only female in the squad, to single-handedly capture the suspect. Why, even Marshal Strellnikoff would personally acknowledge her!

The suspect crossed beneath a street lamp and made his way through the wrought-iron fence that surrounded St. Basil's. Even though he still appeared to be unarmed, she reached into the folds of her coat and grasped the cool, steel butt of her pistol. As she did so, she took several steps forward and greeted him.

"Good evening, comrade. What brings you out on

such a chilly night?"

He began crossing the courtyard with an unbroken pace. There was a cold, distant look of determination in his dark eyes, and Svetlana felt the first stirrings of apprehension. When he was approximately twenty meters away from her, she decided that the time for game-playing was over. In one smooth movement, she pulled out her pistol, clicked off its safety, and aimed its barrel at the exact center of his chest.

"Okay, comrade, freeze!"

Completely oblivious to this warning, he continued his advance. Svetlana shouted again.

"Are you deaf, comrade? I said to stop in your tracks, right now, or I'll blow you away!"

This command seemed to do the trick, and the suspect suddenly halted in mid-stride. Only a few steps away from her now, she watched as he proceeded to silently appraise her figure. He appeared to like what he saw, for a satisfied smirk turned the corners of his thin lips. The light was bad, and Svetlana had trouble making out the suspect's facial features, but his apparent cockiness positively infuriated her. A vile, putrid odor wafted by her nostrils, and she sensed that he might be sizing her up for some sort of sexual encounter.

"Wipe that smirk off your face, and get those hands overhead!" she yelled forcefully.

When he failed to obey her, she cocked the hammer of her pistol and readjusted her aim to take in his right shoulder.

"I said hands up, comrade, or say good-bye to that right arm of yours!"

Much to her disgust, the suspect reached down to his groin and began seductively rubbing his crotch with the open palm of his right hand. She knew that this show was meant for her, and she reacted furiously.

"Why, you sick bastard!"

She followed up the invective by pulling the gun's trigger. There was a deafening, explosive blast as the hollow-point bullet sailed out of the barrel in a cloud of white smoke and smacked squarely into the suspect's shoulder. Yet unbelievably enough, not only did no blood flow from this wound, but the suspect remained standing as well!

A strange red gleam sparkled in his eyes as he met Svetlana's astounded gaze and let loose a booming, deep-throated howl that caused her knees to weaken. She felt herself losing control as fear and doubt clouded her perceptions. Then the suspect approached her once again.

The horrible smell rose to an almost unbearable level. Doing her best to hold her breath, Svetlana aimed the barrel of her pistol at the suspect's chest and squeezed off four quick shots.

Though she was at the point of questioning her own sanity, she remembered seeing her target momentarily stagger. She even saw the tight pattern of holes that indicated where her bullets had slammed into his sternum. Yet still he stood, and his wounds, which surely should have proved fatal, remained completely dry of any blood.

Certain that he must be wearing some sort of armored jacket, she put a bullet into each of his thighs. When this failed to stop him, she spent her last shot on his bare right foot.

By this time, Svetlana's hands were shaking too badly for her to put in another clip. What sort of horrible creature was she facing, anyway? Her entire body shivered uncontrollably when he finally reached her side and delicately touched her cheek with his outstretched left index finger. A wave of dizziness possessed her, and she found herself beyond fear.

She was persuaded to let the man have his way with her. The last thing Svetlana was aware of as she fell to the ground were the shrill blasts of distant whistles and the hollow sound of rapidly approaching footsteps.

Vlad heard the sounds also and angrily turned to see where they were coming from. Charging toward him were dozens of running mortals. Each one of them carried a flameless torch in one hand, and one of those incredible firesticks in the other.

Vlad cursed his predicament. The mortals were quickly closing in on him, and if he wanted to avoid a major confrontation with them, he would have to run for shelter without further encumbrance. Thus he made the painful decision to abandon the young woman and try to make his way back to the catacombs.

He turned and sprinted across the courtyard. Like a deer, he gracefully leaped over the low fence that surrounded the domed structure and took off running into the immense square that lay beyond.

His stride was loose and powerful, but the mortals relentlessly continued their pursuit. Vlad could clearly hear them screaming out in their puzzling language, and he even heard several firesticks discharging. Certain that he could outrun them, he glanced upward as a muffled, chopping roar sounded from somewhere in the cloudy night sky. Seconds later, the astounding source of this racket showed itself in the form of a monstrous flying beast, which had some sort of powerful torch set into its nose. He guessed that it was another one of the mortals' remarkable inventions. Vlad could actually feel the downdraft created by its apparent power source.

It hovered above him like a bothersome fly, with its light illuminating the square around him. Trying hard not to let this extraordinary device distract him, he tried to make his way back to the fortress. Then several horseless carriages roared into the square and headed directly toward him. They traveled with an incredible velocity, and Vlad could never hope to outrun them all, but no other alternatives were open to him. He did his best to increase his stride, and sprinted off for the shelter of the tower.

He spotted the distinctive red torches of this building in the distance, yet doubted if he could reach it before the horseless carriages got to him. The hand of fate determined his course. A long line of marching mortals suddenly moved around a corner before him. Without a moment's hesitation, he headed toward this column, hoping he would be able to evade the horseless carriages by losing himself in their midst.

The last-minute protest march was Petyr Ginzberg's idea. It was designed to catch the authorities off guard and to create greater publicity for their cause. The fiery, twenty-one-year-old economics student had come up with the idea during breakfast. By dinner, he had the support of more than a hundred fellow students.

As planned, they had arrived outside of Red Square via the Metro and congregated in an empty warehouse located behind the state-run GUM department store. Here they finished working on their banners and signs and listened as Ginzberg reaffirmed their grievances in a short, passionate speech.

Not only were they fed up with the government's unresponsiveness to the average Soviet consumer's needs, but they were also upset with the new university chancellor's recent decision to sharply limit their selection of elective courses.

With his troops roused to an almost revolutionary fervor, the precocious Jew from Irkutsk led his fellow protestors into Red Square. Here they planned to march to the entrance of Lenin's mausoleum, where the Western journalists that Ginzberg had spoken to earlier had promised to be waiting with cameras ready.

Because they were undertaking this gathering without an official permit, they were risking arrest. Most of those assembled had been in jail before for similar protests, and each was positive that the risks were well worth it. Their arrests were likely to spark both local and international attention, and the state would thus be forced to at least acknowledge their demands.

They were nearly halfway across the square, with the red spotlights of their goal clearly in view, when Ginzberg sensed trouble. Nine distinct explosions sounded in the distance, and the Jewish dissident could have sworn they were gunshots. This was followed by an assortment of whistle blasts and the appearance of a helicopter which had swooped down out of the black sky.

His roommate spotted the troop-filled, armored personnel carriers that were roaring out of adjoining Kuybyshev Street, and Ginzberg realized once again that the state was overreacting. A murmur of concern swept the line of protestors, and several of the students questioned the wisdom of proceeding with the march under such threatening circumstances.

Ginzberg's only thought was that there had to be a spy within their ranks. Why else would the government troops practically be waiting for them here? He raised his hands over his head and turned to address his fellow marchers.

"Comrades! Just look how our great state reacts to the peaceful pleas of but a small handful of its students! It only goes to show that our cause is just, and that they fear us even more than we fear them.

"So, tell me, comrades, should we run and cower like children, or continue with our protest? For we share the same spirit that brought Vladimir Ilyich Ulyanov and his followers to this same square almost a century ago!"

"Let's go on!" cried a voice from the pack.

"I agree!" shouted another who recognized Lenin's real name. "For the eyes and ears of the world are awaiting us at our beloved leader's tomb!"

Just as the line was about to begin moving forward once again, Petyr Ginzberg noticed a single individual headed straight toward them from the direction of St. Basil's Cathedral. Dressed all in white, the figure was running with incredibly long, fluid strides. Oddly enough, the helicopter and the rapidly approaching personnel carriers seemed to be paying more attention to this long-haired sprinter than to the students themselves.

As the figure dashed through their lines, the dissident leader realized that the soldiers had not been sent to arrest the protestors as he had assumed, but to capture this fleeing figure, who must be an escaped criminal!

Petyr looked on in horror as the soldiers plowed into their startled ranks, following this undoubted escapee. A violent melee ensued as students vainly attempted to protect themselves from what they thought to be an act of pure state-sponsored aggression.

The butt of a rifle sent Ginzberg dropping to his knees in pain. As the blood began dripping down his forehead, his vision blurred, and he could just make out the back of the still-fleeing runner as he disappeared into the blackness beyond. Aware of the surrounding tangle of fallen bodies, which prevented the soldiers from freely continuing their pursuit, Petyr dimly wondered if the malefactor appreciated their painful sacrifice.

18

The American linguist, the redheaded archaeologist, and the holy warrior from the Order of St. John the Pursuer left the Institute of Culture well-supplied with charts, hip-boots, and flashlights.

Dr. Lopatin drove them to their immediate goal in the central part of town. There they entered the catacombs by way of the Kropotkin Metro station. One of Yelena's maps showed that they could gain access to the ancient maze of subterranean passageways underlying this portion of Moscow by traveling down an adjoining sewer tunnel.

With Nicholas leading the way, they began to follow the tunnel to the east. According to their maps, this would take them all the way to the river, and the spot where Lieutenant Antonov last reported sighting the Beast.

Their route was formed primarily of limestone blocks and was shored up by large wooden timbers. Though his traveling companions halted occasionally to explore a promising relic, Nicholas set a blistering pace. He carried the elongated wooden case containing the holy spear he had last seen inside the Abbey of the Pursuer. That fated moment seemed to have taken place in another lifetime, yet in reality it was less than a week before.

When they reached a fork in the tunnel, Nicholas conferred with them. "It appears that we are now faced with a choice of two separate passageways. Does this junction show up on your charts, Dr. Lopatin?"

Pulling out her map, Yelena traced their route and solemnly shook her head. "No, it doesn't. Look, I told you that these charts were incomplete at best. What does the compass say, Richard?"

"It looks like the tunnel to our left points almost due north," Richard said, squinting at the compass in his hand. "The one to our right extends a bit more easterly."

"Then that should be the one that will lead us to the river," reflected Nicholas. "Are both of you fit to continue? As I said earlier, I'm quite capable of accomplishing this task on my own."

"You won't be getting rid of me that easily," replied Yelena. "How about you, Richard?"

The American nodded. "Actually, I wouldn't pass up this chance for anything in the world. After all, how often does a foreigner get to see this side of Moscow?"

"Or a native Muscovite, for that matter," said Yelena with a wink.

"Very well, my friends. May the one Father be with us," said Nicholas, ducking into the tunnel to their right.

Forty-five minutes later, when they had still not reached the river, the monk halted once again. The passageway was becoming increasingly narrow, and Nicholas could barely stand upright.

The monk peered out into the darkness. "Well, my friends, what do you think? Shouldn't we have come across the river by now?"

Richard checked the compass. "I don't know about that. It does appear that this tunnel has been taking us more northward than we originally wanted to go."

"That would most likely put us somewhere beneath the Kremlin," observed Yelena. "Do you want to go back to try the passageway that we passed?"

"No," returned Nicholas. "Let us stay on this path until we see where it leads. We can always retrace our steps later."

Yelena briefly caught Richard's glance. "Okay, but let me take the lead for a while. Maybe our luck will change."

Nodding, Nicholas shifted the case into his other hand and then followed the archaeologist into the pitch black void beyond.

Vladimir arrived at his subterranean lair completely exhausted. The mortals had pursued him relentlessly, yet fate had been with him, as he had been able to duck inside the secret passageway and escape once again.

Never before had he witnessed such a conglomeration of puzzling contraptions! This was especially the case with the vehicle that soared through the air like a monstrous bird. And that tremendously bright torch that shined from its body—it lit up the square with a light as strong as the sun's!

Thankful for the tranquility of the catacombs, he climbed down to the floor of the central chamber. Here he was greeted by a chorus of high-pitched squeals, and his eyes went immediately to the smooth stone shelf where he had laid the blond woman. Waiting for him were thousands of swarming rats in the midst of a feeding frenzy.

So thick were these rodents that Vlad could no longer even see the mortal's body beneath them. The only portion of her that he was able to view was a long strand of

blond hair that stuck out of the swarm like something
unnatural.

His gut filled with rage and loathing. Vlad ran to the
stone shelf and scattered the rats with a single sweep of
his arm. Hardly recognizable beneath them was a carcass
of torn skin, fragmented muscle, and gnawed bone.

Vlad pounded his fist angrily. Now he would be forced
to spend yet another night alone, with only his insatiable
hunger to keep him company.

Backing away from the stone shelf, Vlad lamented, if
only he could break the curse of immortality, then at
least he would have the peace of the grave to look forward to. But even this hope was denied him.

Vlad backed against the wall and buried his forehead
in his icy palms. His interlude of self-pity was brief, however, for a barely audible disturbance soon diverted his
attention from selfish concerns. Cocking his sensitive ear
upward, he picked out the distant sound of approaching
mortals. Strangely enough, the sounds were emanating
from deeper inside the catacombs, and not from above,
as he had expected.

Even more upsetting were the peculiar vibrations he
was beginning to detect. There was something about
them, something . . . Vlad begain to shiver uncontrollably. It came to him in a flash. These mortals carried with
them the only weapon that could confine him to yet
another millennium of sleep—the holy spear of the one
Father!

Vlad struggled to control his shaking. He knew that
there was only one course open to him now. If he took
possession of the spear himself, he would never again
have to fear the thousand-year sleep. Even life without
love was better than the cold slumber of the undead!
Thus he would plan his ambush most carefully.

Yelena Lopatin was beginning to wonder if this trek wasn't a colossal waste of time and effort. The monk had been convincing back in the comfortable confines of the institute, but now she could not help but second-guess him.

They had been following the dank catacombs for a good two hours now, and so far, hadn't come across the slightest hint that someone else had trespassed recently. Of course, they still hadn't explored the portion of the passage that adjoined the underground river, and it was here that the detective had reported actually confronting the creature who was the target of the young monk's age-old quest.

On the positive side, this excursion did give her a chance to see for herself the true extent of the catacombs. Before this trip, she had only explored a tiny portion of them several years ago during the exhumation of several well-preserved human skeletons. Since it was apparent that the maze of twisting tunnels extended throughout the central city, there was no telling what archaeological treasures lay buried here. Hopefully, one day soon, she would have a chance to return with a proper crew to could give this remarkable ancient site the attention it deserved.

Stifling a yawn, the redheaded scientist diverted the beam of her flashlight to illuminate the tunnel's distant meander. For the last quarter of a kilometer, the footing had become increasingly slippery. Water dripped constantly from the stone walls and ceiling. Settling onto the floor in large puddles, the stale liquid made progress even more treacherous than it already was.

Behind her, she could hear the sloshing footsteps of the others. Throughout this entire excursion, the American had not voiced a single word of complaint. Yet like herself, he had to be having second thoughts as to just what he was doing down here.

Brother Nicholas was a different story. He was one of the most intense, determined individuals Yelena had ever met. Guided by his faith, he would most likely continue his exploration of the catacombs until forced to the surface for food and water. There could be no doubt that he was a man with a purpose, and that he would allow nothing to stand in the way of his sworn goal.

The legend he had shared with them was absolutely fascinating. If Nicholas was right, they were in the midst of a manhunt for a bloodthirsty creature well over a thousand years old!

Yelena had to admit that such a thing sounded ridiculous on the surface. But if it was indeed so preposterous, just what was she doing down here risking her life to prove the truth of it?

The archaeologist used her flashlight to illuminate the walls of a large chamber. Her eyes opened wide with wonder upon spotting the many recessed ledges that were carved into this portion of the passageway. An incredible assortment of bones lay exposed here. Quick to begin an examination of this exciting discovery, which appeared to be a burial crypt, she identified the bleached remains as being most definitely human. They looked just as old as the five-hundred-year-old skeletons she had pulled up out of the southern reaches of the catacombs several years ago, and these seemed to have been undisturbed by outsiders.

While intently studying a recess that was filled with nothing but human skulls, her flashlight dimmed and went out. The blackness fell upon her immediately. Since she had loaded the flashlight with brand new alkaline batteries only a few hours ago, she supposed that a mechanical failure of some sort caused the breakdown. Cursing the shoddy workmanship, she turned to see what was keeping her associates.

The darkness was all-encompassing, and she could see no evidence that they were anywhere close by. Certain that they would catch up shortly, she cautiously reached out to orient herself. Her left hand passed over the smooth cranium of one of the skulls she had been examining. Though she was certainly no stranger to such relics, she nevertheless pulled her hand back abruptly. Her pulse quickened, and she castigated herself for letting such a ridiculous thing frighten her.

It was then that she became aware of a sour, putrid scent that reminded her of the smell of spoiled meat. The odor seemed to increase in strength, and Yelena fought back not only the desire to vomit, but her own rising apprehensions. Could her associates have possibly taken a wrong turn and lost her? Or maybe one of them had fallen and injured himself, while the other was forced to stop and attend to him?

Trying hard to ignore the vile scent that was making even the act of breathing difficult, she turned her attention back to her flashlight. After flipping the switch again with no results, she decided to unscrew the cap and try to repack the batteries. The pitch blackness made this normally simple task a difficult one, and while she was carefully emptying the batteries into her palm, one of them escaped her and fell to the ground.

"Damn it!" cursed Yelena out loud.

Not normally a squeamish person, she found herself reluctant to drop to her hands and knees to find the battery. Still, she had no other choice.

Fortunately, the stone floor was dry and relatively

smooth. Groping blindly with her right hand, she started by searching the floor near the wall. Then she
methodically worked her way toward the center of the
chamber. The floor was a bit more uneven here, and it
cut into her knees and palms. Yelena wondered if this
futile search was even worth the effort involved.

Suddenly her hand made contact with an alien object
lying directly before her. Oddly enough, it seemed to be
a piece of smooth fabric of some kind. Such a modern
remnant certainly did not belong here. She longed for
her lost battery. If only she could turn on her flashlight
and inspect the object.

Her hand next touched some sort of smooth rock
shelf. To get a better idea of its size, she cautiously began
to trace its outline with her outstretched hand, starting
at its base, and working her way up. She had to stand to
explore it completely. After determining that it extended approximately to her waist, she reached out to feel
what its upper surface was composed of. Meeting her fingers was a revolting combination of torn skin, ligaments,
and bone.

Sickened by this substance, Yelena yanked her hand
backward and let loose a cry of disgust. The blackness
seemed to close even tighter around her, and the stench
seemed to intensify.

Her disgust turned to fear when a muted, rustling
sound echoed in the distance. Struggling to keep control
of her emotions, Yelena fought back her panic and
shouted out into the black void that surrounded her.

"Richard, is that you?"

The rustling sound repeated itself, and she vainly
peered out into the darkness in an attempt to identify it.

"Richard, Nicholas, where are you?" she screamed at
the top of her voice.

Yelena anxiously listened for a response, almost faint-
ing from joy when a blindingly bright shaft of light cut
through the blackness beyond, followed by a man's deep
voice.

"Yelena! Are you all right?"

Richard Green was first to enter the chamber behind
Yelena, with the young monk close behind. Yelena ran
into the American's arms. While the linguist tried to
calm her down, Nicholas scanned the room with his
torch's beam. Taking in the piles of human bones that
were stored in the various recessed wall niches, he spotted a torn woman's skirt on the ground below. Close
behind this garment, and occupying the center of the
room, was a low rock shelf. Little was the monk prepared
for the gruesome sight that awaited him on the shelf's
surface.

It was evident that the mutilated corpse laid out there
had once belonged to a blond-haired young woman. Her
entire upper torso was ripped open, with many of the
inner organs still visible. Nicholas approached the body
to study its neck and realized that amid all this carnage
not a single drop of blood was visible. His heartbeat
quickened upon spotting the two deep puncture wounds
that lay on the side of the victim's throat, and in that
instant, the young monk knew his quest had not been in
vain.

"What in God's name is that?" questioned the startled American from close behind.

"I would imagine that not long ago she was a most
attractive young lady," replied Nicholas somberly. "But
you only have to look at those wounds on her neck to
know exactly what evil was responsible for her demise.
He's very close, my friends! This discovery proves it."

Nicholas set the elongated wooden box down on the

ground. Richard took a deep breath and gasped.

"Do you smell that awful odor?" he said. "Could it be coming from the woman's body?"

The monk knelt beside his case and prepared to open it. "That's extremely doubtful. It doesn't appear that she's been dead long enough for such decay to set in."

"I first smelled it earlier, when my flashlight gave out," managed Yelena, who had finally regained control of herself.

"Maybe he's got another body stashed away down here," offered Richard, who returned Yelena's concerned gaze. "Don't you think it's best if we go back and inform the authorities of our discovery?"

The monk looked up and replied directly. "I think under the circumstances that it's best if you two do just that."

"And what about you?" Yelena broke in.

Nicholas twisted the lock on his case. "Don't worry about me, my friends. I'm most capable of taking care of myself."

Richard was set to argue this point when his flashlight went dead. At the same moment, the monk's torch also failed and the chamber became engulfed in darkness.

"Oh no, not again!" cried Yelena, desperately reaching out for Richard's hand.

"He's close, my friends! Very close!" boomed the apocalyptic voice of the monk.

Yelena valiantly fought back yet another wave of anxiety. But just then, her hand made solid contact, and she inwardly sighed with relief. But the palm that she grasped felt unnaturally cool. Maybe she had linked hands with Nicholas by mistake, Yelena dared to question.

"Richard, is that you?"

Turning, Yelena gazed at a sight that left her breath-less and dazed. For glowing in the darkness were two spi-raling spheres of crimson flame. They spun with a frenzied rhythm. The flickering flames had an almost mesmerizing effect on her, and before she could cry out, another icy hand wrapped around her mouth and pulled her forcefully backward. The last thing she heard, as she was dragged off into the black depths, was the distant voice of the American calling, "Yelena, where in the hell are you?"

When Mikhail Antonov found the Moscow River entrance to the catacombs closed by a detachment of burly Spetsnaz commandos, he doubted if he and his partners would ever be able to track down the three civil-ians. He had been counting on finding them near the spot where they had found Anna Markova's body earlier. Since even their MVD credentials would not gain them entrance into the passageway that lay beside the river, he knew there was no way that Dr. Lopatin and her two civilian companions would have been able to pass by the line of soldiers.

With this disappointing realization, the detectives plotted their next move.

Yuri came up with the idea of telephoning their sewer department contact to find out if there were any adjoin-ing access routes nearby. As it turned out, the nearest entrance to the catacombs was beside the Kropotkin Metro station, and the three investigators decided to give the site a try.

Much to their delight, they not only found the proper passage, but also evidence, in the form of footprints, indicating that three people had passed down the same tunnel only minutes before. Their expectations were high as they began the tedious trek down the blackened subterranean maze.

Mikhail and Yuri let Pavl choose the way when the tunnel unexpectedly branched into two. There were no visible footprints indicating which route the three had chosen. The photographer picked the tunnel to their right, and it was in this direction that they continued.

There was a special urgency to Mikhail's steps. He was hoping to catch up with the three civilians before they needlessly endangered themselves. Since he had been the one to open up to them, Mikhail felt responsible for their actions. He had to prevent a tragedy from occurring.

What he feared most was a cave-in or some other type of natural disaster. Such a calamity could snuff out their lives just as quickly as a homicidal murderer could. He still had not quite made up his mind as to the legitimacy of the threat outlined by the monk Nicholas.

Mikhail pushed himself even harder. He did not want to think about the difficulties he and his associates would incur if the American was involved in an accident of any kind. Oblivious to the complaints of his coworkers, he raced down the passageway as swiftly as his tired legs would take him.

After a good half-hour, his cramped muscles forced him to slow down. Yuri and Pavl were nowhere to be seen, and Mikhail wondered if they would ever catch up with him. Suddenly a beam of bright light teasingly beckoned ahead. At once his second wind was upon him, and he took off sprinting down the tunnel.

The first person he came upon was Dr. Richard Green, the American linguist whom he had met back at the institute. The foreigner appeared highly agitated.

"Oh, thank God it's you, Lieutenant! Did you find

her?"

"Find who?" asked Mikhail, shielding his eyes from the American's flashlight.

"Why, Dr. Lopatin," returned the linguist. "Are you certain you didn't come across her back there?"

Conscious that the man was bordering on panic, Mikhail softened his tone. "Yes, comrade, I'm certain. Now why don't you take a second and tell me what's going on down here."

Richard pointed back toward the shadowy depths from which he had just emerged. "Come, you can see for yourself."

Beckoning the detective to follow him, Richard led the way down the passageway. Mikhail instinctively reached inside his jacket to pull out his revolver.

As they rounded a broad bend, he saw the beam of yet another flashlight. This torch belonged to the young monk, who carried some sort of spear at his side.

"Perhaps you can tell me what's going down here," said Mikhail. "Where's Dr. Lopatin?"

"That's what we'd like to know," responded Nicholas. "We had just made a most unpleasant discovery in an adjoining chamber, when our flashlights simultaneously failed. And when they popped back on seconds later, she was nowhere to be seen. I'm afraid he might have abducted her."

Still not sure just who the monk was referring to, Mikhail followed him into a nearby chamber. Here he was shown the mutilated corpse of the blond, with the monk taking particular care to point out the two deep puncture marks cut into the throat.

"I hope you don't doubt me now, Lieutenant. And you can put away that gun of yours, for I hold the only weapon that can harm the Beast responsible for this despicable crime."

"We've got to find Yelena before he does the same thing to her!" pleaded the American from the opposite corner of the chamber.

Mikhail took a moment to scan the chamber where he now stood, and only then spotted the collection of human bones lining its walls. "Maybe there's another passageway nearby that leads aboveground."

"We were searching for just such a thing when you arrived, Lieutenant," said the monk.

"Well, you've got another pair of eyes to assist you now, comrades. Two more, if my colleagues ever show up."

No sooner were these words out of Mikhail's mouth, than Pavl stumbled into the chamber, clearly out of breath. Yuri was close behind.

"So you found them after all!" exclaimed the photographer. "Why, it's a virtual miracle!"

Mikhail shook his head. "Unfortunately, we're one short. Dr. Lopatin is missing, and it's feared she's been abducted from this very passageway."

"What makes you say that?" asked Yuri, fumbling for a cigarette.

Mikhail diverted the beam of his flashlight to illuminate the top of the rock shelf. "I'm afraid we've found yet another victim, comrades. Though there's not much left of the body this time, the familiar bite marks on the throat can't be mistaken."

"Well, I'll be," said Pavl. He picked up the camera that dangled from his neck and began snapping photos.

Content to take Mikhail's word, Yuri stood back and thoughtfully inhaled a deep lungful of smoke. "So our madman has struck once again. Did anyone actually see him abduct Dr. Lopatin?"

"He was here, all right!" exclaimed Nicholas. "And although we never did see him, it was his chicanery that caused our torches to fail. That's when he grabbed her. You could smell his evil essence, just as if the putrid pits of Hell had opened up before our very noses!"

Yuri listened impassively and turned to Mikhail. "Now what, partner?"

With Pavl's strobe lighting up the bone-filled chamber, Mikhail answered. "Now that we're all down here, I think it's best if we spread out and try to find out if there are any short cuts to the outside world. Something tells me that's where we'll find both Dr. Lopatin and our suspect."

Yuri remembered the wild tale that Mikhail had shared with them during the drive up from the institute. Though he remained utterly skeptical about the existence of the mythical monster that the monk was supposedly on the trail of, he kept his doubts to himself. Such beasts only existed in fairy tales and bad dreams. As far as he was concerned, the man they were after was but a human being with a twisted mind. He was certain that all those involved in this strange case would soon come to the same logical conclusion.

Meanwhile, Yuri was prepared to do his best to locate the secret accessway Mikhail had mentioned. He decided to begin his exploration in the back of the chamber, away from the others. Using his flashlight, he examined a narrow tunnel that adjoined the room here. With his cigarette protruding from his lips, he squeezed into the passage in an effort to see how far it extended. As he did so, two things immediately caught his attention. One was the fact that the tunnel seemed to be gradually twisting upward. The other was a rubber hip-boot wedged between two blocks of limestone.

19

The helicopter landed with a jolt. A single, massive figure jumped from the cabin door and signaled the pilot to take off. There was a roar as the rotors increased their rotation. As a powerful downdraft blew dust and debris, the chopper returned to the air. Only then did Igor Strellnikoff stand erect. After making a quick adjustment to his eye patch, he turned to greet three rapidly approaching figures.

"Marshal Strellnikoff!" said the uniformed leader of this trio. "I'm glad you could join us."

"Like hell you are, Captain Vorkuta," said the Spetsnaz commander. "I had to get down here before these incompetents you call soldiers let the suspect slip right through our fingers!"

Stung by his comment, the captain responded. "How was I supposed to know that those university students would pick this time and place to let the whole world know of their petty grievances? If it weren't for that bunch of spoiled malcontents, we would have captured the suspect for certain."

"I don't know about that," spat Strellnikoff. "For some reason, I get the feeling that he would have escaped the trap even without the help of those protestors. What's their status?"

"Per your instructions, we escorted them into the lobby of the Historical Museum, where they are currently being held under armed guard. The paramedics are taking care of the wounded, while the more serious cases are being transferred to the hospital."

Strellnikoff grimaced. "This is all I need at the moment, a damn political incident on my hands! Did you explain to them what the troops were doing in the square?"

Vorkuta nodded. "That I did, sir. To satisfy their curiosity, I told their leader that we were on the trail of a foreign agent who had made an attempt on the premier's life. I'm certain he believed me."

The marshal seemed satisfied. "At last you've done something that shows some intellect, Captain. Now, tell me about your briefing with Lieutenant Svetlana Nikulin."

A bit more confidently, Vorkuta replied. "I know this might sound unbelievable to you, sir, but Comrade Nikulin swears that she shot the suspect eight times, at practically point-blank range. One of these 9mm hollow-point bullets struck him in the shoulder, four were directed at his chest, one was pumped into each thigh, with another sent into the man's foot. Though she saw the bullet holes herself, he remained standing, with absolutely no bleeding whatsoever, just as if her shots had no effect on him."

"He must have been wearing some type of body armor," reasoned Strellnikoff.

"That could be," returned the captain. "But that wouldn't explain why her shot into his bare foot didn't stop him, for Nikulin was positive that he was wearing neither socks nor shoes."

The marshal's tone shifted. "Who else knows about

this, Captain?"

Beckoning toward the two junior officers who stood behind him, Vorkuta answered. "Just my assistants here. When Lieutenant Nikulin was relieved after the incident, she was practically in a state of shock. She spoke to us only after she was given a tranquilizer."

"How fortunate for us," reflected Strellnikoff. "Though I'm sure we'll eventually come up with some sort of rational explanation for her bullets' ineffectiveness. Right now, one thing we don't need is a wild rumor spreading among the men. Make certain to keep her silent."

Vokuta alertly nodded. "I have already taken that precaution, sir."

Strellnikoff looked up when a helicopter swooped low overhead. The clatter of its rotors was deafening as the vehicle whisked off toward the Kremlin and began crisscrossing Lenin's mausoleum with its spotlight. After noting that the nighttime heavens were almost completely obscured by the rapidly thickening cloud cover, Strellnikoff began scanning the rest of the square.

"What is the status of the armored column?" he questioned, examining the massive structure that housed the GUM department store.

"It has only just taken up its position on Oktabra and Kuybyshev streets, sir," replied Vorkuta.

"And what about our ground troops?" continued the marshal impatiently.

"After Lieutenant Nikulin's encounter, I took the liberty of calling in the squads that had been searching the southern portion of the Kremlin, to concentrate the most men possible right here in Red Square."

Satisfied, Strellnikoff grunted. "Since it's obvious that he's somewhere in the vicinity, let's have the men form a human chain and begin sweeping the square, beginning at St. Basil's. That will flush out the bastard!"

Captain Vorkuta was set to relay this order when his two-way radio suddenly activated. Quickly bringing the receiver to his ear, he listened to a report, then cried out excitedly.

"We've sighted him, sir! Only seconds ago, the helicopter crew spotted the suspect breaking into the rear entrance of the mausoleum. Not only did they get a positive identification on him, but it seems that he's not alone, for they could also see that he carried a woman over his shoulder."

Turning to face the mausoleum, Strellnikoff shouted out commandingly, "Then what are we waiting for, comrades? Captain Vorkuta, call in the armor and send in those troops! We'll put a wall around him that he'll never escape from!"

The interior of the building that Vlad had chosen for his new lair was solemn and somber. Constructed solely of hard red granite, it was vastly different from the other structures he had explored in this strange city. But since there did not appear to be any mortals inside it, it would serve his purpose well.

With the unconscious redheaded woman he had recently captured secure over his left shoulder, Vlad furtively crept down a dimly lit stairway. His immediate goal was to find a secure spot, where he could lay down his precious load and satisfy his newly awakened lust. Just thinking about the pleasure that would soon be his caused his loins to tighten. He stepped off the last of the stairs and entered an immense, brightly lighted room.

Situated in the exact center of this chamber was a strangely familiar object that caused Vlad to gasp in

wonder. Set here was what appeared to be a massive sarcophagus carved out of a peculiar material that allowed
one to clearly see the corpse inside. Anxious to examine
this strange coffin more closely, he crossed over to study
it further.

What awaited him inside the clear casket was a wondrous sight, and Vlad found himself trembling in awe.
For displayed here was a near twin of the black-robed
sorcerer whom Vlad had last seen standing over his own
deathbed another lifetime ago!

Taking in the corpse's neatly clipped black mustache
and beard, his thick, bushy eyebrows, and sharply
etched cheekbones, Vlad was absolutely positive that
this was the same individual his father had hired to bring
him back to life. Vlad had often wondered what his fate
would have been if this sorcerer had not been summoned to heal him. His father had gone to great efforts to
locate this black magician, and had even willingly
offered him a say-so in the future development of the
fledgling town of Moscow as payment for his services.

Vlad's body shuddered in rage. Though it was the
flying beast's bite that had originally infected him,
here was the man whose evil incantations had sealed his
doom. It was this man's spells that had called Vlad's
soul back from the portals of death. And it was his evil
doings that helped to curse Vlad with his immortality
and insatiable blood hunger.

Tempted to smash the casket and desecrate its
remains, Vlad realized that this was certainly not the
peaceful spot he had been searching for. Thus he
thought only of leaving the somber chamber and putting as much distance between himself and the dead sorcerer as possible.

The stairway once again led him upward, this time to

the structure's roof. Here he hoped to feed in solitude, under the cover of the black night sky.

"For the sake of Lenin, just look at this reception!" observed Yuri Sorokin. He led the others out of the secret passage he had discovered and onto the cobblestone pavement of Red Square.

Positioning himself at his partner's side, Mikhail Antonov took in the distinctive granite mausoleum that lay before them and the hundreds of armed troops and armored vehicles that surrounded this same structure. Mikhail had to practically scream to be heard over the earsplitting clatter of a circling helicopter.

"So this is why we've been called off the case! Do you think the army has enough men here to get the situation under control?"

Shaking his head at this facetious remark, Yuri reached into his pocket for a cigarette. As he lit it, the American's voice came from behind.

"Isn't that building in front of us Lenin's mausoleum?"

Before anyone could answer him, Nicholas took a step forward and pointed at the structure's roof. "He's up there. I tell you, I can just feel it!"

This forceful observation was apparently verified when the helicopter's spotlight began focusing on the mausoleum's roof.

"I believe you may be correct with that assumption," Pavl said as he lifted up his camera to snap a picture.

Yuri spotted a detachment of grim-faced soldiers approaching them on their right.

"Heads up, comrades," he said matter-of-factly. "It looks like we've got some company."

Seconds later, the lead soldier lowered the assault rifle

he had been carrying and coldly greeted them. "This area is off-limits to all civilians. You must leave here at once!"

Yuri was quick to pull out his identification card. "We are here on official militia business, comrade. We have reason to believe that a woman has been abducted and is currently being held somewhere inside the mausoleum."

"You can verify that with our supervisor, Colonel Kukhar, if you'd like," interjected Mikhail. "But our case is an extremely important one, and it's a matter of life and death that you allow us to continue without further interference."

"That's out of the question!" snapped the soldier. "You'll have to bring up the matter with our superior."

"Of course. We'd love to," retorted Yuri impatiently. "So lead on, comrade. Time is of the essence!"

The five newcomers found themselves being escorted to the front entrance of the mausoleum, where a group of anxious officers were gathered before the main doorway. Upon being notified of their presence, one of these officers, a giant of a man with a black patch over his right eye, stepped forward to intercept them.

"What is the meaning of this nonsense!" he cried out angrily. "I don't care if you are personal representatives of the premier himself! I have total authority here, and there is no time to deal with outsiders."

Daring to voice himself, Mikhail nervously cleared his throat. "Excuse me, sir, but you're Marshal Strellnikoff, aren't you? My name is Lieutenant Mikhail Antonov, and we briefly worked together on a drug investigation while I was in charge of the MVD office back in Charbarovsk."

The senior Spetsnaz officer scratched his dimpled chin and responded. "Of course, I remember you, comrade

Antonov. I believe you showed yourself to be a dedicated, responsible young man at the time, and I'm certain that you understand my predicament here. We are after a most dangerous criminal, and you will only be endangering your lives if you remain."

"We'll take that chance," said Mikhail. "For not only have we been on the trail of this same suspect for several days now, but we also happen to personally know the woman he has just abducted. She is a leading historian of the Motherland."

Strellnikoff quickly scanned the faces of the newcomers and shrugged his massive shoulders. "It's your funerals, comrades. I guess I should tell you that we currently have the suspect trapped on the roof of this very building. He has indeed been spotted with this woman you speak of. Our plan is to send a crack unit up there to take him into custody. Yet if he should resist, I have full authority to eliminate him."

"He'll resist, all right," shot back Brother Nicholas, who had been strangely quiet up till now. "And as far as attempting to eliminate him, good luck, my friend. Bullets aren't going to stop him. In fact, only a single weapon on this planet can take him down, and I happen to be carrying it right here at my side."

As the monk held out the tapered lance that he had uncrated and carried up from the catacombs, Igor Strellnikoff pondered the brown-robed stranger's puzzling words. Only moments before, he had stood in the square and listened as Captain Vorkuta related Lieutenant Svetlana Nikulin's bewildering encounter with the suspect. Hadn't she reported firing at him eight times, at point-blank range, and then looking on in horror as these shots had absolutely no effect? Unable to even comprehend what such a thing meant, Strellnikoff listened as Mikhail interjected.

"We don't expect you to make rational sense out of this, sir. We only ask that before you send in your men, you give us a chance to prove our point. Allow us access to the roof, and let us try to put an end to this madness before other lives are wasted."

Allowing them to supersede his authority was against everything Strellnikoff believed in, but for some reason he found himself giving in. "I don't know why, but I'm going to approve your desperate plan. I'll give you ten minutes to apprehend him before we move in."

"That's all we'll need," responded Nicholas confidently.

Mikhail turned to address the monk. "Well, comrade, I hope this weapon of yours is all it's cut out to be."

Stroking the spear's pointed tip, Nicholas nodded. "Don't worry, my friend. Just get me up there, and I'll take care of everything else."

Wishing he could share the young man's faith, Mikhail pulled out his pistol and rammed a fresh round into its chamber. Beside him, his partner did likewise, as a deep voice broke from the mausoleum's entrance.

"Come on, comrades! Let's get on with it before I change my mind."

With Strellnikoff cautiously leading the way, the others followed. Taking up the rear, Richard Green felt oddly out of place. Yet his fondness for Yelena Lopatin gave him the courage to walk by the line of somber-faced soldiers that stood beside the mausoleum's entrance, and to continue on inside.

Unlike his previous trip to this structure, he soon found himself walking up a relatively short granite stairway to the floors above. Lenin himself was buried in the basement, and it was to this portion of the building that

Richard's past wanderings had been limited.

Richard was well aware that great men such as Stalin, Kruschev, Brezhnev, and Gorbachev had climbed these same steps while on their way to the reviewing platform situated on the roof. Yet how very different was the nature of his current visit! He was excited to have been included, but he still did not have the vaguest idea of the true nature of the Beast they would soon be confronting. He entered a wide hallway where his colleagues were assembled. The one-eyed army officer pointed to a sealed iron doorway that was set into an adjoining wall.

Running over to this portal, the two detectives pulled out their pistols and signaled to the others that they were going to try to open it. Richard felt his pulse quicken as Mikhail yanked open the door. Then, with his gun outstretched before him, he quickly ducked through the opening. His balding partner went next, with the army officer and the photographer following close behind, leaving only Richard and Nicholas alone in the hallway.

The American watched as the brown-robed monk closed his eyes and initiated an intense silent prayer. Richard found himself questioning his very sanity when he noted that the point of the monk's spear suddenly began to glow.

This miraculous phenomenon intensified until the entire lance was aglow with a pulsating golden aura. Finding himself speechless, the linguist looked on as Nicholas emerged from his prayer and began to make his way through the doorway. Richard followed, entranced.

Outside, an almost unearthly scene greeted him. Hovering above in the cloud-filled night sky was a helicopter. Its powerful spotlight clearly illuminated the rooftop reviewing platform with a blazing light. Perched menacingly on the edge of this platform was a tall, gangly,

long-haired man who was dressed in a pair of tattered
white coveralls. In his arms was a single, unmoving
figure—Yelena Lopatin. Although he did not know
whether she was alive or dead, he cringed upon spotting
the assortment of lethal weapons currently aimed in her
direction.

"Put the woman down!" cried Mikhail Antonov passionately. "No one's going to harm you if you'll only
cooperate!"

"Don't waste your breath, my friend," said the monk
as he slowly closed in on his quarry, his spear cocked
before him. "You see, he doesn't come from our time,
and he doesn't understand our language, either."

Suddenly inspired by this simple truth, the linguist
made an effort to make contact with the suspect himself.
To do so he spoke in Ancient Slavonic, the language that
had been spoken in this region a millennium ago.

"Greetings, Prince Vladimir, if that is indeed your
name."

These words seemed to produce instant recognition,
and the suspect curiously peered out at the American,
answering him with a voice hoarse from years of disuse.
"How is it that you know my name, mortal, and speak
the language of my people?"

Since his conversational skills in this tongue were limited, Richard did his best to formulate the proper phras-
ing. "I am a teacher, and your language is but one of
many that I speak."

"Yet how do you know me?" repeated Vladimir.

"You are a part of our history," answered the American. "Your exploits are known to many, even though it's
been a thousand years since you last walked the earth."

"A thousand years, you say?" cried Vladimir, who
finally understood why the surroundings were so confus-

ing to him. "And may I ask the name of this great city?"

"Why, of course," replied Richard. "Its name is Moscow."

Clearly staggered by this information, Vladimir scanned the surrounding cityscape as if viewing it for the first time. He teetered on the edge of the platform and almost toppled over.

Strellnikoff stepped forward, his rifle still held out before him. "We'll have plenty of time for chatter back at the Lubyanka. Since you apparently speak his tongue, tell him to put down the woman and surrender himself peacefully."

Richard sensed the officer meant business, and at once conveyed his demands. "We would like to continue this conversation in more appropriate surroundings. Therefore, please release your prisoner and come with us peacefully."

With this request Vladimir let out a deep, booming peal of laughter. "Are you asking me to surrender? Why, it's you who should be begging leniency, while I am the one who will be issuing terms here!"

Again he roared with laughter, and Strellnikoff raised his rifle and prepared to fire.

"The woman!" protested Mikhail.

"To hell with her!" shouted Strellnikoff. "I will not be jeopardizing the success of this operation for the life of a single individual."

"Go ahead and lower your rifle," advised the monk. "Its bullets are useless anyway."

An angry scowl painted Strellnikoff's face as the monk stepped in front of him and blocked his aim. At the same time, he raised his spear and began cautiously moving toward the reviewing platform.

"Prepare to die, Vladimir Dolgoruki!" he shouted

defiantly. "Your time of earthly release is over!"

All eyes were on the monk as he continued his approach.

"Hand over the weapon!" screamed Vladimir, his voice tight with fear. "And if you do so, I'll give you the woman."

"He wants to trade Dr. Lopatin for the spear!" translated Richard.

"Tell him there will be no bargains with his kind," said the monk.

This time it was Strellnikoff who replied. "Don't be foolish, comrade. Give him this spear of yours. Then we'll have the woman, and we can finish off the bastard. Why, we could stop an entire invasion with the troops I've assembled below."

Caught in the midst of this dilemma, Nicholas wondered what to do. He did not want to endanger the life of the archaeologist. His vows had instilled in him the belief that all life was sacred. Thus he had no choice but to be prudent.

Taking a last look at the smirking demon as he stood on the raised platform, Nicholas laid the spear on the smooth stone floor beneath him. Then he called out to the linguist.

"Tell him he can have it the moment he hands over Dr. Lopatin."

Richard conveyed this offer, and Vlad wasted no time in delivering his answer.

"Take the bitch. Once the spear is mine, I'll have my pick of mortal women anyway."

It was the American who offered to make the dangerous transfer. Hardly noticing the still-circling helicopter, the lightninglike flashes of the photographer's strobe, and the assortment of guns still aimed at the suspect,

Richard nervously approached the platform and pre-pared to take possession of Yelena. The putrid scent that he had first smelled back in the catacombs was overpow-ering as he reached Vladimir's side and looked up into his piercing stare.

"You are an extremely brave one, mortal who speaks the tongue of my people. Perhaps I'll have pity on you and kill you quickly when it's time for you to die."

Unable to respond, Richard merely held out his trem-bling arms. Once again, Vlad addressed his remarks to the brown-robed monk.

"Transfer the spear to me, and I'll hand over the wom-an!"

Nicholas needed no translation as he lifted up his foot and proceeded to kick the spear forward. As the lance began rolling toward the platform, Vlad carried out his part of the bargain and handed over Yelena. Richard took her in his arms and quickly backed away.

The instant Vlad bent down to take possession of his prize, Strellnikoff let loose with a volley of expertly placed automatic rifle shots. In the space of a minute, fifty 5.45mm rounds smacked into Vlad's body. Even though they were not able to take him down, the sheer force of the imploding shells caused Vlad to momentari-ly stagger. This was all the time Nicholas needed to leap toward the platform and regain the spear.

The monk angled the point of the lance upward, dar-ing the infuriated creature to take further action. In response, Vlad let loose a bloodcurdling howl, and heed-less to any danger, leaped forward.

Nicholas lunged at his quarry's exposed chest. Vlad countered with a lightninglike parry, using his forearm to deflect the point of the spear upward. At the same moment, he reached out with his other hand and was able to grasp the lance at its midsection. Nicholas struggled to keep his own hold on the weapon as he battled Vladimir for the spear's possession.

From an adjoining portion of the roof, Igor Strellnikoff snapped a fresh ammunition magazine into his rifle. He raised its barrel and attempted to take aim.

Seeing this, Mikhail cried out in alarm. "You can't be serious, Marshal! At least wait until you have a clear shot."

Strellnikoff's response was tinged with unconstrained rage. "No man alive can cheat death when I'm at the trigger! You'll see, these armor-piercing shells will stop him!"

Cringing in disbelief, Mikhail looked on in horror as the burly commando proceeded to depress his rifle's trigger. There was a deafening series of blasts, and almost instantly, a circular pattern of bullet holes formed in the suspect's back.

For one glorious moment, this seemed to stun Vladimir, and he abandoned his struggle and fell to one knee. Yet the monk had also taken one of these rounds, and he collapsed to the floor, the spear clattering noisily to the ground beside him.

Mikhail hardly noticed it when a woman's hysterical screams sounded from behind. Instead, his attention was riveted on the reviewing platform's edge, where their long-haired suspect was staggering to his feet once again. Cursing Strellnikoff's insensitivity and realizing that conventional weapons were useless, Mikhail decided that the only object that would do the job indeed lay on the ground beside the prone body of the monk.

Mikhail made his move, feeling as if he were in the midst of a ponderous nightmare. It seemed to take forever to get to the reviewing stand's edge, where the spear still lay. Vlad, who had shaken off his wounds, also scrambled for the lance. The two reached it at the exact same moment.

A vile, putrid stench greeted Mikhail as he reached out for the lance. He managed to grasp it by its tip and its base. Meanwhile, Vlad had grasped it squarely by its midsection. A temporary stand-off ensued, with Mikhail being able to counter the suspect's superior strength only because of his better leverage.

Fighting to control the urge to vomit, Mikhail looked up and caught the smug expression on Vladimir's face. With this single glance, Mikhail realized the Beast was only toying with him. He learned this fact for certain when Vlad suddenly began lifting his arms in earnest. Still holding onto the lance for dear life, Mikhail soon found that his feet were off the ground and that the suspect was now carrying him over to the roof's edge.

Mikhail turned his head in panic and could see the headlights of the dozens of tanks and other armored vehicles that lay on the square below. Conscious of the monotonous whine of the still-circling helicopter, he knew that he had but one option. He let go of the spear and fell to the floor of the reviewing platform with a dull thud.

Vladimir raised the spear triumphantly. While he looked out over the city to glory in his victory, Mikhail caught a sudden movement behind the suspect. His partner's bald head became visible, and it suddenly dawned on Mikhail just what Yuri was trying to do.

Mikhail performed his part perfectly as his partner continued his approach until he was immediately behind Vladimir. As he went down to his hands and knees, Mikhail rose and charged into the suspect, who then fell backward over Yuri's hunched body.

The shock of this fall was sufficient to dislodge the spear from Vlad's grasp, and it rolled off the platform, finally coming to a halt immediately in front of the stunned linguist. As Richard Green hesitantly reached down to pick up the weapon, Vladimir tried to stand. His legs had become intertwined with Yuri's, however, and while he struggled to untangle them, he turned his wrath on the bald-headed detective.

Mikhail watched as the suspect's iron grasp went to his partner's neck. And realizing that there was only one thing that could save Yuri, Mikhail cried out to the American.

"Use the spear, comrade!"

Richard Green heard these words and realized with a start that they were directed at him. As he watched the struggle that was taking place on the raised reviewing platform, his grip on the lance tightened. Though never before had Richard even raised his fists against another person in anger, Yuri would soon die if he did not intervene.

There was an unexpected, tingling warmth in his palms. A golden, pulsating light seemed to gather around the weapon. Along with this mysterious aura came a sudden dawning in his consciousness, and Richard knew in that instant that he had been chosen to take the fallen monk's place in this eternal fight against the Evil One. New purpose guided his actions as he lifted the holy spear high overhead and charged blindly forward.

Seconds before the lance's tip plunged deep into the Beast's back, the creature known as Vladimir looked up and briefly met the American's gaze. He seemed to have been expecting the attack, and for a moment, appeared almost pitiful. Yet Richard had seen the remains of one of his victims back in the catacombs, and knew that such a bloodthirsty beast could be dealt with in only one way.

The spear point embedded itself firmly into the flesh between Vlad's shoulder blades. Yanking the lance free, Richard prepared to stab him again, but soon saw that this would not be necessary. For the creature already seemed to be fatally wounded as he staggered to his feet and turned to face his attacker.

"So you are the one to deliver the final blow," managed Vladimir between painful gasps. "And now the deathlike sleep shall be upon me once more. I never asked for this curse, brave mortal. Know this fact, and reveal it in your history. For I shall awaken and walk this earth again, with loneliness and blood hunger as my only companions."

With these words, Vlad's face flushed with anguish and he stumbled back to the very edge of the mausoleum's roof. A look of both sadness and wonderment filled Vlad's expression as he briefly scanned the surrounding city. Then his body sagged over the roof's edge and plummeted to the square below.

As the Beast's body struck the pavement, a squad of soldiers ran to encircle it. A startled corporal was the first one there. He arrived just in time to witness a mystifying event, which he was later convinced by an army psychiatrist was the result of an overactive imagination. Still, he could have sworn that he had seen two spiraling, crimson spheres of flame form in the corpse's glazed eyes and then soar upward into the sky above.

At once Marshal Igor Strellnikoff radioed his men to completely cover the fallen body. When he was certain that this task had been carried out, he turned his attention back to the handful of civilians on the mausoleum's roof.

He found them huddled around the prone body of the brown-robed fool who had stepped into his line of fire. The redheaded kidnap victim had regained consciousness and was delicately holding the monk's head in her lap while the American linguist attended to his wound. The bullet had penetrated the lower portion of his abdomen, and if an artery was not severed, he would most likely survive.

"Did we stop him?" the monk weakly mumbled.

It was the woman who responded. "Don't worry, Nicholas, we got him, all right. And you can thank Dr. Green here for taking your place and using the spear to finish the Beast off."

"Thank the Lord we succeeded," reflected the monk, as he struggled to raise his head. "Now, we must ensure proper containment. The Evil One must be buried in the same sarcophagus that you brought up from the Carpathians. When this is done, you must make certain that the holy spear is returned to the Abbey of the Pursuer. And you must brief the abbot there of this entire incident."

"There will be no such briefings!" interrupted Strellnikoff. "In fact, I must demand a signed affidavit from each one of you, in which you will swear to keep knowledge of this incident to yourselves for the rest of your lives. I believe I can help facilitate the monk's first two requests, on the condition that you all sign this document.

"Those who fail to do so will be dealt with accordingly. Not only will the government flatly deny that such an incident took place, but it will order the immediate arrest of any person who openly speaks of this matter. You can then be assured that you will spend the rest of your days in the gulag, undergoing psychological treatment of the most severe nature.

"And since it appears that we have a foreigner in our midst, you must understand, comrade, that this warning goes for you also. We have ways of dealing with you, even after you leave our borders. And don't forget that you can still be brought up on charges of murder if we so desire."

Mikhail Antonov had been nearby attending to his bruised partner and could clearly hear the marshal's crude threats. Beside him, Yuri Sorokin could hear them also, and the bald-headed investigator gestured knowingly.

"So much for this case, Misha. How about handing me a cigarette, and then seeing about getting us transportation back home? I don't know about you, but I'm exhausted!"

"Don't you think you should have a doctor take a look at that throat of yours before you start with those cancer sticks?"

Yuri grinned. "Come off it, partner. After what we just went through, the very least you can do is indulge me this one time."

Mikhail grinned and rolled his eyes. Before he could reply, Pavl Barvicha walked up to his side and discreetly dropped something into the pocket of his jacket. Before Mikhail could identify what it was, Strellnikoff joined them.

"And that vow of secrecy goes for you three also," he warned. "You will not even report this . . . occurrence to your supervisor. I will speak to him personally, and thus free you from having to document this incident."

Beckoning toward Pavl, Strellnikoff added, "That's a good-looking camera you have there, comrade. May I see it?"

In no position to deny this request, Pavl reluctantly handed it over. No sooner did Strellnikoff get the camera in his grasp than he climbed onto the reviewing stand, walked to the roof's edge, peered down, and dropped the camera to the pavement below. He then returned to the shocked photographer's side.

"Send me the bill, comrade," the marshal said coolly. "Also, you will now hand over to me all the rest of your exposed film."

Not waiting for Pavl to fulfill this request, he began to frisk him. Only when the desired film was in his grasp did Strellnikoff turn and casually pick up his weapon.

Mikhail caught the photographer's concerned glance and suddenly realized what Pavl had so secretly slipped into his pocket. It was a roll of exposed film! Although there was no telling what portion of their extraordinary encounter was preserved there, other than the corpse that lay in the square below, it was the only solid piece of evidence that could prove that the beast called Vladimir Dolgoruki had ever existed.

> "And I saw an angel come down from Heaven, holding in his hand the key to the bottomless pit and a great chain.
>
> And he laid hold of the Evil One, that ancient serpent who is also called Satan and the Devil, and bound him for a thousand years,
>
> And cast him into the bottomless pit, and shut him up, and set a seal upon him, so that he should feed on the nations no more, till the thousand years were expired. And at that time, he shall be loosed once again."
>
> —From the *Divine Revelation of St. John*, as recorded on the island of Patmos; Chapter 20, verses 1-4.

ABOUT THE AUTHOR

Richard Henrick is a native St. Louisan, and a 1971 graduate of the University of Missouri, with a Bachelor of Arts degree in Ancient History. While in college, he composed a rock opera entitled *Bloody Monday*, which concerned the rebirth of the Antichrist. The setting was a graveyard at midnight, and the group's vocalist emerged from a coffin to begin the show. *Bloody Monday* was a critical success and toured for more than two years. It was just such a vehicle that eventually led Richard to Los Angeles, where he traded in his guitar to work in the movie and publishing fields.

His current interests range from nuclear warfare to the occult. Single, Richard has bases in both St. Louis, Missouri, and Plano, Texas. *St. John the Pursuer: Vampire in Moscow* is his first book for TSR.